Sarah Dykins was born in London and studied Developmental Psychology at the University of Sussex. She is a teacher who has worked in schools in London, becoming a deputy head at the age of 27. After having her two daughters, Sarah has lectured part-time on Early Childhood Education, and is a voluntary helper and governor at her children's school. Now living in Brighton, Sarah and her husband run a property development business.

LESSONS FROM AN ANGEL

A Novel

Sarah Dykins

The Book Guild Ltd
Sussex, England

First published in Great Britain in 2001 by
The Book Guild Ltd
25 High Street
Lewes, East Sussex
BN7 2LU

Typesetting in Baskerville by
SetSystems Ltd, Saffron Walden, Essex

Printed in Great Britain by
Athenaeum Press Ltd, Gateshead

A catalogue record for this book is
available from the British Library

ISBN 1 85776 588 5

ACKNOWLEDGEMENTS

I'm grateful to many people who helped me while I wrote *Lessons from an Angel*. Firstly, to Alan, who is nothing like the conventional Norman, and has had to put up with a few sidelong glances from people wondering if he is! His wholehearted support has never wavered, and he has cheered me every step of the way. My wonderful friend Daphne saw me through many hurdles and never doubted that this book would be published. I'm grateful to my children, Rachel and Chloe, who always have faith in what I do, and to the girls in the book circle for their valuable advice and enthusiasm. Also to my brilliant mother, and excellent mother-in-law, who stand firmly in my corner and bear no resemblance to the characters in this book in any way whatsoever! In no particular order, I'd like to thank Annie, Ann and John, Naomi, and Sarah for always being on the end of a phone with encouraging words when I needed them. Friends like these make life pretty good. And finally, I'd like to offer a sincere thank you to the angel who woke me up with the idea for the book in the first place. All I had to do was listen.

Far out in the infinity of empty space, the Universe plays in an eternal pattern. The spiralling orbs and planets continue on their majestic path and the stars sound the music of creation in crystalline harmony.

Sometimes, however, there is an infinitesimal pause in the measured rhythm. It is in this minute silence of the firmament that an angel is born.

Then, like a clear shaft of light, a single immaculate note of exquisite clarity streams out through the silent blue aeons of the cosmos. Triumphant as a trumpet blast, the birth of an angel proclaims messages of salvation, redemption and love.

At this moment a journey is begun.

APRIL

Bethany Taylor woke on Tuesday morning to see the sun streaming through the curtains, trying to remember what it was that had just been said to her. She turned her head cautiously and, seeing the sleeping form of her husband, realised that he hadn't spoken.

Norman asleep was a very different man from the one who emerged into wakefulness. Watching him, Bethany wondered why she could only see his vulnerability when he slept. Furthermore, she wondered if he had by now, after 48 years of dutiful endeavour, managed to hide his vulnerability so effectively that even she could not see it any more. She sighed quietly and studied his face.

Norman was lying curled up with his head pressed deeply into his pillow, so much so that one half of his face was obscured. He had his mouth slightly open and a small trickle of saliva was making its way down his chin onto the pillow. His hair was grey, thin and somewhat receding, and there were deep furrows of worry between his brows that even sleep could not erase. His glasses sat neatly on the cabinet next to him, together with the glass of water which he placed carefully down on its Formica coaster each night, and emptied away each morning in the bathroom basin before shaving. As Bethany watched, Norman stirred slightly and grunted. She held her breath, wanting these few quiet moments to herself to try to remember the idea that was nagging at her, but which remained elusive.

She glanced around the room, letting her mind wander, in the vague hope that the voice would repeat what she was sure had been important.

Bethany and Norman Taylor's bedroom was inoffensively decorated in shades of pale green and peach, Bethany having reproduced the room in each of their flats and houses since they had first set up home together 22 years ago. She had once wondered why this was, and remembered that the colour scheme had first been hit upon to match the peach polyester sheets and green

1

bedspread given to them by Norman's parents as a wedding present. These had long since been updated as she had, in a rare burst of defiance, bought a continental quilt in 1974, much to Norman's mother's disgust. Marjorie had fixed her with an icy look at the time as she said, with violent disapproval, 'I don't hold with foreigners peddling their fancy ideas over here, and I'm most surprised that you do, Bethany.'

Somehow, the colour scheme had stuck and Bethany realised that even her dressing gown, which was hanging on the door in a prim, dispirited sort of way, was peach with green trim. Norman had bought it for her last Christmas. She had asked for some bulbs from the Wallace and Bar catalogue. She had even sent away for the catalogue without much hope, it was true, and left it lying on the kitchen table with the pictures displayed, but it had remained there until she had thrown it in the bin.

The sun was now reflecting off the dressing table mirror, and Bethany knew that she had five minutes until the alarm went off at 7.10 a.m. She concentrated her mind, with a vague sense of something needing to be done.

SWITCH IT ON AND MOVE.

Bethany started as though she'd received an electric shock. The voice was so imperious and demanding, and so unexpected that she automatically sat up in bed and stared around the calm bedroom, her heart hammering and her palms suddenly damp with sweat. She caught sight of herself in one of the three mirrors that formed part of the dressing table and instinctively looked for someone else, the person who had intruded so roughly into her mind. No one. Then what . . . ?

The alarm's shrill bleeping pierced the heavy stillness of the bedroom and she slid down into the warm bed. Norman awoke calmly and reached out his arm, depressing the alarm button in the same unhurried way as he had on Monday morning, and every other morning apart from Saturdays and Sundays. Norman's reassuring predictability was one of the things that had attracted the 19 year old Bethany, then so full of turmoil and misery.

Certainly she was experiencing a great deal of turmoil now. The voice, for that is what it had undoubtedly been, reverberated in her head, and she barely registered the fact that Norman was getting up. Norman put his feet into his brown plastic slippers, shouldered himself into his brown paisley artificial fibre robe, and went into the bathroom. Bethany was so shocked that she was still

2

lying in bed, staring at the door, as Norman returned. Immediately, he was alert to a possible difference in routine, and glared at her irritatedly. Anxious to avoid the interrogation that would surely follow as to her state of health, she gave herself a mental shake and quickly got out of bed, straightening her side of the duvet automatically as she did so.

Norman regarded her somewhat myopically without his glasses for a moment and then, reassured that all was well and the world continued to run on well ordered lines, began to go about the absorbing task of getting dressed for work. He always dressed slowly and deliberately, checking that each article of clothing was exactly right before picking up the next from its place on the chair or from the wardrobe. This was in direct contrast to Bethany who, although she was never careless and always paid attention to whatever it was she was doing, put on her clothes without much interest in how they looked, and rarely studied herself closely at all, brushing her hair without looking in the mirror.

Bethany at 43 retained much of the look of the girl she had been at 20. Her large brown eyes peered worriedly out from underneath thick brown hair that was still glossy, though now streaked with grey. People seeing her thought her mildly pretty, as good-natured kindness showed in her eyes and around her mouth. They were sometimes surprised to see her face light up with amusement or delight, and then thought her beautiful. Bethany laughingly thought of herself as 'wrinkled and lumpy'. Certainly there were lines beginning to show around her eyes and forehead, and she had begun to thicken around the waist in recent years, although she was far from fat.

She dressed quickly and went downstairs to the kitchen as Norman reached the sock stage of his clothes assembly. He liked to do things in the same order: pants, vest, socks, shirt, trousers, tie, jacket, shoes. Norman dressed as though his day depended on it.

Bethany filled the kettle at the sink and looked out at the garden. The sun shone on the little lawn, and bright gold and purple crocuses glowed in the morning light. Daffodils had begun to spike the borders with their cheerful green, and there were blue and white anemones sprinkled in the beds, together with neat fat clumps of late snowdrops trembling with dew. She had cleared the winter debris and the garden looked delightful against the clear blue sky. A blue-tit hopped on the lawn, head on one side, then flew off startled as Bethany moved to make breakfast.

Norman liked a full cooked breakfast at weekends, but during the week he had one four-and-a-half-minute boiled egg, a pot of English breakfast tea, and two rounds of toast spread with butter and Coopers Oxford marmalade. Norman had always eaten Coopers Oxford Marmalade. It was what his mother always served. He had been appalled and annoyed by its absence one fateful morning when Bethany had produced the supermarket brand instead. He had gone off to work without meeting her eye, leaving his second cup of tea on the table to congeal in cold reproach. Bethany had wretchedly gone down to Tesco's as soon as the front door had shut behind him, and bought two pots.

She had just laid out the breakfast when Norman appeared. He sat at the table and waited while Bethany served his breakfast. She cleared up as he ate, removing his hard-boiled egg and putting the toast in front of him, sponging crumbs off the sideboard and putting the plates into the sink. When they were first married they used to eat breakfast together, but somehow over the years they had fallen into this ritual. Norman did not read the paper, which lay folded beside him, but made humming noises as he ate. Suddenly he looked up, his mouth tight with suppressed irritation. He looked around the table and located the green and yellow lumpy butter dish which was supposed to resemble primrose clusters but didn't really. It sat near his right elbow. He sighed heavily and picked it up. He placed it down firmly beside his left elbow. Bethany did not respond. She was still thinking about the voice, and this meant that Norman's suffering went unnoticed.

Later, when Norman had departed in silent martyrdom, closing the door carefully with a click behind him, Bethany sat in the quiet kitchen. Norman had avoided her eye as he left, proffering his cheek coldly for a kiss. He was punishing her for her carelessness over the butter dish, but she was too preoccupied to mind. Recently she was reminded more and more of Marjorie, Norman's truly dreadful mother. Marjorie was responsible for most of the gifts in the house that she disliked, including Norman's dressing gown and, she now recalled, the butter dish itself. Bethany quickly suppressed the thought and looked around the kitchen, ready to begin clearing up.

SWITCH IT ON AND MOVE.

She jumped to her feet and stared wildly around the kitchen, realising for the first time that the voice was truly not part of a

4

dream but a reality, insistently prodding her into action, but to do what? She had no idea.

* * *

He awoke to the sound of the dawn chorus outside his window. He came to consciousness gradually, peacefully, as he always did, slowly absorbing details with his eyes closed. He could hear a blackbird outside in the plum tree and smiled, picturing it perched among the plump white blossoms, clear against the blue sky. It was April, and one of those lovely mornings which arrive after days of changeable showery weather. As he opened his eyes, he could see the white lace curtains moving gently against the window, which was set closely under the eaves of the house. He had to be at the church at ten o'clock. He glanced at his watch which read 7.30 a.m., then stretched and sat on the end of the bed, looking out at the view that he loved.

The garden, with its little orchard of plum and apple trees, sat serenely in the foreground of what was a truly peaceful and calming landscape. He let his eyes travel along the gravel paths, down to the little hedge that surrounded his vegetable garden, and then over the stream to the blue and green hills beyond. Much of the original wood had gone, to be replaced by fir trees, owned by the Forestry Commission. He and Claire had been part of the village campaign opposing the sale of the land, and had achieved some measure of success, not the least of which being the camaraderie that the campaign had engendered. Thinking of Claire brought him sharply back to the business in hand. He sighed and reached down for the shiny black shoes by the bed. He could see his dark suit, stiff and unfamiliar, hanging on the back of the oak cupboard in the corner of the room. It spoke of solemnity and duty, of family celebrations and the marking of time. Most of all it reminded him of the past, of days thankfully long gone, of work and commuting, of bustle and jostle and the anger of his fellow commuters. He began to get dressed, steeling himself for the day that was to come.

* * *

Bethany was having a dreadful morning. The voice was becoming ever more insistent, jolting and jostling her into a state where she was literally jumping with fright each time she heard it. Desperately she moved around the house, cleaning and tidying, although it scarcely needed it.

SWITCH IT ON AND MOVE.

She almost ran to the understairs cupboard and pulled out the vacuum cleaner. It was one of those bulbous models that the user pulled around after them. Bethany had chosen an upright hoover, thinking it functional and sensible, but had been overruled by Marjorie who had accompanied her and Norman on the shopping trip. Norman had sided with Marjorie, and so Bethany now pulled the vacuum cleaner around. She always imagined it to be a little dog, following her about and tripping her up. As she switched it on, the thought occurred to her that perhaps this was what was needed. It certainly involved switching something on, and she couldn't really vacuum without moving. However, the rational part of her mind was protesting that it was ludicrous that she had woken up with the instruction to hoover the living room.

Bethany slotted in the attachments and passed the hose along the mantelpiece, lifting the shepherd and shepherdess that sat either side of a flat-faced china Pekinese (another birthday present from Marjorie). There was silence, save for the droning of the hoover. She exhaled deeply and relaxed.

NO, THAT'S NOT IT.

Bethany put down the vacuum, switched it off and sat down heavily on the grey-green chair by the fireplace. She was seriously considering the idea that she was losing her mind. She forced herself to breathe deeply and slowly, concentrating only on being calm, her fingers clutching at the rough velvety feel of the chair's brocade cushions. She considered the possibilities. The first, and she had to admit rather appealing option, was that after years of dutiful service to Norman and Marjorie's idea of wifeliness, some kind of long-suppressed rebellious spirit was somehow breaking out and taking over. Meditating on this, she reluctantly realised that this was unlikely. It would not explain the mysterious and insistent instructions she was hearing, nor why working out how to obey them was so difficult. If she truly was rebelling, the voice might have something specific to say along the lines of Coopers Oxford Marmalade, or butter dishes. Besides, she was not by nature a rebellious or independent kind of person, and apart from rare incidents such as the duvet-buying, which were not spoken of, she had long ago given up asserting herself from day to day. This left Bethany with other, less appealing possibilities.

She had read about people hearing voices in Norman's *Daily*

Express. They were usually poor, blighted creatures who were prompted to acts of violence, leading to articles on page six of the supplement, and debates about care in the community. Bethany could not believe that she herself was one of these people, but she turned the idea over in her mind. The voice definitely was not hers, of that she was certain. Each time she heard it her body reacted as though a charge of electricity had been passed through her veins. However, from what she could gather from the *Express,* the voices mostly instructed people to jump off buildings, or worse, to stab strangers with kitchen knives. Her only instruction seemed to be telling her to switch on the vacuum cleaner. Bethany examined this last thought. She had certainly chosen a distinctive form of mental instability.

She stood up and, leaving the vacuum cleaner still plugged in, walked towards the door, avoiding looking behind her as though the owner of the voice might suddenly pop out from behind the standard lamp in the corner. Once in the hall, she again took a deep breath and reached for her sensible tweedy green coat from the hatstand by the door. Jamming her hat on her head, and without looking in the mirror, she walked quickly out into the avenue, feeling for her keys in her pocket as she did so.

Scarcely knowing where she was going, Bethany hurried along the pavement, hardly noticing the semi-detatched houses and neat front gardens. Instinctively turning away from the small parade of shops at the end of the road, she walked briskly up the slight hill towards the park. It was an undistinguished addition to the pleasant little suburb, with a few municipal tennis courts and straight-edged beds full of roses, at present standing in dispirited rows, twiggy arms stuck disconsolately out in the spring sunshine. It had been raining for a few days prior to this lovely morning, and Bethany was dimly conscious of the sweet aroma of fresh earth, mixed with the pungent smell of dog dirt, as she scuttled along the broken tarmac paths.

She paused beside a damp bench below a sign laying out the bylaws of the suburb. Teenagers had scrawled graffiti across it, and Bethany automatically began to read their clumsy messages of hope and desire. She had always rather enjoyed these glimpses into other people's lives, and was too often hurried along by Norman or Marjorie, or by the need to get the shopping home. Now as she read the awkward declarations of love and longing ('Sumpy for Jane', 'Sue luvs?') her breathing slowed and her heart was no longer beating so hard. She sank down on the bench and looked around her. An old crisp packet was lying by her foot and she

7

picked it up and put it in the litter bin, scattering rainwater onto her tights. She sat down again. She became aware of the sights and smells around her as the modest little park awoke to springtime. It wasn't beautiful like her beloved garden, but here and there Nature was softening the straight lines laid out by unimaginative council planners. The tarmac paths were uneven from the winter frosts, and soft green patches of moss had broken through. A blackbird was perched watchfully on a pile of old leaves and pine cones left over from the autumn, and here and there daffodils were beginning to poke their leaves above the ground.

Noticing and taking pleasure in her surroundings had trans-formed the routine monotony of Bethany's life. It was a habit that she had nurtured as a secret refuge from her situation, and it had become precious to her over the years. In fact, had she but known it, her mindfulness of her surroundings was her salvation. Paying attention to little things had pulled Bethany from misery in the early years of her partnership with Norman, and given her a serene and tranquil acceptance of her lot. Any deviation from routine was regarded by Norman as very threatening, and Bethany had grad-ually surrendered her desire for new experiences. Instead, she had evolved a way of making her ordinary life exceptional by paying total attention to whatever she was doing. The simplest of menial labours was somehow transformed through the way she performed it. She was not fully aware of what it was that had changed over the years, only that her mindfulness had granted her the ability to accept her life, and obtain pleasure and joy in small things. She had become ever more isolated, withdrawing from the hurt of a loveless marriage largely into her own thoughts, but gaining a way of coping and enriching her existence.

Restored by her few moments of contemplation, Bethany turned her mind back to the task in hand. The voice had communicated with her, answering her thoughts. It had said 'No, that's not it' when she had switched on the vacuum cleaner. Therefore it wasn't just some kind of persistent thought that wouldn't go away, like an advertising jingle or a snatch of song. Was she actually going to have some kind of dialogue with it? Bethany instinctively shied away from this idea. She couldn't, just couldn't start asking herself questions, and then answering them. She needed to talk to some-one. Sitting there in the park she realised that, in spite of living where she had for over twenty years, there was no one she could talk to. She had no friends or social life. She and Norman did not go out, except to have tea with Marjorie. She somehow managed

8

to pass her days smiling at neighbours and shop assistants, but never having more than a snatch of conversation with anyone.

Fortunately, Bethany enjoyed her own company and did not normally feel her isolation keenly. Early on in her married life, she had wept tears of bitter loneliness, and desperately sought human contact, but gradually she had accepted her lot, and no longer felt the sharp pangs of insularity. She was secure in a daily routine that cushioned her from thinking and protected her from the extreme emotions that had scarred her past. She still had periods of loneliness, but in general had taught herself to subdue her need for company and submit to the constraints of her days.

Now, however, she found herself in a situation which she felt she could not deal with alone. The possibility of mental instability filled her with fear. She could not imagine Marjorie's reaction should she lose control of herself. Norman certainly would not forgive her. What should she do?

As Bethany deliberated, two girls of about 14 approached along the path which led past her bench to a playground. The playground was small with a single slide, see-saw and two sets of swings. It was the cause of mixed pleasure and resentment for the mothers and their children who used it. The children all adored it, but often tripped and fell on its uneven surfaces and cut themselves on the glass that the teenagers had left scattered around. The mothers resented it for the fact that there was nowhere else to take their young children. Vandals frequently set fire to the swings, and the only bench to sit on had one slat broken so the mothers could not sit comfortably and chat.

The girls stared at Bethany with truculent defiance. She knew that they should be in school, but admired their independent spirit and smiled timidly at them. They did not return the smile, but put their heads down and hurried on to sit on the swings, dragging their feet on the ground as they twirled the chains half-heartedly. They were drinking from a single can of Coke, which she presumed would be left to litter the playground. There were no bins in the park.

Bethany looked at her watch. It was 11.15 a.m. Tonight, Norman was having a small gammon steak, scrubbed new potatoes and peas, with a slice of white bread and butter. She knew that none of this would take very long and that she had some time on her hands.

Suddenly she felt sick and realised that she had had no breakfast. Getting up from the bench, she followed the path until she came to the small alleyway that was a cut-through to the high street. She bought two doughnuts from the Baker's Oven shop and ate them, enjoying their cloying stickiness and heaviness in her stomach as her feelings of nausea subsided. Bethany hesitated, wondering what she should do next. Although she was outwardly calm, she felt decidedly unsettled, and was dreading hearing the voice again. She slowly retraced her steps and turned into the avenue where she and Norman lived.

The houses were mostly 1930s semis, with neat front gardens, a mixture of pocket handkerchief lawns and small beds, intersected with concrete drives or gravel paths. Each house was slightly different – a source of pride to the occupants, who maintained the tone of the area with cautious expressions of individuality. Wishing-wells and garden gnomes were much in evidence and hanging baskets were looked upon favourably. Sometimes there were tubs of begonias by the front doors and number 30 was much admired for its selection of shrubs, ambitiously clipped to resemble birds and animals.

The avenue was unimaginative but pleasant, its cohesive ambience maintained by a largely middle-aged or elderly population. Children were regarded suspiciously, and did not in general trouble the road, it being of little interest to them, and the houses unattractive to young families. Bethany liked children and would have chosen to move to a more lively area of the suburb. However, it was not to be, and she and Norman were a comparatively young couple steeped in the conventions of a rigidly conservative area. Norman enjoyed its conformity and enthusiastically complied with the avenue's weekend etiquette, cleaning his car and edging his gravel path and pocket lawn. Bethany disliked the front garden intensely, preferring the seclusion of her beloved garden at the back of the house.

During the week the residents largely withdrew indoors. Their net curtains shielded their rooms and guarded the houses from unwanted intrusions. Bethany was the only person walking on the pavement, and felt she was being watched resentfully from the bay-fronted houses by unseen eyes affronted by her deviation from routine. She did not usually venture out at this hour.

As she closed the front door behind her, Bethany paused in the hall, listening to the sound of the clock ticking in the front room and taking in the familiar smell and feel of the house. It all seemed reassuringly normal, and she was once more beginning to believe that the voice of earlier that day was a mere figment of her imagination. It just seemed too fantastic, especially now, in the house, where nothing out of the ordinary ever happened. It again began to feel like a fleeting memory of a dream, hanging like early

10

morning mists but vanishing like dew in the ordinariness of the day.

I'M NOT, YOU KNOW, AND YOU HAVEN'T SWITCHED IT ON.

Bethany's knees gave way and she sank down to the floor and covered her face with her hands. How long she crouched there she had no idea, but it seemed as though hours passed as she breathed in and out, taking in her hall from this unusual angle, lulled by the clock's steady ticking. Even now, a part of her quite enjoyed seeing things just that little bit differently. Suddenly the loud snap of the letter box shattered the calm, and she half stood, startled, staring at the door as the post dropped through. She listened to the postman's retreating footsteps and became uncomfortably aware that she needed the bathroom. She turned and climbed the stairs, still wearing her hat and coat, leaving the letters on the doormat.

Bethany sat down gratefully on the toilet and thought. As the morning progressed her agitation was beginning to lessen and her practical sensible nature was starting to assert itself. Although the presence of the voice was still shocking, she was beginning to face the idea that it was not going to go away, at least not until she took some kind of action. It had always been her experience that action was energising. Indecisiveness made her feel powerless and her problems tended to grow, whereas when she did something, even something that might possibly be wrong, she usually felt better and things began to sort themselves out. Turning the problem over in her mind, she began to look actively for a solution.

The first problem was to tackle her fear. In spite of her new-found resolve, Bethany was still very frightened that she might at long last be having some kind of breakdown. Usually when she was confronted by a nagging pain or an ache that she couldn't explain, Bethany's first port of call was the small library situated just off the high street, where she headed upstairs to the reference section. There she would settle down with *Family Doctor – A Home Guide*, thumbing through until she found what she wanted. She had often experienced moments of surging relief on discovering that she didn't have a terminal illness through this method, although it did have its drawbacks. Norman had once had a bad case of athlete's foot which she thought matched exactly with the early symptoms of leprosy, and she had suffered agonies of indecision as to the best course of action before she realised her mistake. Remembering this, and also considering the seriousness of her situation,

11

Bethany reluctantly abandoned the friendly *Family Doctor – A Home Guide* and mentally squared her shoulders. She must take the bull by the horns and make an appointment with the doctor.

Having come to this decision, Bethany returned downstairs, hung up her hat and coat and picked up the post. She was experiencing a mixture of emotions. Although she was relieved to have decided her next course of action, she was also fairly worried as to how she was to gather up enough courage to be able to carry out her plan. Everything in her cried out at the thought of exposing her possibly fragile grip on sanity to a stranger, but she could not think of an alternative. She carefully put the letters on the small table in the hall and sat down in the chair by the telephone. Before she had time to change her mind, she picked up the receiver and dialled the number.

* * *

After they had lowered the coffin into the grave, and the vicar had said all that could be said, they slowly walked back to the little church car park. Everybody lived so close that there was no need to drive, so most people walked together along the verdant lane to the house. He moved a little apart from the rest, who allowed him the space, sensing his need for solitude.

He loved the way the high hedgerow enclosed the lane, bending protectively round it as a mother her child. The green verges were banked high either side of him, and the hedgerows were filled with lush fern, honeysuckle and wild fuchsia. Claire had laughed at him when he had said that he felt invisible there, like a small animal in a safe green tunnel. They had walked in the lane often in the long summer evenings, revelling in its scents and serenity, and he now smiled at the memory of the closeness they had shared.

As they neared the house he returned to the group, adjusting his pace to theirs and instinctively set about the task of putting them at ease, thanking them for coming, and assuring them of the rightness of their presence. Immediately the mood became less sombre, as he gently encouraged them to share their memories, listening attentively and granting them the balm of knowing that they eased his sadness. His smile came easily, and by the time they flocked into the sunlit drawing room for sherry, the atmosphere was filled with friendship and the gift of healing. There was none of the awkwardness that sometimes accompanies a funeral; rather there was an air of solace and comfort, and each person there believed they were contributing to the ambience, as indeed they were. The afternoon passed slowly and all in the golden room were encompassed by its warmth.

Finally the time came to depart and they took their leave of him, sadness returning because of the solemnity of the occasion, but in some way they were secretly relieved. They could now return to their homes and families and distance themselves from the emotion of the day, satisfied that they had done all that could decently be expected of them. He stood under the white wooden porch in the evening light, and saw them go with gentle courtesy. Only after the last guest had departed did he bow his head and turn back towards the house whose welcoming windows cast pools of light onto the dark grassy path. At the door he hesitated, unwilling to go in, and turned back towards the garden. The night sky was completely clear, and studded with a myriad of stars. The moon hung low on the horizon, casting soft radiant light on the world below. He stood still, head tilted back, taking in the majesty of the constellations, feeling dwarfed by the canopy of heaven. Then he took off his shoes and socks, and stood on the wet grass gazing at the cosmos. He stretched out his arms in a gesture of acceptance and thanksgiving, making his own private benediction for Claire, and all that they had shared.

That night he slept deeply, and as he slept, he dreamed.

A woman was sitting in the darkness. He knew that she had been sitting in the dark for a long time. She was holding something in her hands and was studying it reverently, but he couldn't see what it was. In front of her was a high wall, but behind her the space stretched out endlessly. He saw that the woman was not alone, but that an angel was standing next to her and speaking aloud, although she appeared not to hear, bending her head down looking intently. He could hear the words quite clearly.

THE FIRST LESSON IS ALREADY IN YOUR HEART, AND IT IS THAT OF MINDFULNESS.
DIRECT ALL OF YOUR ATTENTION
ON WHAT YOU DO NOW, IN EACH PRESENT MOMENT.
DO WHAT YOU HAVE TO DO SELFLESSLY AND LOVINGLY,
FOR ITS OWN SAKE.
THEN YOU WILL BE FREELY TRAVELLING THE JOURNEY
OF LIFE.

The woman raised her hands, and he saw that the thing she was holding with such loving attention was a flower. The angel continued.

WHILE YOU ALREADY KNOW AND PRACTICE THE FIRST
LESSON, THE SECOND WAITS TO BE DISCOVERED.
YOU ALREADY HAVE ALL THE MEANS TO TREAD THE PATH
OF INNER JOY.
THE SECOND LESSON IS ACTION.
ACT WITH PURE INTENTION, AND YOU WILL BEGIN TO
ENGAGE WITH LIFE.
EVERY JOURNEY MUST START WITH THE DECISION
TO TRAVEL:
DO NOT LINGER IN THE STAGNANT POOLS OF LETHARGY.
RATHER, FIX YOUR EYES ON WHERE YOU WANT TO BE,
AND STRIKE OUT WITH HOPE AND COURAGE.
DO NOT BE AFRAID. YOUR THOUGHTS ARE THE FIRST STEP.
HOLD YOUR INTENTION.
THROUGH PURPOSEFUL ACTION, YOU WILL BE LIFTED UP
INTO THE REALMS OF JOY,
AND YOUR JOURNEY WILL BE BLISSFUL.

The dream faded but before it receded he saw that the space was becoming flooded with translucent, limpid light, and that the woman was lifting her head . . .

When he awoke he remembered nothing of his dream. He heard the soft rain outside his window, and lay in bed listening to the sound. Then he got out of bed and began the day.

*   *   *

Bethany woke up and lay listening to the rain that was pelting down against the double glazing. She half-closed her eyes again and the room became a tranquil green and peach blur. The thoughts that were going around in her head were peaceful and contented, which was strange, considering her unsettled state of mind the previous day. In some indefinable way something had changed and she had ceased to be frightened that the voice would invade her mind. Why it was she had no idea, but she felt calm and no longer full of fear. It was as though in her sleeping state she had managed to come to terms with something, and regard the future with equanimity. She felt as though she was on the verge of a discovery, and powerful enough to cope with whatever it was that she would find out. It was all most extraordinary, but she viewed it as a good sign and vowed to talk to the doctor honestly and openly. Yesterday, when she had made the appointment, she had toyed with the idea of inventing a distraught neighbour or friend with her symptoms. Bethany was by nature an honest person

14

and had not been happy with this solution. Now she felt glad that she had gained courage from somewhere, almost as if it had seeped into her skin in the night. Then the alarm went off and abruptly interrupted her reverie. The day had begun, no differently from many other days in the small house, except that something had changed. Norman went to the bathroom to shave, and she got up and straightened her side of the duvet.

The doctor's waiting room had a bench running around three sides where all the patients sat avoiding each other's eyes. Its foam cushioning could not disguise the fact that it was too narrow, so that everyone had to sit leaning slightly forward, unwillingly thrust into the line of each other's symptoms, perching uncomfortably on its edge, willing the time to pass quickly. When Bethany arrived, there were three other patients there before her, each sitting against one of the three walls of the room so as to provide maximum space between them. There was a man who sat with legs wide apart, his elbows resting on his knees so that he leaned well forward into the room, and occasionally hung his head to look at his shoes. There was a mother with a baby on her shoulder and a toddler leaning against her knee, and a florid middle-aged woman who was wheezing alarmingly. The room had no windows but a harsh neon strip light in the ceiling. One could almost see the illnesses of everyone who had ever sat in the room swirling around in the air.

The receptionist was cheery and welcoming, and deservedly loved by all the regular patients. She never forgot a face, and always had a sympathetic word and a smile for all those who approached her little window. Bethany did not know her, but instantly recognised her as one of those rare people who truly cared for those around her. She dispensed appointments and repeat prescriptions with efficiency and cheerfulness, and did much to soften the harshness of her surroundings. Bethany smiled at her and received a warm greeting in return. She hesitated at the doorway of the waiting room, deciding where to sit. The other patients were avoiding her eye in the casual way of people who are secretly, grimly praying that they will not have to be the one to give up their space. Bethany chose the wall with the young mother and her children, and sat down near the corner with the magazines. She picked up a BBC *Good Food* magazine and began to read an article on how to prepare the ultimate fish pie. Suddenly, the man opposite her broke into a paroxysm of coughing, fishing out a filthy handkerchief and covering his mouth as he bent over, hawking phlegm into its grey, crumpled folds. Bethany resisted the urge to hold her breath, as she knew she wouldn't be able to last long enough anyway. She shifted imperceptibly to her right, moving her knees slightly towards the tired-looking woman with the two children. The toddler's nose was running with a thick green mucus and, as she watched, he pushed his hand over his face, smearing it up his cheek. Then he put his hand on the bench, rubbing it up and down on the foam cushion. Bethany swallowed and closed her eyes. She heard the doctor call for the next appointment, and opened her eyes to see the wheezing woman waddling into the surgery. As she passed, a waft of suffocating body odour reached Bethany's nostrils, rancid and warm. This time Bethany inhaled shallowly through her mouth for a few breaths, but when she breathed again the atmosphere around her was still solid and reeking. She felt waves of nausea breaking over her, and stood up to get some fresh air. Muttering something to the understanding receptionist, she walked briskly out through the heavy fire door at the end of the passage, and leaned against the brick wall outside the surgery. After a while she felt less sick, and went back to the waiting room.

The young mother was dragging her unwilling child down the passage. He was screaming and streams of mucus pouring from his nose now mingled with the torrents of tears rushing down his scarlet cheeks. Bethany flattened herself against the wall as the poor woman manhandled the toddler and her baby towards the door. The baby had started to cry as well and dropped its dummy over its mother's shoulder. As the mother bent down to pick it up, the blue and white changing bag that she was carrying slipped off her shoulder, and nappies, a trainer cup full of purple liquid and nappy-rash cream all rolled out onto the floor. Before she had time to think, Bethany went to help and together they managed to get everything back in the bag.

'Thanks,' the young woman said. 'He doesn't want to leave the toys, does he?' and she jerked her head towards the empty waiting room. As Bethany looked, she noticed that there was a plastic washing basket lying on the floor with an assortment of grubby-looking playthings, which the little boy was desperately trying to get back to. On the spur of the moment she reached out and put her hand gently on the woman's arm.

'If you like, I'll bring him out to the car while you get your baby into the seat.'

The woman looked at her doubtfully.

'Would you? He can be a right little sod,' she said, but she let go of her son's arm and took the baby out the heavy fire door, holding it to one side with her hip, as she swung her bag and the baby through it.

The little boy stopped crying and put his finger in his mouth. Bethany crouched down and looked at him.

'If you're a good boy I'll give you a sweetie, but it has to be a secret, and you have to come out to the car with Mummy.' The toddler stared at her and then nodded. Bethany felt in her pocket and took out a packet of fruit pastels. She had a sweet tooth and always carried a packet of something in her coat. The little boy went with her peacefully, sucking his sweet, and got into the car. She gave the mother the rest of the packet of pastels to go home with and waved to the child, who strained round in his seat to watch her out of the back window.

Feeling astonished at what she had just done, Bethany returned to the welcoming face behind the glass screen.

'Nothing to it, is there?' the receptionist said. 'I always think, when you've had your own, you never forget. Hard work at the time though, isn't it?' Bethany hardly heard the words, she was so thunderstruck at what had just happened. She couldn't remember when she had last reached out to another fellow creature and received warmth in return. She realised how consistently she avoided it. She was about to sit down when her new acquaintance said: 'Oh, Mrs Taylor, Doctor's waiting for you.' Hardly pausing to think, so surprised was she at how easy it had been to make intimate human contact, she walked distractedly into the doctor's surgery.

The doctor had been wise when she had chosen the arrangement of her rooms, in the same way as she had when choosing her receptionist. In contrast to the unwholesome waiting room, the surgery was spacious and well-proportioned, with a patterned carpet and wooden shelving. Light from two windows illumined a large desk, on which sat a computer and various articles of medical apparatus. At one end of the room there was a high couch covered with white paper. The doctor herself was sitting sideways-on to the desk in a swivelling chair, looking down at a fat brown envelope bulging with pieces of paper. Bethany, who never visited a doctor unless she had no other option, gazed at this envelope wondering how on earth the medical profession had managed to amass so much data from her few encounters with it. Suddenly she realised that the doctor had asked her a question and was looking at her impassively, waiting for her to speak.

'I'm sorry, I do beg your pardon, I didn't quite catch . . . ?'

The doctor was a middle-aged woman with dark hair and half-moon spectacles. The impression Bethany received was of a kind, no-nonsense sort of individual.

'I said, what is it I can do for you, Mrs Taylor?'

Until now, Bethany had assumed that she would begin speaking and that the conversation would unfold along certain lines, but she realised that it wasn't going to be that easy. As she prepared to speak she had a strong feeling that what she was about to say simply wasn't relevant, not that she would not be able to express herself, but merely that she was in completely the wrong place, talking to the wrong person. She was unaccustomed to receiving such strong intuitive impressions and this unsettled her still further, making concentration difficult.

Finally she blurted out, 'I've been hearing a voice.'

The doctor looked rather taken aback. This was obviously not at all what she had been expecting, and there was a short, slightly baffled pause while the two of them looked at each other, equally disconcerted.

The doctor was the first to recover, clearing her throat and assuming a brisk, professional manner.

'I see. A voice. Do you suffer from depression at all, Mrs Taylor? Have you ever had post-natal depression, for instance?'

Bethany, who was distracted by the ever stronger feeling that she was in the wrong place, pulled herself back to the present and muttered, 'No, no, I've never had children.'

The doctor raised her pen as if to write something, and then thought better of it, and laid it back down on the desk. She leaned forward intently. 'And what sort of things is this voice saying? Who do you think it might be – I mean, do you think that it is benign, or some kind of demon, for example?'

The horrified Bethany had an instant memory of being instructed to do the hoovering and she recoiled and burst out, 'Oh, no! I'm sure it's nothing like that. Look, I think I've been very silly, and you're so kind to give me your time, but I think that I'm wasting it, it's awfully nice of you and I'm sorry to be so stupid . . .' So anxious was she to get out of the surgery that she had half-risen as she was speaking and was hurriedly trying to push back the heavy chair to stand up fully. The doctor also stood and attempted to stem the flow of Bethany's apology, stepping forward to keep pace with her as she edged backwards towards the door.

'Really, Mrs Taylor, please don't concern yourself. It's not as unusual as you might think, and you mustn't be afraid to consult me if you feel you do have a problem.'

As the words registered, Bethany stopped short in her frantic attempt to escape, and said more calmly, 'No, truly, Doctor, I don't think I'd thought this through, and you have been most kind, and I will come back if I get worried, but I feel so much better. Thank you.'

By this time they had got to the empty waiting room and were passing the receptionist, who was putting on her coat. She looked up curiously at the sight of the doctor escorting a patient out into the street. Bethany scuttled out into the watery sunshine, leaving the doctor still staring after her, with her pen in her hand and the envelope of notes hanging down limply by her side.

It had stopped raining although the pavement was full of puddles, and the air glistened with moisture. The sun shone out from behind clouds in a slate-grey sky and thunder rumbled far off in the distance. Bethany realised that she had left her umbrella behind and instantly dismissed the idea of returning for it. She decided to risk the impending downpour, and set off at a steady pace, weaving her way through the puddles, her heart feeling lighter with each step. Suddenly, the farcical element of the whole experience struck her and she began to laugh. She stopped by a hedge carefully screening a hideous crazy-paving forecourt and laughed out loud until she gasped for breath. She didn't even care if anybody saw her, so funny did it all seem. Luckily nobody passed by and she recovered herself, continuing on her way, her mind busy with ideas and reflections.

When she got home, she first checked that she had not forgotten any of the elements of Norman's tea, and that they were all in the fridge (he was having a small piece of smoked mackerel, a baked potato and a green salad), and then she put the kettle on for a cup of coffee. She went to the cupboard and found a large bar of Cadbury's milk chocolate with hazelnuts and broke off eight squares to have with her drink. She put the coffee into the mug and added the hot water and the milk. By this time she had eaten the eight large squares of chocolate, and so she was about to break off eight more. Then she saw that this would mean that there would be only four squares left of the bar. It seemed silly to put four squares back in the cupboard, so she took the rest of the chocolate over to the kitchen table with her coffee. She knew that she'd put on weight recently, but really it was so lovely to eat chocolate that she didn't care. All the time she was waiting for the voice to speak, because she knew instinctively that it would. It was as if it had been silent, waiting for her to act on her intuitive feelings, and be ready to hear it again. She rested her elbows on the table and drank her coffee. The main outcome of the otherwise disastrous visit to the poor doctor was that she knew, irrevocably and without question, that the voice did not mean her any harm. Who or what the voice belonged to, she had no idea, but when the doctor had asked her if it was a demon, she had felt a wave of emotion overtaking her from inside that had surprised her. The emotion had been overwhelming indignation.

Now she waited, wondering what she would do if the voice did not speak. It was such a complete turnaround from her feelings of yesterday that she smiled again. All the rest of that afternoon and evening, Bethany waited and thought about the voice, but it never came. Norman arrived back from the office and ate his supper and then, in the evening, they sat in the front room while he read the paper and Bethany watched the nine o'clock news. After they had gone to bed and Norman was asleep, she was still weighing up her thoughts in her mind and quietly trying to come to some con-clusions. As with most things that happened in her life, she gave it her full attention, and then tried to act on her resolution. Before she finally fell asleep she had decided that the voice not only meant her no harm, but that it was here for a reason, and that she missed its presence. She resolved that if it spoke again she would try her utmost to learn what it was it wanted from her.

The next day was different in that Norman was not coming home from work that evening. His company were bringing in a new computerised system in Accounts. Norman always called it 'Accounts', with an invisible capital A, and Bethany now thought of it as such. The company were sending Norman on a two-day induction course. He was very agitated about it and had set the alarm one whole hour earlier than usual so that he could finish packing his clothes. He had even put in some aftershave that Marjorie had given him, tucked neatly into the corner of his overnight bag with his spare shirts, socks and underpants. He had asked Bethany to buy him a new toothbrush, and this had been packed in a neat little zip-up bag with his shaving kit. All this meant that Bethany would be alone in the house until the weekend, free to spend time as she wished in the evening.

After Norman had left, Bethany changed the sheets and loaded the washing machine on the whites wash program. She carefully made up the load with two of Norman's work shirts and set it off. Then she took a yellow duster and some spray furniture polish out of a kitchen drawer, and went into the front room. When she had finished the polishing, she took out the vacuum cleaner and starting at the top of the stairs, worked her way carefully down, making sure that she picked up all the little pieces of fluff close to the skirting board. She was absorbed in her labour, doing the mundane tasks for the sake of the work itself, and then moving on. She climbed the stairs again, having put the hoover away in the understairs cupboard, and went into the bathroom. There she carefully cleaned the toilet, and took a cloth and some lemon Jiff and started on the bath and the basin. Once she had done these, she steadily cleaned and polished the taps and rinsed away the Jiff. All this time she was aware of no thought at all, except the absorption in her work, and the peace and joy that she got from it. It wasn't even the result of her labours that gave her the satisfaction, rather the tranquillity of the rhythm and the effect of her immersion in it. It was almost like the feeling she got from singing in church at Christmas. She did not know it, but it was actually more like a prayer.

The first thought that Bethany had after finishing the bathroom was why it was that the people who made the Jiff bottles never made the little plug on the cap long enough to stop the Jiff solidifying in the lid. She wondered if its manufacturers listened to housewives, and if they would like to receive a letter from one about their product. Bethany did occasionally gratify her desire to be of service to her fellow human beings by sending helpful suggestions to the manufacturers of household products. She had once been sent a free sample of furniture polish by one such company, and had been absurdly pleased to have been acknowledged.

Now that she had finished her housework for the morning, she felt that she needed to talk to somebody else, or go somewhere else to find out more about the voice. Just as she had known instinctively that the doctor's surgery had been the wrong place to go, she suddenly knew where she would try next. She went downstairs and out of the house. She double-locked the front door behind her and walked along the road into the warmth of the morning. As always, it was very quiet in the avenue, but the air was especially heavy and still after the rain the previous day, and even the birds were silent. The earth in the front gardens steamed gently and the atmosphere was damp and humid.

Bethany walked steadily down the high street until she came to a small archway. She ducked her head underneath it even though it was easily high enough to let her pass, and followed the time-worn brick path through a graveyard which was studded with lichen-covered gravestones. These were so old and weathered that the inscriptions were no longer visible, and they stood crookedly on mossy banks either side of her. The quality of the air was different here, untouched by the bustle of the busy street beyond, as if steeped in the prayer of generations. The tranquil stillness was broken only by the sound of moisture dripping gently from the gnarled old yew trees onto the warm ground. Bethany paused outside the ancient church. Up one side of the arched door was written 'This is the House of God', and down the other 'This is Heaven's Gate'. She stood with her head on one side attempting to make out the old-fashioned lettering. Then she went into the venerable porch and pushed open the heavy oak door which led to the church itself. The atmosphere inside the building was such that she felt impelled to kneel in one of the dark antique pews and take it in. She was not especially religious, but it was impossible to remain unaffected by the holiness of the place. The air was fragrant with candle wax and incense and the thick stone walls seemed to have absorbed the scent of flowers brought as offerings through the centuries. Bethany had often passed the church, which attracted tourists wanting to view its thirteenth-century nave, but she had never been inside. Now she wished that she had. The place stood secure and steadfast, a sanctuary from the stresses and strains of modern life. She might have been able to take refuge there sometimes. Its sturdy walls were a reminder to those who entered that their daily burdens could be laid down for a brief period while they acknowledged the existence of something more important. Indeed, as Bethany looked around, she noticed a little plaque in her pew saying 'This place exists for the glorification of God'. Sitting in the cool, scented silences of the ancient church gave her time to think about what had happened to her.

Still the voice was silent. In spite of this Bethany felt that she might be in the right place. She was conscious of a sense of harmony and peace, looking upward at the incandescent light streaming in through the stained glass windows above her. At the head of the nave a vast window illuminated the aisle, depicting saints and stories that she didn't recognise, or dimly remembered from assemblies at school. A brass lectern in the shape of an eagle with folded wings stood to one side, and a painstakingly arranged display of yellow forsythia was placed a little self-consciously on the other. Bethany sat for a while, oblivious of the passage of time, resting her mind and soul. Then she got up rather clumsily and walked down the aisle, trying to quiet her footsteps even though there was no one there to be disturbed by her.

As she emerged into the light, the warmth of the air struck her forcibly, as it had been very cool inside the thick stone walls. She looked round the gravestones for a little while, and then left the cloistered graveyard and returned through the archway to the shops. Before she went home she stopped at the fishmongers and bought a pound of haddock.

As soon as she stepped in through the front door, and put her keys on the hook by the hatstand, she knew that something was about to happen.

<h3 style="text-align:center">SWITCH IT ON AND MOVE.</h3>

Bethany went through to the kitchen and laid a piece of paper and a pen on the table. She sat down, and started to make a list of everything she could think of that could be switched on and that would involve moving. She felt ready to begin to understand and take action that was both practical and methodical. Looking round the room she began to make her list: toaster, kettle, oven, grill, fridge (although this was cheating a bit, she thought), light switch. She came to a halt. None of these was right. Thinking further she produced: television, lamp, radio,

<h3 style="text-align:center">YES.</h3>

Radio? Bethany thought. Switch on the radio? She went through to the front room, squatted down awkwardly behind Norman's television chair and opened a small cupboard where she and Norman kept things that were rarely used. There was a bottle of sherry that they sipped from on special occasions, and glasses laid in a segmented box, and some china given to them as a wedding present that they kept for visitors that never came. Towards the back of the cupboard there was an old transistor radio encased in black leather. Bethany had no idea where it had come from but she was relieved that it was still working. She twiddled the tuning knob as she returned to the kitchen and found a classical music station and then sat down.

<h3 style="text-align:center">NO.</h3>

No. Bethany turned the knob again and tuned in to a discussion programme about dog licenses on Radio 4, without much hope.

<h3 style="text-align:center">YOU HAVE TO SWITCH IT ON AND MOVE.</h3>

The next station was playing popular music. Feeling totally ridiculous, she got up and began to shift her weight awkwardly from foot to foot, scarcely noticing the music that was playing, so hotly self-conscious did she feel, trying to dance in the place where the most unconventional thing she had ever done was serve the wrong kind of marmalade. Little by little, however, as the music played, she forgot her embarrassment and began to enjoy herself. She started to make herself a sandwich, and to dance around the kitchen fetching what she needed. There was a medley of songs from the Beatles, and she really threw herself into the movements, swinging the cupboard doors backwards and forwards to the beat of 'Back in the USSR', and wriggling her hips to 'A Hard Day's Night'. Then she sang along at the top of her voice to the words of 'Love Me Do' as she laid the table for herself. She was breathless with the unaccustomed exertion, elated with the joy of moving with such lack of inhibition and, as she collapsed at the table, she was flushed and beaming all over her face. She felt as though she had been lit up from the inside, in a way that she hadn't felt for years. She revelled in the feeling and was momentarily transported to another time, when she felt blessed and carefree. Then, all of a sudden, she was frightened of her happiness, and the fear extinguished her joy like unexpected storm clouds blot out the sunlight on a summer's evening.

At that moment a song began to play and a chill entered her heart. She was seized with a foreboding so great that her chest was filled with physical pain. A violent trembling took hold of her and she stood deathly pale, unable to reach out her hand, powerless to stop the words that she thought would echo forever in her mind. It was a popular song from around 20 years ago, the words of which triggered memories she desperately wanted to forget. She knew what became of the broken-hearted. She did not want to hear the melody again.

The song came to an end, and still she stood there in her own private anguish, transfixed with the pain of her memories. It had been so long since she had remembered, that she had supposed herself anaesthetised to the agony, deadened to the gnawing ache of grief and loss. Indeed, she had overlaid the pain deep inside herself with so many layers of silence and denial over the years that she had believed it was no longer there. Year after year she had continued to lock up her suffering somewhere in her own private prison, telling herself that it was dead and gone, and bartering for her release from pain. Her life with Norman was a narcosis, a waking sleep that she had exchanged for the agony in the belief that she was incapable of coming to terms with what had happened. All this she had done willingly, trying to make a life for herself out of the ashes of her history, thinking that she had done so. Now the pain was back, cruelly piercing her as sharply as it had ever done, torturing her with the realisation that all her efforts had been in vain, and her fragile peace was exposed as a laughable sham.

Stiffly, moving like a wooden marionette, she switched off the radio, and shuffled trance-like out of the kitchen. She went upstairs and sat on the bed, staring ahead of her, her lips blue-white in her ashen face. Then she began to cry for her past for the first time in 23 years. Once she had started she was incapable of stopping, the overwhelming force of her desolation like a thundering torrent, consuming all in its path. She was wracked with devastating sobs shaking her body in an ague of grief. Strange animal sounds escaped her, forcing their way out from some subterranean buried place deep inside and she gave way to them, unaware of her surroundings, lost in a world of pain. Finally her lament died down and she fell asleep where she was, crumpled up on the bed, fully clothed.

When she awoke, it was night, but the room was flooded with an unearthly silvery light, a milky brilliance that transfigured the room so that she did not know where she was, so otherworldly did it seem. Then she saw that the moon was sailing in a cloud-rent sky, casting its radiant beams into the room. She lay there drained of all her sorrow, calm and languid, enveloped in warmth and weariness, merely observing with eyes that were dry and steady.

I'M SORRY.

'Why did you do it?' she asked in her exhaustion, although she half knew the answer.

IT'S NECESSARY TO REMEMBER. YOU MUST LIVE IT ALL
AGAIN, AND THEN LET IT GO.

She did nothing, but lay there for a while, watching the moonlight, as helpless as a newborn infant, registering her senses, but not analysing the information. Her mind was focused on what the voice was saying to her. Then she fumbled clumsily with her tired brain and asked the question that she had avoided right at the beginning, days ago, in this room, where it had all begun, in another lifetime. 'Who are you?' There was a pause and, she felt, uncertainty. Then

I DON'T KNOW.

This surprised her, and she asked, 'Are you me?' The voice came back, more confident now.

No.

Lying there in the silvery translucence of the room, Bethany remembered the stained glass windows in the church, and she asked a final question. 'Are you . . . are you an angel?' Again there was a pause, and then

Yes. I think I am.

Bethany listened to her angel, and understood that she was being offered a choice. The choosing involved both courage and pain, but it also gave her a chance to live again. In that moment, she accepted what was being asked of her, and humbly affirmed that she would embrace the lesson the angel was here to teach, no matter what the outcome. The angel was silent for a moment, and then spoke again.

This is the third lesson, and it is the Lesson
of Healing.
The present moment is the only thing
of importance.
The past and the future are created by your mind,
and do not exist in reality.
Do not allow pain to enslave you by holding onto
it, because the only way to be free in the present
is to let go of the past that binds you.
You think that remembering is pain,
but in reality, Remembrance is Healing.
So learn to embrace and release the pain of your
past, lovingly forgive, and move on.

Bethany turned this over in her mind, wondering what the first two lessons were. She thought about asking, but she felt too tired for any more revelations and instead watched the moon in the cloud-filled sky. It was one of the most beautiful sights she had ever seen and she fixed her eyes on the heavens. The clouds were dark in the moon-bright sky, and looked to her like islands floating in a distant ocean. The sky was a silver sea filled with blue-black reefs which the sailing moon was navigating on its hazardous journey.

26

As she watched she knew that the hazards were not real, as the reefs would dissolve before the moon which would pass through them unscathed. Her eyes closed, and her last waking thought wondered if this too was a message.

MAY

It was Friday, and Norman would be back that evening. After Bethany had dressed she had her breakfast, revelling in the freedom of not having to boil an egg, and instead crunching her way through a bowl of Special K. Then she cleared the table. All this time the radio was playing in the background. She looked at the scantily clad lady in the red bikini on the cereal packet and momentarily wondered if she would slim down a bit faster if she ate another bowl of the stuff. Dismissing the idea as ludicrous, she did a little dance to Elvis Presley's 'Hound Dog', and once again experienced a lifting of her spirits which fortified her for what she knew she had to do next.

When the kitchen was tidy and clean, she went into the front room and sat in the most comfortable seat, adjusting her position so that she was sitting very straight, her back supported by the high back of the chair. She placed her hands on her knees, and turned them upwards in a gesture of supplication and acceptance. Instinctively she held herself erect but relaxed, so that her breathing became regular and even, its calmness transmitting itself to her body and then her mind. Mentally telling her angel that she was ready, she steeled herself and slowly, deliberately, she began to remember. The years fell away until she had travelled a long way from the suburban room and she was back in the sunlit pathways of her past. She made herself remember all of it.

*   *   *

Her childhood had been unexceptional. Mr and Mrs Jones had been childless until their forties and had fully expected to remain so until Bethany had been born late one chilly autumn afternoon in the maternity ward of the local cottage hospital. Perhaps because her parents were so well established into the pattern of their marriage, the new baby had not had such a dramatic affect on the household as is usual in such cases. She had been a placid, obedient infant, and her mother had undertaken her upbringing in much the same lugubrious way as she went

28

about most other household labours, such as feeding the cat or cleaning the oven.

Her father had been a school caretaker in the city's largest secondary school: a dark, oppressive building casting its Stygian shadow over the terraced back-to-back housing that made up their part of the town. He departed before it was light in the winter mornings, and brought the gloom of his job back into the house with him when he arrived home. The building depressed all who worked there, children and staff alike, and its lightless presence seemed to have entered his soul. As it turned out, it had entered his body as well. The building was condemned one January when it was discovered it was riddled with asbestos. The council offered Bethany's father another job in a school in a neighbouring borough. Refusing to accept the loss of a job that he had hated with all his being, it was as if his lungs refused to breathe healthy air. Mr Jones went into stubborn and rapid decline from an undiagnosed sickness, and was buried late in February of that year. Bethany had not known him well, and stood by the frozen graveside in the dreary cemetery, seemingly untouched by the event.

Mrs Jones had from that moment nursed her disappointment in life more tenderly than she had ever done her infant daughter. Always hard done by, she now became bitter, and her dissatisfaction hung like a cloud around her, so strongly as to be almost visible to those who saw her. She never remarried and so, from then on, Bethany bore the burden of her mother's general dissatisfaction. Mrs Jones began a retreat from life, governed by a belief that nothing could change her lot, and no matter how hard Bethany tried, she could not bring happiness into their world. As a child, Bethany was unable to separate her own actions from her mother's reactions, and thus lived with a permanent impression of unease and a sense that she was somehow lacking because she could not make her mother happy. She was too young to know that if a person is determined to live life a certain way, there is nothing anyone can do about it.

Mrs Jones was master of the martyred silence. She lived with sighs and innuendoes and rarely expressed her dissatisfaction directly. A charitable observer would have said that there was genuine sadness behind her despondency, but in truth her unhappiness was self-imposed. As the years went by, her fear of taking any risk prevented her from changing her circumstances, and she resentfully and defensively attacked those who attempted to help her. She had fallen into the destructive habit of seeing the worst in every situation, and in every person. She guarded her right to judge others and find them wanting and, in consequence, was herself isolated and miserable, cut off from the joy of living by the invisible cordon of her own paralysing pessimism. The phrase most often on her lips was 'You go ahead, don't worry about me'. This was usually uttered in a tone indicating strong disapproval, and it had the immediate effect of spoiling the pleasure of those around her. When particularly aggrieved, Mrs Jones was determinedly vivacious and acidly bright. She would make a friend easily and then, just as quickly, the acquaintance withered. She simply did not have sufficient interest in those around her to sustain intimacy. All her energy went into bemoaning the misfortunes of her life. Bethany became used to people coming and going, and developed a quiet self-sufficiency that served her well through the years ahead. She also learned that passive acquiescence saved her from the vitriol of her mother's sharp tongue.

Perhaps because she was quiet and shy, Bethany did not make many friends at school and, although she was popular enough, never formed a close friendship, although she would have liked to. She never invited anybody home. She was a good student, well thought of by her teachers, who sometimes took the trouble to stay behind after school to explain a point to the quietly absorbed pupil. Bethany blossomed under this attention and, although she rarely spoke in class, worked hard at her homework, especially English literature. One day she discovered an old poetry book in the dusty school library and read the poems of Walt Whitman. It seemed to her that the words were bespangled with hope and light, and she began to read poetry avidly, soaking up the works of Milton, Wordsworth and D.H. Lawrence, hugging the new ideas to herself and realising that there were many ways of seeing the world. She began to feel sorry for her mother, even though she could not escape her control.

Academically she did well and, in spite of her mother's veiled hostility to the idea, took two A Levels in English and History. She also took a typing class as an extra option after school. She did this partly because she had no idea what she was going to do when her time at school ended, and had a vague idea that it would be useful, and partly as an excuse to stay out of the house. Mrs Jones increasingly suffered from ill health. It was as if illness was attracted to the house by the clouds of hopelessness that hung over it, and came rushing on dark wings to dwell in the body which was governed by defeated and angry thoughts. Bethany remained happily and stubbornly healthy, and the unspoken assumption was that she should spend her time attending to her mother's needs.

Inevitably, more and more of the household chores fell to the girl, and she found school a blessed refuge from the dispiriting atmosphere at home. It was almost as if the damp cloud of depression was spreading outwards from her mother into the house. Sometimes Bethany wondered if eventually the whole town would succumb to the power of Mrs Jones's dissatisfaction.

When she left school at eighteen, Bethany managed to obtain work in the sorting offices at the Main Post Office. Her English teacher had written her a reference for the job, which was as a typist in the typing pool. There it was that she formed the first friendships of her adult life.

The girls in the typing pool were 'bettering themselves'. Prospects of employment were limited to the nearby steel factory or the market stalls in town. Most of the girls had relatives who worked in these places, and were pleased to have obtained the qualifications to be doing clerical work. In truth, they had not moved far from their origins and the atmosphere in the typing pool was as raucous and happy as the nearby market. There was much good-natured banter between the girls and the young postmen who passed the office window at regular intervals and whose earthy comments caused much hilarity and gossip. At first the typing pool was terrifying. Bethany was as timid as a mouse, and kept her head low over her desk, hoping not to be noticed. It all seemed so sophisticated to the unworldly girl, whose sheltered life with her querulous mother had not prepared her for the robust cackling ambience of the post office. However, the kind-hearted typists would not allow her to sit quietly for long. She became a mascot for them, and they enthusiastically set about improving her prospects, both because they genuinely liked her, and because it was a welcome distraction from the tedium of their jobs.

In particular, there was one girl who took a special interest in Bethany, and the two became friends. They were an odd couple to look at. Sylvia was as curvy as Bethany was slight, as blond as she was dark, and as bubbling over with fun as she was serious. Sylvia loved to 'have a laugh' and often did. She was the youngest of four sisters who all shared her flirtatious good nature. In their lunch hour the pair would go to the canteen and have sausage and chips, and then out into the town to Woolworth's to try the cheap lipsticks and pout into tiny hand mirrors. Bethany felt a little self-conscious at first, but was surprised and pleased to be included, and gradually her self-confidence grew. With her first wage packet she bought a book of Wordsworth's poetry. Her mother was furious and coldly rounded on her for her feckless and frivolous waste of money. She retreated to her room with a headache and stayed there in angry silence until Bethany wretchedly apologised and promised that she would from now on give over the wages for household expenditure only.

One foggy October evening Bethany was walking home up the steep hill that led to her road. Although it was only six o'clock it was dark already and the street lights were switched on. Their pale globes cast haloes of sallow light in the mist, which pooled below each post, but did little to illuminate the town. Chestnut trees lined the path, and condensation from the mist dripped steadily from their overhanging branches. Her footsteps were muffled by the dead leaves lying damply on the ground and the mist deadened any other sound save for the dripping moisture. She walked slowly, dawdling up the hill, wanting to delay the moment when she would have to go into the brooding house and meet her mother's demands. It seemed to her that as she neared her street, the atmosphere grew damper and the mist thicker.

She also had another reason for wanting to prolong her walk. Today the subject of the annual works summer trip had been raised. It was the custom for those who wished to, to put some of their wages aside each week into the fund, and then go to the seaside for a week in August. Sylvia had been last year and had enthusiastically described the joys of the South Coast pleasure spots. It was a 'real laugh', she assured Bethany, and as this was the highest accolade the typing pool could award, Bethany was longing to go. All day the talk had been of the piers and the bingo halls, the fantastic fish and chips, and the freedom to do what you wanted 'of an evening'. Bethany was eighteen and had never left the small Welsh town where she had been born, and she was filled with a fervent desire to see a different horizon, to breathe different air, and perhaps even to be a different person for a while. She had read of faraway places in her books and was filled with a yearning so strong that she thought it would consume her. How could she possibly go? Her mother would never agree, if only for the practical reason that there would be a drop in wages each week. Mrs Jones was almost animated on a Friday evening when Bethany handed over the crisp oblong packet with her money for the week, and certainly knew down to the last penny how much her daughter was bringing home.

She neared the street where they lived. Although the old school building on the hill was long gone, she instinctively raised her eyes upwards behind the houses. On a dark evening like tonight she could imagine its brooding presence dominating the landscape, and it seemed to her that the terraced houses on the sharply rising road still cowered in its shadow. Even though she was a young woman now, it would for ever symbolise the unease of her child-hood, the sense she had of something uncomfortably wrong that she was never able to make right in spite of her childish labours. Her thoughts returned to the present, and her steps echoing along the wet pavement. Bethany was still young enough to enjoy the novel sound of her new high-heeled work shoes clicking down the empty street.

As she turned and lifted the latch of the small wooden gate to her house, her next door neighbour opened the door and put her head out. Mrs Willow was a diminutive and determined-looking little Welshwoman. Her bright dark eyes looked inquisitively out onto the world with great interest and curiosity, and she didn't so much move as bustle. She always wore an apron over her clothes, and often this was covered in flour from her baking. Despite her tiny size she was the unquestioned sovereign of her extensive family, who respected her rule as second only to that of the deity that they paid homage to in chapel on Sunday mornings. Her five enormous sons worshipped her, and she was held in awe by her various daughters-in-law, who knew that she was a firm but kind mother-in-law. She was always ready to look after her numerous grandchildren and asked in return only that she be kept fully abreast of all the news and interest of their lives.

'Hello, Mrs Willow,' said Bethany brightly. 'It's a very foggy . . . '

'Shhhh,' hissed her neighbour conspiratorially. 'You don' want *er* to know you' back, do you?' Craning her neck with difficulty to see into the next door garden, Mrs Willow was reassured by the stillness of the curtains covering the brightly lit window. 'Come on in now for a little sup of tea, why don' you?'

Hesitating only for a minute, and casting an anxious glance at the still motionless curtains, Bethany quietly lowered the catch on the gate and took the few steps necessary to reach next door where she was immediately enveloped in the ambrosial warmth of Mrs Willow's front room.

Mr Willow was snoring quietly by the gas fire, warming his stockinged feet on the tiled surround. He lolled gently to one side in his armchair, his arm hanging down to the carpet where he had dropped his paper, and his head drooping on his chest. Mrs Willow snorted dismissively, and gestured to the far end of the front room at the kitchen. She followed Bethany through and shut the door firmly behind them. 'Now we'll be cosy,' she said, lowering herself comfortably into a chair and reaching for the teapot in its flowered teacosy. Mrs Willow's kitchen was filled with the smells of deep-fried chips and newly baked cake. It was the backbone of the house, and the essence of all that went on there. It was crammed with vitality, almost bursting with the flotsam and jetsam that Mrs Willow accumulated in the course of her busy productive existence. Washing piled high in wicker baskets nudged bright pots and pans stacked in precariously leaning towers, plants lined the window sills and knick-knacks of all varieties perched on the edges of shelves, table ledges and surfaces. A marmalade cat lay curled up on a pile of freshly ironed tea towels, and a family of kittens purred in a basket in the corner of the room.

The walls were lined closely with brightly coloured plates, which clamoured for attention, drawing the eye to their messages and pictures. Views from the Pyramids jostled scenes from Majorca and Minorca, and landscapes from the Lake District vied with beach vistas from Cyprus and Malta. The effect was not discordant, which was surprising considering the sheer number of places represented. Perhaps this was because each plate was regarded with affection and pride by Mrs Willow, who often said that she had no need at all to travel, because she had the whole world right there in her house. She had been born, married, and raised children in her house, and fully expected to die in it. She firmly refused any offer to take her out of it, even for a day trip to the countryside. However, her vast numbers of friends and family who went on holiday brought her these plates back, knowing that Mrs Willow obtained deep vicarious pleasure from their wanderings. The kitchen was warm and steamy and, once Bethany had become used to the assault on her senses, she began to enjoy her tea. The scrubbed wooden table in the centre of the room had a space at the end for partaking of refreshment, and it was here that Mrs Willow sat. Mr Willow had been using the other end for taking cuttings from his geraniums, and she could smell their agreeable pungent aroma mixing with the other smells in the room. Bethany lifted a pile of pillowcases from a chair and put them carefully behind her on the dresser, between a large china cat and a dish filled with clothes pegs with 'A Present From Blackpool' written on it. Then she sat down, cradling her green china mug of dark milky tea in her cold hands, and smiled at Mrs Willow.

The old lady regarded her steadily with a gaze that was both knowing and compassionate. 'Tell me about this outin' then,' she said. Bethany gasped. Even though she knew that Mrs Willow knew all there was to know about everything that went on in the town, it was still a shock to hear her talking about the trip as though it was common knowledge. She looked at her neighbour, mouth agape. 'Why, bless you, it's not so odd, so don' go lookin' at me like that.

34

Close that cake'ole of yours before the flies get in.' Then, patiently, as Bethany was still lost for words, she said, 'Our Shirley popped in in 'er lunch hour and talked of nothin' else, didn't she, so you might as well tell me all about it.' Shirley worked at the Post Office and was married to the second of Mrs Willow's five sons who was a postman. Her other sons were all working. One owned a haba-dashery stall on the market, another was a foreman in the steel factory, a third had a profitable window-cleaning round in the valleys, and the fourth worked at the local telephone exchange. Her daughters-in-law all had jobs in the area, and so did many of her grandchildren so, one way or another, Mrs Willow always had access to any information that she could possibly want to acquire.

Bethany closed her mouth and then opened it again. All her longings and hopes about the trip came pouring out, together with her fears that her mother would never allow her to go, and the impossibilities of contributing the money. Finally she stopped, and stared despondently down at her mug, aware that she had said everything there was to say, and that there was no solution to be found in any of it. There was silence in the kitchen, and the cat could be heard washing her kittens. Mrs Willow was thinking. She had a very soft spot for her neighbour's child and knew what a constrained life she led. Long ago she had had a 'falling out' with Mrs Jones next door, and the two women were as unlike as two women could be. Mrs Willow firmly believed in making the best of whatever life handed her, and did not hold with bemoaning her lot. You just got on with things, in her book, and took life's ups and downs just the same, as part of the pattern. Consequently, Mrs Willow's life was a lot more enjoyable and richly studded with happiness than her next door neighbour's. Bethany, who was extremely observant, had thought about this often, and had come to the conclusion that whether people were happy in life had very little to do with the things that happened to them. From what she could see, it had much more to do with the way that they reacted to events rather than the events themselves. Mrs Willow would say, 'There's no use worrying about things you can't change' and make the best of whatever was going on. Her mother would add the newest setback to a long line of misfortunes stretching back to her childhood, and use it to reinforce her belief that she was the unluckiest of women, one whose life was an endless stream of suffering. Both of them believed what they were saying, and both statements became true for them. Bethany could see why her mother had an unhappy existence, whereas Mrs Willow was very happy in hers. She would remember this all her life.

35

Finally, Mrs Willow spoke. 'Now you just leave it with me, my ducks, and I'll see what I can do. There's no such thing as a problem that can't be solved, it just needs lookin' at from all sides. Just you run along back to that house of yours and I'll put my thinkin' cap on.' She was rewarded by a hopeful look from Bethany, who regretfully pushed back her chair and stood up. She would have liked to have stayed longer, but knew that she could not put off the moment when she had to go home. With a quick stroke of the cat, who arched its back to get the full benefit of the caress all the way down to its tail, Bethany made her way out of the crowded kitchen to the front room, where Mr Willow still slumbered peacefully. Her efforts to move quietly were wasted, for Mrs Willow gave her husband a sharp nudge as she bustled majestically past. With a wink to Bethany and a wealth of sarcasm in her voice she spoke to her drowsy mate. 'When Milord is ready for 'is tea, 'e can come and get it in the kitchen.' With a comforting pat on her arm, Mrs Willow gently pushed Bethany out of the door, saying 'Don' you worry now. Good things come to those who deserve them. Off you go.' She then turned and bustled off towards the kitchen, anxious to be busy with her next task. Bethany looked wistfully back into the cheerful room, returned Mr Willow's twinkling smile, and went reluctantly out into the night.

After the warm welcome of the Willows' house, the evening seemed even chillier and more dank. Bethany shivered and lifted the latch of her own gate once more. She went up the path and fumbled in her pocket for her key, her stomach tense with worry about the reception she was sure to get from her mother for being late. She went in. She could hear the television on in the front room, and called with forced cheerfulness, 'I'm home, Mother.' There was no reply and she knew that she would have to go in. She hung her coat up on the row of hooks in the hall, noticing that the mist had come in with her in the form of tiny droplets sparkling on the fabric. Then she went into the front room where her mother held court.

Mrs Jones was lying on the couch in front of the television with a tartan rug covering her legs, watching *Coronation Street*. Her expression was one of deep hurt bravely concealed, and she kept her eyes fixed on the television without looking at Bethany.

'I'm sorry I'm late, Mother, but I popped in to the library on the way home.' Still Mrs Jones did not speak, but Bethany detected a slight wince and a purse of the lips. Her heart beating fast at the prospect of unpleasantness, she forced herself to continue brightly. 'Have you eaten, or shall I fix us something up?' Only now did her

36

mother sigh heavily and look at her with eyes that were cold and angry, belying the words that she spoke.

'Please don't mind me, I shall be perfectly all right, I've only been waiting and worrying about you since six o'clock, imagining all sorts of things happening to you, and not able to do anything about it.' Bethany looked at her helplessly as she continued. 'If only I had the health and heedlessness of youth and was able to stay out until all hours enjoying myself, but instead I haven't even the strength to rise from this couch and cook a meal for my daughter when she finally gets home. I'm so weak that I'm no use even for that, and I feel quite faint from hunger and worry, but please don't worry about me. I'm sure I wouldn't feel easy asking you to get me anything. I expect that you'd much rather be putting your feet up and reading one of the books you were so eager to get from the library.'

Mrs Jones shot one more coldly furious glance at her daughter, and then turned back to the television, refusing to look up again, leaving Bethany standing by the door, uncertain as to how to proceed. In her experience, nothing would retrieve the evening now, but if she left her mother, as she desperately wanted to do, Mrs Jones's resentment would simmer for much longer. She knew that she had to stay, heart thudding and stomach tight, and keep going until the evening was ended by her mother retiring to her bed. 'Look, Mother, I really am terribly sorry, I should have realised that you would be worrying. Please let me get you something to eat . . . ' She trailed off as she saw that her mother was intent on the television and was not going to meet her halfway. 'I'm going to open a tin of tomato soup and have some cheese on toast with it. Shall I bring you some?' A slight shifting on the couch indicated that Mrs Jones was listening, so Bethany went down the hall and into the kitchen.

She turned on the neon strip light, and the cheerless kitchen glimmered a ghastly green-grey in the flickering glow. She wished she'd kept her coat on, as it felt cold in the room. She busied herself opening the soup tin and putting the bread under the grill, then bent down to get the cheese from the fridge. A small bit of lettuce lay on the floor, stuck down onto the brown carpet tiles. Bethany stared at it, feeling more depressed than she had done since she had left school. It all seemed so pointless and hopeless, somehow, and she wondered if this was all there was going to be, just her and her mother living from day to day with nothing changing except that they got older and older. Smelling the toast burning, she pulled herself together, picked up the lettuce fragment, and continued with the meal. Then she placed the bowls and plates onto a large tray and went back to the living room.

They ate in silence, except for the hissing of the gas fire, and the soothing noise of the television. Every so often the content of the programme would penetrate Bethany's consciousness and she would begin to enjoy watching lemurs struggling to survive in Madagascar. Then her mother would sigh, and the tension in the room would mount again, bringing with it the added guilt of having forgotten her mother's suffering for a moment. Bethany thought that things were always much worse if she wasn't suitably penitent.

The bitterness of words unsaid hung in the room, and she could hardly swallow her food. The anger had a density of its own, occupying the space between Mrs Jones and her world, and coagulating into a thick mass which could not be dissolved. Bethany felt as though it had even managed to permeate her own body, congealing into a knot of lumpish gristle in her throat, rendering her unable to speak. She felt the tightness of her neck and shoulder muscles and no longer knew what emotion she felt, so overpowering was the force of the other woman's unspoken fury. She sat on the far corner of the sofa, inwardly shrinking from the touch of her mother's foot under the blanket, but not daring to move in case it was perceived as an imagined slight. Not a word was spoken for the rest of the evening, until eventually the ten o'clock news was shown. At 10.15, during the advertisement break, Bethany helped her mother rise from the sofa, kissed her proffered cheek, and with relief heard her climb the stairs to bed.

An onlooker would probably have been oblivious to the play of violent emotions in the room during the course of the evening. Mrs Jones would have vehemently denied to her dying breath any suggestion that she was angry with her daughter, and so Bethany herself was denied the power of reply. The older woman's refusal to acknowledge her violent discontent had bred in Bethany a fear of confrontation and a passivity which sapped her ability to confront the situation. All her life Bethany had been robbed of the power of defence, because there was never any open attack. Instead, the feeling of depression that had overtaken her earlier in the evening now returned, and she stayed motionless in the rapidly cooling room, staring at the unlit gas fire, her mind numbed both with the exhaustion of having been in the presence of so much strong emotion, and relief at its longed-for absence.

After a while she stood and picked up the tray of bowls and plates and took them back into the kitchen. She ran the water into the sink and began to wash up and stack the plates onto the draining-board. When she had finished she left them to dry before checking that the back door was locked and the chain securely fastened on the front door. Doing these tasks made her feel better, and already her spirits were lifting.

She remembered her next door neighbour's parting comment about good things coming to those who deserve them. Mrs Willow often said that Bethany was made of 'the right stuff' and would someday 'come into her own'. She wasn't sure that she deserved such praise, as she never felt very certain of herself, but it was so nice to have someone as shrewd as Mrs Willow saying so. Meanwhile, she had the resilience and optimism of youth and rarely stayed miserable for long. Things never felt so bad in the morning, when she didn't feel tired. Tomorrow she would see Sylvia and talk things over with her, and perhaps Mrs Willow would be able to help. As she climbed into bed, Bethany reflected on how very kind most people were, and how lucky she was to have made such good friends merely through the pure good fortune of being in the right place at the right time. Life was pretty good, all in all. She fell asleep, unaware of the damp sheets and the brown patches on the wall, but instead heartened by the prospect of good things to come. The bright promise of clear seaside skies suffused her dreams with gold.

The next day Bethany escaped from the house before her mother was up. Mrs Jones was feeling especially ill that morning and hadn't been able to rise from her Bed of Pain. Bethany had taken her her breakfast in bed and then went out into the wet autumnal morning. She made her way down the hill towards the town centre, where she took a shortcut through an alley at the rear of the imposing Town Hall, to the empty shopping centre beyond. By this time it was raining hard.

The exposed plaza acted as a corridor for the wind, which whipped Bethany's coat against her legs and blew her wet hair across into her eyes. She put her head down and hurried towards the far corner of the square which offered shelter in the form of a concrete overhang. Pressed back against the blank glass doors of C & A, she paused to catch her breath. The top part of her body was shielded from the wind and so was kept fairly dry, but her ankles and calves were still at the mercy of the elements, and were uncomfortably wet from the rain that drove against the building. She surveyed the scene in front of her.

The shopping plaza, which was packed full of people during opening hours, was deserted, save for a few pigeons. They were pecking half-heartedly around the overflowing litter bins, or hunched dejectedly on the back of the concrete benches lining the edge of the square. Old wrappers from the previous day's fish and chips flapped wetly around on the paving and a milk bottle was rolling noisily between the bollards where shoppers padlocked their bicycles. The single green island in the sea of grey concrete was a small plane tree blighted with rust and nearly bent double in the wind. The base of the tree, which was planted directly into the stone and edged with brick, acted as a magnet for the litter, which converged in an untidy heap around its spindly trunk. All in all, it was a depressing vista, and Bethany shivered as she waited under the concrete awning. She looked at her watch, but didn't really worry that Sylvia was late. Sylvia was usually to be found rushing frantically from one appointment to another, arriving flushed and giggling, and full of apologies. It was always so lovely to see her that Bethany (who was punctual to a fault) never resented her friend's tardiness, and only began to expect her after the arranged time to meet had passed.

A loud shriek over by the disused fountain next to the deserted cashpoint machines alerted Bethany to Sylvia's arrival. A bedraggled figure was clattering towards her on impossibly high heels. Teetering through the rain, Sylvia had just stepped into a huge puddle spreading across her path and this had caused her to scream, curse and yell with laughter at the same time. She didn't let this impede her progress, but continued at top speed through the rain, hurtling towards Bethany in a series of lurching movements, driven continually off course by the buffeting wind. She tacked backwards and forwards like a small dingy blown across a stormy harbour, all the time shouting breathlessly at the top of her voice. Bethany could only hear one word in several that were being blown towards her, and as usual found that her spirits were cheered at the mere sight of her eccentric friend. It was no use at all telling Sylvia to wait until she got nearer, her words would have been blown away in the gale and, anyway, Sylvia never listened to advice unless she had already previously convinced herself of the right course of action.

Finally the two friends met at the edge of the square, and hugged each other affectionately. 'Oh, Lor', I can't believe how wet it is and I didn't even bring my brolly and of course I was late this mornin' and our Da' couldn't give me a lift into town today what with the van bein' broken down an' that and of all mornins to break my nail and then that *puddle!*' Sylvia paused to draw breath and then gave another scream of laughter. 'Did you see me bein' blown all over the place? Perhaps I don' need to go on that diet after all. Oh, come on, ol' Droopy Drawers'll be going potty if we don' get to work soon.' Bethany could never bring herself to use the typing pool's nickname for Mrs Evans, the most experienced typist there, who acted as a kind of unofficial steward of behaviour for the wilder girls and who waged war on those, like Sylvia, who were perpetually late. Bethany had a healthy respect for the older woman, and secretly admired her attempts to bring order into the sometimes chaotic office. She knew that it would be a waste of time to say so, and contented herself with quietly following her own standards of behaviour, while at the same time happily enjoying Sylvia's healthy disregard for all things she considered 'borin''.

The day progressed much like any other until their lunch break, when the two girls met as usual in the corridor outside the ladies' loos. In spite of Sylvia's flippancy, she was a good typist and was glad to have the job. Some of Bethany's seriousness had rubbed off on her and, although Sylvia loved a 'good laugh' and was always ready to join in the office banter, she worked hard during office hours and the two did not talk too much at their desks. Consequently, it was 12.30 before the pair had the opportunity to talk about the events of the day before. Sylvia knew about Bethany's mother, and her problem of how to manage the works outing. She had once been to tea at Bethany's house and was completely mystified by Mrs Jones, and consequently failed to make any of the right sympathetic responses to her references to Suffering and Life's Thorny Path. When Mrs Jones had been holding forth at some length, and Sylvia had made a few futile attempts at conversation, she caught Bethany's agonised eyes and had been overcome with a fit of uncontrollable giggles. Snorting into her tea, and spluttering bread and butter all over the table, she had tried unsuccessfully to pretend she was coughing. This had only made her hysteria worse, and she had had to rush to the bathroom. Eventually the two girls had escaped and had leaned thankfully against the front door, both weak and exhausted, but for different reasons. Bethany was overcome with embarrassment for her friend, and relief that it was all over. Sylvia was quite simply shaking with fresh fits of laughter. 'Oooh, I nearly wet me knickers. I'm sorry, Bethany, but it was worse than being in church.' When Bethany returned to the house, her mother was stony-faced and at a loss to understand her daughter's choice of friends.

'A very peculiar young girl, and I would hope that you would never dress that way if you were invited to tea. She was barely covered up.' The visit had not been a success and had never been repeated, but Sylvia had not forgotten the experience and understood the enormity of Bethany's problem.

The girls left the post office and walked through the now busy shopping centre towards Woolworth's. The rain had stopped and the wind was bracing, but nothing like the howling gale of earlier that morning. They pushed open the glass doors and walked through the rows of Pick 'n' Mix to the back of the store where there was a cramped cafeteria filled with people eating pies and gravy. The place was gently steaming as wet coats and headscarves dried in the heat, and the floor was slippery from dozens of pairs of wet shoes and galoshes. Nevertheless the atmosphere was cheerful and homely and made a welcome change from the office. The girls joined the queue and then carried their selections on Formica trays to a table near the window. Sylvia wrinkled her nose and moved an ashtray onto the nearby windowsill, and then balanced both their trays in the crook of her arm while Bethany quickly fetched a cloth from the cleaning station opposite, and wiped the tomato sauce and gravy smudges from the table. They knew from long experience that this was the quickest and most hygienic method of enjoying their lunch and had now perfected the routine so that it took no more than a few seconds.

The girls sat in the green plastic chairs and then went through the contortions of removing their coats and putting them behind them. Sylvia carefully removed her transparent plastic headscarf and patted her silvery blonde hair, automatically glancing at the window to check her reflection and then realising that the glass was so fogged with condensation that the move was futile. She caught Bethany's eye, and giggled. 'My mascara's not run in this weather, has it? I'm so glad I had this perm otherwise I'd be like a drowned dormouse what with all this wet. At least it can't ruin nails, can it? Anyway let's eat, I'm just starvin'.'

They tucked in with relish and Bethany sat in contented silence, listening to her friend chatter in between mouthfuls. They finished their meals and began to drink the sweet, cloying hot chocolate that they both ordered instead of a cake or pudding. Woolworth's cafeteria looked out onto the bus station and, although the window was misted and wet, Bethany could hear the buses revving their engines, and the hissing of their doors as they unloaded their cargo of shoppers. The sounds were rhythmic and steady, and the café was warm and steamy, and Bethany found herself drifting into a pleasant trance as she drank her comforting warm drink.

Suddenly she realised that Sylvia was looking at her and laughing. 'You 'aven't 'eard a word I've been sayin', 'ave you? Here I

42

am, pourin' my heart out and you in a brown study, not even listenin'. Come on then, let's be 'avin' it. It's the trip, isn't it? What we goin' to do about it? You've got to come, so we'll 'ave to work it out, won't we? I was talkin' to Mam last night and we all want to help. It'd be such a laugh if you came, and it wouldn't be the same without you. What are we goin' to DO?'

Bethany sighed and set down her empty mug. 'I just don't know. There's so many problems I don't know which one to deal with first . . . I really do want to come, but I can't see how it's to be done.'

Sylvia, for all her flirting and light-hearted approach to life, could be very practical when she wanted to be. She was silent for a moment as she scraped the dark sludge of chocolate out from the bottom of her mug with a scarlet, and beautifully manicured, finger. She sucked it thoughtfully and then said, 'Well, as I see it, there's only two problems really. First, how do we get the money for the contributions without your mam findin' out, and second, how do we get you away for the week when it comes to it, without her havin' a blue fit?' She looked so pleased to have summed it up so logically, that Bethany burst out laughing.

'Oh well, I'm glad that's all we have to worry about then. I can't think why I'm so concerned.' In spite of her laughter she felt the impossibility of the situation more keenly than before. Last night she had hoped for a solution, but in the cold light of the wet October afternoon she was cast down into the depths of despondency once more. Such was her preoccupation that she only roused herself when she realised that Sylvia had said something extraordinary. Bethany stared at her friend.

'What did you say?' she asked in amazement. Sylvia gave her a good-natured shove.

'I said, dopey, that you could just go, you know. I mean, you are eighteen, and you don' have to really ask permission any more, do you? It's not as if you're doin' anythin' really dreadful or anythin', you're only wantin' to go on a bit of a holiday and you'd have chaperones. I mean, you could just go . . .' She trailed off and her words hung in the air as Bethany continued to stare at her. She giggled nervously. 'What? Stop starin' at me, you lemon, what did I say?' She reached across the table and pushed Bethany's arm again in an effort to rouse her friend from her trance.

Bethany shook herself and looked at Sylvia and opened her mouth to speak. She closed it again, as the impact of Sylvia's words took effect once more. The sheer simplicity of 'just going' took her breath away, and she was stunned that this solution had never presented itself to her before. She wondered why this was, and decided that it was because she had been trained in obedience from an early age. Any childish defiance had been dealt with so firmly by her parents that the possibility of rebellion had been gradually extinguished. The way that they had reacted to her wrongdoings had not been harsh in the sense that they had ever applied physical punishment. However, they had made her feel so much in error, so wrong, that Bethany, who like most children was anxious to please those she loved, effectively learned to accept that she had no right to question her parents. Quietly, she had become used to taking the easy path of compliance, while at the same time doing her best to suppress her feelings of guilt when she strayed too far from her mother's wishes. She learned to keep her experiences, and the thoughts that she drew from them, separate from her mother's world. Her friendship with Sylvia was one such instance. She could not give her friend up, but after the one futile and disastrous attempt to integrate the two worlds, now did not mention her to her mother. In this she was helped by Mrs Jones's lack of interest in her daughter's life.

Compliance was not something she found difficult, since it was the way she had learned to reconcile her own needs with her mother's. Conflict was another matter entirely. The thought that she might meet her mother in a head-on collision simply had not occurred to her, and now the possibility was at once both exhilarating and terrifying. The logical part of her recognised the irrefutable truth in what Sylvia said, while at the same time another voice was screaming. This was the voice of her childhood, which would always be frightened of the consequences of rebellion.

For the first time, Bethany wondered if her compliance contributed to her mother's predicament. Bethany hadn't developed or grown up, and up to now, Bethany supposed she had seen this as all her mother's doing. Now it occurred to her that, although her mother was incapacitated by fear and anger, she too must take some responsibility. Perhaps it really was time to make the decision and choose to change, although it was frightening. Maybe she could even help her mother as well as herself. All these thoughts were whirling in her brain as she continued to stare unseeing at Sylvia across the plastic table of the Woolworth's cafeteria next to the bus station.

Poor Sylvia was by this time getting alarmed. For the life of her, she couldn't understand what she had said that had provoked Bethany's stunned reaction. She had been accustomed to defying her mother from an early age, although she was the first to admit that Our Beryl, her second oldest sister, was a right one for that, and that she was quite docile in comparison. Mrs Jones was an old bat in her opinion and it was high time that Bethany stood up to her. After all, as she had already pointed out, a holiday was a perfectly reasonable thing to want, and her friend deserved a break; she often looked as though she was carrying the weight of the world on her shoulders, Mam said. And now all she'd done was say so, and Bethany had gone all sort of funny. Sylvia looked down at her Minnie Mouse watch and let out a scream of concern. 'Come on, we'll really catch it from Droopy if we're late.' This finally roused Bethany, and the pair of them grabbed their coats and set off at a run through the store, Sylvia cannoning off the lipstick stand with yelps of merriment and relief that everything was all right again. They ran all the way back to the office, and their afternoon was so busy that the subject of the works outing wasn't raised again that day. Sylvia just had time to whisper. 'You had me worried then. What was all that about?' There was no time to answer, but Bethany's grin reassured her. Syliva was relieved to see her friend was looking normal and that everything was just as it always had been. She didn't know that her words had awoken possibilities in Bethany's heart, and that things were about to change.

A few days later, Mrs Willow was outside the pet shop buying catfood for the marmalade cat and her kittens when she bumped into Sylvia's Mam who was there buying pansies for her back yard. The two were old friends and, since they hadn't seen each other for far too long (at least three days, they agreed), it was inevitable that they would end up having a nice cup of tea and an Eccles cake in the tea shop on the corner of Morton Street. This was their favourite place for a break, as it not only served lovely Eccles cakes, but also offered an excellent vantage point for seeing everything that was going on in the street. For this it was essential that the window table was obtained, and for a nasty moment it seemed as though this was not to be. An elderly couple had just entered the shop and looked very much as though they were going to take the coveted table. However, Mam managed to manoeuvre herself as if by accident across their path, while at the same time Mrs Willow fixed them with a beady and censorious eye, and by sheer force of personality beat them down. The elderly couple retreated, muttering, to the table next to the aspidistra in the corner, not at all an unpleasant table, but Mrs Willow and Mam would have died rather than occupy it with any self-respect.

Flushed with success, they settled themselves comfortably and ordered a pot of tea for two and two Eccles cakes. While they were waiting for these to arrive, they began to catch up with all The News. The News was a source of unfailing satisfaction to both, and they were united as kindred spirits by their enjoyment. Being first with The News was a point of honour, and both Mam and Mrs Willow were foremost in their field. There was a certain amount of good-natured rivalry and Mam had scored the latest points with the information that Mrs Cockerel had run off with the milkman from Lower Ladygate Street. This morsel was much enjoyed by both women, as Mrs Cockerel had long been regarded as a flighty piece and had needed her Come-uppance. Mrs Willow would have liked to be first with this item, but was somewhat mollified both by the fact that she had predicted Mrs Cockerel's Come-uppance the previous week, and the fact that she had been first with The News that old Arthur Davies had had one too many at the Dog and Duck and had broken his ankle falling down the steps at closing time. This was particularly satisfactory, as Mrs Davies was considered by both to be a bit above herself and had particularly offended Mam recently with the suggestion that she could be 'making a bit more of herself' now that her children had grown up.

There was a short silence. Mam then imparted the information that Our Maureen was expecting again, although this item was felt by both not to count for much, because Mam would know this first, being Maureen's mother, and Mrs Willow could hardly be expected to be party to the item. This led them briefly into the agreeable conversational cul-de-sac of Mam's daughters and the dance that Our Beryl was leading her young man. Mrs Willow was somewhat disapproving of Our Beryl, and just stopped short of unflattering comparisons with Mrs Cockerel and the milkman from Lower Ladygate Street. She was glad that she had refrained as she really was very fond of Mam, and Our Beryl wasn't really a bad girl, just flighty, and would settle down in the fullness of time. Once the subject was exhausted and the tea and Eccles cakes had arrived, they chewed contentedly, gazing out of the window. Following the previous conversation, Mrs Willow turned her thoughts naturally to Sylvia, and then of course to Bethany. Mam had been following exactly the same process, and both began speaking at once.

Once they had got over the slight disappointment that each knew as much as the other about Bethany's predicament, they quickly settled down to discussing what, in their opinion, should be done to help the poor girl. Both were unanimous in their disapproval of Mrs Jones, and convinced that Bethany should have a holiday, and if they could help, then they would. Mrs Willow began by saying that the poor child was in a right proper stew about it all and had 'poured 'er 'eart out'. She felt it her bounden duty to do something, and Mam agreed wholeheartedly. There was a short pause, whereupon Mam confided in her that Sylvia had put the idea into Bethany's head that she could just ignore her mother's reaction and go on the trip in spite of her. Both pursed their lips doubtfully. Defying mothers was not a strategy that, as a rule, was championed by either of them. However, after due consideration they came to the conclusion that, in this instance, perhaps it was the only way. The plan itself raised difficulties of its own. Mrs Willow was very doubtful that Bethany would be able to withstand the months of unpleasantness that would surely follow the announcement of her intention to go to Brighton. Mrs Jones would not take this lying down, she predicted darkly, and she felt in her bones that the poor child would crumble over the weeks and months it would take to contribute the money to the fund.

Finishing the last morsels of Eccles cake from her plate, Mam was distracted at this point by the sight of Mrs Williams pushing her new baby down the street in a dark blue pram. She tapped on the window, and both women waved at the young mother, mouthing 'how are yous' and 'how's the baby', with much nodding and gesturing. Mrs Williams continued on her way. 'Bless 'is little cotton socks,' said Mam fondly.

Then she came up with an idea. If Bethany could find some way of getting the money to Roy, the young postman in charge of collecting the contributions for the trip, without taking it out of her wages, the moment of defiance could be put off until nearer the date of the holiday. It would be a kind of 'fay taccumplee' she thought. Mrs Willow was impressed in spite of herself, and rapidly turned her thoughts to how this could be managed. Suddenly, inspiration struck. Gareth, her third son, ran a haberdashery stall on the market, and was always looking for someone to do little odd jobs. Only last week he had been bemoaning the fact that he had to spend time, which would be better spent elsewhere, winding wool from the long skeins he got from the wholesalers into the compact and colourful balls he stacked on the stall. As the winter drew in and Christmas approached, the stall got more and more busy, and Mrs Willow was certain that he would welcome Bethany's help. Winding wool could be done in her lunch break, and the money earned could be passed straight on to Roy each week.

The two women looked at each other happily. They loved to solve problems, and were delighted to be of help to young Bethany. Having accomplished everything to their great satisfaction, they

47

both realised that they ought to be getting on. Mam craned her head to see the clock above the hairdresser's on the opposite side of the road, and then let out a gasp. 'Ooh, look, there's Shirley Davies, having 'er roots touched, and she swore they was natrel.' Mrs Willow looked. Of one accord they rapidly gathered up their bits and pieces, paid the bill, and set off down the street past the hairdressers' and the unfortunate Mrs Davies. Things were looking up all round.

The arrangement with Gareth and the wool-winding worked very well. Every day before work, Bethany would call in on the stall, collect several skeins of wool and put them in her large shoulder-bag. Then, during the lunch break, she and Sylvia would sit and wind wool into balls in the Woolworth's cafeteria until it was time to go back. They found that they easily had enough time to eat their sandwiches and then chat to their heart's content as they worked. Sylvia insisted that she would take her turn at the task as it was no trouble, and two pairs of hands were better than one. Then each evening, Bethany would drop the balls of wool off on her way back home. On Thursday evening Gareth would solemnly count out the money from his cash register and put it in a large manila envelope which Bethany pocketed with glee. The money covered her contributions and there was a little bit left over for spending money. This she gave to Mrs Willow for safe keeping, who put it into a china pot on her mantelpiece.

So the months passed, and the entries in Roy's book grew until they covered four pages, and Mrs Willow's pot began to overflow. Christmas came and went, and the days began to grow warmer, and the evenings longer. One morning in late May there was a neatly lettered card in Roy's handwriting on the staff noticeboard. It announced that all contributions were complete and the book was now closed. If anybody cared to buy him a drink for his efforts, they were very welcome. There was much laughter at this and it was generally agreed that Roy was a real card and should be a right laugh on the trip. Bethany was giddy with excitement and relief that the first hurdle was over. She hugged Sylvia and the pair danced in the corridor. 'It's goin' to be so great,' Sylvia giggled. Later that day they went to thank Gareth for his help and to tell him they no longer needed the job. For the first time in many months they sat in the café without skeins of wool hanging on the back of the chairs. Bethany treated them both to melted marsh-mallows in their hot chocolate to celebrate.

As June passed into July, and the date of the great departure grew near, Bethany grew increasingly apprehensive about telling her mother what she was planning to do. Mrs Jones lived such an insular and withdrawn existence that she appeared not to notice her daughter's obvious agitation, although, as Mrs Willow commented acidly, anyone with half an eye would know something was up.

One warm July evening Bethany made her way home after work. It was Friday and the end of a gloriously sunny week. The talk in the typing pool had all been of weekend plans and making the most of the wonderful weather. The air was warm and soft and most of the houses had their doors wide open to catch the last of the sun's rays. People were out in their front gardens talking to their neighbours and the smell of cooking wafted down the street. Cats guarding the outposts of their domain lounged languidly at the ends of the paths right next to the pavement, soaking up the sunlight and gazing watchfully through slitted eyes at the passers-by. As Bethany neared home, she saw that the door to her house was firmly closed, but that Mr Willow was sitting peacefully in his front garden smoking his pipe. She could smell the aroma of the tobacco wafting towards her and breathed in its heady smell, thinking, as she always had done, of the frankincense and myrrh of the three wise men. In spite of her preoccupation she smiled at her childhood thought and her smile was answered on the kindly lined face of her next door neighbour. Mr Willow, perhaps because he was married to Mrs Willow, or perhaps simply because it was his nature, was a man of few words. He took refuge in his pipe and listened more easily than he spoke. Bethany knew that not much escaped him, however, and although she more often confided in his garrulous and kindly wife, she valued his advice greatly. Now she was glad that she had the opportunity to speak with him, as she wanted to discuss what was on her mind.

Mr Willow stood up and held out his arm towards his faded deckchair in welcome. Putting down her handbag and the bag of shopping that she was carrying, she arranged herself on the grass next to him, refusing his gallant offer of the seat, being more comfortable on the ground anyway. She tugged at blades of grass but said nothing and then leaned back on her hands. The marmalade cat appeared from nowhere as if it had second sight, and pushed itself up against her legs. Bethany picked it up and put her face down near its soft fur, listening to the comforting clicking sound of its purring. Still nothing was said and the shadows began to lengthen as dusk gradually settled on the front garden. The sky turned a pale violet and greeny blue, and the air began to cool as the long hot day turned into a peaceful summer's evening. Further down the street they could hear the clink of milk bottles being put out on a doorstep, and a mother calling to her children to come in for dinner. Mr Willow waited quietly, sucking on his pipe tranquilly. Suddenly Bethany said, 'I think everything's going to change soon, and I don't know if I want it to.'

There was a silence as Mr. Willow took his pipe from between his teeth, realised that it had gone out, and cradled it between his roughened hands. Looking down at it, he reached unhurriedly inside his ancient leather waistcoat and took out a block of tobacco. Gently teasing out the strands, he took a pinch and pushed it down into the bowl of his pipe, concentrating deeply. His hands trembled slightly, but his movements were without haste or rush. Next he took a box of Swan matches from the other pocket of his waistcoat and lit the pipe, never taking his eyes away from the task. All this time Bethany waited. She knew Mr Willow well, and was glad of the peaceful way that he considered before speaking. Her words hung in the air, however, and it was a relief when he finally spoke.

'Are you happy, pet?' he asked.

'Yes. No. Oh, I don't know really, I suppose it depends how you look at it . . . well, no, I suppose not really . . . '

Mr Willow's eyes were bright and kind as he said, 'I know it's not easy, but change is part of life, love.' Stretching forward, he reached out a finger and prodded a little green caterpillar sitting on the round leaf of one of his prizewinning geraniums, which were a glorious salmon-pink in the dusky light. 'I'm sure that little fellow over there doesn't think there's anything else but that leaf, that's the world to him, but things must change, and I daresay he'll be glad of his wings when he gets them. Things will be how things will be.' This was a very long speech from Mr Willow, who tended to keep his own council and let his wife do the talking. Bethany sighed and stood up, her palms slightly muddy and criss-crossed with the indented patterns of the grass. She felt stiff, and arched her back experimentally to determine if she could move freely. Mr Willow also rose and stood courteously by the gate, pipe in hand. It had gone out again. Bethany looked at him.

'Then I suppose I can't put it off any longer, can I?' Her neighbour said nothing, but as she turned to go, reached out a hand and gave her a clumsy pat on her shoulder.

'You know where we are, love, if you need us.' Immeasurably touched, Bethany felt a lump rise in her throat. With a heavy heart, she felt in her pocket for her door key, and let herself in to the airless house.

She walked straight through the house to the kitchen at the

back, and opened the door to let the air circulate. By now it was getting dark and the atmosphere was velvety soft and held the scents and smells of the evening. The comforting smell of onions frying wafted from somewhere, and Bethany felt hungry. She went back into the passageway and hung up her jacket, calling, 'I'm home, Mother.' As usual there was no reply. Bethany never knew if her mother did not answer because it was too much effort, or if it was her way of getting her daughter to come to her rather than calling out. Whatever it was, Bethany never stopped wanting her mother to answer her, and she also never went straight away to find her mother when she went in. There was a subtle locking of wills in the house, which Bethany was starting to recognise. This did not help her with what she knew she had to do, and she felt the need of some food to sustain her before she tackled Mrs Jones on the subject of the holiday. She couldn't put it off any longer, she knew, but it could wait until they'd eaten.

Bethany unpacked the shopping. She'd stopped off at the fish stall in the market just as they were packing up and had picked up some fresh plaice. She decided to bake it in milk and have it with potatoes and the fresh peas Sylvia had given her from her Da's allotment. She loved fish, and her mother approved of this way of cooking it. It seemed to speak somehow of invalid menus and convalescence and building up one's strength. Bethany looked out of the back door, thinking about what Mr. Willow had said, while the food cooked. Then she arranged the food on the plate, and put it all on two trays. She walked through to the sitting room, where she knew her mother would be waiting, and put the first tray down. She then carried her own tray into the room, and sat with the steaming food on her lap ready to eat.

Mrs. Jones was not at her usual place on the couch in front of the television, although the noisy chattering of a game show filled the room. Instead, she stood with her back to the room, by the window that overlooked the street. The curtains had not been drawn, and she was staring blindly into the darkness. The street-lamps had not yet been switched on and there was nothing to see, but she stood motionless, arms folded around her, ignoring Bethany's entrance with the food.

'Mother, I've brought you your supper, why don't you come and eat it before it gets cold?' Puzzled by her mother's lack of response, Bethany went over to the window and stood by her mother. Mrs Jones never failed to rouse herself at mealtimes, even though she often protested that she wasn't very hungry. 'Mother, come and eat, it's baked plaice, and some lovely fresh peas that Sylvia's Da' sent us and mashed potatoes . . .'

Bethany trailed off as her mother turned to look at her.

'Don't speak to me in that patronising tone; I'm not a child, nor in my dotage, and I see a lot more of what goes on than you think. I saw you go and sit in the garden with our neighbour, and I saw you talking about me behind my back when you could have been home to see me.' Her voice rose as she continued. 'Why do you go there instead of coming to me with your problems? I've never understood it. Heaven knows it's been the same ever since you were a child, always wanting something more, always challenging me, always thinking you know best. You think you're better than me, you always have, hanging around with those common girls and laughing at me behind my back, plotting and scheming about goodness knows what. You're an ungrateful, deceitful, selfish girl, Bethany, and I know how it's all going to end. There'll be nothing but trouble come to you, I know that. What's the point of anything, anyway?' Horrified, Bethany saw that her mother's eyes were bright with tears and, although her mouth was bitter, she was genuinely hurt. She had no idea what to do and stood there helplessly, until her stomach gave a huge rumble.

Quickly she took her mother by the elbow, and said, 'Mum, our supper's getting cold, come on.' This was perhaps not the most profound of responses, but the words were out of her mouth before she had time to think, and she seized gratefully upon a practical way of gaining time. As she sat down, she was jolted afresh by the clear pain and despair in what her mother had said. She had so often seemed resentful and angry about so little that it was a shock to see that she really did suffer, and that she herself was in no little way responsible for the hurt. Both began to fork up the mouthfuls of food from their separate trays as though their lives depended on it.

All the time she was eating, Bethany was filled with a mounting apprehension, knowing that she had to speak. What her mother had said required a response. She glanced across at Mrs Jones, whose head was bent over her food. She was eating with a rhythmic, mechanical motion, carelessly slopping her food around her plate. She had dropped some peas onto her skirt and paid no attention to them, even though she was normally a fastidiously tidy eater. Trembling, Bethany laid down her fork and began to speak. Her voice cracked and she cleared her throat and started again.

'I'm so sorry I've hurt you, Mother. I . . . I just didn't realise that you wanted me to talk to you about things. You always seem so tired . . . ' There was no reply, although Mrs Jones was looking at her steadily. Taking her silence as encouragement, Bethany continued. 'Mum, I know that I should have talked to you before about this . . . The thing is that there is a works outing next week and . . . and I'm going to go. Please don't try to stop me, because I'm determined, and it's only a week, and I won't be in any danger, and I'll have chaperones and . . . ' Her words hung in the oppressive silence. Her mother closed her eyes and leaned back into the chair. There was no sound anywhere. It felt to Bethany as if the whole world was waiting.

Finally her mother said, 'What makes you think that I'm going to try to stop you from going?' Now it was Bethany who was silent. Of all the replies that her mother could have made, this was the last one that she was expecting. 'Bethany, my life is over. I never expected very much from the world, and I certainly didn't get it. I've tried to tell you that life is hard, and that becoming attached to anybody leads to pain and loss. You won't listen to me when I say that it's better not to expect too much from people, because you have your own ideas. I knew that I would be alone one day, and that you would leave like all the rest, because that's how it's meant to be. In spite of all I've told you, you carry on in your own way, and your life will end in pieces as mine has. I never pressed you to confide in me, it's true, because I saw very well that you valued our next door neighbours and girls from your office more highly than me. I don't pretend it didn't hurt, but I wouldn't demean myself by poking my nose in when you very obviously didn't want me to. I've done all I can do, and you're grown now, and you must make your own way. It's over.' Mrs Jones finished and Bethany saw that, during the whole of her speech, she had remained leaning back against her chair with her eyes closed. She looked drained, as though with each sentence the very life force was draining from her. Now her skin had a greyish tinge, and the dark shadows under her eyes showed strongly. Bethany was genuinely concerned for her.

'Mum,' she said, for the third time that evening using a term of endearment that she hadn't uttered for years. 'Look. I'm so very sorry. I haven't meant to hurt you, really I haven't. Can't we talk about this? Is it all right for me to go to Brighton on the trip or . . . ' She was about to say 'or would you rather I didn't go' but she stopped herself just in time. Her mother would rather she didn't go, and she couldn't give up now that she'd come so far.

Without speaking, Mrs Jones put her hands onto the arms of the chair and raised herself out of it with difficulty. She appeared to have aged in the course of one evening. She began to walk slowly towards the door. Bethany stood up and stood in her path.

'Mum, please, talk to me. I really would like to talk and we can make things better . . . ' She trailed off again as she realised that the older woman was impassive, merely waiting for her to move out of the way. Now it was Bethany who was close to tears as the realisation dawned that nothing she said was having an effect. Mrs Jones was not looking at her, and continued to wait for Bethany to move out of the way. Bethany made one last imploring effort. 'Mother, it's not too late. If you want me to talk to you instead of to other people, I will, it's all I ever wanted, and we can tell each other things and be friends, and when I come back I can tell you about all the things I've seen and done, and it'll be so wonderful, just how things should have been all along between us . . . '

While she was speaking she moved aside, carried along by her words, beginning to pace the room in her eagerness. Surely this was what her mother wanted too: the closeness, and the sharing of things that would give them a bond. Maybe one day it would even be possible to laugh together. Her mother had been hurt by her actions. This must mean that she wanted deep down to repair the jagged tear between them, to start finally to mend the gulf that had separated them for so long. Saying 'it's over' was a way of asking Bethany to open her heart, to make the first move of openness and reconciliation which would lead to the new relation-ship of trust and love.

The hope that had sprung in her as she spoke died abruptly as she realised that her mother had simply walked away. At first, Bethany did not understand, and then the sound of the door closing brought her sharply back from her dream. Desperately she ran into the hallway as her mother was climbing the stairs. 'Please, Mother, please, talk to me.' Mrs Jones turned to look at her daughter and her face was blank and emotionless. When she spoke, it was flat and drained of expression.

'You're wrong, Bethany. It is too late. Much too late. It's done. Now leave me be.' It was her face rather than her words that finally convinced Bethany that she would never build the bridge between herself and her mother that she had longed for all those years. She knew that the love and companionship that she wanted could not happen, and that there was no longer any point in trying. Her grief stabbed her all the more sharply with the realisation that perhaps her mother had wanted something more once, and that maybe they could have salvaged something if she had tried harder to penetrate the despair that surrounded her. Bethany cried bitterly for the loss of the mother she had never had, and for the mother who had seen her, and judged her wanting. At that moment she believed all that her mother had said about love and pain and loss, and wept for her, and for herself.

After Bethany left for the Brighton trip, she never saw her mother again. She didn't return to Wales even when her mother died. One day she received a letter from a firm of solicitors, telling her that her mother had died. Among her effects had been a specific request that her daughter not be allowed to sort out the house or her things. She left all of her possessions to a distant surviving cousin, and no message for her daughter, save that she was requested not to attend her burial. Bethany occasionally thought of her mother during the years, alone in the cold dusty rooms of her childhood home, but she never went back. Mrs Jones had meant what she said when she said 'It's too late.'

* * *

Bethany took a deep breath. She had no idea how long she had been sitting there in the high-backed chair, remembering her childhood. It had been years since she had thought about her mother, because she had not been able to endure the pain she had felt at the rejection, and had locked the whole memory away where it could no longer hurt her. Now she turned the past over in her mind. Just the mere fact of looking at it made it somehow more bearable, and she realised that there was the possibility that she could come to terms with what had happened. What was it her angel had said? 'Remembrance is Healing', and something about embracing the pain of her past. That needed quite a bit of thinking about.

She got up to go into the kitchen, and found that her foot had gone to sleep. Staggering, she almost fell down and this brought her thoughts sharply back to the present. Laughing at herself, she tottered into the kitchen to put the kettle on. It felt good to smile. She saw that remembering the rejection that had seared her with pain had no power to stop her smiling. She struggled to remember more of what the angel had called the Third Lesson. A pen and paper would help if she was really to work on it. Glancing up at the kitchen clock she found with a shock that it was two o'clock in the afternoon. She had been sitting remembering since early this morning, and it was no wonder that she was faint and queasy with hunger.

She made herself a cheese sandwich and devoured it rapidly. Fishing around in the back of the fridge, she found a low-fat yoghurt and ate that as well. She wished there was some chocolate but knew without looking that she'd finished it yesterday, or was it the day before? Since the angel had first made its presence felt, she'd rather lost track of time. Friday afternoon; only three days since she'd first heard the voice, and yet it felt like a lifetime. Norman would be home in four hours and she felt she had changed completely. She wondered if he'd notice. Probably not, since the changes were on the inside, and their relationship didn't really concern things that weren't immediately visible to the naked eye. Poor Norman, she thought, momentarily considering what he'd do if she told him about the voice. She smiled again. Luckily it had nothing whatsoever to do with him. It was for her, and her alone, that her angel was speaking. She had a flash of gratitude, and resolved anew that she wouldn't let it down. She would learn her lessons.

Although she wasn't quite sure how, it appeared she already had three, and it very much sounded as though there were going to be more. She found the pad of paper that she usually wrote shopping lists on. On the front was written 'Switch it on? toaster? kettle? oven? grill? fridge?' She tore it off and threw it away in the pedal bin under the sink. It needed emptying, but it could wait. Then she reached for the radio and switched it on so she could listen to music while she thought. She twiddled the knob and found a classical station playing something orchestral. For a moment she gazed into space, entranced by the pure loveliness of the sound. It felt as though her body was filling up with the rich melody, and she breathed deeply and closed her eyes. After a few moments, she opened them and picked up her pencil.

She stared at the blank sheet of paper and wondered what to do. What could she remember about what she had been told? When she focused her thoughts, she realised that it was all there as though resting in a book in the corner of her mind. The first thing was that the present moment was the only thing of import- ance, and that she was creating the past and the future with her thoughts. She realised that the first thing she noticed about her memory of her mother was that she could hardly make a picture of what she looked like without feeling miserable. She concen- trated on seeing her face without being unhappy, or feeling the tight sadness of rejection and inadequacy. She could do it. She experimented further. She made her mother smile in her memory, putting the loving happy smile she always wanted to see on her face, shining from her eyes. She could do that as well.

Bethany came back to the present. She knew that she was

56

imagining her mother happy, and not finding a real memory, but it made things feel different somehow. If she could look at the past and not feel the misery deep in the pit of her stomach, surely she was well on the way to the next stage: to let go, by lovingly forgiving. She felt tears pricking her eyes, in part influenced by the glorious music which was reaching a crescendo, in part at the thought that she could let go of her pain and let the love for her mother through. Could she change things around and forgive her mother? What would happen to her if she did? According to the angel, she would be free, healed, and ready to move on. That was worth trying to embrace the pain of her past for. Bethany imagined her mother once more, and this time saw herself there as well. She was reaching out her arms and her mother was crying. Bethany stopped and laid her head down on the table, overcome with emotion, but at the same time filled with love and pity for her past. There was a lump in her throat, and she knew she had a lot more to do, including remembering real memories with forgiveness. But already she felt different.

The music came to an end and there was a short announcement that the composer had been Bruch. Turning to the back of her pad Bethany wrote 'Bruch', and underlined it. Then she wrote 'Poetry?' and turned back to the front page. She then wrote out as much as she could remember of the Third Lesson, under the title, 'Healing'. She took the little pad and put it under her side of the bed. Then she emptied the pedal bin, washed up her lunch things, and went out for a walk. She was going to practice letting go of the past that bound her.

JUNE

Norman wanted to go to see his mother. It was around half past five and he was driving home from work in his Austin Allegro, an activity he usually found soothing in its reassuring predictability. He knew exactly when it was essential to change gear to take the corners smoothly, knew that the traffic lights at the top of Shenley Drive would be turning orange and then red just as he drew up to them, knew that he had precisely 34 seconds to wait before they changed to green again. He knew because he noticed these things, and catalogued them in his mind because they were important. You had to learn to observe things, in his experience, because in that way you could draw conclusions about the way things worked. Traffic lights were a case in point. How many people, he wondered, passed this way every day, just as he did, and had no idea how long they sat waiting for the lights to change? They caused themselves so much unnecessary worry because they hadn't bothered to catalogue the information and draw conclusions from it. So much of life's uncertainty could be avoided if only people would take the trouble. It made him annoyed just to think about it. It was so unnecessary.

Norman had drawn out of the office car park and then was forced to stop at the zebra crossing almost immediately before he was even out of the high street, because a group of schoolchildren were already crossing. Just as he was about to shift into first gear and pull away, an elderly man stepped into the road. Norman let out a hissing breath between his teeth and drummed on the steering wheel impatiently. This was too bad. He looked at the clock on the dashboard. He would have to make up these wasted minutes before he got home. The journey should take precisely 27 minutes. He accelerated sharply before some other person could delay him further. As he coasted down the hill which took him out of the town towards the open fields, he relaxed a little. If he increased his speed to 50 m.p.h., he could make up the time. It was irritating because he usually only needed to do 40 m.p.h., but of course the old man on the crossing had put paid to that.

Norman put the thought firmly from his mind. No sense in getting angry again, as what was done was done. 'What's done is done' was one of his mother's sayings, and he found it calming to repeat it to himself when he knew he had failed to predict and control events in spite of all the precautions he took to eliminate uncertainties. Mother understood how much work he put in to see that everything ran smoothly, and she appreciated his sense of responsibility. That was why he knew that she would understand when he told her of his worries, and why he was contemplating paying her a visit.

What was holding him back was that it was Thursday. Marjorie lived only 4 miles from Norman and Bethany, but he never dreamed of calling unannounced. If he wanted to speak to her about something, or she to him, they waited until they saw each other at the appointed time. Bethany and Norman called at Marjorie's bungalow on every second Sunday of the month at half past three, stayed until half past five, and then came home. They had pilchards on toast in the winter, and tuna and cucumber salad in the summer. Once a month, on the third Sunday, he took the Allegro and picked his mother up, and she took tea with them until he drove her home again later in the evening. It would be unheard of to visit in the week. Neither Marjorie nor Norman approved of changes in routine. It showed weakness, and was entirely unnecessary. However, this evening, just for once, Norman knew that he would have welcomed a more casual arrangement. He wished that he could call round, as though there were no reason in the world why he should not, and then nonchalantly, during the course of a cosy chat about nothing in particular, bring up what was on his mind.

As he imagined this scenario, he realised the impossibility of such a turn of events. Marjorie would want to know everything, and be involved. What he longed for was a person who would not judge, but instead listen to him and let him come to his own way of solving the problem. However, he knew this was not the way that his mother dealt with things. Even when he was quite a small boy he had known this. If ever his mother had found out that he had difficulties in class, or in the playground, she would march straight up to the school. He had suffered agonies of humiliation when she confronted his teacher in front of his friends, or worse, made him point out the boys who had scuffed his new brown sandals. His mother wanted to take charge. She simply had no time for another point of view. It was unnecessary. He had grown to respect this in her, and valued this quality she had of organising her life. His wife certainly didn't have it.

However, he had learned very young that the best way of dealing with things was not to let others take over. That way you were less likely to be humiliated and hurt by somebody else. You had to make sure that everything was regulated, and that way you could guard against losing control of events. He had never respected his father. He seemed to just drift along in life, as ineffectually as a leaf in a stream, led this way and that by circumstances beyond his control. Norman could not imagine anything more threatening than losing control. If things had been left to his father's ill-advised methods of dealing with things, there would have been chaos, the nightmare of never knowing what was round the corner, and a casual expectation that 'things would work out'. From as early as he could remember, Norman had recognised the superiority of his mother's vision. His father had just failed to understand the necessity of forward planning. It was his mother who had to organise everything, and arrange events so that life ran to an ordered plan. Everything would fall apart if it wasn't managed.

Norman prided himself that he had assembled each aspect of his life with the precision of a jigsaw, each piece fitting neatly into the next with no irregularities or peculiarities. He had a job that offered security if not the possibility of advancement, and he worked with figures. The important thing about columns of figures was that they were unlikely to offer any unexpected surprises, and you could predict their outcome. He had a well-appointed house in one of the most respectable roads of the suburb. His car was both spotlessly clean and totally reliable, thanks to vigilant attention to specks of dirt, and scrupulously regular servicing.

As Norman ran through the well-ordered, neatly fitting segments of his existence, he knew that he was avoiding an important piece of the jigsaw, and it was this that had been worrying him for some days. In fact, it had been worrying him long before he had been able to put his finger on what it was. For several weeks before he had recognised the problem, it had begun to make its presence felt, like a crouching grey thing just outside the line of his vision. It was intangible, a feeling of growing unease that all was not as it should be, a dread that he felt clutching at his heart when he woke in the morning, a sensation of something imperceptible growing, threatening his security. Suddenly Norman was seized by such an acute sense of panic that he did something he had never done in all the years he had been driving backwards and forwards from his office. He braked sharply and drew into a small lay-by at the edge

60

of the road. He switched off the engine, and took his hands from the steering wheel. They were wet and shook slightly. He smoothed them over his trousers, drying them. Then he took off his glasses, rubbed the bridge of his nose and stared blindly at the passing traffic. He saw with awful clarity that, while he thought he had been assembling a jigsaw puzzle, his secure and safe life was much more like a tower of bricks. Up to a few months ago he would have said that this tower was a solid fortress against the uncertainties of fortune. Now he realised that each piece rested upon another, and that one element was threatening the stability of all the rest. His car ran smoothly, and his house was snug and could weather the elements. His work was routine and he was able to control the routine difficulties that arose there. The problem was far more worrying. The problem was his wife. B had begun to act very strangely.

Norman never called Bethany by her full name. It sounded too foreign to him, and he had never felt comfortable with it. Early on in their courtship they had been to see a James Bond film together, and he had jokingly told her that he would call her 'B'. The nickname had stuck, and even now it sounded strange to him when Marjorie called his wife by her full name. Marjorie insisted upon it, managing to inject disapproval into each syllable. Norman did not know whether her veiled criticism was of B, for having such an outlandish name, or of him, because he shortened it in rather a childish way. It was often difficult to know precisely what attracted his mother's censure, and Norman did not ask. It was better not to.

Norman looked at his watch. It was 6.10 p.m. There was still time to go and see Marjorie before she went to her bridge club at eight o clock. If he did, what would he tell her? That he thought that his wife was having a breakdown, or at least was falling victim to a personality disorder? Marjorie would demand facts, as of course she was entitled to do. Norman forced himself to think clearly, pushing through the fog of fear that enveloped him at the thought that everything might fall apart, and that something dark and grim was about to happen unless he could avert it. For a start there was the singing. B had begun a horrid humming a few weeks ago, and three days ago he had even heard her break into fully fledged snatches of song. It was as he came down the stairs for his breakfast and he heard her lift up her voice quite clearly. She had stopped as he had come in, and continued to prepare his boiled egg, but if it hadn't been so preposterous, he could have sworn she had been dancing as well. It was outrageous, and Norman was so bothered he did not want to think about it.

Then there was the music. A horrible little wireless had appeared from nowhere, and he knew that she had it playing all hours of the day, because sometimes he heard it as he was putting his key in the front door. One day he had come very slowly up the path so that his feet didn't crunch on the gravel. He had gravelled the path for the very purpose of thwarting intruders, and as he tiptoed up it, the realisation came to him that any burglar worth his salt would easily foil his carefully laid plans. This thought was bitter indeed, but the bile of angry fear rose in his throat as he crouched down below the sitting room window and peeped in to see his wife vacuuming. Marjorie would truly have been horrified to see how B was treating the vacuum cleaner. It was true that she was cleaning the room, but in shocking fashion. She had her back to him, and the wireless was obviously on. She was twirling the hose and its attachments above her head and swinging her hips about in a manner that Norman could only describe as unseemly. He swiftly ducked lower down under the window as she turned around. She was oblivious to his appalled scrutiny, and appeared to be miming, like some dreadful popular singer, into the dusting attachment that mother had selected with such care. Norman shuddered.

Just as he was about to turn away, he had an uncomfortable suspicion that he himself was being observed. Slowly he straighted up and turned round to see his neighbours from number 120. Mr and Mrs Prodfoot were considered to be of some standing in the Avenue. Mr Prodfoot was the chairman of the local Conservative Association, and his wife was captain of the weighty ladies' golf team at the local club. The couple were standing open-mouthed in their gravelled drive by their newly waxed Volvo. Mr Prodfoot's hand was suspended at the point of opening the door, and both were staring at him with amazement clearly written on their florid countenances. Before he could mumble an explanation they rapidly avoided his eye, and suddenly became very interested in other things. Mrs Prodfoot climbed into the car, wrapping her car coat tightly around her, while her spouse began to clean the windscreen furiously with a car cloth. Norman had felt the hot blush of mortification creep upwards from his collar as he let himself into his hallway. He now felt hot all over again at the humiliating memory.

He continued to catalogue B's strange behaviour. He had found notes lying around, and there was a book on the sitting room table that had certainly not been there before. It was full of poetry, and his wife had underlined passages in pencil. He couldn't make head nor tail of it.

Next there was the question of B's absences. Every morning of their married life Norman had been accustomed to getting up on the alarm's first shrill beeping, and putting on his glasses. Then he would go to the bathroom, and while he was there, B got up and made the bed. Next she would get dressed and go downstairs and begin making his breakfast while he got dressed. This arrangement had served them perfectly well for 23 years and it was a sensible, economical use of the time. It was what they were used to, so why in Heaven's name would B feel the need to change it? Norman felt the anger and panic rising in him again, because he simply did not understand what was happening. It was just . . . unnecessary. Now what happened was that he would wake up at the alarm's sound as usual, fulfilling his part of the arrangement, and his wife simply wasn't there. He hadn't, in fact, noticed this until he rose from the marital bed, only discovering the stunning fact as he reached for his brown slippers. The first morning it had happened, he had felt quite dizzy with shock, and had had to sit down heavily on the bed again, unable to make his mind function. Then he had rushed to the head of the stairs, only to hear B coming out of the living room into the hall. Overcome with terror that she would find him on the landing, he fled hurriedly back into the bedroom. B came in quietly, and he waited for an explanation. None came, and she began to dress with a serenity he found astounding. Quivering with suppressed indignation and filled with secret misgivings as to what he would find downstairs, he retired to the bathroom. When he came out, B had gone downstairs and all appeared normal.

Try as he might, he could not discover what it was she had been doing as he slept. He had vowed to find out, but to his intense private frustration he had found himself unable to wake up in time. Each morning he tried to wake, and each morning he failed in his endeavour, coming to consciousness to find B gone. In some ways he found cause to congratulate himself that his body was so well-regulated and ensconced in routine that it refused to wake up a minute earlier than it always did, but it made the problem of discovery very difficult. Setting the alarm earlier would defeat the object of surprising his wife in her guilty secret and besides, something deep and primeval in him was violently resistant to the thought of changing a routine that was part of his secure and steady existence. It was a matter of principle. So for the time being he was forced to remain baffled.

Finally, and undoubtedly the most disturbing of all, was his wife's general demeanour. She had changed, and certainly not for the better. If, in the past, she had transgressed from their unspoken agreement to maintain routine, the mere fact that he pointed it out would ensure her meek acquiescence and mute apology. He had thought they were in accord over this and, in fairness, recognised that her errors were mainly due to carelessness rather than a deliberate attempt to sabotage their life together. He was quite prepared to be generous in this and had assumed that she valued his magnanimity. Now, however, everything had changed. Each time there was an error on her part (and Norman had to admit to himself that these were increasing daily) he pointed it out generously and in the proper spirit and was met with a hitherto unheard of reaction. It was true that B did not actively defy him, but she certainly displayed no indication of being chastened. She merely smiled at him and rectified her mistake. It was the smile that was so unnerving. What business did she have in smiling so radiantly, when everything was rocking on its foundations? Why was she so serene and content when she was wrecking his peace of mind? How could she be so indifferent to his happiness? She had even held out her arms to him the other day and he had thought that she was actually going to attempt to embrace him. Horrified, he had hurriedly turned his back on her, feigning an interest in checking the cutlery on the table, but all the same it had been appalling. What was happening?

Norman ran the catalogue of awful happenings over and over in his mind. It was certainly time to do something, but at present he was paralysed in a way he found humiliating and terrifying. He let out a trembling sigh. With shaking hands he turned the key in the ignition. Not even the fact that the engine turned over smoothly the first time could console him. Bethany had been wrong when she assumed that Norman would not notice the coming of her angel.

*   *   *

Bethany woke at 6.30 a.m. and lay quietly, luxuriating in the warmth of the bed, enjoying the sun's clear light shining through the curtains, and relishing the sound of the birds singing in the garden. She had never understood people who complained about the dawn chorus. It was one of the most joyful affirmations of the morning's promise that she could imagine. Listening to the birds, she planned the hours ahead. She had begun to do this last month, one of the many results of the lesson of Healing. Her days had begun to take on a significance that they had not had previously,

64

and she looked forward to them with keen anticipation. It was strange, but she had begun to wake a few minutes earlier each morning, until she had seemed to settle naturally into this time of 6.30. She was grateful for this, as it gave her exactly the right amount of time to begin the day joyfully.

A few weeks ago she had begun to work at the lesson that her angel had given her. She had been told to let go of the past and be free in the present. She had to 'heal her pain' so that she could 'receive into her outstretched hands', and she had to 'lovingly forgive'. Knowing what to do was comparatively easy. What was more difficult was finding a way to do it. Bethany was, by nature, practical and methodical. She was used to giving her full attention to daily tasks and had never in her life encountered something that she viewed as more worthwhile. Therefore, she spent a good deal of time mulling over the angel's words, and working out a systematic method of following the lesson.

The first thing that she decided was that practice was crucial. Learning anything new involves diligent, regular practice if it is to be accomplished, and she understood that changing her thoughts and her memories was no different in this respect. Therefore she had realised the importance of setting aside a regular time to practice her lesson. Being a morning person, she had resolved to begin shortly after Norman had departed each morning to work. Much to her surprise, shortly after she had made this decision, she had started to wake up earlier and earlier each morning. As Bethany remembered how surprised she had been when this had started happening, she smiled.

As time went by she was gradually coming to the conclusion that very little was happening by chance. Everything was unfolding smoothly and exactly as it was meant to. All it took was for her to trust in the process, and things just kept going right, leading her further and further along the path she was meant to travel. So, once she had discovered the fact that she needed to set aside a regular time to practice, the angel provided her with one. And of course it was exactly the right time. Beginning each morning by focusing on her lesson imbued her days with clarity and purpose, transfusing events with her intention to love and forgive. It was as though she was washing her days with colour, charging everything with significance and beauty.

So what was it Bethany was doing each morning while Norman tossed and turned in frustrated slumber in the bedroom above? Quite simply, she was being still. She had realised that the intensity with which she had remembered her Welsh beginnings and her mother's love was different in quality from mere reminiscence because of the way she had done it. Seemingly by chance (although she now suspected that it was not merely accidental) she had hit upon a method of focusing her mind. When she had settled herself in her chair and steadied her breathing, she had become calm and serene. And this was what she practised every morning, steadily and with a discipline that purified her intention to learn.

Bethany was learning with a pleasure that delighted her. She had never expected that letting go of the past would give her such joy in the present. She had thought that her childhood was something that she had experienced, that had formed her, but that she had put it behind her. Now she realised that she had simply tried to forget it because it hurt her, and that by doing this, it was always going to hurt her. This new way she was learning was different. As she practised truly letting go by loving her past and her mother, she understood that she was free and filled with joy. She began to give herself permission to think of things that would give her pleasure, such as reading and listening to music. She could perform her daily chores as usual, but because she was enchanted with the bliss of her new-found freedom, her days were full of sparkling happiness. As Norman had noticed, she had begun to sing and dance, because she couldn't help herself. She smiled because she was happy, and people in the street responded to her serene contentment, and smiled back.

One thing that worried her was that she could not share her happiness with Norman. Several times she had wanted to hug him out of sheer delight, but he hadn't noticed, and turned away. However, she told herself that this would probably change if it was meant to. She tried not to let it bother her, and for the time being she concentrated purely on the angel's message.

Then, after some time had gone by, and she had practised every day, and experienced the resulting joy, Bethany had begun to wonder what was going to happen next. She couldn't help but congratulate herself on the progress she had made, to say to herself that she had really moved on and learned to forgive the past. She knew that she accepted the way things had been between her and her mother. She could lovingly forgive her and acknowledge that she had brought up her daughter the best way she could. She was no longer angry and hurt, but felt love and forgiveness and joy. Perhaps this was what the angel had come to teach, and now she knew the way, she was on her own. As the days drew into weeks, and Bethany had still not heard the angel, she experienced a tiny sense of disappointment. It seemed as though learning the lesson meant that she would not encounter her angel again, and she felt the loss keenly.

One day Bethany got up and went to the drawer where she kept her notebook. She looked back to where she had written 'Healing' and all she could remember of what the angel had called the third lesson. Underneath were the words 'Paying Attention ????' and 'Do something – take Action ??????' These comments represented her attempt to unravel the first two lessons. For a while after the angel had given her the lesson of Healing, she had been puzzled that it had never outlined lessons one and two. Being of a logical and practical nature, she had deduced that this was perhaps because she was meant to work them out for herself. Certainly the angel remained stubbornly and uncharacteristically silent when she attempted to engage it in conversation about what they might be. During the weeks that she had practised the third lesson by sitting in silence and holding its message in her mind, her intuition had become sharpened and she came to trust her instincts as much as she did her more logical thought processes.

Finally, some time in late spring she had decided that the lessons represented the sum total of the knowledge that she had gathered from her married life with Norman. When she thought about it that way, it didn't seem much for 23 years, but she knew that it was knowledge hard won and tempered in the fire of experience. She had made these rough jottings when the thoughts had come. Perhaps now it was time to try to write out the first two lessons more formally. Bethany sucked the end of her biro and thought.

She had come to the conclusion that the first lesson had something to do with her gift for paying attention to what she was doing, for immersing herself in the present. By concentrating totally on the mundane tasks that filled her day she infused them with meaning and purpose. The second lesson might be something to do with her habit of using activity as a means to banish misery. All too often in the early years she had found herself sunk in lethargy and despair, realising that she was isolated in a marriage to a man who did not understand her, and feeling that there was no purpose in her life. Eventually she had stumbled on to the realisation that taking action was the simplest way to break out of her lethargy. Her actions were limited to rousing herself and undertaking little projects such as her garden, or going for walks to observe the changes of the seasons, but each time she immersed herself in action she felt better.

Bethany continued to stare at her little book. Gently, she tore out the page with her notes on it and neatened up the edges of paper sticking out of the spine. Then she smoothed her hand over the clean new page and wrote carefully:

Lesson 1. Attention.

She underlined it, and then looked at the word, which, for some reason failed to satisfy her. It sounded somehow military, and it wasn't exactly what she meant. However, it would have to do for now. She chewed the end of her biro for a while and then wrote: 'Do everything for its own sake with love. Live in the present and don't expect things to turn out a particular way.' Next she wrote:

Lesson 2. Action.

She drew a neat black line underneath this and quickly wrote: 'Doing something makes you feel better, and through action you can change things. Purposeful action starts with the decision to act.' Finally she wrote:

Lesson 3. Healing or Forgiveness.

Next she copied out what she could remember of the third lesson. This was more detailed, as she had written it down the day after her encounter with the angel on the moonlit night in May. It included the sentences that had sparked her reconciliation with the memories of her mother, the ones that read 'The past and the future are created by your mind. Do not allow pain to enslave you by holding on to it. Learn to embrace and release the pain of your past and move on.'

Bethany felt pleased with herself. She now had three lessons to work on.

WELL DONE.

Bethany smiled to herself. She hadn't lost the angel after all. 'Well, the ones I've done aren't as lyrical as yours, but if you won't tell me the actual words ... Attention, Action, and Healing. Is that right?'

YES ... ATTENTION IS GOOD, BUT 'MINDFULNESS' IS MORE APPROPRIATE.

'Thank you. Yes, that is much more what I mean when I pay attention to what I do.' Bethany looked at the lessons in her little book for a little longer, and then closed it and went to the understairs cupboard to fetch the hoover. She thought about the lessons and tried to put them into practice all that day, and for the next few days.

Then, one morning in late June, after Norman had gone off to work, Bethany went upstairs to strip the bed ready to wash the sheets. A song called 'Lady in Red', was playing on the radio, so she carried it upstairs with her and set it down on the dressing table. It needed dusting, she noticed, so she went back downstairs to fetch a duster, humming under her breath. Leaping up the stairs two at a time so that she wouldn't miss the song, she realised how healthy she felt these days.

When she had first heard the angel, she had been constantly tired, dragging herself around and hardly able to function on some days. She hadn't been eating well, constantly skipping meals, and then feeling faint and nauseated, in a lethargic cycle of tiredness and neglect. Now, because she was happy, she was filled with physical well-being. Her hair seemed glossier, her eyes brighter, and she noticed that she had a lot more energy. She knew that she was more than a few pounds heavier than she used to be, but she didn't gorge on chocolate much any more, so maybe even that would change. She dusted the dressing table carefully and then turned towards the bed. Then the angel spoke.

YOU HAVE TO GO ON.

As usual, there was no introduction, no letting her get used to it gently, Bethany thought contentedly. She sat down on the bed and listened. There was silence. Nothing more. Puzzled but unconcerned, she waited peacefully to hear what would come next. Surely she had proved that she was able to fulfil what was asked of her, and perhaps even merited some praise for her efforts. As the minutes passed, her complacency began to ebb and a faint annoyance pricked at her mind. Why couldn't the angel be more direct and give her the next lesson? Then she rebuked herself for her impatience. If there was one thing she had learned, it was that things unfolded if she allowed them to. She would know everything if she waited patiently. 'What do you mean, go on?' she asked. 'Haven't I done it already?'

YOU HAVE TO REMEMBER ALL OF IT.

Bethany held her breath. A creeping, cold sensation was spreading through her body, settling in her chest. This was asking too much. This she could not do. 'No,' she said abruptly, and stood up. There was silence. She moved awkwardly over to the radio and turned it off. Then she began to strip the bed with angry, jerking movements, tearing at the sheets with claw-like hands that clutched and

69

scrabbled and finally wrenched the bedding into her arms, which were clumsy with distress. Without knowing that she did so, she was muttering to herself. 'No, no, it's too much . . . you can't ask me to go on . . . I've done enough . . . and I can't do any more . . . what can possibly be gained by unearthing all of it over again . . . it can only do harm, not good . . . please don't force me to do this . . .'

Still there was no reply from the angel and Bethany took the washing downstairs and loaded the machine. Now she too had lapsed into silence and carried on working swiftly and mechanically, moving around the house angrily, dropping things and slamming doors as she went. Finally, as she went into the kitchen, her elbow caught the side of the door and she gasped in pain. Miserably she rubbed the spot that hurt. Whoever named it the funny bone was just plain stupid, she thought unhappily. But the pain had stopped her moving around rapidly, and she found that she had also banged her hip against something during the course of her erratic progress around the house. Wearily she sank down at the kitchen table. 'I'm not strong enough, I just can't do it,' she said aloud. Her words hung in the air and she listened to them. A tear slid down her cheek and she rubbed it away sadly. It seemed as though she had come so far only to fail her angel after all. If she tried to do what it asked, the pain would envelop her again and she would go back into the dark place from which she had fought for so long to escape. Bethany went upstairs to the bathroom. Her body was leaden and it was impossible to imagine that she had flown so lightly up the stairs just a few moments ago. She reached for some tissue and blew her nose. 'I'm sorry . . .' she said, and there didn't seem anything else to say. She went downstairs again to think about what Norman would be having for his tea. She left the radio where it was.

Three days later, she was having a cup of tea at the kitchen table and feeling miserable. She missed practising her lesson, and was deep in a depression that had descended on her as a result of not having a focus for her day. She wished the angel would talk to her again but feared it had gone forever, disappointed in her cowardice. After a while, the gentle query nudged at a corner of her mind again, and refused to leave. The thought was tentative, infinitesimally small and hesitant, yet it persisted, and continued to hover around her at various moments since her refusal a few days ago. She gave it space in her mind. Could it be that she was wrong about her own strength? The angel had been right about the lesson of Healing. Was it possible to open herself to the raw pain involved in learning the next lesson, and trust that it would be all right? Could she, perhaps, take the risk and expose herself to the agony again, or would it destroy her as it almost had before?

TRUST ME. IT WILL BE ALL RIGHT.

Bethany let out a shuddering breath of relief mixed with resignation. She dreaded the next step that she was going to take, but knew that there was no going back and that she was committed to following the angel's lessons through to the end of her journey, wherever that might be. Now that she had started, she knew she would never return to the place she had been before, and didn't really want to. Her angel and the lessons had changed the way she thought, so life could never be the same. She drew a breath and spoke aloud. The words were as much for herself as for the angel. 'I do trust you and I know that I can learn the next lesson. But you have to give me time; it will be so hard for me, and I have to find the right time.'

I UNDERSTAND.
I UNDERSTAND THAT THIS IS HARD FOR YOU,
BUT IT WILL BE ALL RIGHT.
TRUST ME.

Bethany closed her eyes. She had once again affirmed her willingness to go on, and felt better than she had done for days. She was ready for the next lesson, and now it was just a question of waiting for the right time. She thought that the time would probably be soon.

That evening Norman announced that he was being sent on a team-building course with the other members of Accounts. He would be going next Monday, and not be coming home until Thursday evening. The course was to be in Hull, and the department were paying for them all to stay in an hotel for the whole week. Norman was obviously excited, but also oddly evasive. For some reason he refused to meet Bethany's eye, and changed the subject rapidly when she enquired about the trip. In truth, Bethany was far too preoccupied to notice Norman's evasive behaviour. She was still reeling from the immediacy of the opportunity that had presented itself. She had known that the angel would provide her with time for her lesson, and give her a respite from dealing with her daily chores, but all the same it was rather a shock to have it

71

presented so quickly. She made a mental note to try not to be surprised at the way events unfolded in the future.

*   *   *

It was late June. All day he had been unusually restless and, as the afternoon progressed and the bees buzzed sleepily in the flower beds, he felt the need to get away from the house and the garden, and breathe the warm evening air deep into his lungs. He dismissed the idea of a stroll in his beloved lane, and instead drove the car out to the hills during the late afternoon. He parked at the top of a winding road and began to climb the steep hillside without looking back. The grass was springy and sounded hollow under his feet, and he knew that rabbits had been busy making their warrens in the sandy soil beneath him. Soon they would be venturing out as the day gave way to evening, and he wanted to be still before then so that he wouldn't disturb them. He quickened his pace, reaching the crest of the hill and turning at last to take in the view that stretched out around and below him.

The sun was low in the sky and he turned his face towards it, closing his eyes for a moment, feeling the light on his eyelids. When he opened them he looked to the west and saw that the oak woods which covered the purple hills were beginning to flame red and gold, their foliage tinted by the ruby light from the blazing sky. Looking ahead, he could see the reservoir, silvery and shimmering in the evening light, and the sky to the east was the palest green and turquoise, a perfect complement to the deepening colours over the woods. He felt the restless mood that had possessed him draining away and precious tranquillity returning. He sat down on the springy turf and rested his elbows on his knees. He watched the magnificent sky changing as the minutes passed, marvelling as always at the beauty and peace of it all. It was as if the brilliance of Heaven was emblazoning its splendour across the sky for all to see, and yet in all the world he was the only one there to marvel at the miracle. He imagined that the brightness of the scene was washing his eyes and soul with colour, and he smiled. What was it? Something about the sky being a pavilion for the sun, exulting as it makes its way across the Heavens. He thought for a minute, and then stood, stretching his stiff muscles, and turned down the hill. He quoted softly to himself as he made his way back to the car. 'See how the skies proclaim God's glory, How the vault of heaven betrays his confidence.'

Humming quietly under his breath, he continued on down to the car, jingling his keys in his pocket. When he reached it, he turned for one last look behind him. The sun had gone, leaving its glowing impression on the burnished sky, and the moon hung bright and low on the horizon. Wishing for a moment that he had someone to share all this with, he eased himself into the front seat of the car. Another snatch of quotation occurred to him as he turned the key in the ignition. He was fond of the Psalms, and odd lines popped into his head at times of great joy or sadness when his own words seemed inadequate. Now he jumbled two separate verses together, partly because he couldn't remember with total accuracy, but partly because he thought the occasion warranted it. 'I will lift up mine eyes to the hills, and sing to the Lord a new song, A song of wonder at his doings.'

He mentally apologised to King David for the muddle, and to the teacher at his school who had made him learn things by heart, and thanked both most sincerely for the gifts they had given him. While he was at it, he gave thanks for the beautiful evening, and the renewed peacefulness it had brought him. As he drove home, he once again marvelled at the beauty that was all around him, and the many blessings that filled his life. It was true that he did sometimes feel lonely without the familiar companionship that Claire and he had experienced for so many years. The feeling was especially sharp at moments like tonight, when he would have loved to share the sights and sounds that filled his spirit with joy. He wound the window down as he drove along the narrow country lanes, and breathed in the sweet summer scents.

He realised he had slowed almost to a standstill and was glad that there were unlikely to be any other cars coming along fast behind him. That was yet another advantage of living where he did. The road widened slightly and he pulled the car over into the passing place. He had nowhere to go and was in no hurry, and the whole evening was so obviously there to be lived in and enjoyed that he simply gave himself up to the moment.

His thoughts turned to Claire. For a time after her death he had hardly been able to think about her, and had functioned automatically, performing the tasks that had needed to be done as gracefully and gently as he could. Now that the sharp unhappiness of her loss had subsided, he found that he could remember her without pain. He did miss her, but often felt her presence in the house and sometimes even talked to her when no one was around. It also happened that he had discovered how kind people could be. Since her death, neighbours from the village were constantly calling around, and rarely came empty-handed. He seemed to have more casseroles in the freezer than he could possibly eat and, rather guiltily, had secretly disposed of the uneaten ones which were growing greyish fluff at the back of the fridge. Mrs Leadbetter from the Vicarage had knocked at the back door with a bundle of runner beans just as he was scraping the fluff into the bin, and he had hidden the plate in the pantry. Sometimes he felt overwhelmed by their well-meaning kindness, but generally it was yet another thing to be thankful for. He knew why he had come out at the end of this perfect day. It reminded him that he had not been able to stop and register his thankfulness for some time, and he had known that he wanted to. Whenever he considered the gifts that had come to him in the course of his existence, his blessings appeared to multiply almost without end. He had cultivated the habit of trying to see good in all that happened, and this had become second nature to him. Since Claire's funeral, he had had little time to himself, and it was only now, after several weeks had passed, that he could collect his thoughts and take stock of his life.

He had been miserable for a while, but gradually his natural serenity was restoring the balance which was so much a feature of his life. In this he was certain that he could hear Claire's gentle murmur of approval. Gratitude for what they had shared sharpened his appreciation for her, and it was right that he should remember without pain. It only strengthened the affection that had bound them together in life, and would not alter in death.

He sighed. It had all worked out just as she had been so certain it would. Claire had been wonderful when they had first come together, soothing all his early doubts about whether he was being fair to her in marrying her. They both knew that she was not the great love of his life, and he had suffered agonies of conscience when she had suggested that they share a lasting partnership. In the end she had been so right, and for this he had once again been overwhelmingly grateful. How had she known? Gently and gradually she had mended his aching heart and soothed his doubts. She had held him and healed him with her undemanding love and now, all these years later, he paid tribute to her strength. He knew that he had made her happy throughout their time together and now could marvel at the amazing rightness of it all. He had never believed that such abundance and wonder could have come from such sorrowful beginnings, that such a secure relationship could have blossomed from such fragility. He found himself remembering even the events before Claire with a semblance of peace and acceptance. Perhaps in time he would even be able to look back without regret. As he turned over in the double bed later that night and switched off his reading light, he counted his blessings and was grateful, both for the present and for the past.

JULY

Bethany let her breath out slowly and allowed her shoulders to relax. It was funny that even when she thought she was at her most calm, her shoulders always seemed to carry residual tension, and it was only since she had been sitting quietly listening for her angel that she had realised this. She was sitting in her favourite chair with her back to the window, and preparing to receive the next lesson, the one the angel called the Fourth.

Norman had at last departed, still avoiding her eyes. He was to pick up someone from the department on his way, and they were going to drive up to Hull together. Bethany had anticipated the moment when he finally closed the door behind him with a mixture of relief and trepidation. She had stood at the front bow window, holding back the net curtain, for a full five minutes, gazing out at the quiet Avenue. She needed to reassure herself that he really had gone, and found herself unable to tear her un-focussed eyes away from the deserted drive. The departure had taken quite a while, since Norman had suddenly become unac-countably jumpy and nervous. He kept losing his nerve and could not steer the Allegro into the road. Reversing and braking, he finally managed to back his car out of the drive after a seemingly endless series of cautious manoeuvres. So intent was he on his progress that he stared straight ahead of him, and did not see Bethany at the window with her hand raised in a smiling wave. In truth, she had stood there for so long that her smile had become rather fixed, but since Norman wasn't looking, it didn't really matter.

Eventually she had forced herself away from the window, and gone to clear away the breakfast things. All the time her thoughts had been on what was to come. Now the moment had finally arrived. She pushed her back deep into the chair and closed her eyes.

For a short while, there was nothing but the sound of her breathing. Her body relaxed and she continued waiting. This process had become habitual, and she knew that it might be a while before she was ready to remember. Much to her surprise, the angel spoke before she had time to focus her thoughts.

ARE YOU READY?

For one wild moment, Bethany considered going back, and simply refusing to hear or try, or move on. It was only momentary, however, and she was curious to know what her angel had to teach her. She had to remember all of it before she could have the next lesson. So she nodded, and began to travel back in time to when her life had all begun to fall apart.

WAIT.

Startled, Bethany opened her eyes and looked around her. Ridiculous as she knew it to be, she still half expected to catch the angel out, and see it standing or hovering before her in the room. She felt its amusement, and smiled shamefacedly. Then it spoke again.

I KNOW THAT YOU ARE READY TO BEGIN,
BUT IT IS IMPORTANT TO REMEMBER IN THE RIGHT WAY.
YOU ARE FEARFUL.
IS THAT RIGHT?

Bethany nodded. She could not rid herself of this habit, even though she knew that she must look faintly ridiculous, nodding in the empty room. She knew that she had only to think or feel and the angel would know her thoughts, but she still wanted to nod, or speak out loud, even after all these weeks. The nature of her communication with the angel had changed since she had first heard its voice. To begin with, she had been shocked and frightened by what she felt was an intrusion into her mind. As the months went by this was no longer the case. They now communed, rather than communicated. Often their exchange was emotive, rather than in words, and she was no longer surprised when the angel made itself known. They had become connected in some way, and although she felt that the angel was a distinct presence, and an entity in its own right, it was also part of her in a way that was hard to explain. Paradoxically, it was her growing sense of oneness with the angel that was helping Bethany to understand its separateness as a being. She and the angel were company for each other now, and she could not imagine living her life without it. She couldn't have put it into words, but was comforted by the fact that this sense of unity was mutual, and that the angel wanted her to feel as serene and calm as it appeared to be.

All this flashed through her mind in an instant, and the angel waited and then spoke again.

REMEMBER THE LESSON OF HEALING.
THE WAY THAT YOU CREATE THE PAST WHEN YOU
REMEMBER IT IS IMPORTANT.
YOUR PAST HAS NO HOLD OVER YOU IF YOU CREATE IT
WITH LOVE.
HOLD THIS LESSON IN YOUR MIND AS THE FOURTH
LESSON UNFOLDS.

THE FOURTH LESSON IS THE LESSON OF GRATITUDE.
EACH AND EVERY LIFE IS BLESSED WITH GIFTS THAT POUR
FORTH FROM THE UNIVERSE.
GIVE THANKS CONSTANTLY FOR SUCH ABUNDANT BOUNTY
FLOWING FROM AN EVERLASTING SOURCE.
OPEN YOURSELF UP TO THE JOY OF BEING ALIVE.
APPRECIATE AND BLESS ALL THAT COMES TO YOU
AND YOU WILL FIND MORE AND MORE TO BLESS
AND APPRECIATE.

The angel was silent, and Bethany stayed still and quiet in her chair. She wondered why the angel had stopped her from remembering when she was finally ready to face the pain in her past. Then she remembered the words 'It is important to remember in the right way'. She resumed her calm breathing as she attempted to focus with love and acceptance on the events that had unfolded so long ago, but still cast their long shadows through the years, reaching her even now in the sunny room in which she sat.

*　*　*

A large, brown, cracked leather suitcase was propped up at the end of Bethany's bed. It had come from Mr Willow, who had stopped her at her gate one evening, and asked her if she had a bag for her holiday. Bethany had frowned wearily, for it was a problem that had been perplexing her ever since the idea of the trip had become a reality. She wanted to save her precious store of money for Brighton, and was reluctant to spend any more of it on a suitcase.

Smiling, Mr Willow had bent down and heaved the large, unwieldy case over the fence into Bethany's grateful arms. 'I don't want it back, love. It's been in the shed under my potting bench ever since I was demobbed. It's no beauty, but it'll serve its purpose.' After thanking him with shining eyes, Bethany had lugged the case back to her room and laid it at the end of her bed. To do this she had had to go past the firmly closed door of her mother's bedroom. Her mother had gone to bed the night that they had talked about Bethany's trip, and had not got up again. Her door remained tightly shut, and she had not uttered a single word to her daughter for four days.

Bethany had tried over and over again to get her to respond to her tearful pleas, but her mother seemed frozen in dark ice, and only stared straight ahead of her through the gloom of the dust-filled bedroom. She would not let Bethany draw the curtains, and until she was alone in the room again, refused to eat from the trays of food that her daughter brought for her. Eventually Bethany had broken down and, weeping at the foot of the bed, sobbed brokenly that she wouldn't leave and wished things could go back the way they had been. Mrs Jones had stared into the darkness, and said nothing. The house grew colder each day. When Bethany had been younger she had fancied that wreaths of mist gathered around her house, which always seemed surrounded by denser fog than any of the others in her street. Now, rejection and indifference had hardened the damp into cold which cracked in the walls, even in the height of summer. The chill emanated from her mother's room and permeated every corner of the house. Bethany's lips became dry and cracked, and her hands and feet were numb.

Each day, Bethany went to work and did her job mechanically, blindly going about her tasks without thinking or feeling. The typing pool was buzzing with excitement and so preoccupied with the arrangements for the trip that her quietness went unnoticed by all but Sylvia. Concerned, all she could do was reassure her silent friend that it would all come out all right in the end, and a holiday was just what she needed 'to take 'er mind off things'. Bethany could only gaze at her dumbly. Things felt so bad that she could no longer cry. She had not shed a tear since her mother had refused to listen to her begging to be allowed to stay. It was as if her tears had frozen in the ice of her mother's indifference, and now her whole body was desiccated and without sensation. Even her mouth seemed to have dried so that she could not taste her food. There was no saliva to swallow, and speaking was an effort. And so the days passed.

Then, in the last week before the trip, Bethany was surprised to see both Mr and Mrs Willow standing side by side at the garden gate waiting for her when she came home from work. The sight of them pierced the bubble of misery that enveloped her and drew a smile to her face. In spite of their diminutive size, the united couple presented a vision of dependability and strength which radiated out towards her along the street.

'Come on in, love, we want to say somethin' to you,' said Mrs Willow. Without waiting for Bethany's reply she had turned, and was already bustling down the path towards the front door, which was left on the latch. Mr Willow stood gently aside, as though holding open the gate for her, although in reality it had not moved from its welcoming wide-open position for years. Unlike its next door neighbour, which was kept firmly latched, this gate was pushed up against the clipped hedge where a small stone had been placed to keep it from swinging shut. Over the years grass had grown around and through it in dense wedges so that it would be almost impossible to shut it now, even if someone had wanted to do so.

Bethany walked up the uneven path and into the warm light of the Willows' front room. Mr Willow closed the door behind them. 'Come on through, love, and take the weight off your feet,' called Mrs. Willow from the kitchen. Rather to her surprise, Bethany saw that Mr Willow was following her in from the front room. Usually he remained by the gas fire when his wife was holding sway over the teapot in the heart of the house.

The kitchen took on a slightly different character, depending upon who was occupying it, and at what time of the day. Early in the morning, while the light was still bluish and sharp from the dawn, and the birdsong carried clear and melodious from the open garden window, Mrs Willow made breakfast, moving quickly between the stove and the sink. The room took on the rich aroma of frying bacon and eggs, and sang with the energy generated by her smooth and rapid activity. Later, when she left for town on her errands, the kitchen became quieter and more reflective.

Now was the time when Mr Willow took charge, moving gently around the room. The mid-morning sun made golden pools of light on the table and floor, providing amusement for the cats who played with the dust motes whirling in the shafts of light from the window. Their mother stretched luxuriously in the sunlight, watching them through slitted eyes. Humming quietly, Mr Willow would spread newspaper out over his end of the wooden table to take cuttings from his geraniums or laboriously prick out seedlings into seed trays. The clock, which could scarcely be heard when his wife bustled around the room, ticked gently on the wall. All was tranquil. He always carefully removed all traces of soil, gathering it up into the newspaper, which he shook out into the back flower beds. Later on Mrs Willow would return, presiding over her domain again, kneading bread, energetically pounding the dough which was then left to rise in yeasty mounds in the warm corners of the room.

The kitchen adapted itself to all the numerous uses its occupants chose for it. Now it was still and peaceful, perhaps surprised, as Bethany was, to see both of its owners sitting at its table at the same time.

Bethany's surprise increased, as she looked from one to the other. Both seemed to be uncertain as to how to begin. Mr Willow looked at his wife. For a startling moment, Mrs Willow appeared to be struggling for words. Never had such a thing been known to happen before. It was so extraordinary that all three people in the room seemed taken by surprise. Even the cat stopped washing herself and stared unblinking at the silent group. The clock ticked away the seconds, and still Mrs Willow was seized by uncharacteristic diffidence.

Finally, Mr Willow prepared to step bravely into the breach to aid his wife, and cleared his throat. This brought Mrs Willow sharply to her senses. It would be unthinkable of her to neglect her duty as spokesperson and allow her silent husband to take on the burden of what had to be said. She too cleared her throat briefly and then began with a rush, her words falling over one another in her haste. 'Now look 'ere, my Lovely, there's no sense in hiding it, we know you're un'appy, an' we know that it's your mum who's makin' you miserable. Neither of us 'old with interferin' in family business, and for that reason we 'aven't said anything so far.' Mr Willow looked very much as though he would like to be lighting his pipe, but he never smoked indoors. Instead he nodded as his wife spoke, and gently put his hand on her trembling arm.

Mrs Willow continued gamely in a voice that had a trace of a shake, but was otherwise firm. 'You 'aven't said nothin', but it's as plain as the nose on your face that you're thinkin' of leavin' this trip and stoppin' 'ere.' Bethany nodded, her eyes bright with unshed tears, and the lump in her throat threatening to stop her swallowing. Seeing how close she was to breaking down, Mrs Willow rushed onwards, her words now tumbling over one another in her haste to finish what was so important before she was cut off. 'Well now, you're like a daughter to Ewan and me, and we can't stand by and let you throw away your chance. Don't you see, Love, that if you weren't to go now, you never will, and you'll be stuck with 'er until she ends 'er days as miserable as she begun 'em. You can't change 'er, Love, it's the way she is, and 'avin' you there will just make 'er bitterness all the stronger. Leavin' now is the natrel way of things, and you 'ave to take your chance to make a new life for yourself. Don't throw it away for the sake of 'er. She's 'ad 'er chance and made 'er bed. Go, and don't come back until you've made somethin' of yourself, for our sakes if not for your own. We just can't bear it, can we, Ewan?' At this point Mrs Willow, who had been wringing her hands as she spoke, now sniffed loudly, and began fumbling in her sleeve for a handkerchief. Mr Willow reached inside his waistcoat and pulled out a snowy white, neatly-hemmed square, and passed it silently to his wife, who blew her nose loudly. He put his hand back comfortingly on her arm, and patted her gently. Then he cleared his throat in the now silent room, and said gently, 'She's right, Love. You got to go, or you never will.'

Bethany swallowed with difficulty, and looked from one kind familiar face to the other. She had no idea what to say. It had all been so unexpected. She had always loved the Willows, who had been her kindly neighbours ever since she could remember, but she had never known that they felt so deeply for her. Both had a self-imposed code about what was proper and a dislike for 'over-familiarity'. Now she realised that their feelings were strong enough to have broken their silence, and given her such uncompromising advice. She was unutterably touched. But there was more to come. As she stared mutely at them, Mr Willow rose and went over to the china pot where his wife had been keeping Bethany's holiday money. He solemnly tipped the pot out onto the table, and pushed the contents over towards her. 'We want you to have this. It's not much, but it will be enough to see you through until you get settled where you want to be. You can pay us back if you like, when you get the chance. You don't have to thank us, we've agreed and it's what we want to do, so go on, Love, take it with our blessing.'

Bethany looked at the money. The notes were neatly packaged together with an elastic band, and the coins were in little transparent plastic envelopes. The loving warmth which had gone into the gift was what thawed Bethany's frozen heart and caused the tears to come. Mr and Mrs Willow stood behind her, Mrs Willow rubbing her back and repeating over and over, 'There there, my

Love, there there.' Feeling something more was needed, she added, 'It's only the egg money and we shan't miss it.'

Bethany continued to sniff and, after some hesitation, Mr Willow produced another handkerchief which he put on the table in front of her. She eventually stopped crying and he sat down again and waited.

'Do you mean that you think I shouldn't come back here again – ever?' Bethany said in a voice that was muffled by Mr Willow's handkerchief, but completely steady.

Mrs Willow returned her level gaze. 'Yes, Love, we do, at least for a while. You know you can come back to see us if you need to, but it's time to leave and not come back until you've made somethin' of your life, good and proper. She'll take everythin' you got to give otherwise, and throw you out like a dried-out husk one day. We don' want to see you go, Lord knows, but we've come to see it's the only way, haven't we, Ewan?' Mr Willow nodded, and laid his hand once again on his wife's shoulder.

So that was how the decision was made. A few hours later, Bethany was standing at the foot of the bed. She went to the huge suitcase and put her hands over the slightly rusty catches. She slid them sideways and the latches snapped open. She began to pack all of her possessions into it, moving slowly and tiredly. In spite of this, the task was accomplished quickly, considering she was packing everything that had made up her life so far. She put her poetry books in last, stroking their worn covers gently. Then she put the case at the end of her bed, took one last look round the room and went out, closing the door quietly behind her. A shiver ran down her back, and she walked past the closed door of her mother's room and went downstairs. She was going to eat with Mr and Mrs Willow tonight in the warmth and comfort of their kitchen, and then tomorrow she would take her case and go out, as if to work as usual. Everything would be as normal. The only thing out of the ordinary was that tomorrow was Saturday, and she did not work on Saturday. She knew that there was no use bidding farewell to her mother, so she would not be opening Mrs Jones's door and saying goodbye as usual. The only other thing was that she would be leaving her home and everything she had ever known, and she didn't know if she would be coming back. Otherwise, it would be a normal day.

* * *

It had started to rain as they gathered behind the municipal centre where the coach was waiting for them. It was hot and humid, and the drizzle moistened everyone's cases, which were standing in little groups on the gritty car park surface. The dusty air was buzzing with barely suppressed excitement. Knots of people converged and were either involved in animated conversation, or half-heartedly chatting with one eye fixed on the waiting coach.

As Bethany and the Willows approached, she could see that Roy was weaving his way between the groups like a soldier ant taking messages between one cluster and another. Laughter followed his progress as he confidently ticked off names on his clipboard. When he saw Bethany, he left the group he was with and walked towards her, smiling. 'So you made it, did you? It was touch and go right up until the last minute, I suppose.' He included the Willows in his smile, and they returned it, in spite of the tension they felt.

Everybody liked Roy. He was so good-natured, and always ready to crack a joke or see the funny side of things, that it was hard to stay miserable when he was around. He turned to Mr Willow and began talking about the weather, and the possibility that it might cause traffic delays on their journey. Bethany listened to the courteous exchange and reflected once again that people tend to have the lives they themselves create. Roy was so easygoing and friendly that those around him relaxed. He enjoyed company, and was never short of people to buy him a drink, or share a story with at the bar. Bethany had once heard him comment that 'there's good in all sorts, and most people were decent when it came down to it.' Roy enjoyed people, and was always ready to see the best in them. Consequently, what he saw generally was the best, and his experience mirrored his belief.

Seeing Bethany lost in thought, Roy grinned and nudged her. 'Penny for 'em! Cheer up, we're going to the seaside, and it won't be raining there.' He looked down at his clipboard and made a quick check. 'We're all here bar one, and that was to be expected. When she gets here we can be making a move, I think.' Roy was about to go over to the coach driver, who was glancing at his watch, when he gave a shout of laughter. 'Here's your mate now, and needing a hand by the look of things.' Before she turned around, Bethany could hear Sylvia's progress across the car park. The familiar shrieks and giggles drifted through the air, and people smiled to see her. Roy tucked his clipboard under his arm, and strode determinedly towards her friend. For the first time Bethany thought how similar the two were. Sylvia was scatty, but she had the same good faith in human nature, and her desire to 'have a good laugh' generally meant that others had one too. The thought pleased her and, smiling, she left the Willows standing by her suitcase, and went to help.

Sylvia was attempting to drag along two large cases which kept getting stuck in the rutted stony surface of the car park. She had a carrier bag under each arm, a shoulderbag which kept sliding to her elbow, and a large fluorescent pink handbag, the handle of which was clenched between her teeth. Her nails were brightly painted as usual, and she was teetering along on a pair of pale pink high-heeled sandals. All in all, she was a sight to warm Bethany's heart, especially since, on seeing her friend, she dropped everything on the ground and let out a delighted scream and then a peal of giggles. 'Oooh, I can't believe it, we're all here and we're actually going on 'oliday. I was so excited last night I barely slept a wink, did I, Mam, and now it's here and it's going to be brilliant. I'm so glad you made it, you'll see it'll all work out OK. Oh Roy, you are a darling. Thanks ever so. Let's sit together on the coach, Bethany, up the back.' She threw her arms around Bethany, who was enveloped in Woolworth's scent. Bethany just had time to catch Roy's amused glance before Sylvia swept her over towards the coach. 'Come on, let's get on, shall we? What's everyone waiting for? We can get on, can't we?' Roy picked up Sylvia's suitcases and strode to the side of the coach. He handed her the carrier bags and the shoulderbag, and began to pass the baggage to the coach driver, who stacked it away in the hold. Mr Willow followed him, and was joined by other men eager to be doing something, and wanting an end to the standing around.

Mam came over to Mrs Willow, and Bethany stood slightly apart from the pair, who fell into easy conversation. They were standing right at the front of the coach. The rain had stopped but had left marks on the thick grime of its surface. The air shimmered from the heat of the running engine and she felt the heat on her cheeks. Her nostrils were filled with the acrid smell of exhaust fumes. Suddenly, she experienced the strangest sensation. It was as though everything was quiet and still, and that she was standing outside time. She slowly reached out her finger, just as she would have done as a child, and made a little mark on the edge of the coach, next to the door. She could hear snatches of conversation, and sensed people moving around her, but felt detached from it all. She looked at her fingertip, which was black from the dirt, and for a moment her immediate sensations of vison and smell were magnified. The exhaust fumes, the heat, and the grime on her hands filled her vision and she was in a place of great calm and silence. She listened to the stillness. She had heard the expression

'Time stood still' but had never experienced it before. It was as if she was outside herself observing everything that was going on. It was most peculiar.

Her reverie was abruptly broken as Sylvia remembered that she had forgottten to say her goodbyes. She rushed up to hug Mam. Goodbyes were said, and motherly advice given, and Mam was still talking as Sylvia hurtled across the car park in search of Da'. Da' was deep in conversation with a group of cronies debating the merits of cold frames when starting the first crop of early lettuce. He broke off and fondly hugged his youngest daughter, telling her sternly to be sensible. 'Don't be silly, Da', it's only a week. I'll see you Saturday.' With these parting words, Sylvia clambered up the steps that boarded the coach. This manoeuvre took a little time as the steps were steep and narrow, and she was still weighed down with her assorted bags. The tightness of her skirt and her high heels made the task more difficult, as she kept dropping the bags in order to pull her skirt down. Being Sylvia, she became helpless with giggles and gave up before she reached the top of the steps. She turned round to wave, and the pink handbag rolled out from under her arm and opened as it slid down the steps. A torrent of lipsticks, powder compacts, tissues and other assorted items cascaded out and rolled in all directions, clattering noisily underneath the coach.

In the hubbub that ensued, Bethany turned towards the Willows. She had been dreading the moment of farewell, but Sylvia had put a smile on all of their faces, and she held on to the feeling as best she could. Mrs Willow held out her arms, and Bethany bent down to hug her, lost for words. 'Don' you say anythin', pet, everythin's already been said.' Mr Willow hugged her. 'Let us know how you're gettin' on, won't you, lovely?' he said. Bethany nodded, her eyes bright with tears. Mrs Willow fumbled with her handkerchief and then gave her a little shove.

'Go on, my love. You've a place saved for you at any rate.' Sylvia, who had eventually been installed complete with her bag and its contents, was waving and gesturing from a window seat near the rear of the coach. They could see her mouth moving and knew she was talking ten to the dozen as usual. Gratefully, Bethany squeezed Mr Willow's hand and then clambered aboard. She sat down on the seat next to Sylvia and craned her head to see out of the window.

The coach driver started the engine, and they slowly rolled forward. Mr and Mrs Willow were standing next to Mam and Da', and all were waving. Bethany had never been on a coach before, and it felt strange to be looking down from so high. She felt as though she were rising up from the ground and flying away from them. She joined Sylvia blowing kisses until the little group was out of sight.

'Are you all right?' said Sylvia. 'It'll all work out, see if it doesn't, and I know your mam didn't want to come and say goodbye, but she'll've got over it by the time we get back, honest she will.' Seeing her friend's anxious blue eyes, Bethany was quick to reassure her that she was fine. In fact, now that the moment of parting was over, she felt a surge of excitement. Her great adventure was about to begin. She determined then and there that she would seize her opportunity with both hands. She knew what kind of a person she wanted to be, and the kind of life she wanted to have. She wanted to really live, not be closeted in some unremarkable house in some dreary town, wondering where all the time had gone, and what had happened to her dreams. She turned to Sylvia, who was delighted at the radiance of her friend's smile.

Behind her, those sitting on the back row had started singing 'Oh I do like to be beside the seaside'. Sylvia strained to turn around and see who was in the best seats. She met Roy's amused twinkling brown eyes and smiled back. 'Bethany, would you mind if we swapped places so I can be on the outside?' she asked. Sighing resignedly, Bethany edged out into the gangway and Sylvia began the laborious task of getting herself and her bags into the aisle. Amid cheers and catcalls, the operation was accomplished and Bethany eventually found herself looking out of the tinted glass at the familiar sights of her home town, which were passing rapidly by as the coach left for the motorway.

She leaned back into the comfortable seat. Sylvia had twisted right around into the gangway and was joining in enthusiastically with the singing. They had finished 'Oh I do like to be beside the seaside' and were going through all the songs that nobody really sings except when on a journey. After 'One man went to mow', someone started 'The quartermaster's stores'. This provoked a great deal of hilarity as the verses involved choosing somebody's name and then rhyming it. The chorus of 'My eyes are blind, I cannot see, I have not brought my specs with me' was a catchy one, and Bethany was gradually drawn in and was soon singing as loudly and cheerfully as the rest. They tailed off eventually, as nobody could think of a rhyme for 'Sylvia', and everybody paused, breathless and laughing. Someone half-heartedly began 'One hundred green bottles, standing on a wall' and was hushed up with good-natured groans and 'give it a rest' from Roy. Everyone settled back into their seats and there began a more peaceful way of passing the journey, looking out of the windows or talking quietly together. The half hour of singing had strengthened the feeling of camaraderie on the back two rows of the coach, and Bethany and Sylvia were beaming as they turned back to face the front. Sylvia leaned back against the headrest and Bethany looked out of the window again.

They had left the town far behind and the uniformly grey buildings had given way to the patchwork colours of open fields and farmland, as the coach sped along the motorway. After a few moments of watching a distant tractor moving slowly along the crest of a hill, Bethany came to a decision. She had been wondering how to broach the subject of her future. Part of her had been hoping that it would be possible to merely wait until the last minute, and then tell Sylvia that she wasn't coming back with them. That way, it would be too late for anyone to try to persuade her to change her mind. Now, flushed with happiness after the singing, she knew that it was time to leave this childish hope behind. It was time she took charge of her own future. Telling her friend would be a way of making it definite, an acknowledgement of the new life she was going to make for herself.

Quickly, so as not to give herself the chance of changing her mind, she said, 'Sylvia, I'm not coming back after the holiday. I'm going to get a job and see what the world has for me. Something is waiting, but it's not at home, it's out there. It might even be somebody, I don't know, but it's so close I can almost touch it. I have to go to meet it.'

The words tumbled over each other in her haste to get them out. She was rather surprised by what she had said, but for the moment she was only interested in Sylvia's response. Clutching the armrest of her seat, she waited anxiously for her friend's reaction. It would make it so much harder if Sylvia were against her plan, and tried to change her mind. There was a long silence, which was the last thing she had expected. Bethany had never known Sylvia quiet for so long. She turned to look at her friend's face. Sylvia had fallen into a doze, her head lolling against her pink shoulder-bag. Bethany smiled at the top of her blonde head. The big announcement would have to wait for another time. All the same, she felt a new resolve strengthening her. In spite of the fact that nobody had heard her speech, just saying the words out loud had reinforced her conviction that she was doing the right thing. It had taken her a while to build up her courage, but now she was certain.

In the silence that followed she had time to mull over what she had actually said. What on earth had she meant by something waiting for her? She had certainly not planned to say any such thing, but now she came to think of it, it was true. Somehow she felt that something was about to happen to her, and that she was meant to be making this journey. 'Destiny' was not something she had considered before, but there was a certainty inside her that she was going to meet hers. Oddly, for no particular reason, she remembered the peculiar little moment of silence in the car park. For a moment she had the fanciful impression that someone had spoken to her, that she had heard a voice. It was like trying to remember a dream, and she couldn't at all think why it had come into her head. She left the thought behind, and looked out of the window.

The smooth motorway was leading them steadily through the featureless landscape. They were eating up the miles inexorably, leaving Wales behind them, cruising effortlessly further and further from familiarity, and onward on their journey. Somehow, Bethany had expected it to be more exciting, but the motorway itself cut through the land, effacing the natural landmarks and creating its own. Huge blue signs marking junctions and service stations, and ugly concrete bridges arching the lanes, made far more of an impact on her vision than anything she could see either side of her. She leaned her head against the glass and gazed, her mind drifting without focus.

Her reverie was broken as the coach began to slow down. They were approaching the huge steel and concrete structure that was the Severn bridge. As they drew into the nearside lane with the tollbooths for the widest and slowest vehicles, Bethany could see vast expanses of wide grey sandflats edging the steely water, which lay leaden and inert below the bridge. Once they were on the bridge itself they had no impression of its size or magnificence, although Bethany could well believe that it was an impressive sight from the ground. She wondered if perhaps travelling was like this, more interesting from a distance than actually doing it. Perhaps Mrs Willow had been right to stay in her kitchen all these years and collect plates. The coach was buffeted by the wind as they crossed and then they were on the other side. Bethany was now in England.

They had set off from the car park outside the works building at four o'clock in the afternoon. After two hours they were all ready to get off the coach to stretch their legs, and were shifting in their seats as Martin, their driver, pulled into the car park of the service station. As they shuffled down the steps, he gave the cheerful instruction to be 'back in forty-five minutes or miss the off'. When they had left Wales, the hazy drizzle had stopped and the skies had cleared, and their journey had been made in bright afternoon sunshine. This made the stop all the more inviting, although the service station was not picturesque. Sylvia and Bethany clambered off the coach and Bethany squinted upwards into the sunlight. White clouds were scudding across the deep azure sky, and a strong breeze was blowing. She took a deep breath, her first gulp of English air. Grinning, she followed the group who were all picking their way through the blue puddles in the car park, heading determinedly towards the glinting modern building housing the cafeteria, and more importantly, the loos.

Inside there was piped music and a strange cold antiseptic smell from the air-conditioning, mixed with fried food. Neither of them had been in such a place before, and they meandered towards the cafeterias looking at the luridly coloured animals on stands that rocked backwards and forwards when you put a coin in the slot. Sylvia wanted to sit on a bright pink elephant which reached just above her knee, but Bethany dragged her away. They both felt light-headed with happiness and were laughing in a way that Bethany's mother would certainly have disapproved of if she had been there to see it. When they got to the self-service cafe they were both shocked at how much more expensive it was than Woolworth's, and only bought a sandwich and a cup of coffee. Undaunted, they looked around a little more, and then they turned back and wandered towards the sliding glass doors that led to the car park.

Martin opened the coach door with a hiss of rubbery smelling air and welcomed them aboard. 'Wotcha, first ones back you are; in a hurry to be off, are you?' Sylvia wanted to turn around and go back, but was laughingly persuaded to sit down in her seat. The others were returning in small groups, and gradually the coach filled up again. There was much rustling of paper and plastic bags, as everyone showed off the purchases they had made. Roy made a quick head count, and they were off again. The next part of the journey took them towards London. Bethany had been very much looking forward to seeing the city, but it seemed as though they were not to see any of the more famous sights. All that happened was that there was more and more traffic, and the coach had to stop and start at traffic lights. Binbags full of rubbish lay on the pavement. She told herself that, when she was settled, she would see all of the landmarks: Buckingham Palace, Trafalgar Square, Covent Garden, the museums and the galleries.

Her mind became more and more hazy as she imagined all of the delights to come, and she sank back into the comfortable seat. She suddenly felt very tired. She had not slept well last night. In spite of the welcoming hospitality of the Willows' kitchen, the previous evening had felt strange, and full of unaccustomed silences. They had all been thinking of the next day, and could not be natural with one another. In the end she had gone back home and tossed and turned in her bed. Her worried thoughts had chased each other around and around her head, and she had imagined one alternative future after another, and lain awake into the small hours. Now, in the warmth of the coach, her lack of sleep was catching up with her. Her eyelids grew heavier, and she gradually sank into a dreamless doze.

When she woke the coach was on a smaller motorway and the view outside the window had changed. Instead of the cramped urban sprawl they were now in open countryside. Woods and fields spread out either side of them and, for the first time, Bethany sat forward in her seat and really began to enjoy the view. They were now travelling through the rolling landscape that was the Sussex Downs. It was evening and the coach's shadow moved over the grassy verge alongside them. Hillsides were familiar to all of them but, to Bethany, who was used to the blue-black severity of the Welsh Valleys, these hills seemed pliant and gentle. The wide expanses of softly waving grass and chalky outcrops which rose either side of the road ahead appeared to be beckoning them onward, inviting the traveller to wander over their high open spaces. This was in sharp contrast to back home, where the hills hung over the towns distrustfully, warning the unwary traveller to beware of hidden dangers in their dark crags. Bethany had always disliked the hill behind her street, and had wanted to live some-where flat, but now she saw the possibility of these hills, and craned her head eagerly out of the window to see more. The others on the coach were doing the same, and everybody realised they were getting nearer their destination. On the steeply rising verges either side, there were white and yellow flowers, and clusters of bright poppies waving in the breeze.

They passed two large grey pillars either side of the road, and someone said 'It's the five mile marker.' Now everybody was really sitting up and looking around them, and there was a stirring of excitement on the coach. They were slowing down as the road changed to a two-lane highway edged with houses. Sylvia wriggled next to Bethany.

'We're really here!' she said, and the pair grinned at each other.

Next, Roy got up from his seat and shouldered his way down the bus. He dug Sylvia playfully in the ribs on his way down and she squealed and giggled. 'Oh, 'e's such a card that Roy,' she said to Bethany, and then fell silent expectantly as Roy began to talk to Martin, their coach driver.

There was a loud electronic screech followed by catcalls and good-natured jeers as Roy struggled with the microphone. 'Twiddle your knobs!' someone shouted to gales of laughter.

Grinning, Roy replied, 'Come up here then, if you can do any better.' The heckler, Big Hugh, so called because of his generously proportioned beer belly, made as if to rise from his seat, and was pulled back down by his wife, Carol, and his sister-in-law June, both of whom were as large as he was. The three of them took up a large proportion of the back seat, and all chortled merrily at Big Hugh's remarks. The seat shook as they elbowed each other and told each other to be quiet. When the noise died down, Roy continued. 'OK, well, we're getting close now, and we should be arriving in the next ten minutes. Make sure you've got everything, as Martin will be going back to London, and it'll be a different coach that takes us back. We'll be stopping at the coach station, as the road with our hotel is a bit narrow for the coach to park. It's only a short walk, so I expect you'll all be glad to stretch your legs. I've not got much more to say, except thanks to Martin for driving us, and get ready for some fun!' There was a huge cheer at this, and the front rows began a chorus of 'For he's a jolly good fellow'.

Bethany and Sylvia shivered with excitement, and Sylvia squeezed Bethany's arm. 'See, I told you, didn't I, just you wait till you see the pier, and the sea, you'll love it, honest you will.' Then she began to pack up all of the debris from her bags, scrabbling under the seat and twisting round to get stray crisp packets and sweet-papers behind her back. When she had tidied up, she fished out her compact and her lipstick and began doing her face. 'Watch out!' she said sharply, as a sudden movement from Bethany jogged her hand and she smeared her pink lip gloss. Bethany had half risen out of her seat and was gesturing wildly. There were incoherent sounds coming from her wide open mouth.

'Oh, that, I know, it's the Pavilion. It's really amazin', isn't it, sort of like it should be on a chocolate box or somethin'. Some king or prince built it, 'e must 'ave been a bit daft, don' you think?'

Bethany had by now turned right around in her seat to follow her first sight of the remarkable building called the Pavilion. She had never seen anything like it in her life. It was like a huge iced cake, a fairy tale palace for a confectionery princess, so exotic and outlandish that it sat in the green space that surrounded it as though it had dropped out of a giant Christmas cracker. She wanted to find out more about it immediately, but by now everyone was craning to look in front of them. Martin slowed the coach right down, and they had a clear view of the Palace Pier directly ahead. The sun had gone down, although it was not properly dark, and what they saw presented such an attractive vista of gaiety and pleasure that they felt like cheering. The lights from the attractions and rides filled their eyes with colour, and they could hear the music from the funfair. It was all a clarion call to Sylvia, who was by now bouncing up and down in her impatience. 'Come on, come on, let's get to it, and park and get out. Oh, I can't wait.'

Martin steered the coach expertly into the coach station and spoke into the microphone. 'Well, 'ere we are, ladies and gentlemen, safely at your destination. 'Ave a great 'oliday and don't do anything I wouldn't do, which gives you plenty of elbow room.' He shouldered himself out of his seat and down the steps in one easy movement, and began to open the baggage hold under the coach. Everybody was hurriedly packing up the debris from their journey and some were squeezing into the aisle. Suddenly Bethany didn't want to get off. It had been such a steady and comfortable ride, so safe and enclosed, and now it was time to leave. She wanted to stay where she was, and travel back home, dozing and looking out of the window at the world passing by. She didn't want to go out into the thick of it all, and face the uncertainties of the future. But it was too late to turn back. So, taking a quick look around, she stood up and followed Sylvia down the aisle. She was the last one out of the coach, and the others were already beginning to sort out the bags which were being piled carefully on the tarmac.

Bethany found her case and looked around her, taking in the first impressions of a new environment. The first thing she heard was the sound that all travellers recognise as the sound of the ocean, the sound that heralds the start of a holiday. The seagulls were calling noisily, asserting their sovereignty of the skies and sea. Their squawking, screaming cries rent the air as they wheeled far above in the patch of blue above the coach station. The night air was warm and the smells familiar, and yet somehow different. Bethany breathed deeply. There was the tantalising aroma of fish and chips mixed with the sweet heavy smell of frying doughnuts drifting up from the seafront. She could hear the buzz of excited crowds wandering along the pavement beyond the bus station, and the faint sound of the funfairs on the pier. She had experienced some of the sights and smells back home, but these were mixed with something else, something indefinably exhilarating that she couldn't pinpoint. She listened again and the wild crying of the gulls pierced her ears. The sound threaded the sights and sensations of the evening like beads on a necklace, binding them together into a unified whole.

Roy, who was standing next to her, saw her drinking in the air, and took a deep breath himself. 'Great, isn't it? I'll never forget the first time I smelled the sea.' Their eyes met briefly in understanding. He gave her shoulder a friendly pat and moved over to talk to Martin. Bethany marvelled at how surprising people could be sometimes. Roy was always the centre of a crowd, cracking jokes and apparently never sparing a thought for much other than having a good time, but often he had a knack of saying just what you were thinking, of putting himself in your place in a way that most people couldn't do.

Bethany was reminded again of Sylvia. To most people, she was a great girl, good for a laugh, but there was not much going on in her head. People laughed at the oddness of their friendship, but only a few of them knew how kind Sylvia was, and how observant she was of other people beneath her frivolous exterior.

Bethany dragged her case over to her friend and they smiled at each other. Roy waited until everyone was ready and then set off through a narrow lane threading itself between tall concrete buildings.

Almost immediately, they emerged into a large open space with bright flower beds filled with pink and white petunias. There was a large fountain in the middle with three huge fish at its base, made of some kind of greeny bronze metal. Glancing quickly back and to her left, Bethany could just make out the fairy tale Pavilion lit by phosphorescent green-white light. There was no time to stop and stare, however, as they needed all their wits about them negotiating the busy roads that surrounded the Old Steine. They passed the white and grey building that was the Royal Albion Hotel and Bethany stared wide-eyed at the huge number of windows. They had nothing like this at home. She had no time to dawdle however, as Roy was leading the party across the traffic lights and up the road which climbed alongside the seafront.

On the other side of the road the pale ornamental railings separated the promenade from the traffic, and beyond that the sea stretched endlessly into the distance. Although it was late, the water wasn't dark, but a kind of milky grey-green flecked with white waves. It seemed to have its own light, opaque and glimmering. Bethany put down her case with a bump and gazed, drinking in the wonderful sight. A shout from Sylvia ahead brought her sharply down to earth and she was just in time to see the party disappearing into a road which appeared to be their final destination. She quickly lugged her case up into her arms again and turned sharply left to catch them up. Behind her was the sea and the pier, and at the end of the short street she could make out another road full of shops. Almost every building was either a small hotel or a guest house offering bed and cooked breakfast, and it was in front of one of these that everyone had stopped. 'This is it, ladies and gentlemen. Please walk this way.' Roy held out his arm in imitation of a conciege, at the same time helping Sylvia up the steps and into the foyer.

Bethany climbed the two wide, rounded steps which were covered in a diamond pattern of black and white tiles. There were large dark oak doors with glass panels in them that were hooked back against the wall, and which led into a square, high-ceilinged entrance foyer. She put down her suitcase and sat down on a sofa. Directly opposite the main entrance where the group were gathering, there was a solid bar laid out with register and bell, and pigeon-holes with keys in them. The lighting was unlike any she had ever seen before. There were a series of brownish, yellow plastic cylinders on stiff cable suspended from the ceiling in differing lengths. They were so thickly indented to resemble cut glass that they didn't shed much light, except in pools onto the swirling plaster of the ceiling. The eddies of this plaster were echoed by the carpet which had whirlpools of red and brown, and covered not only the hall, but the solid staircase with its curving banister. There was a smell of cigarette smoke and stale steak and kidney pudding, and a faint tang of cat. It was reassuringly respectable and comfortable. On the half-moon table beside her there was a rack neatly laid out with leaflets labelled 'The attractions of Sussex'. They were covered with bright photographs of families waving from the top of traction engines and face to face with flamingos at wildlife parks.

Sylvia trotted over from the bar, triumphantly brandishing a room key with a large red plastic tag on it. 'Come on, this is ours, it's got two singles and a camp bed in, so we'll have to get someone else. Who d'you want, I'm easy really, how about Doreen, she's good for a laugh? DOREEN! Come over 'ere. D'you fancy sharin' in with us? I've got our key, me an' Bethany are in number 25, d'you wanna come in with us?' Doreen shimmied up in a tight pencil skirt and heels almost as high as Sylvia's. She did her typing two desks along from Sylvia and Bethany, and was engaged to Joseph who did the Bridge Street round. She was an easygoing, dimpled brunette whose talk was much involved with bridesmaids and wedding breakfasts, and who wasn't expected to stay long in the typing pool. Mrs Willow and Mam darkly suspected that she was no better than she ought to be, and if it was going to be a white wedding it would be a tight squeeze in more ways than one to get it in before the Christening. Bethany and Sylvia liked Doreen and were pleased when she readily agreed to share. Other groups and pairs were beginning to sort themselves out, and one by one they all staggered up the stairs, heaving their heavy cases and then trundling along the corridor in search of their rooms.

'Come on, dopey, I wanna go and get some fish and chips,' said Doreen, as Sylvia fumbled impatiently with the unfamiliar key and lock. ''Ere, give us a go.' In the end it was Bethany who let them into their room, which was as Sylvia had described, with two single beds and a pull-down camp bed under the window. They made a brief inspection of their accommodation. The walls were off-white, and there was a small basin with a cloth tucked into the pipes underneath it. The carpet was a rather marked beige-brown colour, and the curtains were of a dark green hessian. Otherwise the room was bare, apart from a small table with a drawer wedged tightly into the small space between the beds and a narrow wardrobe in one corner. The floor and the wall did not form a proper right angle, but sloped gently away from each other, causing the wardrobe to lean rather tipsily into the room. Someone had tried to wedge a square of folded newspaper under the near edge in an attempt to keep the cupboard from rocking, but when Sylvia pulled the door, it swung drunkenly out and rocked gently, revealing a dusty square of mirror loosely fastened to the inside. The metal hangers clinked quietly together, as Sylvia automatically peered into the tarnished mirror, checking her face. Doreen jumped onto the bed and pulled open the drawer of the little table. 'Ooh, look, 'ere's something to read in the evenings, girls! We can 'ave Prayer Meetins.' Cackling, she tossed a Gideon Society bible onto the nylon bedcover where it bounced and lay open at Corinthians.

It was very warm. The air in the room was stale, and Bethany lifted the net curtain and struggled with the metal catch on the window. With difficulty she slid the sash up several inches, where it stuck firm. They were at the back of the building, and the view was unremarkable. There was a black fire escape and the grey concrete fascias of the backs of the buildings from the next street. She could hear the seagulls screaming to one another again.

Sitting down on the end of the bed Doreen was on, she closed the bible and put it back on the table. 'Who's going to have the beds?' Sylvia made a short running jump and landed on the bed opposite.

'I know, let's do "paper, scissors, rock".' It took them a few moments to work out how to do it with three people, as no combination seemed really fair. This was compensated for by the fact that none of them really minded where they slept, it was just fun to decide. In the end Doreen and Bethany went first. Bethany won, so she chose one bed, and Doreen played Sylvia. Doreen won, so Sylvia had the camp bed. Plonking her suitcases down on its end, so that it tilted precariously, Sylvia had had enough of the room for a while. 'Well, we're here, let's not waste time, girls. Let's go out and get something to eat and then go down to the pier. We can see if the others want to come.' They readily agreed, Doreen wanting to catch up with her Joe anyway. So, leaving everything just as it was, they locked the door behind them, skipped down the stairs, left the key on a hook in the lobby, and ran out into the road, laughing with excitement.

*   *   *

Bethany squinted at her watch in the bright sunlight. She was lying down on the pebbles by the edge of the sea and the time said 7.30 a.m. The waves were barely lapping a few feet from her bare toes and the sound so lulled her that she was dozing and drifting in the morning sun. Her senses were filled with the sea. The seaweed smelled strongly, and there was a faint breeze carrying the salt through the air. Her skin was alive to the sensations of the sun and warm air on her face and arms, and most of all she was listening. The combination of waves and the cries of the seagulls was so intoxicating that she had barely noticed the half hour that she had spent by the water's edge. Her thoughts turned to the night before.

It had been a perfectly lovely evening on the pier, filled with movement, laughter, lights and music. They had all been silly with happiness and ridden the rides until late into the night. Later some of them, including Sylvia and Doreen, had gone dancing, but Bethany had come back tired but happy, carrying a huge stuffed tiger that someone had given Sylvia. She had been so sleepy that she hadn't heard them come in, and slept a deep, dreamless sleep until she had woken to the screams of the gulls early next day. The others were both snoring loudly, Doreen in a tightly

97

curled up ball under her covers, and Sylvia with her arms flung wide and her bedding on the floor. Bethany had gently picked it up, put it back over Sylvia, and then pulled on her clothes as quietly as she could, glad of the chance to explore on her own. She had tiptoed along the corridor and through the deeply carpeted foyer to the fresh air outside. It was a beautiful clear morning, and before setting off for the beach, Bethany stopped only to stroke a small black and white cat that was sunning itself on the steps. She had walked along the promenade and then down onto the steeply banked stones near a large breakwater which stretched out into the sea. Here she had sat down, meaning only to look out over the blue water for a moment, but gradually succumbing to the sensations around her. Now she was stretched out with her trousers rolled up, gazing up at the blue sky through narrowed eyes.

The light was fringed by her eyelashes. A seagull wheeled in the space above her, and then glided effortlessly through the air. She could see its pure white shape sharply outlined against the blue of the sky as it looked down on the beach below. The bird seemed to her to define freedom itself. The fierce joy of its flight, and the wildness of its cry awoke a deep response in her. For a moment she experienced happiness so complete that she closed her eyes again, wanting to prolong the feeling. Never before had she felt the rightness of everything, the certainty that all was well in her world and that she was where she was meant to be. She resolved to try and always remember this moment, and turned over onto her stomach. The pebbles were bright and hard beneath her chin, and she dug her hands into them, enjoying their smooth coolness. Her mind was clear all of a sudden and she stopped drifting through the memories of the night before and thought through her plans.

She knew that she had the skills necessary to find a job. Her shorthand was good, her typing very good, and she had an organised brain which made her useful as a secretary. Brighton seemed the perfect place to settle, and towards the end of the week she could begin to look for work. Once she had a job, a room would not be hard to find, and she would begin to make her new life. It all seemed simple this morning, out in the sunshine, smelling the salt in the air and listening to the seagulls. It was more than just the pleasantness of the morning, however. Ever since that moment of silence on the journey, Bethany had been filled with a calm expectancy. With every hour that passed, she was more and more certain that something important was going to happen to her, something that would mark her life, and form her future in some way. She had not felt this way before, and was rather surprised that she did so now. If she had had to put the feeling into words, she would have found it very difficult.

Suddenly the air cooled. A single, small cloud had passed in front of the sun. Bethany sat up and her stomach rumbled. It was now eight o'clock, and the others would be coming down to the panelled dining room for plates of egg and bacon. Squinting up and down the beach, Bethany said goodbye to the waves and seagulls, and then clambered hurriedly up the pebbles towards the promenade and a hearty breakfast.

The first morning there, everybody who had been on the coach made their way down to the beach. They basked in the sun together, and took turns to get ice creams and drinks for the group from a small café on the seafront. They took over a whole section of the pebbles with their towels and suntan oil, spreading the familiar jokes and camaraderie far and wide, the women whistling at passers-by, and the men eyeing bathing beauties in bikinis. Gradually the freedom and ease of the holiday atmosphere began to seep into them, and they relaxed and became more confident in their new surroundings. Later that morning, they wandered noisily through the streets in search of lunch. At this point, everyone realised that it wasn't really practical to stay together as a whole group for the whole holiday. For one thing, the cafés and pubs couldn't cope with the size of their party. More importantly, they began to realise that they wanted to do different things. They stood indecisively in the main shopping centre, knowing that they would go their separate ways, but strangely reluctant to trust that the holiday would be as wonderful if they weren't all together. After a little while, with the agreement to 'meet back at the bed and breakfast', some decided on the pub, and others on a large familiar burger bar that was part of a national chain. There was one in their home town. Others, more adventurously, set off down the hill towards the part of town that was filled with smaller shops and cafés. Bethany and Sylvia fell into this last category.

Down the hill from the main shopping centre they came to a pedestrian area crammed with market stalls and quirky little boutiques selling second-hand clothes. For a while, the girls were so busy looking at all the shops that they didn't feel hungry, but eventually they collapsed outside a small café. It had white slatted chairs and benches, and salt and pepper pots resting on red serviettes in the centre of each, slightly wobbly, table. The menus were handwritten and covered in plastic, and there were the options of jacket potatoes or sandwiches. The two friends had never seen so many varieties of home-made sandwiches. If ever they bought them, they were always wrapped in cellophane, and were cheese and tomato, cheese and pickle, ham, or beef. Here the range of combinations bewildered them and, in the end, each decided on a comforting and familiar potato with butter and cheese, and a large lemonade. They squinted at each other in the sunlight, and decided that their very next purchase would be sunglasses to shield their eyes from the strong, bright sea light.

After they had satisfied their hunger pangs with the enormous brown potatoes piled high with the fillings, they asked for coffees. These came in mugs, tall and frothy and sprinkled with cocoa powder. Each had a little sachet of brown sugar in the saucer. Sylvia scattered her sugar on the top of her foamy cup, watched it sink to the bottom, and stretched back in her chair with a deep sigh of satisfaction. They watched the people hurrying past for a while, and Bethany decided that now would be a good time to tell Sylvia her plans. To her surprise, Sylvia wasn't nearly as shocked as she thought she'd be, but instead was typically enthusiastic and full of ideas as to how Bethany could find a job. Suddenly she clapped her hand over her mouth.

'Oooh, but 'ave you got enough money, an' 'ow will you manage till you get work, let's see what I've got. . . ' and she opened her large handbag and made as if to tip the contents all over the table. Laughing, Bethany told her about the Willows and the generous loan of their savings.

'Well, aren't they just ducky, but of course you'll be able to pay them back and I suppose it's just as well because if I gave you what I've got we wouldn't be able to go shoppin' very much . . . ' She tailed off into silence. Bethany burst out laughing again. Sylvia could never hide her emotions, and every thought that rushed fleetingly through her mind was as clearly pictured as if it were written in large letters on her face.

They carefully divided the bill and Bethany went inside to pay. When she got back, Sylvia was doing her lipstick with the aid of a small hand-mirror. Bethany gave her a nudge. 'Come on, I want to go and see the Pavilion,' and, without waiting any longer, she set off at a steady pace down the street. Sylvia tottered, off balance, behind her, half running, half walking, rummaging in her bag to find the exact amount to pay her share, calling out to Bethany to wait for her, dropping coins on the pavement, and barging into passers-by because she was looking down into her enormous bag instead of looking where she was going. Halfway along the street she caught up with her friend and thrust some coins into her hand.

''Ere, 'old your 'orses, I'm not really sure I want to go to the Pavilion. I saw it last year an' it was only an old building. 'Ow about if we go back to the "B and B" and see what the others are doing?' Bethany looked doubtful.

'Oh go on, I don't want to go back on me own, I'll get lost and there's lots of time. You don't mind, do you?' Bethany reluctantly agreed, at the same time thinking that they too, like the larger group, had the option of being apart. It was going to be odd, spending time away from her friend, but she resolved that she was going to make the most of this holiday, and Sylvia and she were likely to want to do different things some of the time.

As they walked companionably back towards the seafront, Bethany silently reflected that, apart from the times in her room, with her mother's glowering presence downstairs, or journeying home to the miserable prospect of an evening with Mrs Jones, she had rarely been alone. Certainly, she had never had the luxury of spending time doing something of her own free will in her own company without a deadline. Even the few snatched minutes at the library in the evening after work had been overshadowed by the necessity of finding an excuse to explain her lateness. She found herself eagerly looking forward to solitude, and resolved that she would try not to become involved with any of the others this afternoon, but instead treasure the experience of being alone. It was a luxury, and she was on holiday. She found herself grinning with sheer happiness, feeling light-headed with all the possibilities. They crossed a main thoroughfare, skipping quickly out of the way of a bus bearing down on them, narrowly missing a taxi coming the other way, and dived with relief into another maze of pedestrian streets on the other side of the main road.

Almost immediately they saw Doreen and Peg ahead of them, laden down with bags, and called to them to wait as they caught up with them. Jerking her head towards the heap of carrier bags which they had rested on the ground, Peg said, 'We're just off back 'ome to unpack these. D'you wanna see what we've got?'

Shrieking with curiosity and delight, Sylvia cried, 'Ooh, me an' Bethany only looked in the shops, what did you get? We wanna get sunglasses, let's look on the way back. Ooh, give us a look. D'you wanna come back, Bethany?' Bethany repeated that she'd like to see the Pavilion and Sylvia marvelled once again at the strangeness of her friend. If it was a contest between looking at shopping and seeing an old building, she knew which one she'd choose. Reluctantly, she eventually accepted Bethany's reassurances that she would be fine and they parted affectionately. Sylvia, Peg and Doreen set off back for the bed and breakfast, leaving Bethany standing in a patch of sunlight in a narrow street, revelling in anticipation of the enjoyment that awaited her.

Although she did still want to go and look at the Pavilion, Bethany found herself beguiled by her surroundings, and moved to the edge of the narrow lane to look about her. She was at the entrance to a charming maze of pedestrian streets, different in character to the ones she and Sylvia had wandered, but so enchanting that she found herself reluctant to retrace her steps to the busy main road behind her. She felt compelled to venture further into the maze, not knowing what she would find there, but inevitably drawn towards its centre. She was enticed onwards and she began to walk slowly and happily in the sunlight that streamed down into the enclosed streets. There was a myriad of little shops either side of her. The smells of baking bread, cheeses and meats from an Italian delicatessen mingled with the heady perfume of a place selling soaps, bath oils and lotions. Ahead of her she could hear the clear sound of a violin rising above the murmuring and laughter from a nearby restaurant whose tables spilled out onto the pavement. And all around there were shops. Shops selling antiques and jewellery, shops to buy things in and shops to sell things in. A notice to the left of her said 'We buy rubies, sapphires, diamonds and emeralds'. Bethany felt she could be in some exotic fairy tale land. It was intoxicating. And all the time she was drawn onwards, not knowing or caring where she was going, merely revelling in the growing feeling of happiness that was filling her up. This was truly her time out of time. Real life, as she had known it, had ceased to be, and she was in a place outside all her worries and fears. She was content not to think of the future or the past. She was merely going to enjoy the present moment, and the wisdom and clarity of this decision rang like a clear bell inside her. All the while her happiness was growing.

She turned a sharp corner, and at the end of a street whose shops crowded even closer either side, she could see a building which stood calm and peaceful amid the hustle and bustle of everything going on around it. She made her way towards it, up the red brick lane which sloped slightly, with her eyes fixed on what she saw ahead of her. The building was set back from the rest, behind a pair of wrought iron gates which were half open. They rested between two solid brick pillars. Either side of the gates, twisting and turning above and around the pillars, were two trees that Bethany had never seen before, but reminded her of ancient olive trees with their buckled, ravelled trunks. They looked as though they had stood there for a long, long time. Bethany walked right up to the building and stood just inside the gates. The notice on the double doors in front of her said 'Friends' Meeting House', and another said 'Rear entrance, please enter from front. All welcome'. Bethany, who had never heard of the Quakers Society, was both intrigued and delighted by the name. How lovely to have a building emanating such serenity and joy, devoted to the meeting of friends. Once again, she was drawn without knowing why, and decided to find the front of the building.

This turned out to be easier said than done, as the streets twisted and turned, one leading to another and then turning sharply again until she realised that she was in a place that she had already been in a few minutes before. This had not mattered up to now, as previously she had wandered without direction in the maze of streets, content to luxuriate in the mindless pleasure of meandering happily without destination. Now she set her mind on finding the front of the building and, after one false start, set off in the right direction. She emerged out of the lanes with the sea in front of her, and a beautifully proportioned Georgian building standing to her left. It was covered in bright strands of Virginia Creeper and the light seemed to dance off its golden windows. Bethany looked curiously to see who owned it and laughed out loud with sheer joy to see the brass plaque on the gatepost. It was emblazoned with the solemn Dickensian legend 'Woolley, Bevis and Diplock – Solicitors'. To Bethany, who was by now filled with happiness so intense it was like sunlight shining from inside, the names were so funny that she could not contain the laughter which bubbled upwards and outwards. She followed the road round and immediately saw a high stone wall which was solid but not forbidding, and a number of plane trees whose grey smooth branches hung over the wall into the street.

Bethany walked up to the great iron gates which, like those of the rear entrance, stood wide open either side of a stone path. The slabs were worn down by hundreds of feet, and led to a low building with two arching portals. Over the top was chiselled 'Meeting House Of The Society of Friends'. There were benches resting on the grassy spaces, and notices saying that all were welcome. Feeling totally at home, Bethany sat down on one of the benches which was suffused in sunshine, and breathed freely. The plane trees cast dappled shade onto the worn grass beside her, and a little group of sparrows hopped near the path. Once again, she was conscious of the peace emanating from the building – an oasis of serenity in the busy lanes. The place encapsulated her acute sense of being outside of time. She felt that if she were to wait here, no matter what happened to her, the world with all its important happenings would carry on without her. She could step out of time, experience a different life in other realms of possibility, live in eternal and everlasting space, and then return and nobody would have noticed she'd been gone. Stillness surrounded her, and the world receded to beyond the stone walls. She waited.

* * *

Afterwards, neither of them could say what had drawn them there, only that they shared the same sense of destiny, that their meeting was preordained and had already happened maybe hundreds of times before. Some impulse had propelled him to the meeting place just as she had been, and they had finally come together with relief and joy at the familiarity of the other.

Bethany had opened her eyes to see him coming up the path towards her. Their eyes met and it was impossible not to smile in welcome. With the smile came an infusion of warmth and gratitude that enveloped her like a golden bubble, filling and surrounding her with bliss and delight. He stopped in front of her bench, and she could see the same unalloyed happiness in his eyes. He looked down at her. 'Hello,' he said.

'Hello,' she replied, still smiling delightedly. Wordlessly she moved over on the bench and he sat down. They sat side by side in the sunlight, not thinking, not wondering at the strangeness of this meeting, but suffused with delight, separated only by the small space between them, waiting together as the minutes of the golden afternoon ticked by in stillness.

After a while, it seemed the most natural thing in the world to lean towards each other so that their shoulders touched, feeling the warmth of the contact, still not talking, merely revelling in the rightness of their meeting. Finally, as the shadows lengthened across the garden and the noise of the shoppers passing the gateway began to give way to the sounds of those coming out to enjoy the evening, they moved apart, and turned to face each other. 'Well, how extraordinary,' he said. Bethany beamed at him.

'Hello,' she repeated, aware that this was hardly original, but too happy to care. They looked at each other.

He was tall, perhaps a whole head taller than she, and looked older than she was. His hair was a soft light brown, and his skin was freckled and lightly tanned. He was dressed in khaki trousers

104

and a blue shirt, the sleeves of which were rolled back to reveal strong, lean forearms. But it was his face, and most particularly his eyes, that held her attention. They were the deepest blue she could ever imagine, and alight with amusement. When he smiled, as he was doing at that moment, they were surrounded by laughter lines. Bethany knew she could look into his eyes for the rest of her life and never tire of it. Indeed, she could think of nothing else that she would rather do. She continued to beam at him.

'Well, I suppose we should introduce ourselves,' he said, and then let out a shout of laughter. 'It's hardly the most orthodox of meetings, is it? I'm Oliver . . . but you don't already know that, do you? I mean, this is all rather strange, isn't it?' For the first time, uncertainty entered his voice, and she hurried to reassure him.

'Oh, no, I mean it *is* strange, but it's wonderful, isn't it? I sort of feel I am going to know things about you, but not your name . . . I'm Bethany.' She could see him considering this, matching the name to her face, all the time smiling at her, and then pulling himself out of his reverie with an effort.

'It's lovely to meet you, Bethany.' The amusement was bubbling up in him again at the peculiarity of their situation, and he continued, 'How about a coffee, or something to eat?' He glanced at his watch and started in surprise. 'Good Lord, it's nearly six o'clock; do you have to be anywhere, would you like to . . . I think we must talk . . . um . . . '

Bethany wondered if Sylvia would be getting worried. 'Well, actually, I suppose I ought to let my friend know where I am. Could we perhaps meet a bit later after I've told her what . . .' She tailed off, wondering just exactly what it was that she would tell Sylvia.

By now they were standing up by the bench, and she felt panicky at the thought of leaving him. Suppose he went away and didn't come back? She knew that that would be the worst thing that could ever happen to her. Before she could continue, he spoke again. 'Look, I know this is silly, but I really don't want to let you disappear off like this. You might not come back and that would be . . . Perhaps we could go together and then go and get something to eat afterwards?' The relief she felt must have shown on her face and he said no more, merely holding out his arm in a courteous gesture for her to lead the way through the open iron gates onto the street. They both glanced back briefly in gratitude at the building, and then walked towards the seafront. They walked side by side, he matching his stride to hers in an easy and comfortable rhythm.

105

They said nothing more until they reached the wide pavement opposite the pier, and prepared to cross the road away from the sea. The traffic was busy and they had to wait for a while. Suddenly, they heard a familiar voice in the distance calling Bethany's name. They turned to see Sylvia behind them.

They moved apart, but it was obvious that Sylvia had seen them together. She was wearing bright red sunglasses, waving and trying desperately to catch them up. This wasn't easy as she was half staggering, half hopping along. She was holding one of her shoes in her hand and talking, not waiting for her listeners to come into earshot. ' . . . so then the 'eel came off my shoe and Roy said 'e'd carry me but I told 'im 'e'd 'ave a turn and, Roy where are you, where is 'e, and where 'ave you been, I was worried?' All this time she was hopping up and down on one leg, trying to keep her balance, and looking with frank interest at Oliver, and then Bethany. At this point Roy arrived. He was holding the pink heel of Sylvia's shoe, which he handed to her without comment. At the same time, he moved closer to Sylvia and firmly put her hand on his shoulder, balancing and supporting her so that she could stand still. He avoided meeting Bethany's eyes, and she knew that he also had seen Oliver, and was not sure if he approved.

For a moment there was an awkward pause. Then Oliver held out his hand to Roy. 'Hello, I know this must seem odd. You must be Bethany's friends. I'm Oliver, and you are?' He included Sylvia in his open gaze and the introductions were made. Roy visibly relaxed, although he was obviously still puzzled. Perhaps his initial assessment of Oliver as a 'chancer' out to take advantage of Bethany was a bit strong, but the situation still required some explanation in his view. After all, he felt some measure of responsibility for those in the party, especially for Bethany, as she was a bit different from the other girls, less worldly, so to speak. He was going to clarify matters to his satisfaction before they left this chap alone with a young girl who was hardly wise to the ways of men. This would mean that they would have to stay to talk for a while, which was not an altogether unattractive proposition. Staying to talk to Bethany and her mystery man would give him a bit more time alone with Sylvia, a prospect he had begun to relish.

He had long had his eye on Sylvia, and liked what he saw. The friendship between her and Bethany had intrigued him and he had suspected that there was more to the bubbly, fluffy surface that Sylvia displayed happily to the world. He had quietly decided to spend some time alone with her and had seized the first opportunity he'd got with dogged determination. It wasn't easy getting Sylvia alone, and he had pursued her like an earnest butterfly collector on the track of a particularly fine specimen. When she had arrived with Peg and Doreen, and without Bethany at the Bed and Breakfast, he had seen his opening. Listening for a while to the shopping talk, he then informed the delighted Sylvia that he knew a great place on the seafront that sold stylish sunglasses. He could take her if she wanted. For a tricky moment it seemed as though they were all coming, but Peg and Doreen wanted a cuppa, and so Sylvia had come alone. They had just been returning along the front from a successful expedition when they had seen Bethany and Oliver.

Roy was accustomed to trusting his gut feelings, and he now appreciated that Sylvia was not only fun to be with, but she had a kindly and warm-hearted nature. He was beginning to feel increasingly protective of Sylvia, and liked the thought of them spending more time together. Thinking quickly, he said, 'Look, why don't we all sit down over there? Maybe we can fix your shoe, Sylvia?' He jerked his head towards the large expanse of grass in the middle of the Old Steine. He grasped Sylvia's waist firmly and supported her in the direction of the benches and begonias surrounding the ornamental fountain. Sylvia giggled and twisted her head round to the hesitating couple behind.

'Come on, you two, I wanna hear all about it. What are you waiting for?'

Bethany and Oliver were looking at each other in near desperation. What could they possibly say that would explain their meeting and accelerated intimacy? Until the moment Sylvia had burst in on their world they had been enclosed in a private bubble of happiness. So strong was the feeling of recognition between them, the sense of re-knowing each other, that they had been content just to relax into a kind of relief at their meeting. They hadn't stopped to think how odd it would look to the eyes of the world. Now, when the strangeness of the situation was brought home to them fully for the first time, they wanted to absorb it together, alone and undisturbed. Instead, in less than half a minute, even if they walked slowly, Roy and Sylvia would require some explanation. What were they to do?

'Oh God,' said Oliver suddenly. Bethany looked at him and saw his eyes brimming with helpless laughter.

She couldn't prevent the grin from spreading across her own face as she said, 'It's not funny really. What *are* we going to tell them?' Oliver suddenly bent down and began to untie his shoelace. Bethany looked over at Roy and Sylvia. Roy was bending over the heel of Sylvia's shoe, though why Bethany could not imagine, as it was obviously not mendable with bare hands. Sylvia sat very close and was also bending her blonde head close to Roy's brown one. Bethany suddenly saw her friends with great clarity. She was momentarily distracted from her problems and filled with delight. It was a pairing that seemed so right. Roy suddenly raised his head and looked directly over to Bethany, and his eyes met hers. For a brief instant they looked at each other. Both had been caught completely off-guard. Bethany knew that confusion and apprehension was clearly written on her face for him to see. Similarly, Roy had had no time to cover up the emotion he felt for Sylvia, and knew that Bethany saw the strength of his feelings. It seemed as though they read each other's minds. 'Gosh, this is a very strange day,' thought Bethany.

Finally, Roy smiled ruefully, and Bethany knew that they had made some sort of unspoken bargain. Roy was decent and honest, and his natural instincts were to investigate what was certainly an unusual situation, and offer what protection and advice he could. Bethany was telling him that she could manage, that there was more to this than he thought, and he was indicating, cautiously, that he would trust her, and not make difficulties. All of this she knew as certainly as if they were speaking aloud. Silently, she smiled back, communicating her gratitude. He gave an almost imperceptible shrug and sat back, leaning his weight on his hands.

'Are you ready yet?' she asked Oliver, who was still bent over his shoelace, tying it in some impossibly complicated time-consuming knot. He tilted his head back and looked up at her. Doing her best to ignore the ridiculous joy that welled up inside her at the sight of his face again after a whole minute of not seeing it, she made herself concentrate on what he was saying.

'Well, I have to say I haven't come up with anything very much. I've toyed with the idea that I stopped to ask directions and then needed to rest my arm on you, but it doesn't really hold water, does it?' She was forced to agree. 'The only other thing I can think of is that we met by coincidence and we've already met before.' There was no time to analyse this as he was continuing, 'So, do you have any long-lost relatives from the back of beyond? Please hurry up, because we have to do something, and fairly quickly.' Once again the radiance of his smile belied the seriousness of his words, and she knew everything would be all right. After all, it was Roy and Sylvia a few feet away, her friends who wanted the best for her, not her mother, foreseeing disaster in everything she did.

'Right, I'll do my best, only don't be shocked and think badly of me. I'm not usually untruthful. And I've thought of something so you don't have to untie that again.' Oliver grinned and stood up. Bethany braced herself for the explanation she was about to produce, and they strolled over to Roy and Sylvia.

'Did you fix it?' Bethany asked as she settled herself on the warm dusty grass beside Sylvia.

'No, worse luck, I think I'm goin' to 'ave to throw them away; I really liked them as well . . . ' She paused and then visibly brightened. 'Course, I'll need a new pair, won' I, an' this is just the place to get them.' Beaming at everyone, she continued, 'So come on, introduce us. How do you two know each other? I can't wait to find out where you've met.'

Determinedly avoiding Roy's serious gaze and Oliver's barely disguised curiosity, Bethany touched Sylvia's arm. 'D'you know, I can hardly believe it myself, I was amazed when we bumped into each other. It's been a long time, but we recognised each other straight away. D'you remember when Mother and Father and I went to Swansea for that holiday?' Sylvia nodded slowly. She did remember. She and Bethany had been fourteen, and scarcely knew each other at the time, but Bethany had since told her what a miserable vacation it had been. Her parents had driven to the beach most days and then sat silently in the car drinking tea from a thermos, leaving the depressed Bethany scuffing her shoes in the rainy car park. It was the only holiday Bethany had ever had, but she had never mentioned to Sylvia anything about this tall stranger gazing with his mouth slightly open, hanging on her friend's every word. Puzzled, she looked back at Bethany, who continued in a voice that held the merest trace of a tremor, 'Well, we stayed in this house, what was it called, 'The Nook' wasn't it, Oliver, and Oliver's mum was the landlady!' Sylvia's blue eyes were round.

'Oooh, so you were childhood sweethearts. Ah, isn't that lovely, Roy?'

'Oh, no,' said Bethany hurriedly, 'I was only a gawky teenager with braces, and I had a bit of a crush on Oliver. He was really nice to me and took me for walks when no one else wanted me around. You had a little dog and we used to take it for walks on the common: I don't suppose you remember that, do you, Oliver?'

At last Bethany dared to look at him. His mouth was still hanging slightly open, and his blue gaze barely concealed his astonishment. Oliver met her eyes, which were silently pleading with him not to make a hash of it, and pulled himself together. Mentally squaring his shoulders, and pausing only to take a breath, he rose magnificently to the challenge. 'Of course I do. Dear old Muffin, he did

109

all right, considering he only had the three legs. And you weren't that awkward, I recognised you quite easily. But it was a terribly long time ago and an extraordinary coincidence us bumping into each other. Actually, it wasn't 'The Nook', it was 'Bide a Wee'. I can't imagine how you forgot that, Bethany.' Oliver was getting into his stride now. 'Yes, Mum had guests every summer, but she always used to say that there weren't many parents as lovely as yours, Bethany. My mother and yours wrote to each other for years, didn't they?'

Sylvia was now looking a little bewildered. She was ready to believe the story, but the vision of a 'lovely' Mrs Jones exchanging letters with a seaside landlady from 'Bide a Wee' cottage for many years was obviously involving a stretch of imagination. Bethany continued hurriedly with a distracted eye on Sylvia, 'Well, I don't know about letters, but your mum sent Christmas cards to us. I used to put them up on the mantelpiece every December, and we all remembered the holiday for a long time.' Relieved to have finished the trickiest part of the explanation, Bethany turned to Roy, who was listening quietly to the exchange with every impression of relaxed interest. 'Oliver is down here on business.' Before Roy could ask what business he was in, Oliver looked at his watch.

'Gosh, that reminds me, I've got an appointment in ten minutes. It was very nice to meet you, but I'm afraid I really must dash. I'm here for a few more days, so perhaps we might meet up again while you're here?' This was to Roy and Sylvia. Oliver had held out his hand to Bethany and pulled her up beside him as he stood up, and it was obvious he intended that she go with him.

For a moment Bethany hesitated. Then she said, 'Sylvia, Oliver doesn't have to meet his friend for very long, and we thought we might go for a meal afterwards and talk about old times. Is that all right with you?'

Sylvia smiled brilliantly at Bethany. 'Course it is, what are you askin' me for? We're only going to the Bingo tonight so you won't miss much. 'Ave a brilliant time, and you can tell me all about it later.' As Roy shook hands politely with Oliver, Sylvia hugged her friend. She put her mouth close to Bethany's ear and squeaked under her breath, 'I don' blame you 'e's really gorgeous but I can' believe it's happened so quickly. Mind you tell me everything tonight.' She hesitated, and then, suddenly serious, she took hold of Bethany's hands in hers and said, 'I am really happy for you, you look lit up, an' I know this is somethin' . . . special . . . but you will take care, won' you? Don't get in over your 'ead?' The pair stood looking at each other, and Bethany marvelled at her friend. How could she see that this was 'something special'? To watch her listening to Oliver, it would appear that there wasn't a thought in her head except the little dog called Muffin with three legs, and yet her light-hearted airy manner concealed a much deeper perceptive nature. She understood better than Roy that Bethany's meeting with Oliver was not all that it seemed. Impulsively, Bethany hugged her friend again in a rush of warm affection. Pulling away and laughing, Sylvia hopped back to Roy's willing arm for balance. 'We'll see you later then, 'ave a lovely evening,' she called, and the pair began to make their way across the grass towards the bed and breakfast. Bethany and Oliver stood in silence and watched them go.

Only when Sylvia and Roy had rounded the corner and were out of sight did they turn towards each other with the now familiar feelings of delight and happiness. Oliver pushed his hair back from his forehead and sighed with relief. 'Phew, *that* wasn't something I'd like to do again. Your friends were very nice, though I'm not sure Roy was the sort of chap to be entirely convinced by Muffin and "The Nook".' After a short pause he added, 'and perhaps Sylvia knew more than she was letting on as well; she seemed a good friend.'

'Yes, she is, and no, he isn't the sort of chap to be fooled, and it wasn't "The Nook", remember? You said it was "Bide a Wee",' replied Bethany, giggling. 'You see, we've forgotten our stories already. How are we going to carry on with this?'

Oliver looked at his watch again. 'Well, I know that I didn't like fabricating that tale for your friends. It's just that this is so . . . odd, and so new. I suggest we go and sit down somewhere and have something to eat, and we can talk properly. How does that sound to you?' Bethany nodded happily and they began to retrace their steps back the way they had come, moving away from the wide open spaces of the Old Steine and the seafront, towards the more intimate network of streets that housed the restaurants and meeting places of the Lanes. The clear blue light of the day was gradually giving way to the muted softness of the evening and, although the air was still warm, a small breeze was blowing off the ocean behind them. They walked towards the lights and warmth of the eating places.

After a short distance they stopped outside a restaurant. It was still early in the evening so the streets were not yet busy, but the owners of this particular Italian eating house had dimmed their lighting and lit the candles on the tables in the hope of attracting early diners. The effect was cheerful and welcoming and so, with a brief glance at each other, Bethany and Oliver stepped over the threshold and stood looking at the sea of empty tables. 'Where would you like to sit?' asked Oliver.

Bethany looked around indecisively. 'Oh, I don't mind really, just somewhere . . . well, what about by the window?' Since they had no coats, they settled themselves at the table and Oliver looked with interest around the room.

'What a nice little place. I wonder if I can catch the eye of that chap over there who looks like he'd rather we weren't here?' Bethany followed his gaze, and the waiter, who was obviously not overly delighted at the early start to his evening, picked up the menus and walked to their table.

'Would you like a drink before we order, Bethany?'

Again, Bethany hesitated. She had never been out for an evening meal in a proper restaurant before, and although this place wasn't grand, she didn't know whether there were rules she ought to follow. She looked doubtfully at Oliver, who was waiting for her answer. Conscious of her hesitation, he spoke instead. 'Oh, well, I'm pretty thirsty, aren't you? I think I'd like a jug of iced water, and maybe some wine? Would you like red or white, or perhaps a soft drink?'

Bethany thought that the iced water sounded lovely, but also thought she'd like to try a glass of wine.

'Could I have the water, please, and wine sounds great. I haven't drunk much wine, but I do like red, thank you.'

Oliver smiled at the waiter. 'That's settled then. Could you bring us some water and a bottle of house red? Thanks very much.' Bethany noticed that the waiter, who had been somewhat half-heartedly going through the motions of service until then, responded rapidly to Oliver's smile and drew himself up to his full height. He was a small man, but very dapper, with slicked-back dark hair and a little pencil moustache like Charlie Chaplin's. He threw a little white cloth over his forearm with a flourish (Bethany had seen waiters on television do this but had no idea why), and he walked briskly off to fetch the drinks.

They lapsed into silence as they looked at the menu. Bethany's eyes glazed over as she once again wondered if there were conventions she should follow, and what on earth she should choose from the bewildering array of food listed in front of her. She gave up, and instead lifted her eyes and looked around her. Inevitably, her gaze was drawn back to Oliver. His head was bent and he was studying the menu.

112

Taking advantage of his absorption, Bethany allowed herself a few minutes of thought. Beyond the initial first impressions when they had first met, she had been distracted by the familiar feelings of pleasure that filled her when she saw him. Now, for the first time she was able to look at him without his being aware of it. She saw that he looked totally at ease in his surroundings, surveying all around him with interest and openness. Her perception sharpened by happiness, she sensed that no matter where he was, it would always be this way with Oliver. She remembered the way he had chatted to her friends, approaching them with open friendliness, with no trace of guardedness. A sort of joy washed through her, and she began to smile again.

Bethany's musings were abruptly ended and she jumped guiltily as Oliver looked up and met her eyes. 'Hey, that's not fair. I haven't had a chance to look at you, I was too busy deciding what I want to eat. Shall we call the waiter over? Have you decided already?'

Bethany coloured. 'No, not really, to be honest I haven't been looking. I'll just have a salad or something.' She thought to herself, secretly, that she didn't really care about the food, she'd just like to begin talking to Oliver. After the initial euphoria of their meeting, and the afternoon of silent communication, it seemed as though they had had one interruption after another, and she was becoming increasingly impatient to know more about him, and to understand what had happened to them both at their meeting.

Oliver returned to the menu in his hand. 'OK, that's fine. How about a plain bowl of pasta with a salad to start with, and then pudding if we want it? Frankly, it all looks good, and I'm beginning to want it here already. It seems as though we are wasting time with all this. The longer it goes on, the more I want to actually talk to you.' Bethany noticed that their thoughts were running along parallel lines again. She thought that it had happened before during the course of the afternoon, although she couldn't remember exactly when. She was about to comment on this but Oliver was talking to the waiter, who had been hovering at a discreet distance but now appeared magically at their side. 'Hello again. Yes, we'd both like a green salad to start with, and some of this, and plenty of time between courses, if that isn't inconvenient to you. My friend and I have just met again after a long time apart and we want to catch up with each other uninterrupted. Would that suit you, do you think? Oh, and if it's not a bother, we're quite happy to wait for our drinks until you bring the food.' All he said was with the ease and friendliness that Bethany had already noticed. She thought that Oliver was the sort of person that people liked to do things for. She watched as the waiter responded to Oliver's manner and readily assured the gentleman that he quite understood, and that interruptions would be kept to a minimum so that he could enjoy the company of his 'beautiful lady'. This last comment was accompanied by a wink, and Oliver laughed and thanked him. Eventually the waiter gathered up the menus and passed through some swinging doors at the back of the deserted restaurant, presumably to the kitchen.

Oliver picked up the breadbasket and offered Bethany a roll. They both took one and began to go through the motions of unwrapping the little packets of butter, and breaking the bread carefully. Neither of them said anything. Bethany sensed that, although they had both been waiting for the moment when they could begin to talk, neither of them knew exactly how to begin the conversation. For the first time since they had met, the joy they felt in each other's company was tinged with doubt. She wanted to say so much, yet was suddenly fearful that the connection they thought they had made had been some peculiar mistake, nothing more than one of those instances where you think you know someone in the street and they turn out to be a stranger. And yet, she had felt so certain, so convinced that they knew each other on some deep level, and he had appeared to feel the same. So intent was she on these thoughts that she only now realised that Oliver was speaking.

'I'm so sorry,' she said. 'Can you start again? I was lost in thought. I don't mean to be rude.'

Oliver began again. 'Oh dear, I'm finding this hard. I feel somewhat at a loss for words, and I get the impression that you feel the same.'

Although this was a statement, there was a question in his eyes, and she nodded as he continued. 'The way that I see it, is that something extraordinarily amazing has happened but, as yet, we only have our feelings to go on. I'm afraid that it will turn out to be more fragile than I want it to be, that this . . . connection . . . I feel will turn out to be an illusion and we'll go charging in with the banality of words and somehow bash it to pieces . . . ' The misgivings and hesitation on his face so exactly mirrored the apprehension she had been feeling that she drew in her breath sharply. Oliver, misreading her surprise, broke off in dismay. 'Oh, lord, I knew I'd put my foot in it, it's probably all my imagination, and please believe me I don't make a habit of picking up girls and

114

taking them out.' He tailed off again and Bethany began to speak, her words falling over each other in her haste to put him right.

'Oh, *no*, it's not like that at *all*, I was only surprised because you keep putting my thoughts into words so exactly, it's as if we have the same mind. Look, let's not worry about offending each other. It's absolutely clear to me that, for whatever reason, we are feeling the same way and communicating on a level that people don't usually connect on. We've now got to figure out why, and how we are going to go on. It is strange, but I'm sure we'll get used to it. We haven't got the usual rules to go by, that's all, and so we'll have to make up our own.'

Looking across at Oliver, she saw relief written clearly on his face, and this gave her the confidence to continue. 'It's just a case of where to begin, really. Can I ask you a question?'

'Of course, if I can ask you one back. I know, how about this . . . let's take turns and ask questions and answer them until there's nothing more to say.' For a minute they paused, smiling and looking directly into each other's eyes. There was a minute of silence, during which they both began to work out the best way to phrase the first questions. Bethany was thinking about the days and hours before she had met Oliver, of the increasing sense of expectancy she had felt. It seemed to her that the moments of stillness, the spaces outside time, had led directly to Oliver. She had known that the normal rules were not going to apply during this week, that it was to be a 'time out of time'. She wanted to know if he had felt the same way before they had met. As she opened her mouth to speak, he asked his first question.

'OK. I need to know this first. Before we met did you . . . What is it, what's so funny?'

Bethany put her hand up to her mouth and said, 'Oh, nothing, I mean, not really, it's just that . . . '

Oliver looked at her with slowly dawning realisation. 'I see. I suppose you were going to ask what I was going to ask. As I got nearer to this week, I started to feel a bit like you do when you are a kid and it's the day before Christmas Eve, and it starts to snow. Like something wonderful is about to happen, and that no matter what you do it will happen anyway. Did you get that feeling?' Bethany nodded silently, and he went on, 'There was something else.' He hesitated. 'I wanted to ask if you knew that you were going to meet me. I mean, not just that something was going to happen, but that *I* was going to happen.'

Bethany shook her head. 'No, I don't think so. What I remember is the feeling that something was going to mark my life in some way, and affect my future. And I had these lovely feelings of happiness and excitement. But I didn't know it would be you.'

Oliver nodded and thought for a minute. 'I think it's probably your turn, but I'm going anyway. I don't think I'd be able to ask this usually, it sounds so odd. Did you . . . I mean, oh hang it all, did you hear any voices?'

Bethany looked at him, astonished. 'No, did you?'

Oliver pushed back his hair from his forehead and was about to answer when the calm was broken by a loud crash of the swing doors at the back of the restaurant, and their waiter reappeared.

For the next few minutes all was hustle and bustle. He began by carrying in large blue bowls heaped high with pasta. He set them down on the table and there was rather a lot of manoeuvring as they moved the candle and the salt and pepper aside so that he could put down the salad plates. Next, he disappeared through the swing doors with the usual crash, and returned with a big jug of water and two glasses, followed by a bottle of wine and two more glasses. After Oliver's assurances that he wouldn't need to taste the wine and that it all looked great, he went away. Finally, just as they thought that everything was peaceful again, the waiter bustled up with an enormous pepper mill and began to grind pepper onto their food. After all this had been accomplished, the waiter made a little bow in acknowledgement of their thanks, and withdrew again into the kitchen. A few seconds later, the swing doors clacked open again as he reappeared and bent down behind the bar in the corner. The strains of Vivaldi's *Four Seasons* blared out into the restaurant at maximum volume so that they all jumped. Hastily, he ducked back down behind the bar, and the music receded pleasantly.

They looked helplessly at their food. At another time, Bethany would have relished such a meal. Her salad, in particular, was beautifully presented, with pale crisp lettuce nestling under moist heaps of bright, grated carrot, hard-boiled eggs arranged in slices between cucumber and tomato, and drapes of anchovy and spears of tinned asparagus. But now she almost wished that they had chosen to talk sitting under a tree in the park, or walking by the sea. Their meal looked lovely but meant yet another interruption in their dialogue. Oliver had picked up his knife and fork, smiling at her dismay. 'Come on, we can still manage to talk and eat, you know. What was I saying?'

'You were about to tell me if you heard voices. I'm sure *I* didn't.' A doubt fleetingly crossed her mind and was gone before she could pinpoint what it was. Oliver was speaking again, hastily swallowing

116

his mouthful. 'Oh yes, I can't . . . ' He stopped and said, 'This'll only work if you have a go at eating as well, you know.' Obediently Bethany picked up her fork and speared some salad into her mouth, as Oliver went on. 'Yes, I can't exactly be certain, but before we met, I had the strangest feeling of life – I mean life as I usually go through it – being sort of suspended for a while, and hearing someone speaking. Once, when I drew into a garage to fill up with petrol, I switched off the radio, and there was such . . . stillness. Do you know? And in the stillness there was something, someone maybe, speaking. After we met, I kind of thought that it might have been you, and that we had some kind of telepathy.'

Bethany looked at him, thinking hard, and in the pause Oliver doggedly and rapidly managed to swallow several more mouthfuls of his food. 'No, I'm sure it wasn't me, or not that I'm aware of. What was it that you heard exactly?' she asked. She picked up her knife and fork again as Oliver nodded firmly in the direction of her plate. He opened his mouth to speak and then closed it again. She wasn't sure but she thought she saw a faint colour rising on his cheeks, and her heart gave a leap of tenderness. She let her fork with its piled contents hang in the air and said, 'Look, I think we've gone beyond the normal kinds of conversation. Don't be embarrassed if that's what you are feeling, it's just as peculiar for me, but wonderful too, and we do want to take it further, I mean, find out more, don't we?'

He reached across and squeezed her arm affectionately. Her forkful of food dropped back onto the plate. 'Oh, sorry,' he said. 'Yes, you are absolutely right, it's partly that I'm not sure if I really did hear someone or just convinced myself that I did, and I've got a kind of *feeling* for the words rather than a memory of hearing them. Well, I suppose what I heard, or think I heard, was someone saying "It's almost time for us to meet. It will happen soon."' He frowned. 'At least, it was something like that, I think. And you definitely weren't sort of projecting that then?'

'No, I know it wasn't me. All I had was a definite feeling that something was going to happen. But I did have those moments of stillness just like you described. I've never experienced anything like it before. The stillness led directly to this. And . . . ' It was now her turn to hesitate. Oliver said nothing, but waited patiently, until she went on. 'For a while I've been thinking that the time I have here, I mean on holiday here, is meant to be a sort of continuation of those moments. I don't know if it makes sense at all, but that this week should be a sort of "time out of time". The normal rules just don't seem to apply, and I wonder if this time could be lived in a different way from the way I usually live. Does that make any sense to you?' She finished off, and bent her head over her plate, putting a fork piled high with pasta into her mouth.

When she looked up again she saw that Oliver's blue eyes were blazing with enthusiasm. Again, her heart gave a little somersault of happiness, and she gave him her full attention.

'Yes, you are making absolute sense, ludicrous as it may sound. I had exactly the same feeling. In fact, I'd made a sort of resolution for myself that I was going to give myself up to whatever might come in this week. I've got a week here too, by the way. Did you arrive yesterday as well?' He barely registered her answering nod as he continued, swept along by the flow of his thoughts. 'OK, well, we are agreed. Before we talk about how this is going to work out, this "time out of time" idea, I think I ought to say something. I know that we've only just met, and that we hardly know each other, but I'm more certain than I've ever been of anything that this was meant to happen. And I'm pretty sure that we are going to spend a lot longer than just this week together. If anyone had told me this could happen I'd have said it was preposterous, but I reckoned without this certainty that I feel. It's not just from my heart, it's from all of me. And that's the truth.' He stopped suddenly and stared at her.

It was now Bethany's turn to be speechless, but her eyes were eloquent with happiness and assent. She put her hand out over the table and rested it on the cloth. Oliver enclosed it in his, and they were content just to sit for a while in silence. Bethany felt his hand on hers and the warmth of the contact seemed to spread up her arm and flood into her chest. It was though joy itself was filling her body. After a few moments, Oliver released her hand and sighed, looking at the food still on their plates. 'We haven't made much of an inroad on this, have we? And it all looked so good too, but I don't have much of an appetite for some reason.' This was accompanied by such a rueful look that Bethany laughed.

'Nor do I, but we haven't done too badly considering the circumstances. I'm going to eat my salad anyway. It's really good.'

Oliver brightened. 'That's true, and we can finish the wine. But I want to think about what we mean about "Time out of time". It seems important that we carry this through, especially as it appears that we both got such a strong sense of it being important. Why don't we mull it over and see if we can come up with some ideas about what exactly it's going to mean and how we are going to do it? We are going to spend the whole of this week together, aren't we?'

Bethany hesitated only for the briefest of seconds before answering. 'Well yes, if you can manage it. I'm on holiday so I don't have any plans as such, but what about you? Are you working, or on holiday too?'

Oliver was silent for a minute. 'No, I've nothing that can't be rearranged either. So it's settled then? We are really going to do this? I mean, if you have any second thoughts we can always back off a bit. We should give ourselves permission to in the unlikely event that we have misread this whole thing.'

'All right, but I don't think I'm going to have second thoughts. I feel so certain that this is the right thing to do. Otherwise it would be such a joke really. If you knew me at all you'd see how funny this is. I'm not at all the kind of person that this happens to. I'm so ordinary, really. I can't believe that we are here together and talking about living life in a completely different way for a week. It makes me want to laugh.' For a moment, the incredible happiness she felt threatened to swamp her completely and she laughed out loud from the sheer joy of it all.

Oliver looked at her seriously. 'I don't think you're ordinary at all. In fact, you are totally out of the ordinary. It's me, you know. I'm so level-headed and sensible, nothing happens to me that I don't half expect. But this!' He grinned with delight. 'I present to you, the amazing, the extraordinary, the out of this world Oliver and Bethany!' He raised his glass to her and they clinked glasses and drank. 'All right, we were going to think about how this week is going to work. We can make up our own rules totally, you know. It's only us and we are completely in charge of our destiny for at least the next six days, so we can decide.'

This last was said half jokingly, but to Bethany it struck a chord. She felt instinctively that she had met her destiny in some way, and that making a decision to live differently, if only for a week, was the right thing to do. But Oliver was right. They had to decide what they meant by living 'time out of time' and how they were to do it. It was no good having some woolly and vague idea that they were not able to make practical. She realised that Oliver was perhaps as organised and practical as she was. He had said he was level-headed, and she supposed she would have described herself in such a way as well. She liked his willingness to transform their intuitive ideas into reality, and the way he was getting down to the practical details. She looked at him with new respect and affection and he smiled.

'Come on, are you thinking? I am, but I'm not quite ready to put my ideas on the table. How about if I get the bill and we go for a walk and talk? We could always pop in somewhere if we want a coffee or something more to eat later. Let's go and get some air.'

Bethany readily agreed, and they looked around the restaurant in surprise. They had no idea how long they had been talking, but what had been an empty room had now become a bustling and lively eating place filled with people talking and laughing. Their waiter had now been joined by two more, and they were having a hard time keeping up with all the orders. There were even people standing outside, peering at the menu in the window, and looking to see if anyone was going to leave. Oliver looked down at his watch.

'Good Lord! We must have been here ages. I'm going to give our chap a big tip. I hope we haven't taken up valuable table time. How nice of him not to disturb us.' He stood and began putting the plates together in a pile. Bethany helped him, and the waiter, seeing their efforts, bustled over to stop them. Oliver began to apologise for taking so long and thanked him for his kindness, but the little man brushed away his thanks.

'No, no, is no problem. You come again with your beautiful lady. Now go, go, out into the world together. But you pay me first!'

Bethany wanted to pay half of the bill, but Oliver said, 'No, look, it's fine. Don't let's go into all that now. You can buy next time, I'll do it now and then we can go for a walk.'

Bethany decided she would use the ladies before they left, and followed the sign down a little flight of steps. The passage was lined with wood and painted dark green. There were little pink lights on each side, and two doors with silhouettes of a man in a top hat and a lady dressed in a crinoline dress. Bethany went into the latter. After she had used the cubicle, she washed her hands and looked at herself in the mirror. Her eyes were shining and she remembered the phrase Sylvia had used earlier. It was true, she thought. Something was lighting her up from the inside. She was illuminated by the possibility that she was embarking on a great adventure, a week that was going to alter the course of her life forever. And she was going to begin it in a completely new way, in partnership with a young man she had just met. Suddenly, her sight blurred and she felt as though she no longer stood still. She was moving through memories long forgotten and places far away, seeing not through her eyes, but through others, fumbling for an elusive truth like a sleeper awaking from a dream. Sometimes it was imprinted fresh and green in her mind, and then she was groping once more as though in a mist. After a long time her eyes became focused again and she stared at the young woman reflected back at her. She felt that she was returning from a long way away or maybe a long time ago, and she had a vague impression that she should have remembered something important. But one thing she *was* sure of. Her partnership with Oliver was not new, and they had not only just met. They had been together before.

Oliver was waiting for her in the restaurant. Together they said goodbye to the waiter with thanks, and Oliver held the door for her as they stepped out into the street. By now it was evening and the air resonated with music and the smells of cooking that Bethany had breathed in so enthusiastically the night before. The streets were filled with those in search of food, drink and entertainment. Snatches of conversation and bursts of laughter filled the air and Bethany and Oliver were jostled gently by people pushing their way past. No one paid much attention to the young man and woman standing irresolutely on the pavement. Bethany and Oliver found themselves hesitating once more. Again, their train of thought had been interrupted and the momentum that had been sweeping them onward was temporarily halted by the need to make a decision as to where to go next. Both longed for a place where they could talk uninterrupted until there was no more talking to be done.

Bethany sniffed the air appreciatively. 'Mmm, it smells so lovely, doesn't it?' Mingled with all the delicious and appetising aromas there drifted a strain of the tantalising scent that meant freedom, just as the sound of the wheeling gulls conjured in her a feeling of wild happiness. She supposed she had been breathing in the smell of the sea all day long, but in the early evening air it now held a promise of adventure, of heart-stirring excitement. Impulsively taking Oliver's hand, she said, 'Let's go down to the sea.' Readily agreeing, he gave her hand a squeeze and they walked towards the hustle and bustle of the seafront. When they reached the promenade they crossed the busy traffic-laden road and turned away from the brightly coloured lights of the Palace pier, walking instead past the old West Pier towards the quieter end of town. Finally they turned down onto the beach and clambered over the pebbles down towards the sea. In the shelter of an old concrete groin they found a space on the stones, and turned to watch the waves splashing gently onto the shore in front of them.

Light from the town and the distant pier was reflected only in the nearest edge of the water. Beyond this thin strip of fragmented bouncing lights, the blackness of the ocean seemed to stretch endlessly into the night. The waves slapped gently onto the rattling stones, which rolled backwards and forwards on the shore, their movements providing a deep rhythmical base to the light plashing and murmuring of the water. The air was cool and a breeze blew directly off the inky water in front of them. Bethany leaned her head on Oliver's shoulder. He shifted his weight slightly to balance himself, then put his arm around her. Each pursued their own thoughts, listening to the hypnotically peaceful rhythm of the sea.

Finally, Oliver gave a contented sigh, and they drew apart. He lay back on the shingle and looked up into the night sky. 'Have you ever wondered how it is that the sky seems to have its own light? I can't see a moon or stars tonight, but the clouds show really clearly.'

Bethany also lay down and clasped her hands behind her head. 'It's true, I've never really thought about it before. I always thought that the sky was just dark and the lights came from the stars, but it's not like that when I look at it.' They watched the little wispy clouds for a few moments. After a while, though Bethany knew herself to be lying on the beach, at the same time she felt drawn upwards towards the sky. She enjoyed the sensation and kept her gaze fixed on the clouds as Oliver spoke. She could hear his voice close by her shoulder, and knew he was looking up just as she was.

'All right. Let's start. I'm going to sum up what has happened so far, and you chip in when you want to. That all right?' He paused and then said, 'I'll take that "mmm" as a "yes", shall I?'

Bethany smiled in the darkness, and could hear the amusement in his voice as he continued. 'We know that we feel very much the same about the fact that we have met, and that we were meant to meet. We both have a strong intuitive notion that we want to preserve the moments of silence or peace that led us to each other, and we have both experienced this idea that our week here should be lived in a special, different way.' Bethany continued to gaze at the sky, listening intently to what Oliver was saying. 'You talked about "time out of time" and I think that's exactly how I would have put it if I'd thought of it. So, what do we actually *mean* by "time out of time"?' He continued without a pause. 'Bethany, what I think is that we can make our own rules. We have already connected at a very deep level, it seems to me, without any of the normal information that one usually gathers about someone when one gets to know them. We both feel that this week is only the beginning of our being together. So there'll be time to find out all the mundane bits and pieces later on. Do you see what I'm getting at?'

Again he didn't wait for her to reply before continuing. 'Anyway, so the idea I have is that we carry on just as we are. We talk about the important things, the things that matter to both of us, because I'm willing to bet that we feel the same about those. But what we don't do is get all tangled up in facts about ourselves. I don't need to know that your uncle's name is Ernest and he kept a pet hamster called Hiawatha, just as you don't need to know that I was born in Basildon and moved to Berkhampstead when I was seven and three-quarters. That's what we mean about "time out of time". We live this week the way we began, and then at the end of it we can sit down together, find out all the normal stuff, and make plans. Until then, we don't. Find out the normal stuff, I mean, or think about the future.'

Bethany was about to speak when she realised he was talking again. 'Let's make a pact to live only in the present, just for this week. We can live for the moment, and only the present need matter. Of course it wouldn't work forever, but since we know that we plan to have much more than this week together, we could do it, couldn't we? What do you think?'

There was a long pause, and he turned onto his stomach to look at her anxiously. Bethany smiled at him.

'No, really, what do you think?' he asked again. Eventually she opened her mouth to speak and he waited, his mouth slightly open and his blue eyes fixed on hers.

'Well, what I think . . . What I think . . . is that you are very clever and I agree with everything you've said. Totally. Absolutely.' Before he could hug her with relief, she said, 'But there's just one more thing.'

He nodded seriously as she went on. 'With all this defining you've been doing, I think there's one more thing you need to define. Can you just explain what you mean by "chip in when you want to" because I don't think I quite understand the concept. I sort of thought there had to be just a tiny break in the conversation to do that, but I'm probably wrong . . . '

For a moment he opened his mouth and shut it again before he saw the teasing in her eyes. He threw his head back and laughed. 'All right, I know, I do tend to go on. My mother always says . . . ' He checked himself. 'Oops! You don't really need to know that, do you? My mother will come as a lovely surprise in due course. Come on, d'you fancy a coffee somewhere? I'm getting a bit chilly.' She was glad she didn't have to talk about her mother to him, and grasped his outstretched hand as she scrambled to her feet. They went in search of coffee.

And that was how the week began. Supremely confident that they had all the time in the world, and that they were destined to be together, they began the period of 'time out of time' that Bethany would remember all her life. Hand in hand, they embarked on their wonderful adventure, the sun-filled stretch of happiness that illuminated their time of love. They spent every minute they could together. They cherished the pact they had made and were careful only to live in the present. They met every day just after sunrise at the gates to the Meeting House, and when the time came to part each evening, they left each other by the sea. They talked about poetry, about love and death, and pain and happiness, about joy and relationships and about life. Of course, occasionally some detail would slip out and each would mention a person or an event that the other had not heard of, but they carefully avoided pursuing these. And so their partnership deepened, and the joy they felt in each other's company was unparalleled since time began. Or so they believed, in the manner of young lovers everywhere. Some days they explored Brighton, wandering through the streets and by the sea. Another time they hired bicycles and followed the cycle path along the sea and up onto the cliffs. Oliver had a car, and they ventured further afield, the sun shining down on them as they drove through the countryside, stopping to browse in sleepy villages, or wandering happily alongside fast flowing rivers, through leafy woods chiming with birdsong or softly waving fields of grass and poppies.

The days were endless, and often they talked late into the evening in lamplit eating places, or sitting under the stars by the sea. The love they felt for each other was unbounded, and they lived outside time.

One day they met at the Meeting House and the sky was blue, and the seagulls were tossed wheeling above them in a strong, warm sea wind that took hold of them and blew them towards the beach. Bethany and Oliver were buffeted along the stones and their laughter was carried away by the wind to the gulls above. Battling with the gale and the sound of the sea in their ears, they went up onto the Downs and walked until they came to ancient beech woods and they went in. The wind still blew above them and the bright, clean, new green leaves of the trees formed a roof above their heads, and they were alone in the warm early morning. Their heads were filled with the sound of the wind and they no longer knew if it was in the green branches above them or if the sea itself had entered their ears and eyes and hearts. They lay together on the soft grassy forest floor and the trees appeared to draw closer around them. They were protected from everything save each other, enclosed and sheltered by the present. It was then that they no longer knew where one began and the other ended, and they were together, surely, forever and a day. Bethany and Oliver stayed in the wood together as the sun moved across the sky, lost in a dreaming love that knew only possibility, unchained by the future or the past.

Later, Bethany would always remember, as they lay on the cliffs overlooking the sparkling sea, how Oliver gazed out over the bright water and softly quoted:

> As fair art thou my bonnie lass
> So deep in love am I;
> And I will love thee still, my dear,
> Till all the seas gang dry.

> Till all the seas gang dry, my dear,
> And the rocks melt with the sun;
> I will love thee still, my dear,
> While the sands of life shall run.

Many years later Bethany came across Burns's bittersweet poem in an anthology in the library. She read the final verse, the one Oliver had left out, and the tears had coursed down her face.

*   *   *

Someone was breathing softly in the darkness. Slowly, she became aware of the breathing, shallow and regular, and she listened. Gradually, she realised that it was her own breathing she was listening to, and knew that she was still sitting in the green velvety chair, her hands resting in her lap, trying to remember the past with love. She had no idea how many hours had passed since Norman had left her standing by the window, but guessed that she had been sitting for a long time. For a while she stayed motionless, listening to the regular ebb and flow of her breath. Her breathing was the bridge between the world that had been and the room that she must shortly re-enter. Slowly she came back from the past, out of the silence and into the present. Opening her eyes, it seemed for a brief moment that the memories that had been so real were shimmering before her like the lambent translucent surface of a bubble. For a few short seconds Oliver was there in the room with her and she could almost see the soft radiance of love around him. Then suddenly it was gone, and all that was left was the pale morning light filtering greenly through the lace curtains and imitation velvet drapes around the bay window. Bethany took a deep breath and let it out slowly. Then she moved her hands and feet experimentally, finding that they hadn't gone to sleep as she half expected, but moved easily. She stretched slowly and stood up.

To Bethany's intense surprise hardly any time had passed. It was barely an hour since Norman had backed out of the drive, although she had been convinced that most of the day must have slipped away. She went into the kitchen, put the kettle on, and then turned on her little radio. This had become habitual with her since the angel had asked her to 'switch it on and move' nearly five months ago. Music seemed to help her with her third lesson, the one the angel called Healing. Sometimes she listened to the classical stations, and sometimes the more popular ones, carrying the small transistor with her around the house as she went through the routine of her day. She twiddled the dial until she found Radio Three just in time to hear the presenter announce that they would be playing Brahms's 'Violin Concerto'. She made herself some coffee, paused briefly to look out of the window at her beloved garden, then set down her mug on the kitchen table. Leaning her arms onto its Formica surface, she began to order the thoughts that were running through her mind.

She now knew the angel too well to believe that the task of remembering was over. She still had the hardest part to come, but at the same time she understood that there must be a reason why that particular time had shimmered so vividly for her that morning. If she only had to embrace the pain, then why remember all the joy she and Oliver had felt? She remembered the fourth lesson, that of Gratitude. She opened her little book, and found the first three lessons, of Mindfulness, Action and Healing. Under this she added the latest lesson. She wrote:

Lesson 4. Gratitude.

After neatly underlining this she wrote, 'Give thanks constantly for abundant beauty. Open yourself up to the joy of being alive. Accept and love all that comes to you and you will find more and more to love and accept.' Satisfied, she pushed her chair away from the table and stretched her arms above her head.

'So I have the four lessons, what happens now?' There was silence, and Bethany sighed. 'I know I haven't finished remembering, and I really am grateful for what happened early on, but how can I be grateful for all of it? It just seems so hard.'

NEVERTHELESS, IF YOU WANT TO BE FREE IN THE PRESENT
YOU MUST LOVINGLY FORGIVE.

OPEN YOURSELF UP TO BOTH PAIN AND JOY WITH GRATITUDE, AND EMBRACE PURPOSEFUL ACTION.

'All right, I'll try. But not today. There's plenty of time, isn't there, and Norman isn't back until Thursday evening.' All of a sudden Bethany was conscious of a hesitation. 'There *is* time, isn't there? I mean, you aren't going to go away?' The prospect filled her with sudden dread.

WHEN YOU HAVE LEARNED ALL OF THE LESSONS AND ARE FREE AND JOYFUL THEN YOU WILL HAVE NO NEED OF ME.

'But of course I'll need you. Please don't tell me that you're going away! Why did you come in the first place if it was just to leave me alone again? I don't think I can bear being alone again, even if I learn a hundred lessons ... please explain to me, I don't understand.' Bethany found that her eyes were full of tears and that her throat ached. She swallowed painfully. There was a silence and then

I DID NOT SAY THAT I WOULD GO AWAY, MERELY THAT YOU WOULD HAVE NO NEED OF ME. WHEN YOU ARE READY, THEN IT WILL BE TIME FOR US TO MEET.

Bethany was stunned. She sat mesmerised, not able to grasp what she had heard. It had never once occurred to her that she would meet her angel. How would that happen? People only met angels if they went to heaven. What could it mean? Could she be going to die? She was beset with doubts and her mind was racing. One frantic question after another came into her fumbling mind, but she received no answer. Bewildered by the silence and by what she had heard, she put her head down on the table in confusion and doubt. Her breath came in short gasps and there was a pain somewhere in her stomach. She realised that she was feeling faint and unwell, and gave herself up to the sensation. Sweat pricked her forehead and she closed her eyes and rested her cheek on the cool table.

After a few moments she grew calmer, and opened her eyes. The first thing she saw was her little book. She pulled herself together, scolding herself for her panic. Everybody felt ill sometimes and there might well be another explanation for what the angel had just said. There was no sense in going into a flat spin and imagining things that weren't there. All the same there was a lot to think about. She had plenty to be going on with just with these lessons, didn't she? What did the third lesson say? 'The present moment is the only thing of importance.' Well, she certainly had plenty to be thinking about. If she was going to die, then there would be time enough to think about that when she felt a good deal worse than she did today. In the meantime the fourth lesson beckoned, and there was no question that she had a lot to feel grateful for. She was going to be alone for almost a whole week. She could eat what she liked, when she liked, could go out when she wanted to without having to explain herself to anyone, and she could think as much as she wanted. She stood up and gave herself a little shake. The sun was shining, her energy was returning, and she was going to go for a walk. She put the little book in her pocket and went out into the hall. Opening the front door, she was greeted by a burst of warm air and sunshine. It was a beautiful summer's day and she, Bethany Taylor, was free to do exactly what she wanted with it. Life was good. She gave a little skip and set off down the road. She was going to buy herself a huge ice cream.

AUGUST

The days passed and Bethany quickly adapted herself to her new routine. With Norman away she could play her music at all times of the day. She also found the evenings to be a whole new rich source of time that she could fill with activities that gave her pleasure. Bethany sat quietly twice a day now, holding the four lessons in her mind, feeling herself growing stronger and more sure of herself. She prepared herself to encounter what she knew would be difficult, and even found that she was anticipating the pain of memories with less dread than before. She spent long hours in the garden, which was in its full riot of summer colour, and even sat out and ate her evening meal there, feeling the warmth of the day fade and the scents grow stronger in the evening dusk. She loved listening to the birds in the morning and slept with the curtains drawn back and the window open. She rose with the light and enjoyed her shower in the morning. When Norman was home he showered before work, and she sometimes had her bath in the evening while he watched the news. She relished the change.

On Wednesday evening, just after six o'clock, the phone rang. Bethany went to answer it, wiping her hands on her skirt. She had been washing up in the kitchen and her hands were still wet and foamy. It was Norman. 'Hello, B, how are you, how are things going?' Norman's voice sounded rather falsely hearty and she guessed that he was ringing from a public place. She imagined him standing in a hall with a handful of coins for the phone.

'I'm fine, thanks. Would you like me to ring you back?'

'No, no, the others are waiting for me, we're going for a drink in the bar before dinner. It's been a slog today but we've ironed out a number of new parameters in Group Dynamics.' He sounded self-conscious and slightly smug and she wondered if he wanted her to ask what the parameters in Group Dynamics meant.

She could hear laughter and voices in the background. She remembered he had said he didn't have much time, so she said nothing.

129

'B, are you still there? Oh. Well, the reason I'm ringing is that the Team have decided to stay an extra night. I'm taking Friday as a holiday. We're covering a lot of important ground which should benefit Accounts, so we feel it's justified. So I shall be back either late on Friday or on Saturday morning, depending on how long we decide to continue for.' He had raised his voice during this speech and now lowered it again. 'I feel sure that you will be able to manage all right without me, and the extra time may give you an opportunity to think about things.'

Bethany was so surprised that she again was silent. Never had Norman, voluntarily, spent any time apart from her, and it amazed her that he should have noticed that she appreciated time to think. She was surprised and touched by his noticing.

'B, did you hear me, this must be a very bad line. I said that I'd be back at the weekend. I expect you to manage without me until then. I'll have to go now, the others are waiting. I'll be dropping my colleague off on the way home, so I shall be incommunicado for a while.'

Incommunicado, thought Bethany. Really, these four days were having a deep impact on Norman. He disapproved of jargon normally.

'For goodness sake, B, what is the matter with you? I shall hang up now and I'm very busy with work-related matters, so you needn't try to contact me. Any little crises you may have can wait until I get home. All right? All right then, until then. What? Yes, I'm coming. No, no, it's fine, I'm finished now. Are you still there, B? I've . . . run out of money now. I'll see you at the weekend. Goodbye.'

For a moment Bethany stood in the hall, listening to the dialling tone. Norman had hung up, leaving her at a loss to explain this latest development. In twenty-three years they had never spent any time apart, not counting the time that Norman had had inflamed tonsils and had admitted himself to hospital overnight, at Marjorie's insistence, 'for observation'. Now all of a sudden he was voluntarily extending his absence, and there was that cryptic comment about her needing time to think. What could it mean? Bethany realised that she had no idea what her husband was thinking about and for the first time wondered if he too minded the absence of communication between them. She had become accustomed to being alone, and hadn't stopped to wonder if Norman had been feeling lonely too. It was even possible that he had been as unhappy as she had been, but powerless in his own way to change how it was between them. The thought stopped her in her tracks, and she realised she was still standing motionless in

130

the hall with the receiver in her hand. Carefully, she replaced it, then absently sat down on the bottom stair, her eyes unfocused, lost in thought.

Turning this latest development over in her mind, she remained at a loss to explain it. Could it be that Norman had decided that she needed time to think, and was staying away in order to allow her space to do so? Surely that was unlikely. He had never, in all their time together, acted in a way that indicated that he was thinking about her needs at all, and to inconvenience himself was completely out of character. Unless, and this was a really big unless, it could be that the angel was visiting him as well? Perhaps Norman, too, was getting some kind of guidance which would help them reach out towards each other after all this time. It was an incredible thought, but one that was a possible explanation for his acting so out of character. The only way to find out was to talk to Norman. Bethany was filled with new resolve and hope.

Suddenly filled with a wild energy and happiness, she jumped up from the stairs and went back into the kitchen. As soon as Norman came home, and with the first opportunity she had, she was going to talk to him. She put the kettle on and reached for one of the new fruit teabags she had bought at the start of the week. Her tastes seemed to be changing. She used to drink endless cups of coffee, but for the past few weeks the drink seemed to have entirely lost its appeal. She didn't feel like drinking tea either. For some reason, the smell made her feel slightly faint and nauseated, and she had found herself leaving more and more cups half-drunk. However, boiling the kettle and making herself a hot drink was so much part of her day that she missed the comfort of the familiar ritual. She was getting used to fruit tea and, although she couldn't in truth say that she liked it a great deal, at least it didn't make her feel sick. As she poured the boiled water onto the bag and breathed in the tangy blackcurrant smell, the thought occurred to her that her senses might be telling her something.

Once again she returned to the idea that she might just be ill. Could it be possible that something was seriously wrong? She was cast down by the thought, her happiness ebbing away. There was the angel, the periods of nausea, her exhaustion a few months ago and her strong mood swings. On the other hand she generally felt well and full of energy, particularly in the last few weeks. It was true that her body didn't seem to like the same things as before, but perhaps Norman's absence merely accentuated the fact that she had a choice and didn't have to eat what he wanted to eat. Weighing the pros and cons calmly in her mind, Bethany decided

131

that she couldn't come to a decision of any sort at the moment. It was possible that there was something wrong with her health, but until there was more of a deterioration she wasn't going to rush to any conclusions. Perhaps her increased intuition merely meant that she was more attuned to her body and was noticing things she never had before. She was not going to become a hypochondriac, worried about the slightest thing. Sipping her tea, she resolved to continue listening to her body, and if she noticed any more worrying symptoms she would go to the doctor. Not her doctor, as she still felt rather embarrassed about the scene in the surgery, but perhaps there was a walk-in surgery, or something, at the hospital. Bethany put the thought from her mind, but not before she had resolved once again to eat more healthily. Even though she had stopped gorging on chocolate and doughnuts she was still too fat. Her clothes felt too tight, and she'd read about middle-aged spread. That was probably all that was happening to her. It would probably be a good idea to walk a bit faster on her walks as well. Washing up her cup and putting it on the draining-board, she turned out the light in the kitchen and went upstairs to sit quietly and think about the lessons and about Norman.

The next day was Thursday and she heard from the angel again. She had been sitting in the garden enjoying the warm sun on her face and listening to the drone of a bee meandering drowsily around the flower beds. Once again, she was thinking that life was very good. Since she had been practising the fourth lesson of Gratitude, she had been amazed at all the good things there were in her life. 'Appreciate and bless all that comes to you, and you will find more and more to bless and appreciate.' At first she had presumed that this simple statement was a neat way of telling her to be grateful for what she had. However, she very soon came to realise that, as with the other lessons, the angel was giving her much more than a sermon. It was more of a manual, a practical guide which, if followed, did exactly what it said it would do. The more she blessed all that was in her life, the more things there were to appreciate. In fact, they stacked up so fast in her mind that she could hardly keep up, and her gratitude and happiness knew no bounds. Take this morning in the garden, for instance.

A few months ago she probably would have treated this short sit-down as a reward for the chores she had done that morning, and enjoyed the experience up to a point, but it would have been different. She would have been tired, and her mind would have been filled with little resentments or worries. She would be thinking of all the things she still had to do, how long she could spare to sit down, perhaps feeling guilty that she was sitting down at all, and maybe running through an unsatisfactory conversation that she and Norman had had over breakfast. Her back might be aching, and she would probably be noticing jobs to be done in the garden, wondering how she was going to fit it all in, and feeling sad and inadequate that she never quite managed to do all she had to each day. She would gulp down her coffee, scarcely tasting it, and go back inside, returning to the chores. The whole episode would most likely have left her feeling less refreshed than when she went out.

Today she had finished vacuuming the carpets, and then polished through the house with her radio by her side. She had resolved that, when she finished these two tasks, she would take her hot drink outside and sit in the garden for fifteen minutes before beginning the less than envious chore of cleaning the oven. Things went according to plan and she was a mere five minutes into her break and experiencing the unusual phenomenon of having too many things to be grateful for. She had sat down in her chair, and begun listing them.

First, there was the fact that she had done the vacuuming and the polishing and had earned the right to have a break after a job well done. Next, there was the fact that the chair was so light and easy to carry and to open out. Then there was the garden, looking so lovely. The sun was warm and pleasant, and glowed red behind her eyelids when she leaned back in her chair. There were any number of sounds to appreciate, and they were coming almost too fast to list. There was the bee, whose humming was making her feel delightfully relaxed; the soothing sound of the Prodfoot's garden sprinkler next door; the distant drone of a lawnmower; and the faint rustling of the breeze in the leaves of the trees at the end of the garden. Without opening her eyes, she could smell fresh lawn-cuttings, and somebody making coffee. If she opened her eyes a fraction, she could see all the bright colours of her flowers; a cabbage-white butterfly fluttering erratically through the beds; a distant aeroplane making a puffball trail across the blue sky; and the bright green silver birch leaves. All of her sensations were warmed by the golden sun-drenched morning.

Bethany experienced a sense of great well-being and knew that all this had always been there for the taking. The fourth lesson merely gave her permission to enjoy it, to bless and appreciate it, and in so doing, to open the way for more blessings. In the early days, when she had first tried to put the fourth lesson into practice, Bethany had very quickly become stuck. She seemed to get bogged down in what she ought to be appreciating, and very often sighed with frustration that she was so *un*grateful, when it was precisely the opposite effect she was hoping to achieve. The angel had gently suggested that she let go of her ideas of what she ought to think, and instead begin by noticing what was around her. Bethany had been trying to feel grateful that she had her house, her garden, Norman, that she had been born into a life where she needn't go hungry or unclothed. All of this was very worthy but didn't make her feel particularly happy. When she had stopped trying so hard, and began to notice things around her, the lesson began to unfold. She started with her senses, breathing in smells, and savouring tastes, listening gratefully and seeing with more wonder.

Gradually, Bethany came to understand that the fourth lesson of Gratitude could be understood and practised alongside, and through, that of Mindfulness. By living in the present and focusing on her gratitude and joy, she was becoming more and more aware of what the angel had called the everlasting source of the abundant bounty. Reflecting on the connections between the first lesson and the fourth, Bethany noticed other links. The second lesson, Action, was about thinking as well as doing. Thoughts were really the actions of her mind, she realised. When she held an intention in her mind, her actions were more focused. So being mindful, and having the intention to bless and appreciate, were all linked to the joy she was feeling.

As she continued to contemplate the lessons, further links began flowing into her mind. The third lesson talked of healing and forgiveness, but also said that the past and future were created by her own mind. She could choose her thoughts with intention (the second), and choose to live more in the present (the first again). The lessons appeared to be adding up to become more than they were individually, weaving together to form a coherent whole. She had been correct when she had realised early on that the lessons were not abstract, but meant to be practised. They were like a manual, an instruction booklet, which if followed could be a kind of blueprint for living a joyful life. She glanced down at her watch. It was 10.55 a.m. The oven beckoned, but she had a little more time. She gave a contented sigh and lay back further into her deckchair. Her mind was so peaceful when it was free from all those 'what if' and 'if only' thoughts that usually ran around in it.

YOU ARE STILL AND PEACEFUL.

134

'Yes.' Bethany reflected briefly that, more and more, the angel came to her when she was still. At first it seemed as though it was always jolting her out of her thoughts, or intruding unexpectedly when she was busy. Now it simply occupied the silences. Was that because she was more silent and peaceful these days and less continually caught up in the whirl of her thoughts? 'Yes, I'm really enjoying this beautiful day. I feel so happy.'

Now she was habitually noticing and appreciating, her mind formed grooves of happiness. All of a sudden she found herself remembering how she and Oliver had tried to live in the present all those years ago. They had had the right idea, she thought. Living in the present did bring great joy. It was just such a shame that it had brought her pain in the end. Could she bring herself to be grateful even for this? Bethany stopped short. A few months ago thoughts like these would have been unthinkable. She could not allow herself to remember at all costs, lest the memories destroy her. Now she was even contemplating being grateful for the pain. She laughed out loud. Thanks to the angel she knew that she was stronger than her past. They were only memories, and she had the power to choose how to remember them. 'Thank you,' she said.

YOU DID IT. NOT ME.

'Well, I suppose that's true, but I wouldn't have done it without you. It's as though I am able to change because of the lessons, not through any strength of my own.'

NO. THE LESSONS SHOW YOU THE PATH OF
TRANSFORMATION, BUT YOU ARE DOING THE TRAVELLING.
BOTH TOGETHER CREATE THE JOY.
YOU ARE READY FOR THE FIFTH LESSON.

'Oh.' Even though she had suspected there were more lessons to come, Bethany somehow didn't think that the next would be revealed so quickly. She felt unprepared. Although she was relaxed by the sunshine and knew her breath was already calm and her body still, she didn't feel quite right. She couldn't concentrate properly, lying in her deckchair. Instinctively she wanted to be more upright, her body alert as well as relaxed, in order to give the lesson her closest attention. She went indoors and fetched a hard chair from the kitchen and placed it on the grass in the warm golden light. Then she resumed her sitting position and, after a few moments began to calm herself and be peaceful by breathing smoothly. All this was much more natural to her now that she had formed this ritual for herself. As she had practised her lessons she had observed that her thoughts chased each other through her mind, one following the next with very little connection or sense being made of them. She knew that, in order for her to listen more easily, she had to try to get her mind to make less noise. By concentrating very hard on making her breath smooth, she found her thoughts gradually calmed and she could begin to listen better.

Into the stillness came the voice of the angel.

THE FIFTH LESSON IS THAT OF DISCIPLINE.
WHEN YOU TRAVEL THE INWARD PATH OF
TRANSFORMATION YOU MUST STRENGTHEN YOURSELF.
THROUGH DISCIPLINING YOURSELF YOU WILL BECOME
DETERMINED, COURAGEOUS AND FEARLESS,
AND YOU WILL FIND IT EASIER TO DIRECT YOUR ENERGY.
DO NOT IMAGINE THAT DISCIPLINE MEANS CHASTISEMENT:
RATHER IT IS THE MEANS FOR FOLLOWING THE PATH
TO PEACE.
YOUR MIND WILL NATURALLY RESIST SELF-CONTROL
BUT WITH DISCIPLINE YOU CAN PERFORM ACTS
CONSCIOUSLY AND DELIBERATELY
TO FREE YOU ON YOUR JOURNEY.

Bethany opened her eyes. A ladybird was crawling up a blade of grass just down by her shoe. She kept her eyes fixed on the point as it made its way determinedly to the top. As it reached the end of the blade it stopped, then spread its wings and flew upwards. Bethany carried on looking at the grass, thinking. She felt she was going to need to think for quite a while before she understood this fifth lesson. Unlike the other lessons which appeared fairly straight-forward, she didn't immediately understand its relevance. What could it mean by trying to perform a conscious act deliberately to free yourself? She knew from experience that when she had studied the other lessons in more depth, she had found that they revealed new layers of meaning. Also, she knew that the best way to understand was to practice.

The first thing she needed to do was to write it all down so that she could remember the actual words as precisely as she could. She had been out here long enough. With gratitude in her heart, Bethany looked round the sunny garden and, carrying her chair with one hand and her empty coffee cup in the other, she went in through the back door to the kitchen.

The acidic smell of oven cleaner reached her nostrils and her duties beckoned. However, she thought that the fifth lesson must take priority and she reached for her little notebook. She quickly made another heading.

5. Discipline.

Then she underlined it and paused, looking at the word. She remembered that she had mistrusted the word 'Attention' and had later replaced it with 'Mindfulness'. It had to be said that she had similar reservations about 'Discipline'. No doubt she would change her mind when she understood better. She took up her pen again and began to write out the fifth lesson.

When she had finished, she put her book away. There would be time enough to study it in depth this evening. In the meantime, she could see out of the corner of her eye a brown sludgey stain dripping gently from under the oven door onto the kitchen floor. She sighed. She really *didn't* feel like cleaning the oven. It was such a hateful dirty job, and her hands would sweat inside the rubber gloves on this warm day. She wished that she hadn't sprayed the wretched stuff on. She really would much rather be going for a walk and studying her lessons.

She gave herself a mental shake and told herself not to be so defeatist. The whole point of the lessons was that they were about living her own life as it was, not about retreating to some lovely place where everything was as perfect as it could be and it was easy to think about higher things. She now had Mindfulness, Action, Healing, Gratitude and Discipline; and if she couldn't make a good job of cleaning the oven with those, then she was a poor traveller indeed. Just to make a game of it, she resolved to apply all of the lessons if she could. She pulled on her turquoise rubber gloves. All right, discipline was easy. She wouldn't really have chosen to clean the oven, but she was going to, anyway. Action: well, she was going to hold the intention that she was going to do this job as well as she possibly could. Healing. Here Bethany paused for a minute. Then she thought that she could maybe give herself a little bit of forgiveness for not being perfect and embracing the oven with joy. For good measure, she could refuse to think thoughts involving the future and the past, and concentrate only on the oven. This was stretching it a bit, she felt, but to complete the game she resolved to focus on Mindfulness. She would observe all of her senses as she was cleaning, which would bring her close to her actions. And finally, she knew that through all of this she would be feeling happy and grateful for that happiness. Smiling, she began her task.

After a few minutes of attempting to hold all the lessons in her mind all at once, she felt that it was probably a bit of a tall order, and she was not being altogether successful. She sensed a flash of amusement from her angel. She felt a little silly. However, her lack of success probably stemmed from the fact that she had been attempting too much. It would hardly be likely that all the lessons related to all of her life all of the time. She knew, from the way she had been feeling while she worked, that she was on the right track. It was possible to clean the oven with Mindfulness and Intention. If she did this, it transformed her work into practice for herself. Perhaps she could select different lessons at different times.

THAT IS THE RIGHT WAY.
IN ADDITION, YOU DO NOT ALWAYS HAVE TO BE SERIOUS.
IT CAN BE FUN.

Bethany hesitated, a little shocked. Her game had been set as a small challenge for herself and she had not really stopped to wonder if she was having fun. The lessons were very important and she wanted to be serious about them. Thinking about it, she remembered how often the words 'free', 'joyful' and 'happy' appeared in each lesson. They even mentioned singing and laughing. Could something really be all those things, and at the same time serious? Yes, it made sense that they could. Serious didn't mean sad or straight-laced. She could be happy and joyful, play games, have fun in life, and still be deadly serious about the lessons. You probably couldn't have one without the other. Relaxing a bit, she laid down her cloth and put the rubber gloves in the sink with a broad smile. All right, she would be happy and concentrate on one or two things at a time. She would have enough to do just keeping her mind on her work and in the present, for the time being. At other times, she could meditate on the meaning of Forgiveness and Discipline. The challenge was finding the right place for all of the lessons in her life. She cleaned up the kitchen and, on impulse, decided to go shopping.

Her days were less regimented by the lack of preparing Norman's meals at certain times, and she had no need to shop as much. She knew that she had run out of bread. In the normal course of events this would have caused them both much anguish. Today, it just provided Bethany with an excuse to go to the shops. She relished the fact that she did not have to plan all her meals, and had fallen into the habit of browsing and selecting food that took her fancy. She had no need of a coat, so merely reached for her keys, opened the front door and set off down her gravelled drive to the end of the high street to Tesco's.

Reminded of her recent resolution to do something about her weight, she began to walk very briskly, but this very quickly made her feel tired and out of breath. Suddenly a sharp stabbing pain took hold of her at the base of her stomach and she gasped. There was a bench on the pavement and she took refuge on it, breathing heavily. Her forehead felt clammy and her heart was pounding. She was overwhelmed with shock. How could she have become this unfit? It was true that she did not exercise, but she had always assumed that she led an active life and that this would be sufficient to keep her body healthy. It seemed that this was not the case. Over the years she had slowed down, because there simply wasn't reason to hurry. She had gradually adjusted her rhythms to those dictated by the comings and goings of Norman, and these were never hectic. Surely there was no harm in that. Did she really need to run everywhere? Perhaps not, but there was a growing question in Bethany's mind about her general state of health. If a brisk walk caused her this much disturbance, there was something wrong, surely.

Bethany thought that she would call in at the library after doing the shopping and consult *Family Doctor – A Home Guide*. It might furnish her with clues as to whether she was ill or merely out of shape. While she was there she would list any other symptoms and see if a general picture emerged. Meanwhile, her short rest on the bench had restored her and she pushed herself upwards with some difficulty (she found that her legs were still a little shaky) and set off again towards Tesco's. She didn't try to walk as fast as she had been, but still quickened her pace slightly from her usual saunter. She held herself erect and took deep breaths. While she was at the supermarket she bought *SlimWorld* magazine. There was a feature in it about tempting her husband with an exotic cocktail of raw vegetables. She wondered how Norman would react. Probably not well.

Later that evening, after a salad of lettuce, tomato, grated carrot, cucumber and a little dollop of pale cottage cheese, Bethany had a low-fat fruit yoghurt and read the magazine. It was full of before and after pictures of women who had lost weight. She was some-what encouraged to notice that she was not really overweight by the guidlines outlined in the magazine. *Family Doctor* had not been helpful. She had looked up 'breathlessness' and 'stomach pains' but had ended up by following so many cross-references that she lost track. None of her symptoms seemed to relate to one another, and so she had looked up 'obesity'. There was a chart showing how to calculate your ideal weight for your height. Bethany, who had not weighed herself for twenty years, found this of little help. However, she did not appear to be obese. Once again, she concluded that she was overreacting. Her body was just giving her a gentle reminder that she wasn't getting any younger and she needed to keep an eye on herself. That was all it was. According to this magazine, all one had to do was regulate the amount of food one ate, and take exercise five days a week. That shouldn't be too hard. There was rather a lot about raising one's heartbeat as well, so her heart pounding fast on the way to the shops was totally natural. Reassured, Bethany went to make herself a cup of tea. She found herself eating rather a lot of biscuits while the kettle boiled, and then a few more with her blackcurrant tea, but that was all right. She would start properly tomorrow.

The next day was Friday, and Bethany was not sure whether to expect Norman back or not. He had said he would be incommunicado and not to try to contact him. He had apparently forgotten that he had not left Bethany any number where she could reach him even if she had wanted to. She had a lamb chop and some frozen peas for his supper just in case, and reasoned that he would be unlikely to be back before the early evening. She resolved to make the most of her last day on her own. She woke as usual with the light, and went downstairs in her dressing gown. In spite of the fact that she was alone in the bedroom, the living room still felt like a more suitable place to sit. After her morning session of silence, where the angel's words on Discipline appeared to sing in the stillness, she had some cereal for breakfast. Then she packed some sandwiches and a thermos full of blackcurrant tea in a plastic bag and set off for the bus stop.

Bethany felt quite excited. She had never taken the route she had decided to take this morning. In all the years she and Norman had lived in the suburb, they had only ever been on outings together, when Norman drove them in the car. Bethany had learned to drive early on in their marriage. She knew that she could, and Norman had raised no objections to her weekly lessons. She had proved to be a good driver, perhaps even better than Norman, and had passed the test first time.

And then a peculiar thing had happened. While she always meant to drive, and Norman never actually said that he wanted to, it almost always seemed as though he ended up in the driving seat when they went out. He drove to work every morning, and he probably took the wheel automatically, but for whatever reason,

Bethany didn't get many opportunities for practice. The car was only in the drive at weekends and in the evenings. Norman always cleaned it by hand on Sundays, unless it was raining, when he took it to the car wash. Their outings to the country became less frequent, and Bethany had no reason to take the car on other occasions. Norman was always there. They both agreed that they had no need for a second car and, besides, they couldn't afford it. So Bethany did not drive, and hadn't driven for years, now she came to think about it. As with so many other things, it hadn't happened dramatically. It was because she had not wanted to argue with Norman. They both had a dislike of confrontation and all too often she shied away from mentioning subjects that she knew would cause Norman pain. He so needed to be in control of everything, and in the early years it just seemed simpler not to make a fuss. In this way, her resistance had been gradually eroded. If ever she had offered to drive, Norman had tensed and said in an offhand way, 'Well, if you *really* want to.' Bethany had looked at his rigidly outstretched arm holding the keys, and knew that she didn't want to that much.

Since the coming of her angel, Bethany had looked at herself with new eyes. It was as though she had been asleep for twenty years and woken up to find that she was changed. Now, in a few short months, the young woman she had been, and perhaps the new woman she was becoming, was emerging from her lethargy like a caterpillar splitting its chrysalis. The image pleased her. As she waited at the bus stop she looked around her, imagining she was seeing everything for the first time. Although the pavement was dusty, the sun was shining and there was a green hedge behind her that rustled and swayed slightly in the sun. Bethany washed her eyes in the lush greenness until they went out of focus. She felt bathed in the colour. The bus trundled up and she got on.

Bethany took her seat and remembered she had always loved buses. She loved the way that you couldn't hurry them, the way they stopped and started and jerked and swerved through traffic. Her mother had always loathed buses, saying they were coarse. Bethany knew exactly what she meant: the noises they made as they disgorged streams of passengers onto the pavement without saying pardon. The rubbery hissing of the doors, the whistling of the breaks, the grumbling of the engine and the slapping of the wipers when it rained, made Bethany think of a rude old man belching and burping in a public place. During the winter before she had married Norman, she had travelled to work on the bus each morning, and had often not wanted to get off. She loved the condensation on the windows, the warmth of people packed together in the aisles and the regular conversation all around her. It made her feel safe and unnoticed. She had drawn comfort from the fact that the bus was totally impervious to the feelings of its passengers. No matter if they were happy, angry, or even as totally wretched as she had been, the bus carried on getting them to where they wanted to go, with belligerent indifference.

Bethany was going to a local beauty spot for her picnic. The bus drew in to the lay-by and she got off, thanking the driver as she stepped on to the pavement. It was a short walk along the road, and then she turned down a small lane edged with high trellis wiring separating the path from the back gardens of the houses either side. Columbine was running wild all over it and the trellis was thickly hung with dark leaves and white flowers. There was a strong smell of dog dirt and she watched where she was putting her feet.

Ahead of her she could see the glint of water and hear the excited shouts of children. Although it was a weekday, there were plenty of people about, mostly young mothers with small children and older people enjoying the sunshine. Bethany passed through rusty green gates which no longer opened or shut but framed a path that led to an old quarry. Years ago, a local company had mined gravel from the pit, but it was long since disused and flooded. Local people had been attracted to the spot and a thriving business had built up in the summer months hiring out brightly coloured little paddle-boats. There was also a picnic area and a small playground, at the corner of which was parked an ice cream van. The path that Bethany was walking along had a little concrete wall running alongside it which children liked to balance on, holding onto their mothers' hands for safety. Here and there were little gaps in the wall where you could get down to the water, and she paused beside one of these and reached into her plastic bag.

Norman would have thought her impossibly frivolous, she thought. Not only did she want to feed the ducks (a very childish habit), but she was proposing to use some of the new bread that she had bought yesterday. She could just imagine the conversation that would have taken place. Of course if Norman were here, she wouldn't be feeding the ducks. It was a pity, she reflected, because he might have enjoyed it. Not for the first time in her life did she wonder if sometimes her acquiescence did not really help those who were around her. Perhaps if she had said that she wanted to feed ducks, she and Norman might be here together. In the meantime, she would enjoy herself, watching the birds squabbling and splashing over her bread. When it was all finished she carried on to the grassy area on the far side of the water.

Bethany had a lovely day. She took off her shoes and socks and dangled her feet in the water. She hired a paddle-boat and meandered rather inexpertly across the lake, and she swung on the swings in the playground. She ate her sandwiches on the grass and lay in the sunshine listening to the children and mothers all around her. She bought herself a huge soft whipped ice cream with a flake in it and finished it all with great enjoyment. This last activity caused her a little uneasiness, because she didn't think it would help her trousers to become less tight. However, she reasoned that something that melted away was unlikely to be too fattening. It would probably just melt through her body somehow. Anyway, she was having far too nice a time to worry today. She would think about it tomorrow. Finally, towards three o'clock in the afternoon, Bethany reluctantly decided that it was time to go. She heaved herself up and wandered along the path, dangling her shoes and socks from her hand, thinking what a sight she must look, a middle-aged woman behaving like a child. Nobody gave her any odd looks, however, and instead readily returned her open smile.

Bethany caught the bus home. It took longer than she had anticipated, and she had only just enough time to walk in through the front door, unpack the remains of her picnic, and brush her hair, when she heard the sound of a car drawing up in the drive, and a few seconds later, Norman's key in the door.

Norman recoiled with shock as he came into the hall to find Bethany standing right in front of him. He struggled to put down his carryall bag as she put her arms around his neck and stood there, making it difficult for him to move. She was also speaking too fast for him to get a word in edgeways. 'Did you miss me? It's lovely to have you back. I had a lovely time today. I went over to the old quarry. Hasn't it been glorious weather?'

Norman sighed pointedly. Avoiding his wife's eyes, he replied, 'B, I'm very tired, it's been a long day. I would rather not talk now, and particularly not about the weather. I should very much like to have a cup of tea and then eat.' In spite of his cool words Norman felt agitated. His heart was beating uncomfortably fast in his throat. He had expected to find Bethany at the stove preparing his supper. Instead he was faced with her forcing intimacy in the hall, of all places. Trying to slide past her in the hallway, he made a great show of the necessity of unpacking his bag. Bethany remained standing where she was, her smile still warm. She reached out for the strap of his shoulderbag.

'Oh, don't do that now. Come and chat while I make the tea. It really is nice to see you, you know.'

There was going to be an unseemly tussle with his bag, Norman thought. Suddenly he felt furious that he couldn't get away from her. How dare she cause this unnecessary and unwanted scene as soon as he got in? He had to make a stand. Shouldering his way to the stairs, he wrenched the bag with an angry movement, meaning to escape the situation as quickly as he could. If he could only put some space between them, he could perhaps regain control over the ridiculous situation. Unfortunately, the force with which he pulled the bag caused it to snag on the bottom post of the banisters and the strap came away. Somehow he must have left the zip slightly undone, for the whole bag fell and his clothing and washbag scattered onto the floor.

White with fury and humiliation, he scrabbled on the floor grabbing items and stuffing them back inside the bag. Bethany stooped to help. 'Look, Norman, they are all falling out again,' she giggled. In his agitation he had mistaken the wide pocket of his bag for the main section, and clothes were cascading out as quickly as he shoved them in. The sight of Bethany's laughing, happy face as she held a pair of pristine white Y-fronts out to him was the last straw.

'How dare you!' he shouted. The words exploded through his gnashing teeth in a paroxysm of bitter animosity. 'You stupid woman! I've worked hard all my life to keep things going. Everything was satisfactory until you began this ridiculous . . . ' He paused. He wasn't sure what it was that she had begun. 'Until you started to act so impossibly. How dare you do this to us? Turning our lives upside down. And now you crowd me when I've just got home from work and make a . . . situation . . . when it's all completely . . . unnecessary. Just leave me alone and I will sort it out. Go and make the tea. No, I don't want anything to drink, I don't feel like it any more. Just go and do whatever it is you do, and make supper. Leave me alone.' Norman snatched the Y-fronts with a trembling hand, turned on his heel and stumbled blindly up the stairs.

Bethany was horrified. Her smile had frozen on her face, and she stood stock-still, unable to move. She had been completely unprepared for Norman's outburst. She had no idea that she had been upsetting him, and she had never in all their lives together heard Norman shout. He never even raised his voice. Poor, poor

Norman. How could she have disturbed him so much? Stricken, she didn't know what to do. Should she go after him and apologise, or go and make the supper? She decided to go and begin cooking. That was what Norman wanted, and trying to talk would only cause him further agitation. She listened. There was no sound at all from upstairs, so she gingerly turned round and tiptoed into the kitchen. As she opened the fridge and got out the chops and put the kettle on for the peas, she wondered what to do. Her previous plan of talking to him about the angel was out of the question. She had obviously been very wrong when she had thought that Norman had been hearing voices too. He was so upset, and she had done it. She mustn't disturb his equilibrium further. No, she must keep her angel secret at all costs, for Norman's sake more than her own. He would never accept it. She was overcome with remorse. She must make things right. It was awful that she was becoming so happy and at the same time causing Norman so much anguish. How could she have been so unaware? But now that she knew, she must find a way to make amends. She would try very hard to be a better wife to him. Oh, poor, poor Norman.

Upstairs, Norman was sitting on the bed, thinking very much the same thing. His anger had given way to self-pity. All he wanted was some peace and quiet when he got home. He had been working hard for five days, he had even taken a day's holiday so that the team could complete their mission. A fleeting image of them all in the bar last night flashed through his mind and he instantly dismissed it. He was entitled to relax as well. One couldn't work all the time. But when he got home he expected his wife to be there for him. All he wanted was to unwind, eat and maybe have a little conversation in good time, filling her in on the important aspects of what he had been doing.

At first, all had been well. He had drawn up in the car in the happy anticipation of all being as it should be. When he dropped Rita off, she had laid her little hand on his arm and thanked him for driving her home so safely. Looking down at her, Norman had felt a surge of masculine protectiveness. He made sure she was safely deposited at her destination, watching carefully in case she should come to any mishap on her way to her pale mauve front door, and then he had driven the few short miles to his own abode, warmed by a feeling of deep satisfaction. The car still smelled strongly of Rita's scent. The pleasure he had felt in returning to his own home after his travels caused a little smile to play about his lips. As he put his door key firmly into the lock, he had been confident that there would be a routine schedule of events, some of which he would feel free to amend. He would unpack while B occupied herself in the kitchen. He would maybe, daringly, suggest a drink, as befitted a man coming home from a course away. B would be surprised and admiring as he poured himself a sherry, and they would eat while he told her about the course. Not all of it, of course, only the parts he thought she would understand. All would be well, and things would be ordered and calm.

His feeling of manly control had been shattered instantly by the unseemly behaviour of his wife. She had spoiled it all as soon as he had stepped inside the front door. He had not been allowed any time to set the tone of his own homecoming. All of his pleasant and soothing fantasies lay in ruins around him. B should have let him run the evening, and everything would have gone smoothly. It was not too much to ask. Instead she had behaved with appalling lack of decorum and sensitivity. The impropriety of her actions, hanging around his neck like that, had filled him with repugnance. To make matters even worse, she had dared to laugh at him and made him feel foolish. How could she? His blood ran hot and, to his horror, he noticed that his hands were shaking. Norman let out an unsteady breath, and clutched his knees. He longed for a cool and sympathetic hand to stroke his headache away. His mother used to do that a long time ago. His mind briefly flicked back to Rita. He had barely noticed her before this week away, and had been very nervous about giving her a lift. Now he felt differently. She was everything his wife was not. She was ladylike and refined and she had made him feel big and strong and in control. And now he had to go downstairs and go into the kitchen and deal with a situation that he did not want or need. Suddenly Norman felt hot anger coursing through him again. B had caused him to lose control of himself, and that was unforgivable. He would act as though nothing had happened, be cool and dignified and try to put the evening back together. B could act as she pleased, but he would not lose control again.

Later, Norman lay awake on his side of the bed, while his wife slept peacefully. He carefully preserved the distance between them. It was hot, and his polyester pyjamas chafed his neck. He looked at the alarm clock next to him. It was 1.30 in the morning. It was Sunday tomorrow, so he would sleep a full half an hour later than on workdays. That was the reason that they always had 'relations' on Saturday nights. Even tonight, when he had felt nothing but fury for his wife, Norman prided himself that he had done his duty. Norman told himself that he had had relations with his wife every Saturday night of their marriage, and he could draw comfort from that, even if Bethany did not. He turned his head to look resentfully at her back, and then turned over so that he faced away from her. His mind ran over the events of the last few days. It reassured him to remember how he had been. He had felt popular, in control, one of the team. And now he was home. In spite of B's obvious remorse, the evening had been uncomfortable, and he had still not forgiven her. He had told himself that a few days apart would be what she needed to come to her senses. She would miss the routines and schedules that he worked so hard to preserve, and she would realise that she was jeopardising all of it with her selfish behaviour. He had hoped that she would see her ridiculous antics for what they were, and abandon her foolish singing and dancing and . . . general laxity. Instead things appeared to be just as bad as before. She had not used his absence as an opportunity to think about things and see the error of her ways. She knew what had been expected of her – he had even given her a strong hint over the telephone – and still she had failed to act responsibly. He was at first disappointed, and then angry that she had let him down. What was he to do?

In the safety of the dark bedroom, Norman once again allowed himself to think about Rita. Rita was not strictly regarded as part of the Accounts team; but she was the secretary shared by himself and three others, and as such was essential to getting any work done. After a lengthy meeting some time last October, during which various protocols were discussed in depth, it had been decided that Accounts was an egalitarian department, not given to standing on ceremony, provided the proper regulations were followed. It had therefore been agreed in principle that Rita would be allowed to take part in any team-building measures that would be deemed necessary during the course of the development of the department. Norman had thought this over, and decided that he fully supported the decision.

When it had been announced some months later that Accounts would be spending a week in Hull, it was generally understood that this would include Rita. The week itself (which was regarded as rather a 'perk' by some of the more junior members; not himself of course) was to take place some time during the summer. They were to make their own transport arrangements, but would be spending the time in an hotel at the company's expense. When Norman had told Bethany about the trip, he had not thought it necessary to mention that the 'colleague' to whom he was due to give a lift up to Hull had been Rita. For some reason, foolishly he now realised, he had felt somewhat uncomfortable about offering

Rita a ride in his car. He had wondered apprehensively what it would be like, driving all that way, just the two of them. Now, however, he saw that it had been entirely appropriate that he, as a senior member of the team, should offer assistance to Rita, who was clearly not able to manage without a guiding hand. Besides, the circumstances through which this had come about were entirely due to Bethany. In a way she had been to blame for the whole thing, indirectly.

It had started on the previous Friday, when he had gone to work feeling bitterly resentful. It seemed a long time ago now. The angry indignation had been gnawing at him all through the drive, and as he pulled into his space towards the back of the car park, Norman felt helpless and exhausted. He had been grinding his teeth on the journey, and now he had a headache. He was going to have a miserable day. And so it turned out – at least the first part of it did.

B had been mysteriously absent from the bed again that morning, and this, together with her generally uncooperative behaviour, had continued to irritate him. He went over and over it in his mind, a pile of papers lying unseen on his desk. The whole situation was made worse by the fact that he had no one to confide in. If only there was some way of getting it off his chest. Never before had Norman suffered such torment without the cool balm of sympathy or understanding. The previous day he had reluctantly acknowledged the impossibility of speaking to his mother. Marjorie would want him to take action; she would want to become involved, and Norman shrank from the possible scenario of being caught in a dispute between his mother and his wife. Not that 'dispute' would be the right word, but any situation of that kind would be impossible, absolutely intolerable. It would be admitting that he had lost control of his own marriage. No, he would have to manage on his own.

It was in this unsettled state that Norman found himself at lunchtime. He had not managed to resolve anything in his mind, and his headache still nagged at him. His self-pity had by now hardened into truculence, and he belligerently told himself that enough was enough. He was going to take charge. B was not going to disturb him any further. And then events had conspired to cause Norman to act out of character.

Every Friday lunchtime a certain section of Accounts was accustomed to go down to the Dog and Shepherd to 'unwind'. Norman disassociated himself from this crowd, as he thought it unseemly to drink at work. He felt there should be some kind of regulation prohibiting this kind of thing, similar to that employed by the constabulary perhaps. (Norman secretly rather liked the phrase 'I never drink on duty' and applied it to himself.) Of course he never said it out loud. He merely observed disapprovingly that the pub goers returned in an excitable and over-convivial state and that not a great deal of work was accomplished on Friday afternoons.

Norman always lunched alone in the cafeteria on Fridays. It was much quieter than the rest of the week, and he normally appreciated the empty tables all around him. Today, however, he did not relish more time alone with his bitter thoughts, and this had led him to a daring resolution. Norman had decided to go down to the Dog and Shepherd at lunchtime. He was going to have a drink, maybe two, and possibly even an alcoholic one. He deserved it, after what his wife was putting him through.

As 12.30 approached, his heart began to beat in his throat. He was the only one in his section that did not go to the Dog and Shepherd, and every week somebody would invite him. He was aware that they didn't expect him to go, and that the ritual had become rather a joke. He usually waited until they asked, declined, and waited for their laughter to die away, echoing along the corridor. He consoled himself with the thought that he was above it all. Today he was going to accept, and in spite of his belligerent state of mind, was a little worried that he might not be asked. He carefully stacked his paperwork and clipped it together with a little paperclip from his special stock. All around him people were pushing their chairs from their desks and getting ready to go.

Reg sat back in his swivel chair and stretched his arms up above his head, yawning ostentatiously. The chair was a source of irritation to Norman. He could never understand how Reg had managed to get it, as only senior members of management had one. The rest of them perched on regulation grey metal chairs with maroon and grey flecked seats. Reg's chair had padded cushions and a moveable back. The chair was just one of the many things about Reg that irritated Norman. Reg sat at the desk next to him, and this made him very difficult to avoid, something that Norman would dearly love to have done.

Reg was about the same age as Norman, and occupied the same level of seniority in Accounts. They had joined the company at about the same time, and worked at desks that were set side by side, and they shared the services of Rita, their secretary. But in every other way, they were as different as two men could be.

Reg was loud, brash and full of bonhomie. He was considered to be the office wag. No social occasion was complete without him. He specialised in double entendres and suggestive humour. The most innocent of remarks could be turned into jokes by Reg. Norman (who in contrast to his neighbour was reserved to the point of frigidity) could not stand the way he was made the butt of Reg's smutty innuendoes. Worse still was that his anger was not shared by the other members of the office. Everyone loved Reg. Rita simpered and blushed when Reg patted her on the bottom and told her she was looking perky, and his male colleagues laughed uproariously at Reg's jokes. On April 1st this year, Reg had brought in some superglue and stuck all of Norman's split pin fasteners together. He had carefully placed them so that they were indistinguishable from Norman's own system. Norman was so mortified that he failed to notice that all around him other people were discovering Reg's work and greeting it with howls of laughter. Flushed and angry, he convinced himself that the whole office had been aware of Reg's plan and that he had been made an object of general ridicule. 'I had to come in at half-past-seven to get all that done,' Reg had told the assembled company. Norman, who often got to work early, but not to play practical jokes, bitterly resented Reg's popularity. In the months since April he had occasionally passed the time devising a complicated and impractical scenario where he, Norman, became the agent of Reg's downfall and saved the office, to general acclaim.

In the meantime, Reg was invariably the person who invited him to the pub on a Friday. He would say heartily, so that everyone could hear, 'Have you got time for a quick one, Norman, old boy?' This was accompanied with raised eyebrows and a sort of smirk which made Norman want to smash his fist into Reg's beefy red face. Usually the accompanying laughter would carry the drinkers to the door, and Norman would be left impotently swallowing his witty retort that somehow he never had time to give. The bile would rise in his throat as he heard the laughter fade down the corridor, and he would check that the clock said precisely 12.30 before making his way to the cafeteria. Today it was going to be different. He ran through his carefully rehearsed reply.

Reg continued to lean back in his chair with his arms over his head. He was rather a snappy dresser and favoured highly decorative waistcoats and ties, sometimes at the same time. Today he was wearing a mustard yellow waistcoat with silver buttons in the shape of anchors, and a bright blue tie with little pink pigs all over it, under which were written some letters that Norman couldn't make out. Suddenly Reg beat his chest like a gorilla and let out his breath in a rush. Norman jumped, and nearly missed his opportunity.

'Aaah, it's good to stretch out. Well, Norman, old boy, are you coming? How d'you fancy getting your lips round something wet and refreshing?'

Norman cursed inwardly. His reply had been tailor-made to wittily intercept Reg's 'quick one'. He wasn't prepared for this. Nevertheless, he stood up with alacrity, and cleared his throat. His words didn't emerge with the strength he had hoped for, and his voice quavered a little, but nevertheless he managed it. 'Yes, as a matter of fact, I think I will partake of some refreshment, thank you, Reginald.' Reg looked surprised and then slapped Norman on the back with a force that dislodged his glasses.

'Attaboy, Norm! 'Bout time you put a bit of hair on your chest!' Looking round, Reg saw Rita checking her lipstick in a small compact mirror. Raising his voice so that everyone could hear (which required only a slight increase in volume, as he never spoke quietly), Reg shouted, 'Hey Rita! Look after our boy here, he might even treat you to a quick one.'

Seeing his opportunity, Norman quickly produced his prepared witticism. 'We do have the entire lunch hour, so perhaps two quick ones would be in order, Reginald.' There was a brief silence. Norman was aware that Rita's mouth had fallen open, and that the others were looking at him in surprise. Reg suddenly roared with laughter and slapped him on the back again. This caused the others to laugh too, and they all set off down the corridor. Norman was relieved that the worst was over. He surreptitiously wiped his hands on his suit trousers, and swallowed. His throat felt dry and he was now looking forward to that drink.

The Dog and Shepherd stood on the intersection of two busy main roads. It boasted a sign saying 'Home-cooked Food' (although it would be more accurate to say that it was 'Pub-warmed Food'), a dusty beer garden where intrepid drinkers braved the traffic fumes, and a series of rather smeary tables clustered around the bar where one could eat the microwaved pies and chips served up in the name of lunch. They walked past the entrance to the saloon bar, and into the area known as The Snug. This was out of respect for the ladies. At one end of The Snug was a mock brick fireplace which served as a focal point for the room. In the winter an electric flame-effect fire was plugged in and positioned in the space, but as it was summer, a bright yellow coal scuttle and a set of tongs were carefully placed either side of a dusty dried flower arrangement. The walls above the rustically exposed brick were painted two contrasting shades of maroon, and the carpet was violently patterned brown and cherry. The walls themselves were

151

covered with horsebrasses, completing the rustic theme begun by the walls, and there were little plates pinned precariously to the dark brown plastic beams glued to the ceiling. A cheery tea towel was pinned to the space where Norman was standing, explaining the Rules of Cricket to foreigners, and above the bar was a sign saying 'You don't have to be mad to work here – but it helps'. Apart from a young couple deep in conversation near the door marked 'Toilets', The Snug was empty. The sun shone cheerlessly through the grimy windows onto the cherry patterned carpet.

Reg took charge in his familiar hearty way. 'Right, what're we having? Everyone for the usual, is it?' He slapped his hand on the bar and shouted, 'Shop!' There was general laughter, as the seating arrangements were sorted out. Norman stood hesitantly by Reg, uncertain as to whom to sit by. He leaned his elbow on the bar, affecting nonchalance. To his relief, Reg spoke immediately. 'What's your poison, Norm?'

Norman thought rapidly and asked him for a shandy. He fumbled for his wallet. Icy dread clamped his heart and surged upwards through his body. He turned hot and cold and then colder. Of course it wasn't there, why should it be there, he had no reason to bring his wallet to work.

Reg was speaking again. 'Come on, Norm, grab these and we'll be getting round them. Must service the ladies.' He winked, and noticed Norman's hand still in his jacket pocket. 'Oh, don't worry about the boodle, landlord keeps our tab. We'll settle up later, and if you've fallen off the wagon for good, you can join the kitty.'

Norman wanted to throw his arms around Reg right there and then and weep into his mustard waistcoat. He really must get a grip on himself. B had a lot to answer for. He followed Reg with three drinks in his trembling hands. Most of the group were sitting at two dark benches at the edge of The Snug near the cloudy windows. Right against the wall were two red plastic seats facing each other over a table. Known as a Banquette, it was here that Reg was settling himself. Rita and Shirley, another of the secretaries, were already perched on the inside, and Reg slid his ample bottom in next to Rita. This involved much shuffling and nudging, indignant gasps from Rita, and hearty laughter from Reg. The manoeuvre finally accomplished, Reg laid his arm easily along the back of the Banquette.

Norman silently gave thanks that he was of a much slighter build. Norman's waist measurement was unchanged from when he had bought his first suit to marry Bethany. In fact, the suit itself was also unchanged, as he only wore it on Thursdays. He nimbly seated himself next to Shirley, leaving a few precious inches of modest space between them. He found that Reg had ordered him a pint of shandy. The last time he and B had been into a pub it had been Mothering Sunday, and he had escorted her and Marjorie. He had chaperoned the two women into a select establishment frequented by Marjorie's bridge circle, and they had had lunch. On that occasion he had ordered a half, and found that he could barely accommodate that.

Today was different. Norman felt himself to be on his mettle, being in the company of other men. There would be no question of halves today. He squared himself and took a deep gulp of the pale liquid. After a little while, he took a second gulp, and then a third. He ran a clammy finger around his collar, sweating slightly. He noticed that the conversation had turned towards staff management training, something he felt able to contribute to. Perhaps this would not be such an ordeal after all. He cleared his throat and spoke with what he hoped was a confident manner. 'It's all very well sending us on a course, but unless they pay travel expenses, the logistics are going to be very difficult. I have heard that the matter is under discussion at the present time.' Now seemed a good time to have another pull at his pint. Reg nodded affably.

Rita sighed. 'I don't know how I'm going to manage it. It's so much easier if you can drive, public transport is an absolute menace these days.' She pursed her little mouth and took a dainty sip from her gin and tonic. Norman noticed that this left red lipstick smudged on the edge of her glass. His eyes followed the glass as Rita set it down neatly, right in the centre of her mat. He found that he wanted to carry on watching the bubbles floating up to the top of the liquid where they turned pinkish behind the lipstick. With difficulty he wrenched his attention back to what Rita was saying. 'I do envy you men, being able to drive your own cars. I've always been far too nervous to learn.'

Reg laughed heartily. 'Well, "baby you can drive my car" any time. I daresay you get your fair share of "lifts". He winked at Norman, who laughed rather loudly and took several large gulps of his shandy. Reg continued, 'Of course, I would normally offer to assist a damsel in distress, but I'm already getting a lift with Cliff.' Cliff and Reg shared a bachelor pad together and played squash at the weekends. Cliff drove a red sports car with only two seats in it, and he and Reg cut a dash cruising down the high street on Saturday nights. Norman, who secretly wondered what it would be like to drive a red sportscar, knew that it was wildly inappropriate. He had noted waspishly to himself that Cliff's rather portly figure barely squeezed behind the wheel. Both he and Reg had to have the seats pushed back as far as they could go to accommodate their thickening waists, and there was no room at all for any passengers.

Reg was continuing: 'Does anybody know when we are going, by the way?'

Norman was flattered that all eyes turned to him. He was beginning to feel warm solidarity with his table, and leaned conspiratorially towards Reg and Rita, balancing his weight carefully on his elbow. 'Well, there isn't anything definite, but my hunch is that it will be announced that the course will take place the week after next.' Rita looked at him admiringly, and Norman basked in her glance. He was glad that he was the only one in the office who read all of the memos sent down to them.

Reg suddenly said, 'Ah ha! Here come the sandwiches.' He gestured lavishly to the party's glasses. 'Same again, landlord.' The barman set down an aluminium platter of ham and cheese sandwiches covered with cling film. They looked as if they had been made some time ago, but Rita was already daintily peeling the plastic off with her scarlet manicured nails.

'Sup up Norm!' bellowed Reg, and Norman saw with satisfaction that he had nearly managed all of his pint. Then he noticed that another pint of shandy had appeared in front of him, its golden liquid slopping gently out of the glass. He belched softly.

By the end of that lunchtime Norman was firmly established in the group. Reg had heartily pronounced him to be a sound nob. Norman could not believe it had been so easy. He glowed with bonhomie, and thus it was that he found himself, towards the end of the second pint of shandy, offering grandly, if somewhat unsteadily, to escort Rita to Hull in his car. His offer was accepted with alacrity, and Shirley and Rita tottered off to visit the 'little girls' room'.

Reg had slapped him on the back and called him a 'dark horse', a 'quick mover', and an 'old dog'. Norman rather agreed. All unpleasant thoughts of Bethany were receding, and he spent the afternoon in a haze of self-satisfied contentment. He and Reg were men of the world, Herculean athletes who drove their own cars and who assisted damsels in distress whenever the need arose. They were free to act as they pleased, making up their own rules as they went along. Norman even tilted back in his chair and stretched his arms during the afternoon tea break.

By evening, Norman was frantic with nerves and bitterly regretting his rashness. His bravado had evaporated, leaving him twitching with panic. Rita would surely misconstrue his offer, and the intimacy afforded by the hours alone in the car together might encourage a regrettable occurrence. Norman's palms grew damp, and he resolved to act with icy courtesy towards Rita in future, in a manner suited to a senior employee generously offering assistance to a junior one. He bitterly resented the necessity of having to take these precautions and laid the blame firmly at Bethany's door. If she had not caused him so much distress in the first place, none of this would have arisen. Was there no end to the trouble caused by her immoderate behaviour?

Norman had spent the days leading up to the course alternately fuming at Bethany, and agitatedly devising ways of fending off any untoward situation that might possibly arise. He was glacially polite to Rita, and steadfastly ignored Reg's allusions to 'stallions' and 'dark horses'. He was satisfied that neither Reg nor Rita could detect that he was flustered, and that Rita, in particular, would know that he would never welcome advances, in the car or otherwise.

In the end, Norman mused in the darkness, it had all turned out very well. Rita had been respectful and admiring, and behaved in the most exemplary ladylike manner. In fact, her behaviour was so ladylike that it made him all the more conscious of Bethany's laxity. Rita always waited for him to open the car door for her, she always swung her legs out, knees clamped tightly together, and she always wore little skirts and spotless white blouses. Bethany wore trousers, she strode around, and appeared totally unaware of the fact that he was on hand to perform acts of gallantry such as holding open the door. Rita always looked demurely up at him and murmured her thanks. She never behaved with him as she did with Reg.

The return journey home had passed in the twinkling of an eye. It had seemed as though they talked for the entire time, and there was no awkwardness, even when Norman had bought them both lunch at the motorway service station. Rita had confided in him that, although she laughed at Reg's innuendoes, she felt somewhat uncomfortable at times in his presence. She had laid her tiny hand on his arm for the briefest of moments and confessed that it was wonderful to be treated as a lady by a real gentleman. Norman had almost taken his eyes off the road, but instead accelerated manfully into the second lane, causing Rita to draw in her breath in a little gasp of fear or excitement. Norman did not know which it was, but experienced a delightful frisson as he changed gear. Rita later rested her slim fingers absently on the gear stick, stroking it gently, and Norman's hand had brushed hers more than once. Each time Rita had jumped and blushed, apologising for her carelessness. All in all the journey had passed delightfully quickly.

Norman shifted his thighs in the darkness, remembering how he had felt when Rita had gasped at his masterful driving. He thought about Rita's modesty, her spotless white frilled blouse, and the tightly-clamped stockinged legs as she got out of his car. Rita ate daintily, nibbling at the edges of her sandwiches, dabbing fastidiously at the corner of her mouth between each mouthful. When she spoke, her words slid delicately from in between her scarlet lips with a delightfully sibilant lisp, and her laugh was a beautifully refined silvery tinkle. How different from Bethany. When he thought about Rita, his wife seemed coarse, clumsy and immodest in comparison. Norman could not, and never had been able to abide coarseness. The contrast between Rita's refinement and his wife's abandoned . . . laxity . . . had made the scene in the hall at his homecoming all the more painful. Norman tried to breathe quietly. For some reason his thoughts kept returning to Rita's tightly-clamped, stockinged legs. He wondered if she did indeed wear stockings or perhaps tights. He knew that they couldn't be pop-socks, her skirt was too short and tight for that. He was almost sure she must wear stockings. Someone like Rita would, and of course that would make it even more imperative that she kept her legs pressed tightly together. Norman shifted his thighs again. He could not get comfortable tonight. He turned over and stared sullenly at Bethany's back in the darkness. It really was too bad that he had to go through all of this. If she was a better wife, he too would be sound asleep instead of tossing and turning through the night. It really was too bad.

* * *

Bethany was feeling low and dispirited. Norman had been withdrawn and irritable ever since he had returned from his course and, in spite of her best efforts, it seemed as though she could not find a way to communicate with him. Everything she did appeared to be wrong, and she had caught him looking at her with something like disgust on his face. Her efforts to restrain her food intake made her feel tired and were having no noticeable effect on her weight. One evening she had felt so miserable after a day of low-calorie yoghurt and salad that she had gone into the kitchen and began putting one biscuit after another into her mouth as she waited for the kettle to boil. Norman had come in, seen her with her mouth full and both hands full of biscuits, and turned on his heels without a word. She had felt his contempt for her lack of will-power.

Discipline. That was the other thing. That was the most important thing really, the root of all the trouble. She seriously wondered if the angel's fifth lesson was too difficult. Some days she had even lain in bed after she had woken up, instead of going downstairs to listen to the silence and work through the lesson. This made her feel unhappy, and her day would run less smoothly as a result. In spite of her feelings, the routine that she had fallen into over the last few months had become disrupted, its regular pattern disturbed. Bethany felt leaden and depressed.

After several days of seemingly inescapable lethargy, she decided that she must pull herself together. If she did not do something soon, the gains she had made through her new-found happiness would slip away. Positive action must be the way to come out of this. Bethany told herself that a lapse in her study did not mean that she had stopped forever. It was merely because she had missed a few days and did not mean that she could not start again. She had been waiting to feel better before she found the energy to rouse herself. Now she realised that without action, energy was unlikely to return. Rather, she would hope that through action, she would encourage herself to feel better.

The first morning after she had resolved to act, she woke early. She thought positive thoughts and ran through all the reasons why beginning again was a good idea. Before she knew it, the piercing bleeping of Norman's alarm caused her to start guiltily. She then spent her day feeling miserable, trying to be disciplined, and ate too much. It was obvious that she was unable to rise to this challenge. Maybe the fifth lesson was her nemesis, and she had proved herself undeserving of the gifts offered to her. She was fat, stupid, and weak-willed, and she had failed the angel. What was the point of it all? She may as well accept that she had given up and was never going to make any progress. That was the end of it. Finished.

The next day she woke early and got out of bed as soon as her eyes opened. She did not think any positive thoughts, but went quietly downstairs. She slowed her breathing and closed her eyes. It was as simple as that.

When Norman had left for work she went up to the bedroom and opened her wardrobe. She was going to sort out her clothes. Bethany had read about sorting out her clothes in *SlimWorld*. There was a whole article on how your clothes showed what kind of person you were, and that a cluttered wardrobe meant you had a muddled life, and that colours made you feel differently about everything, even being a bit too fat. If you sorted them out, and you only had things in your cupboard that fitted, then you could feel better about everything. She wasn't really sure what she thought about it all, but the article had made her think quite a lot, nevertheless. She had never been the sort of person to worry about her appearance overmuch, and she had always assumed that Norman thought she looked all right, but recently he seemed so angry with her all the time, and she frequently caught him glancing at her with that same look of disgust. Buying new clothes would improve her morale and surely, if her morale was high it would help her be more disciplined. Maybe she was postponing practicing the lesson of discipline, but nevertheless, it was still an important task. Besides, it would be fun.

Two hours later Bethany sat despondently at her dressing table. There was no room to sit on the bed. The heap of discarded clothes lay all over the duvet, and spilled over onto the floor. Bethany leaned her elbows on the dressing table, cupped her face in her hands, and scrutinised her reflection in the mirror. Could she really be this different, and if she had changed so much physically, how could she not have noticed? The simple fact was that hardly any of her clothes fitted her any more. She seemed to be the same height, but everything else had grown. She had struggled into one tight garment after another, failing to do up buttons and zips and vainly trying to hold in her stomach. Even if she managed to get a dress to fall over her waist, the buttons would gape and strain over her chest. How did one hold in one's chest? No wonder Norman was disgusted with her. Bethany put on her trousers again, which were made of a comfortable stretchy material, and slipped her loose silk shirt over the top. She brushed her hair, and then went downstairs to get some black binbags. She systematically parcelled all of her things up and put the bags back into the bottom of the wardrobe. She made herself a sandwich with brown bread and lots of lettuce and cucumber. Then she let herself out of the front door and went to look for new clothes.

Later that afternoon she returned to the house feeling quite pleased with herself. Armed with the magazine's thoughts on colours that suit you, she had chosen three skirts and two matching blouses. The skirts had elasticated waists, it was true, but that would be good for when she returned to a bit more like her old size, and the new clothes really did suit her. Standing in front of the full-length mirror on the landing outside her bedroom, she inspected herself critically. Although she was bigger than she used to be, she really didn't think she looked at all bad. Autumn colours were 'in' this season, she had been told, and the soft green skirt and nut brown blouse brought out the colour of her eyes. Her hair looked glossy and she looked vibrantly healthy.

With a spring in her step, Bethany went downstairs to prepare supper. She had bought steak, which was Norman's favourite, and she was going to fry onions and potatoes and have ice cream afterwards. It was 5.30. That meant that Norman would be home in about 45 minutes. She had better make a start on the table, and peeling the potatoes. It wouldn't do to be late. She wondered if he'd notice that anything was different about her.

At 6.10 Norman phoned to say that he would be late. The meeting that he had told her about was going to take much longer than he had thought. She was not to worry about tea, because he would get something at the pub afterwards. Bethany put the phone back on the hook and wondered what to do. The steaks were already under the grill, and the potatoes and onions were all ready to go in the pan. Carefully, she divided the pile of peeled, sliced potatoes and onions into two heaps. She fried the smaller heap and decanted the rest into two small bowls which she covered with cling film and put in the fridge. She left Norman's steak to cool and took hers on a tray into the living room. She put the tray down on a small table, switched on the television, and looked at her food. Then she leaned back in her chair and thought.

For a long time she sat there, blind to the noise of the television, and to the food in front of her. All day long she had been thinking about the fifth lesson, its words drifting in and out of her head as she sorted her clothes. She acknowledged the sense of purpose that had run through her day, like a thread linking her actions together, leading her towards a goal, and she was aware that that thread had nearly slipped through her fingers. During the past few days she had allowed herself to lose momentum, to stand still. And when she had stood still, she had been losing ground all of the time, becoming depressed and despondent, but still allowing it to happen. After today she was astounded that she had come so close to letting it all go and giving up on the lessons. Perhaps you couldn't stand still in life. She knew from experience that when she stopped moving forwards and growing, she began to stagnate. But supposing that what she thought of as stagnation was really a kind of sinking down and declining? That was what it felt like, and her instinct told her that inaction caused atrophy, that something inside her began to waste away and die if she didn't move forward.

That was why she placed so much store by action. But she had been a long time staying still, trying not to be hurt. Now something had caused her to take stock and begin again. What was it that had made her pick herself up and tell herself that staying still was all right for a while, but that it was now time to take action?

She knew that, by starting all over again today, in spite of the lapse which was threatening to become permanent, she had discovered something important. Abruptly, she stood up and turned off the television. She went into the kitchen and looked out of the window at the garden. The weather had changed in the last few days and the sky was overcast and heavy, and the evening light was fading. A sparrow hopped about the lawn. She watched it absent-mindedly for a minute, and then rummaged in a drawer for her pencil and notebook. Carrying them back into the living room, she made space on the table in front of her by pushing aside her plate.

The page fell open at the last thing she had written. 'Your mind will naturally resist self-control, but with discipline you can perform acts consciously and deliberately to free you on your journey.' Bethany sighed, as the familiar feelings of irritation and frustration took hold of her. Really, she just couldn't connect with this one. Why did the lesson have to be so obscure and difficult? She didn't want to be like Norman. Norman's discipline was restrictive, stulti-fying. No wonder her mind naturally resisted this. And yet, there was something here, something that related to what she was thinking about.

It seemed to her that her whole life had been a series of repeating patterns. She would begin something with enthusiasm, and then that enthusiasm would fade away, and whatever she had been trying to do became too difficult. Gradually it would no longer seem important, and she would start thinking about some-thing new. When she had first married Norman, she had deter-mined that she would try a new recipe every week. She would experiment with ingredients and spices and produce a variety of tasty and interesting dishes. It was true that Norman had been at first amused, and then impatient with her, and that some of her early efforts hadn't been totally successful. But the reason that she had stopped cooking was that she had let several weeks go by when she was too tired, or too demoralised to try. Then she had told herself that it was too late. If she wasn't going to stick to it regularly, then she wasn't going to do it at all.

It was the same with driving. She had let that go because she disliked confrontation, but also because it had to be all or nothing. Either she would drive the car on a regular basis, or there was no point. Once she had lapsed, there was no starting again. Over and over again, Bethany realised that she began things and then gradually let them go. It was very true that Norman disliked change and treated any innovation with suspicion, but Bethany could not lay all the blame at his door. For the first time, she realised that she acquiesced passively to Norman's need to control because of her own tendency towards perfection. If she once lapsed, then that was the end of it. Whatever she was trying to do was obviously not worth doing, because otherwise she would stick to it. It was all too easy to let him take responsibility for her life, because otherwise she would have to admit that she had a habit of giving up. Better to think that Norman stifled her.

Bethany's eyes grew wide with realisation. When had this begun? She remembered her mother saying to her, 'You go your own way, and your life will end in pieces, as mine has done.' She had defiantly resisted the idea, gone to Brighton, started out so long ago full of hope and longing for life. She was going to do so many things, read so many books, travel so many places, and what had she really done? She had met and lost Oliver. And then she had lost her hopes, her dreams and her conviction that life was an adventure. The pain of that loss had caused her to reach blindly out for someone who could numb her grief, and somehow salve the wounds that were tearing her heart. In marrying Norman she had gained safety, security and routine. But had she really reached out blindly all those years ago, or was it a more conscious choosing? Had she done what she had done so many times since – begun bravely, and then turned back, retreating into the safety of what she knew?

Bethany knew that in choosing Norman, she had chosen some-one who disliked change. She had allowed herself gradually to cease resisting, settling for life without pain, giving up each little venture by slow degrees, slowly descending into passivity. She remembered her mother and her childhood home, shrouded in the mists of defeat and bitterness. Perhaps her acquiescence had begun then, all those years ago as a defence against unspoken anger. Maybe she unconsciously repeated her pattern of giving up when things got difficult because the one time she had tried to pursue her own happiness, she suffered so much that she had nearly lost her mind. Maybe it had begun even before this. When she had defied her mother, she had lost her love. Perhaps the roots of her patterns lay right back at the beginning. Bethany laid down her pencil. There was so much to think about, she could hardly take it in. She closed her eyes and thought of the angel. 'I

161

think I am beginning to understand at last. You are making me understand.' There was silence for a minute before the angel replied

IT IS YOU WHO MADE THE DIFFERENCE.
YOUR HABIT IS TO GIVE UP.
BUT YOU DID NOT GIVE UP; YOU BEGAN AGAIN.

Bethany listened, and then looked back at her notebook again. Because the lessons were so important, it had spurred her on to resist her natural impulse, which was to abandon them. 'But why is it so hard? I didn't even know that this is what I have always done until now. It's so hard to change when you don't know the pattern.'

THE FIFTH LESSON HOLDS THE ANSWERS.
DISCIPLINE IS THAT WHICH MAKES THE ROUGH
PATH SMOOTH.
IT IS WHAT SPURS YOU TO TAKE THE RIGHT ACTION.
IT IS YOUR FRIEND.

Bethany opened her eyes. Suddenly she saw it clearly. She understood what freed her from her patterns. She had been angry, because she did not know that she had a pattern of behaviour which stopped her moving forward. Now that she had the knowledge, she could begin to work out the message of the fifth lesson without resentment. She remembered the fourth lesson of gratitude and how, before she had understood, she had become *less* grateful in her life. It was possible that the same thing had been happening with the fifth lesson. She would have another look at it tomorrow. Bethany felt released from her despondency. Choosing to change was entirely different from being forced into something, and she herself was in charge. Not her mother, and not Norman. Poor Norman, how wrong she was to tell herself that he was the one restricting her, when all the time she was the one choosing not to go forward.

THERE IS MORE.

Of course. There always would be more, she supposed. And she knew what the next stage was. Her memories had taken her to a certain point. It was as though she stood at the edge of a cliff, looking down at the sea crashing below, wanting to turn back and retreat to safer ground. Her fear had always been that if she

162

thought about Oliver, about what had happened, she would step off the edge of the precipice, and all that was solid and safe beneath her would disappear. She would begin falling, and falling, and the dark water would close above her head, and she would be sucked down into a chasm of darkness and despair. The fragile wall that she had built to protect herself would come crashing down, and nameless catastrophes would befall her. Even as she contemplated the possibility of going back into the pain, her heart began to beat faster and her brain warned her insistently that she must beware, be very careful, guard against the impending doom. She tried to face the thought, and it eluded her, leaving her only the familiar feeling of creeping fear. But what if there was no need to be afraid? It was possible that the fear itself had become the nameless shape in the darkness that mustn't be exposed to the light. If she threw open the door, would it turn out to be a delusion after all these years? Would the monster dissolve into nothing, a counterfeit fraud that evaporated when she faced it? Her angel was with her, and she could walk up to the cliff and step beyond safe ground. She did not know what would happen, but she trusted in her angel, and also in her own new-found strength. She would do it, and she would soar on wings out over the sunlit ocean and leave the fear of dark far behind. Tomorrow. It was the first of September, the end of summer and the beginning of autumn. A good time to begin.

Bethany was getting ready for bed when Norman arrived home. She had just slipped on her nightdress and was hanging up her new skirt and blouse when she heard the door open downstairs. She started guiltily. Really, it was awful how little she missed Norman, or minded that his comings and goings were more erratic than they used to be. If anything, she was grateful for his absences. She rebuked herself, and resolved to be especially nice to him when he came up. She glanced at the clock. Nearly 10.45. Poor Norman, he would be very tired. She climbed into bed, turning out the bedside lamp, and waited for him.

Norman was trying to be very quiet. It was after 10.30, and B would have gone to bed. He hoped so, as he really did not want to discuss his lateness with her. He had met Rita after work, and they had talked. She had been distraught because her cat, Muffy, had gone astray, and she did not know which way to turn. Norman had bought her a sweet sherry, and patted her shoulder as she had told him in a faltering voice about dear darling Muffy who was her only love. Norman had racked his brains for comfort, and had suggested putting up leaflets in the neighbouring streets with perhaps a reward. Rita had turned her little face up to him gratefully and said she hadn't thought of that, and what would she do without him to turn to? Dabbing her eyes delicately with a lacy handkerchief, Rita had cheered up and they had talked about other things. Norman had even hinted darkly that all was not easy at home, and Rita had nodded sympathetically, sighed deeply, and replied that she was always there for him if he needed her. After all, he had been there for her and Muffy. Norman felt a glow deep down in his stomach at the delicious possibility of confiding in Rita one day. It had been a delightful evening, but the time had passed all too quickly, and now he had to go upstairs to his wife. He felt rising irritation with Bethany. If only she could be more like Rita.

Norman hesitated at the bottom of the stairs and took off his shoes. He told himself that it was ludicrous that a man should have to be tiptoeing in his socks in his own home, and once again blamed Bethany. When he got to the bedroom, it was dark, and he sighed with relief. Suddenly B turned on the bedside lamp, and he froze in shock, shoes in hand. Failing to notice his discomfort, Bethany had turned to him with an understanding smile on her face. 'Oh poor you, you must be exhausted. Come to bed.'

Norman saw her friendly hand patting the duvet beside her and he recoiled in fright. The possibility that she might be inviting intimacy was appalling. Hurriedly, he forced a smile to his face and made an effort to appear normal. He turned the light out and replied under cover of darkness, 'Yes, I'm very tired. I'll be along in a minute.' In the silence that greeted this riposte he imagined B lying there, quivering with anticipation. Hastily, he continued, 'I'm rather thirsty. I'll go and get a drink of water. You go to sleep.' Dropping his shoes where he stood, he scuttled quickly onto the landing. Listening furtively in case B should follow him, he was relieved to hear no sound from the bedroom.

Norman went downstairs and sat in the kitchen and waited for his wife to fall asleep. Gradually he was aware that the two halves of shandy that he had bought in the pub were putting a strain on his bladder. Thus it was that he found himself standing indecisively at the bottom of the stairs for the second time that evening. He shifted his weight uneasily from foot to foot, listening to the house creaking in the darkness. An orange street lamp cast its light into the hall, staining everything with its livid glow. Finally he could wait no longer for the bathroom and he took the stairs two at a time, trying desperately to be quiet. Throwing caution to the winds, he rushed silently through the bedroom on the tips of his toes. He had almost reached the bathroom when he encountered his shoes and hurtled headlong onto the carpet. He stumbled on his knees into the bathroom and closed the door behind him. He relieved himself, and then put his ear close to the door to listen for any signs of movement on the other side.

To his relief all appeared quiet, and he undressed in the cramped bathroom. Switching out the light, he tiptoed noiselessly to the bed and eased himself inch by inch under his side of the duvet. Once Bethany sighed and turned over, and Norman froze. Only when he was sure that his wife's breathing was deep and steady did he continue his infinitesimal descent onto the mattress. Eventually he was satisfied that his task was accomplished, and he lay there trying to control his uneven breathing in the darkness. In despair, he pondered his life. How had it come to this? It seemed only a few short months ago that all had been well, and that he had lived a regulated, dignified existence. Then Bethany had changed everything out of the blue. There was no rhyme or reason to her behaviour, and it enraged him. His assumption that he and B were united in appreciating their life together had been dismantled by her outrageous conduct and steadfast indifference to his wishes. She had shaken him to his core. For a while he had almost begun to wonder if he had imagined his previous existence with his wife, so changed was she. Luckily, his new relationship with his work colleagues, and particularly Rita, had reassured him that he was the sane, reasoned one, and that his expectations of married life were proper and sensible. The thought of Rita gave him new resolve. He was not going to tolerate this state of affairs for much longer. B had no right to subject him to the kind of indignity he had suffered tonight. Norman thought of Rita again. The way she had dabbed away the merest suggestion of a tear with her spotless white kerchief had been so dainty and neat. Her tiny hand had trembled on his arm as she thanked him for his kindness to Muffy, and he had noticed how her tight white frilly blouse had heaved with emotion. The movement of her breasts beneath the blouse had transfixed him, and it was with difficulty that he had torn his eyes away and taken another gulp of his drink. She aroused strong and tender feelings of protectiveness in him. Norman drifted into a restless sleep, to dream confusedly of fluffy rabbits wearing soft frilly blouses, nestling in soft hollows and burrows and sipping daintily from sherry glasses.

SEPTEMBER

He was gone, and she was alone. She was alone in this grey black room, in the grey black crawling darkness of her mind. The grey world outside was creeping through her brain, or maybe her thoughts stalked the streets, bleeding black onto the pavements. It didn't matter. The rain was moving steadily down the window pane and the roads glistened black like the slate back home. So much black. Strange that the slate was still there somewhere, with her mother in the fog and the mist and the cold. How odd that her mother had been right after all. She had brought disaster on herself, and it was too late to go back.

She leaned her forehead against the cold window and listened to the sound of the wind outside whipping the rain into shudder-ing blasts against the glass. The room behind her grew darker, and she did not switch on the light, but allowed the darkness to seep into the room. The blackness filled the space like an animal, greedily swallowing up the grey and hungrily draining the colour from her surroundings. Still she did not move, but stared with unfocused eyes out into the wind and the rain, listening to the whispering voices. She strained to catch what they were saying, but no matter how long she listened, she could not understand them. But they kept whispering, especially in the darkness, so she concen-trated hard. The insects were crawling inside her head, and they wouldn't stop moving either, so she let them scratch behind her eyes as she waited to understand what had happened. The whisper-ing would tell her if she waited long enough. The insects were gnawing at her mind, and they wouldn't stop crawling.

* * *

On the Saturday she and Oliver had gone to wave the coach off. Sylvia and the others were going home after their week in Brigh-ton. Bethany and Oliver were going to stay on until the end of his holiday. That would be Sunday evening. After he had sorted a few things out, they were going to drive to his parents' home and then they would begin a new life together. Secure in their plans, they

166

had strolled along to meet Sylvia and Roy. The coach was due to depart at midday, but they had arranged to meet earlier in the morning. The four of them walked along the prom, and Sylvia and Bethany fell behind. Sylvia lowered her voice and said, 'Ooh, I can' believe it, it's all been so sudden and so romantic. 'E is really lovely, you can see that by lookin' at 'im.' They both looked at Oliver in easy conversation with Roy. Suddenly Sylvia shivered and clutched at her friend's arm. 'Let's go an' have a drink, shall we? There's loads of time an' I'm all packed an' I really want to talk to you about everythin'.'

Bethany readily agreed and Sylvia called to Roy and Oliver. 'Stop a minute, Roy. Us girls just need to get everythin' sorted out so we'll see you in a little bit.' She patted his arm and gave him a tender kiss on the mouth. Oliver raised his eyebrows and Roy laughed sheepishly, his happiness showing in his eyes.

'I see things have moved on a little,' Oliver said. 'Congratulations.'

Sylvia gave a shriek of laughter, and nudged him so that he almost lost his balance. 'What d'you mean, "congratulations"? I'm not a prize 'e's won, you know.' But she leaned shyly against Roy, who put his arm around her protectively and gave her a squeeze.

'I can't *wait* to go and have a talk,' said Bethany. 'Why don't you two go for a walk or something, and we'll meet you back here in two hours?'

Roy laughed. 'Two hours? Do you think you'll be able to get a word in edgeways, Bethany? You'll barely have covered what she wore on our first evening.' He winked at Bethany as Sylvia opened her mouth to answer and then, as she drew breath, he kissed her again and said. 'All right, all right, I'm only joking. Are you up for a bit of a stroll, Oliver? I'd like to fill my lungs with the sea air before we go, anyway.' Oliver nodded his assent. Unlike Sylvia and Roy, Bethany and Oliver were a little shy of affection in public, so there was a minute pause before Roy, with his usual knack of doing the right thing, slapped Oliver on the back and said, 'Come on then, let's get going and leave them to it.'

Bethany and Sylvia watched the two men as they crossed the road and turned away from them, strolling along the promenade towards the beach. Then they hurried inland, eager not to waste a single moment of their precious talking time. Both were conscious of their imminent parting and the need to reaffirm their friendship before they went their separate ways. As quickly as they could, they found a café and Bethany ordered their hot chocolates while Sylvia went and powdered her nose. As she sat waiting for her friend to

167

return, Bethany wondered when they'd see each other again. Wales seemed so far away, and the life that she was leaving behind already seemed a distant memory. It was as though she was looking at the past through the wrong end of a telescope, making everything seem unreal and tiny. She was poised at the start of a new adventure, and the future was near enough to grasp with both hands.

Sylvia returned just as the waitress was bringing them their steaming drinks, and for a while neither of them said anything. Sylvia blew on the froth on top of her chocolate, and dipped her finger into it. Sucking off the bubbles, she said, 'Are you sure that this is what you want to do? I mean, it is very sudden and all that, and Oliver is lovely, but what do you know about 'im really?' Suddenly interested, she leaned forward and said, 'No, tell, what *do* you know? What does 'e do, bet 'e's got a really posh job, an' where does 'e live, an' where do 'is parents live, an' what are you going to do next, an' where are you going to live, an' are you going to get a job? Oh, this is silly, we 'aven't got nearly enough time for it all an', oh, talk, talk!' She sat back, and took a sip from her mug, her round blue eyes signalling that it was Bethany's turn.

Bethany took a deep breath and began to explain about their pact to live in the present. Before she had got very far she tailed off, noticing Sylvia's horrified expression. 'What, d'you mean to tell me you don' know anything about 'im? Bethany, you're mad, what are you doing?'

Bethany tried again to explain that it wasn't that they didn't know anything about each other, they knew a lot of the important things, enough to know that they would be together, and they weren't going to ignore the practical details for ever. They had met on Sunday evening, and tomorrow evening would be one week from that date. After Oliver had sorted out various arrangements he needed to make, they would meet at the Friends' Meeting House, go for a meal in the restaurant they had eaten at before, and talk and talk and talk, until there was nothing more to say about their mundane lives. Then they would get in the car and drive.

Sylvia was sitting with her mouth open. For a whole minute she said nothing while Bethany waited anxiously. Finally she said, 'Well, it is really romantic, and I suppose it can't do any harm, but promise me you won't go off with 'im if you 'ave any doubts about what 'e tells you. I mean, 'e could be . . . well, 'e could be anything!'

Bethany reached across the table and held Sylvia's hand firmly. 'No, I won't, I promise. Thanks for understanding, I really . . .'

Suddenly she found it hard to carry on, and swallowed a huge lump that had formed in her throat.

Sylvia squeezed her hand hard and her eyes welled with tears. 'No don't, you'll get me started. Ring me, or write to me and tell me *everything*, promise?' Bethany nodded, unable to trust herself to speak, and Sylvia suddenly fished in her bag. 'Well, I don' know why we are wasting time on you, when I'm burstin' with really big news.' She pulled out a small box covered in blue velvet and thrust it across the table. 'Open it, go on.'

Bethany snapped open the lid and let out a gasp of astonishment. There, sparkling in the light was a diamond engagement ring. She looked up and Sylvia burst into peals of laughter. 'Your face! I know, I'm not the one to tell you everythin's very sudden, am I? We're not tellin' everyone till I've 'ad a chance to talk to Mam and Da', so you're not to breathe a word to the others.'

Bethany looked at her friend's dear sweet face, beaming with shy happiness, and stood up abruptly. She lurched around the table and pulled Sylvia to her feet, enveloping her in a warm hug. They held each other tightly for a while, neither able to express their feelings any other way. Then they drew apart. Sylvia was sniffing a little.

''Course, you do know it's Roy we are talking about? I forgot to say that bit.'

Bethany opened her mouth, caught Sylvia's eye and collapsed with giggles. They laughed till their stomachs ached, their drinks cooling in front of them, oblivious to the amused glances of passers-by.

Finally, Bethany managed to gasp, 'No, stop, stop, I can't laugh any more. Seriously, I can't tell you how happy I am for you. Roy is such a good man, and I can't believe I never noticed how right you are for each other until this week. You are going to be so happy, and grow vegetables and keep house, and have lots of children, and grandchildren and . . .'

Sylvia interrupted her, 'Hang on, not so fast, don't make me a grandmother yet, I've still got my figure, and as for vegetables, Roy's not going to be doin' much of *that*, I can tell you. I'm startin' as I mean to go on.' The rest of the hour was taken up with Sylvia's wedding plans, and they steadfastly avoided the subject of Bethany and Oliver. Eventually they knew that it was time to go. Suddenly there were no words, and they paid the bill and set off for the seafront in silence.

When they reached the bus station they could see the familiar knot of people from their group crowding around suitcases. Roy had his clipboard out again, but looked up anxiously as Sylvia and Bethany arrived. Bethany met his eye and held up her engagement finger, beaming, and then gave him the 'thumbs up' sign. Roy broke into a broad grin and seemed about to walk over to them, before being accosted by Doreen, who thought she might have left a case at the Bed and Breakfast. Sylvia and Bethany watched him fondly, as he checked through the baggage and traced the missing case. 'I'm so glad for you,' Bethany said again, and they gave each other another hug.

Sylvia suddenly put her hands over her face and said in a muffled voice behind her hands, 'Look, do you have to wait for the coach to go? I'm not sure I can bear all these goodbyes.'

Bethany had been thinking the very same thing, but had not been able to think how to manage the moment of parting. She looked around for Oliver, who was nowhere to be seen.

As if reading her mind, Roy approached and said, 'Hello, you two. Had a good chat? Oliver wasn't sure if you'd want him around, so he's waiting on that bench over on the prom. He said he'll be right over if you need him.' He looked down at her with eyes that were kind and concerned.

Bethany did not know how to reply, so instead stepped towards him and found herself enveloped in a warm hug. The tears were beginning to roll down her face no matter what she did to prevent them, and as they drew apart she croaked, 'I'm so happy for you. Take care of her, won't you?' Roy cleared his throat and then put his hand in his pocket and pulled out a huge, immaculately ironed white handkerchief. He handed it silently to Bethany, who laughed in spite of her tears. 'How do you do it, Roy? Anyway, I'm going to say goodbye now because we just can't bear hanging around.'

Roy nodded his agreement, putting a protective arm around Sylvia, who was crying openly. 'Go on then, do you want to do a general goodbye, or would you like me to tell them all when we're on our way? They won't notice if you just want to slip off.'

Bethany nodded gratefully. 'I think that would be best, Roy, if you don't mind. You can explain it somehow, and I'll be in touch in the next few weeks. Do you mind?' She gave him another tight hug, and then turned to Sylvia.

Sylvia looked at her and then held out her hands. 'Oh, please don' let's go on too long. Promise you'll write an' ring me, and we'll get together in a few weeks an' talk about wedding plans. It's not like we are never goin' to see each other again, is it? Let's just pretend we are sayin' goodbye after work and go.' It was the strangest after work farewell they had ever had. In spite of Sylvia's brave words, she was sobbing openly, and the tears were pouring down Bethany's face. Finally they broke apart, and Roy took hold of Sylvia's shoulders.

'Now you go and sort out your stuff. I've put it over there apart from the rest, I think I've got it all.' Bethany met his eyes in understanding and watched Sylvia totter over to her pink pile of suitcases and bags. She turned away, and could hear Roy reassuring Sylvia that her mascara hadn't run much; well, not too much anyway, and then heard Sylvia's shriek of dismay when she saw her face in her hand-mirror. One final look back saw Roy shepherding Sylvia onto the coach as she tried to fix her make-up at the same time. Smiling though she felt her heart was bursting out of her chest, Bethany walked away from the bus station towards Oliver.

They spent the rest of that day up on the Downs walking hand in hand along coastal paths and picnicking in a high field among the poppies and cornflowers which were scattered through the waving grass. They bought bread and cheese and salad and a bottle of wine, and soaked up the sunshine, laughing and talking. Late in the afternoon they parked Oliver's car by a little village green and went into a small church. They sat in silence on the cool dark wooden pews and gazed quietly at the stained glass window over the small altar. Both knew that the conversations they shared characterised the ease of their intimacy, but that the silence between them carried the communion of their souls. It seemed that never before had they been so at one with each other, so completely happy in each other's company. In the evening they bought fish and chips and carried them down to the sea's edge. They licked the salt off their fingers and watched the sun sink down into the horizon. Tomorrow they were to spend the day apart because Oliver had things to do.

Both accepted that these arrangements were a necessary bridge from the present to the future, from this perfect week into the practicalities of their life together. One part of each of them even welcomed the next step with eager anticipation. Bethany and Oliver wanted to share their histories. They needed to reveal to the other the places which were special to them alone, the people who were dear to them, and the memories and experiences that made their lives unique. The tapestry of the past had led them to this point, and they wanted to weave the separate strands of their lives together. At the same time both wanted to preserve their idyllic union for the full seven days. They had made a pact, and in so doing had achieved a partnership suspended in time and space for longer than either had thought possible. As this period inevitably drew to a close, and the next stage beckoned, both entered into the game of protecting their intimacy from the outside world with wholehearted conviction. They avoided the subject of tomorrow.

Finally, they walked back to the hotel room which they had booked during the day. Oliver had never been to the Bed and Breakfast, and Bethany did not know where he had stayed. This had been part of the game. They had decided to meet each day without knowing even this much detail about the past. It was only now that the others had gone that it was not practical for Bethany to go back to the Bed and Breakfast alone. Not wanting to go to Oliver's room, they had found a little hotel near the Lanes. Each brought an overnight bag from their own lodgings so that they could be together. The collecting of their luggage could be done at the last minute when they would have Oliver's car.

Only in the final words before they went to sleep in each other's arms did they place the finishing touches to their pact. They would meet at the Friends' Meeting House at precisely the hour at which they had come together one week ago. It would be as if they were again meeting for the first time, and they would discover whole worlds in each other that would be as delightful as the one they knew already. The echoes they had already experienced would be repeated again in a different way. Each would know the other, but not know the other. The choosing of the time and place closed the circle, achieving a symmetry and a finality that was necessary and pleasing to both. It would be both an end and a beginning.

They woke on Sunday morning and smiled into each other's faces. The sunlight shining through the windows and falling in glowing pools on the bed heralded another fine day, and they lay for a time luxuriating in its warmth. After a while they got up, and went down to breakfast together. When they returned to the room, they knew it was time to begin their separate days, and both instinctively hung back from the inevitable parting. They sat together at the end of the bed, and Oliver clasped her hand warmly. 'I think it's time to make a start, don't you?' he said.

Bethany gave herself a shake. 'Yes, you're right, I'm quite looking forward to my last day, really.' Her eyes belied her words, and Oliver moved closer to her, his arm encircling her shoulders.

Suddenly serious, he said, 'You know, we could just spend the day together. It doesn't have to be the way we arranged, we are so close to the seven days after all.' He hesitated, and looked at his watch. Bethany saw him calculating the hours which would have to lapse before they saw each other again, and for a moment she too hesitated. Then, pulling herself together she replied, 'No, we'll be together for the rest of our lives, after all. It's daft to not be able to bear a few hours apart. Besides, I want to buy some presents, and it wouldn't be very interesting. I'm sure it's the same for you. Whatever you have to do is best done alone.'

As Oliver nodded agreement, Bethany reflected how soon the details came crowding in. They were so close to telling each other what needed to be done today. She guessed that Oliver would be telephoning his parents to let them know they would be coming. The thought was strange, a little frightening. She herself wanted to buy some little things for Mr and Mrs Willow as a present from Brighton. She had seen a little shop opposite the Lanes that sold tobaccos and pipes, and another full of china, and noticed that both were open on Sunday from midday. All of this was, as she had said, best done alone. The hours apart would make their reunion all the more joyful. The thought gave her new resolve and she said lightly, 'Look, let's say goodbye here, and I'll be off. I'll see you at 6 o'clock this evening.' They held each other closely for a long while. When they drew apart, Oliver cupped Bethany's face in his hands.

'I'll miss you. I'll be missing you all the time we are apart. I won't be late.' They smiled at each other, gave each other one last hug, and Bethany went down to the street. Looking back up towards their room, she saw Oliver standing at the window. He blew her a kiss, and she set off into the quiet morning.

There was a strong breeze blowing the salt air in from the sea, and instinctively she turned again to the promenade. The sea was a dark blue, with the wind whipping the tops of the waves into white crests. She reflected that every day she had been here the waters and the skies had been completely different, and wondered how long this would go on. She supposed that people who lived here all the time could build up collections of seascapes that they had seen, matching one sky with another that had appeared last week, or noticing the resemblance of the sea today with one last month. They would know that the range of variation was finite, that every possibility had been exhibited before. But what of the patterns of seagulls wheeling across the sky? How could the clouds assemble themselves in exactly the same formation, and how could the curve of the particular wave she could see crashing on the stones this precise minute, ever be replicated? Surely the shapes and colours would go on and on for ever, and never in her lifetime

173

would she see just such a sky, or just such a sea as this again. Bethany lay on her back and watched the seagulls.

She and Oliver would always come back to the sea, she thought. Perhaps they would bring their children for holidays year after year. Children loved the seaside, but perhaps they would visit other beaches, in Devon maybe, or Cornwall, where there was more sand. She and Oliver had walked on the beach late one evening and noticed that, when the tide went very far out, there was enough sand for the children to build castles, but still it would be nice to go somewhere without the stones bruising their soft little feet. She daydreamed about the children she and Oliver would have. She knew instinctively that he shared her love of children.

After a while she stood up and stretched. It was 10.30, and the shop didn't open for an hour or so. Nevertheless, she couldn't sit here all day. She climbed up the stones and crossed the main road into town, an easy task as the traffic was sparse on what was usually a busy thoroughfare. She wandered down the narrow streets looking in shop windows. There was a delicious smell of coffee coming from one of the small cafés. She bought a paper and sat down at one of the little tables set out on the pavement.

Bethany laid the paper down and searched the area immediately around her. She was experiencing a sensation that was entirely new to her. She could feel Oliver's presence close by her, as though he were simply around the corner about to walk into view. At first she had only been dimly aware of something unusual, but the impression of not being alone had gradually grown stronger during the course of the morning. Now that she was sitting still doing nothing, she could almost hear his voice. The sensation was acute, crackling with energy, so strong that she could almost touch it. Involuntarily she looked around, expecting to see him, but of course she was alone. It was a totally novel experience, subtly different from that which had assailed her before she had met Oliver. Before, she had been filled with an overwhelming sense of expectancy, of all-pervading happiness, and of a conviction that something was about to happen. This was something entirely different, more specific, more intimate. She could feel Oliver near her, and it was definitely him, rather than a general sense of not being alone. Bethany had read about telepathy, and wondered if this was how people felt. The more that she thought about it, she was sure that Oliver was feeling her presence too. They were linked together in a way that transcended the limitations of space and time that she was used to.

Suddenly she remembered the intense conviction that she had

174

had early on that she and Oliver had met before. Perhaps this was what she was groping for, this connection that existed between them. It felt so natural that she wondered how she had managed without it. She closed her eyes and tried to imagine what he would say to her now if he were here. For a while she daydreamed, seeing his beloved face in front of her, with his laughing eyes and open smile. All at once, like the instant a dark sky is illumined by the flash of lightning, she was overwhelmed with the feeling that they had indeed been linked together in this way before, and had lost the connection somehow. Her blood chilled and a sudden dread took hold of her. In fear she turned inwardly to him, and was reassured by the immediacy of his presence. A sudden gust of wind flicked her newspaper, and she jumped, opening her eyes hurriedly. She saw that the weather had changed suddenly. The sky, blue either side of her, was dark overhead as a large black cloud obscured the sun. The wind swept a solitary leaf down the pavement, and large drops of rain splattered onto her table. Bethany hurriedly gathered her things together and went into the café to pay her bill. This done, she stood in the doorway and peered at the sky. Although there were fat dark drops of rain falling, the sky looked bright over the sea, and further inland.

The shower would be over before it had properly begun. It served to remind tourists and holidaymakers that summer was almost over, a fleeting messenger from the autumnal season that was almost upon them. The sudden gusts blew the first leaves from the trees, and the seagulls screamed angrily around the dark cloud. Bethany, sheltering in the doorway, remembered the future. She and Oliver had held it back too long, and it seemed determined to rush in on them like the foaming waters of a dam that has been broken. As quickly as the shower had blown up, the skies cleared and people went on their way, blinking in the clear sunlight glancing off the wet pavements, picking their way through bright puddles reflecting the blue above. Gathering herself, Bethany too went on her way, but the gathering clouds seemed to have left a darkness in her day, and she fought a vague unease that she could not name. Still she felt Oliver's presence and gradually her misgivings subsided. She quickened her pace and arrived at the little tobacco shop she was looking for just as the owner was opening up.

She spent a pleasant half hour or so browsing in the tobacco store, and after a while saw the china shop across the road opened by its owner. Eventually she selected a beautiful old pipe with an ivory bowl and a stem polished so that it shone. For Mrs Willow she found an old blue and white china plate with 'A present from Brighton' on it and little seagulls all around the edge. It was so nice that she wouldn't have minded keeping it herself. She waited politely as the owner of the china shop, a tall, thin, stooping man with fumbling fingers, painstakingly wrapped the plate in news-paper, then brown paper, and finally tied the package with thick hairy string. Bethany could picture Mrs Willow unwrapping it, and winding the string again to put in the drawer full of useful odds and ends. Mr Willow might use it for tying back his sweet peas one day. She saw Mr Willow gently unfolding the tissue paper around his pipe and smoothing it out before turning his present over with quiet, deliberate fingers.

So absorbed was she in her thoughts that she was startled to find herself in the dim little shop and not in the welcoming kitchen of her memory. The shopkeeper was waiting to be paid. She handed over her money, and noted with amusement that he rang it into a till where the keys that popped up said '2 Shillings'. It would have made sense of course to make her purchases before the others had left, so that Sylvia could have taken them home on the coach with her. Somehow there had never been the right moment, so instead she would go into a post office tomorrow and post them, together with a letter telling them she was doing well. In a way she preferred this, so that her present and news would come directly from her to them without an intermediary. Standing in the dim light of the china shop, she imagined what she would say to them. She fingered the little tissue-wrapped pipe, laying it down on the counter next to the plate while the shopkeeper counted out her change labori-ously into her hand.

The fear came crowding in on her as she was about to leave the shop. For a moment she was unable to move, but instead stood rooted to the spot, seized by a deep dread which caused her to shudder with panic. Something had happened. Suddenly she turned on her heel and ran blindly out into the road, the shop's doorbell clanging behind her. Gasping for breath, she continued to run back towards the seafront, dodging passers-by and almost falling in her haste. She was so desperate to retrace her steps that she did not hear the faint cry of the shopkeeper behind her, who emerged from his shop holding the brown paper packages aloft with feeble arms.

Bethany ran on, the fear throbbing at her throat, encasing her lurching heart in a vice-like grip that never loosened. All the while Oliver's presence was growing fainter, and fainter, until she could barely sense him. She wanted to stop and feel for him, groping desperately for what was beyond her grasp, but she didn't dare stop running. She reached their hotel. Fighting for breath she halted in the reception in front of a young girl behind the counter. The girl's welcoming smile died on her lips as she noticed Bethany's pale and agitated state. 'My friend. Is he still in our room? I need to go up. Something . . . I need to . . . has he gone?'

The girl looked down with agonising slowness for the hotel register. She moved with languid torpor, her limbs slack and inert. She was barely moving at all, her body appearing to give the impression of being suspended in slow motion. Bethany felt as though trapped in another time-frame. She was like an insect living life at a faster pace than all around her. She could hear her own thoughts whining like a gnat trapped in a room, invisible to the naked eye. She was accelerated by the claws of terror holding her, and the girl standing a few feet away was no longer of her world. Blankly, Bethany stared at her mouth. She was speaking, but the words were a deep droning that were no longer attached to meaning. The meanings were flying around the room like whining insects, and try as she might, Bethany could not weld them to the deep jarring sounds coming from the mouth in front of her. She ran up the stairs and along the corridor. The door to their room stood wide open and she walked in. Oliver's luggage had gone. There was no overnight bag in the corner of the room. She stared at the place it should have been. Her case had also gone. Still the droning continued, rushing in her ears, disconnected sounds with no meaning. She stood still, unable to make her brain function, frozen with fear.

After a while, sensation and comprehension returned. She was sitting on the bed and there were two women with her. One was the concerned receptionist, the other a maid, who had been hoovering their room. The flex of the vacuum cleaner lay in coils, spiralling across the carpet. Although Bethany was returning to normal, and was attempting to concentrate on the words around her, she could only with difficulty wrench her numb mind from the patterns that the flex made on the carpet. They carried the same importance as the voices she could hear.

'She's had a shock. Maybe we should bring up some brandy from the bar? Would you like a cup of tea dear?'

Bethany looked up with dawning understanding and shook her head dumbly.

'I expect there's been a misunderstanding. Your gentleman friend checked out at around midday. Didn't he tell you?' The receptionist spoke kindly, slowly, her hand hovering above Bethany's shoulder. The cleaner had no such reserve. Glad of this welcome diversion from her work, she had plumped herself down on the bed next to Bethany and now gave her shoulders a squeeze.

'What's happened, love, did you leave something behind? I'm sure he's not gone far. Where were you going to meet him?' The naked curiosity in the woman's eyes repulsed her. She stood up shakily, putting her hands down on the counterpane to lever herself up on legs that did not feel like they belonged to her.

'How silly of me. I left something in my bag, and thought I would catch him before he left. Never mind. As you say, I can get it when we meet.'

She turned her head in time to catch the look of disbelief that passed between the two women. Instantly understanding each other, they knew that they had seen this sort of thing before. It wasn't uncommon in Brighton, a young girl misled by a smooth-talking man. Bethany shrank and said, in as cool and dignified a manner as she could manage, 'I am sorry to have troubled you. It was silly of me to have panicked, I'll detain you no longer.' Her lips were stiff and her words felt clumsy. The cleaner's mouth pursed, her eyes hardening, and Bethany knew that the woman did not believe her. Unable to bear the pity in the face of the young receptionist, she drew herself up and walked with unsteady steps back down to the lobby, followed a few paces behind by the girl.

'Are you sure I can't get you anything? I think that Mr Ferris, our manager, is around. Perhaps he can help you?' The girl gestured uncertainly at a closed glass door in the corner of the foyer, and looked as if she needed no prompting to knock on it. Bethany thought she was not a bad girl, merely unwilling to let go of the unexpected drama the situation had provided her with. She wanted to be part of it, to help in some way, and then to regale her friends or her boyfriend with the story. Bethany knew she had to leave quickly.

'No, thank you for your kindness. Do you have the time, please? I arranged to meet my friend at ... at one o'clock somewhere.' The girl looked pointedly at the large clock just above her head, in full view of Bethany's vision.

'It's half past one,' she said.

Bethany found herself sitting on the beach with her back to the stone sea wall, scarcely knowing how she got there. The sun was shining, the skies had cleared, and the brief shower of the morning might never have happened. She stared at the sea until her eyes hurt to look at it. The water was reflecting the clear sunlight like a hard glinting sheet of metal. She took a deep breath and closed her eyes. Gradually calming down, she told herself that what had happened was ridiculous. Everything was perfectly all right. She and Oliver had discussed their plans and she knew that he was planning to check out of the hotel that morning. How stupid of her to have reacted so illogically, so strangely, and made such a scene in front of the hotel staff. One day, when she and Oliver were old and grey, they would laugh about it, and he would tease her about how little faith she had had in him, in their future together. And yet . . .

Bethany pressed her hands to the side of her head until it hurt, and forced herself to examine the facts. Here she was, barely four hours since they had parted and less than five hours before they met again, in a blind panic about losing him. She had nothing to go on, absolutely no reason to feel this way. The gripping feeling she had in her stomach was perhaps nothing more than hunger pangs, and she wasn't going to allow herself to think anything otherwise. She had to gain control over her body, stop the shuddering panic which caused her skin to crawl. She would not allow herself to give in to this irrational fear. She would force herself to go on as though nothing had happened. Nothing had happened. Nothing was wrong.

She moved automatically through the streets by an effort of will. Eventually she realised that she was walking with no direction or plan, afraid that stopping would force her to pay attention to the frenzied thought that hammered repeatedly in her head. She must eat. Buying herself something to eat would give her a reason to walk. She went into a shop but realised that she was staring at the cabinet in front of her, her arms limp by her sides. She had no idea how long she had been standing there. Blinking her eyes hard brought her back to the present, and she bought a sandwich and a drink. Now she would find a park to eat it in. Concentrate on what needs to be done, she thought, desperately blocking out the insistent question in her head.

Bethany walked for miles in search of somewhere. She hesitated on street corners, seized by indecision. She remembered seeing a park one day when she and Oliver were walking, but couldn't think how long it would take her to get there from where she was. She set off in one direction, then decided that it was too far to walk, and turned back. She looked at her watch. It was only two o'clock. Of course she could walk to the park. She had hours and minutes and seconds to fill before she saw him again. She retraced her steps. Her bag was heavy on her shoulder and she was tempted to stop and eat on the pavement. She stopped, and then realised that once the sandwich was gone, she had to find something else to do. Now that she had come this far, she would keep going. Finally she found a stretch of green by a children's playground, and sat uneasily on the grass. She wondered why she had come this far just to eat, when she wasn't even hungry any more. Everything seemed pointless. She looked at her watch, then castigated herself for her foolishness. She peeled the cellophane from her sandwich packet, and drank her bottle of water. It was an effort to swallow every mouthful and she concentrated on the act of eating. And then, only when there was nothing more to do, no meaningless actions with which to avoid the inevitable, she was forced to face the fact that something was wrong. She couldn't feel Oliver's presence any more. Shortly after one o'clock she had felt his absence. There was quite simply a blank space where he had been. Where was he? What had happened?

Bethany spent the rest of the afternoon waiting. The minutes ticked by with agonising slowness, and her eyes ached from staring at her watch. She walked without knowing where she went, and remembered nothing of the things she had seen. At five o'clock she took up her place on the bench outside the Meeting House and continued to wait. She steadfastly refused to listen to the voice inside her that said that he would not come, was never coming. Instead she willed herself to be with the part that would not give up hope, would never give up, not if she waited all her life. If Oliver did not meet her, then something must have happened to him. He had promised he would come, and she would be there waiting when he did. She looked at her watch again. There was still half an hour to wait. It wasn't even time yet. She would not give in to the fear.

The light left the sky and the darkness crept into the garden as the hours slipped away. She waited motionless, while her limbs grew numb and cramped and the pain in her head threatened to explode out from her eyes into the world beyond. The coldness began to seep into her body, and still she didn't move. After a while it began to hurt to breathe. The effort of breathing in, and then breathing out, seemed too hard. She stared with unfocused eyes out into the darkness, the pain holding her chest like a vice. The hours passed. At some time during the night a stranger approached, but she did not hear his words. She was waiting only for Oliver, and it seemed to her that she would not see or hear anything until she could see or hear him. Shortly before dawn it began to drizzle with soft rain. There was a grey light somewhere

180

on the horizon, although the garden was still dark. Still Bethany waited, unable to leave. She held herself very still. If she moved, the pain would surely crush her.

Finally the dawn arrived. The street sweepers began to clean the wet streets and the still air was broken by the shouts of men and vans delivering to the shops nearby. The first seagulls began to scream. Bethany turned her head and focused her eyes. Numbly she groped for a thought. She must stand up. Then she must walk, pushing her feet forward, moving to a place that was not here. She barely understood the impulse that forced her to get up, battle with the pain in her cramped limbs, compelling her to move away from the bench in the garden. Blindly, moving like an old woman, Bethany began to walk. She fixed her eyes ahead of her and did not look back. She returned to the Bed and Breakfast room that she had shared with Sylvia. She stood in the dark foyer and waited for someone to come. She did not notice the odd looks she received, but stood motionless, staring ahead of her. She could not remember what happened next, but later thought that someone must have recognised her and given her a key to her room. She moved her cold wet limbs down the corridor and fumbled with the key. Her suitcase was still in the corner of the room, and she lay down on the bed. Her head burned with pain, and her body shuddered, but she did not close her eyes. If she closed her eyes, the dark would come and she would be lost. She would never find her way out of the darkness again. She stared unseeing at the ceiling.

Hours passed. The whispering began. At first she was indifferent. Nothing mattered any more, because he was gone. She carefully walled up the thought and returned to staring ahead of her. She must not think, she must not move. She would guard herself carefully in case she entered the darkness. Later the insects began crawling behind her eyes. She did not know what to do. She must not go into the dark.

At some point she ran down the corridor to the small bathroom and was sick. The sweat from her cold forehead dripped onto the linoleum and she grasped the toilet bowl with shaking arms. The pain that was in her head and chest now enveloped her whole body, her stomach cramped with waves of excruciating nausea. She retched over and over, convulsed with agony. At last she stopped, and lay down on the cold floor. All her strength had gone. In the emptiness that was her body and mind, the thoughts flowed, and she watched them dispassionately in a moment of lucidity. He was gone, and she was alone.

Bethany laid her hands across her navel. She could feel the blood pulsing, the insistent rhythm of life beating on and on. She had no desire to live and yet she had no choice. She could not die, and therefore she must live. Because of this she must find out what had happened to him, must not leave until she knew. She must get strong again. Turning onto her side, she used her weary arms to push herself up. She stared into the mirror, and splashed cold water onto her face. Shivering, she let herself out of the bathroom and went along the corridor. On the way back she met a maid cleaning the rooms. The doors were open, and there were piles of sheets on the carpeted corridor. Bethany put her hand out to the trolley full of soaps and teabags to steady herself.

'Excuse me,' she said. The sound that issued from her dry throat was a mere croak, and she had to repeat herself before the maid heard her and turned. 'Excuse me,' she said for the third time. 'I am not well. I think I need to spend a bit of time in my room. I hope this isn't inconvenient. Please, could you try to see that I am left alone?' Exhausted by the effort of speaking, Bethany swayed as her vision swam. Red and black circles started to float off the carpet and press around her neck. She wanted to sink down into the red and black, but she knew she had to get back to her room. Turning around, dimly aware of the maid saying something behind her, she muttered, 'Please, I will be all right if I can go to bed. Please leave me alone. I'm sorry to be rude . . . please.' She found the door to her room wide open, just as she had left it in her flight to the bathroom. She closed it carefully behind her, and began to pull off her wet clothes. She climbed into the bed, pulled the covers around her shaking body, and closed her eyes.

She did not know how long she stayed there in the room. She knew that someone knocked on the door once and that she had replied. She listened to the footsteps dying away down the corridor and then drifted back into the fevered dreamlike visions of Oliver that consumed her. She saw the shadows move across the room and thought that day drew to a close and the night began, but she did not know for sure. She saw it was day again because she stared dry-eyed at the patch of blue sky she could see from the window. Gradually her mind came to distinguish between her waking nightmare, and the ones she had while she slept, and gently she began to test her strength. She tried to contemplate a world without Oliver and held the thought for as long as she could. Each time the anguish overcame her and she retreated into her world of visions, but always she returned to the room in which she lay. Slowly, painstakingly, she gathered together frail shreds of courage, drawing pathetically fragile defences around herself, attempting to shield her mind from the marauding demons in the darkness.

She opened her eyes. It was light, and from the angle of the sun's rays streaming in through the window, it was late morning, or even afternoon. There was a small golden window of light glowing on the muddy carpet that she could see without turning her head. She knew that the sun had to be high in the sky for it to cast light like that, because the buildings were high and blocked out the sun in the early morning. She watched the little squares of light for a while, watching the dust motes whirling like tiny beings in a miniature ocean. She tried to focus on one single speck, following its path, but she lost it among the crowd of other specks. She imagined that they were alive like her, and that there was some other huge being watching her just like she was watching them. All she was was a tiny speck of dust, her suffering minuscule and insignificant. Again she laid her hands across her navel, knowing that she was alive. She had lost Oliver and, although in her heart she knew that they would not meet again, a part of her needed to know what had happened to him. She knew deep inside her that he must have died. Nothing else would explain the emptiness she felt. It would be impossible for them both to be alive and not to experience the connection between them. So now she had a task to perform, and then she had to begin the rest of a life lived without him.

Bethany sat up wearily. She was weak from lack of food and drink, and her skin was dry and shivery, but the fever had left her mind and her body. She knew she would have to go slowly, muster her strength and guard it carefully lest she find herself unable to complete her labours. The first thing would be to wash herself, and to put on clean clothes. Then she would arrange to stay a little longer at the Bed and Breakfast, and get something to eat and drink. Then she would see. If she felt strong, she would go out. If not, she would come back to this room and rest until her resolve strengthened. She would take each step like this, not going too far ahead into the future but doing the little she could manage. Suddenly the aching sorrow pierced her again, and the weight of her grief pressed down on her like an iron vice. Tears rose in her throat and eyes, and she gasped in pain. She must not be caught unawares like this. If she allowed herself to think about what she might have had, her heart would break under its crushing burden. She could not accomplish what needed to be done if she thought of him. She must block out what had been. What had happened was irrecoverable, gone, and she must not hold on to it. They had held back the future together once, and she must now block out the past alone.

And so Bethany began the slow process of finding out what had happened to Oliver. Such was her single-minded determination to preserve her fragile strength for the task in hand, she never once contemplated going back to Wales, or ringing Sylvia for help. She could only afford to hold on to the way she had chosen to move forward. If she once let go, she would fall back into the darkness. There were days where she did nothing but lie on her bed, fighting with every ounce of her determination for the strength not to be beaten down by her burden. She could not allow the tears oozing tiredly from her aching eyes to become a torrent carrying her away into uncontrollable grief. On other days she was able to do more. She retraced her steps to their hotel and found that Oliver had taken his car from the car park at about 12.30, and checked out. She sat on her bed for hours attempting to remember the registration number plate of the car, hoping against hope that she would recall some information that would help her track him further. She stood outside the police station once, but turned away in despair after minutes of indecision. She could not go to the police. What could she say, other than that she had known a man who had disappeared, whose name was Oliver. The hospitals would not be able to help her either, because she did not know what she was looking for.

Every day she went to the Meeting House. She sat for an hour or so, and then walked through the streets of Brighton, stopping and looking everywhere she and Oliver had been. She went down to the sea and stood at the water's edge, narrowing her eyes against the glare in the hope that she might see his beloved figure strolling down to meet her. She did all of this in spite of her conviction that she would never see Oliver again. She knew that a part of her would always be waiting for him at their meeting place, even though she might never go there physically again.

Finally, Bethany had to face the fact that she could no longer stay in Brighton. The weeks passed, and her supply of money was dwindling. She could not afford to stay at the Bed and Breakfast. The summer was over, and the town was shutting up its tourist attractions and settling into autumn. She was reminded of Oliver in every turn of every street. Even the wild keening cries of the gulls carried an unbearable memory, rending the wind-tossed sky with bitter calls of loss and grief. She would never give up, but she must face the fact that she would never know how they had lost

184

each other. She must summon every particle of resolve and move on.

And now Bethany wrestled with the decision that would affect the rest of her life. She was standing on a path that took her on towards the future. It divided sharply, one way leading back to the home she had left, and the other leading into the future towards a destination she could not see. She had to decide what to do. She thought of Mr and Mrs Willow, and Sylvia and Roy and all the friends she had left behind. They cared for her and she could turn to them. She would probably be able to get her old job back at the sorting depot. But if she did that, what would it mean? Of all the people back home, only Roy and Sylvia knew Oliver. Everyone else would know nothing except that she had lost him. The loss of Oliver would be more a part of her life than the time they had together, and every day she would be reminded of his absence. She could not bear the agony of being talked about, or tolerate being the object of their pity. If she returned she would have to explain, and see the thoughts in their eyes. She would be face to face with what had happened, and everyone would know. She would never be able to hold him secretly in her heart.

Bethany went over and over the decision in her mind. One night, she was sitting in her room, looking at the suitcase she had never unpacked, and her thoughts returned to the moment that Mr Willow had given it to her. She remembered the evening in their kitchen when he had tipped out their money onto the table. Suddenly she heard Mrs Willow's voice. 'Leavin' now is the natrel way of things, and you 'ave to take your chance to make a new life for yourself. Go, and don't come back until you've made somethin' of yourself.' It was almost as if her friends were standing in the room with her. Bethany let out her breath with a heavy sigh, and then went over to her case and snapped its lid shut. She would settle her bill tomorrow. Then she would go to London. She would not buy a return ticket.

Bethany rose early in the morning and walked the streets to the Meeting House. She stayed for an hour, her heart aching, and then threaded her careful route back towards the sea. She went to the sea's edge and waited one last time until she could no longer bear the ache in her throat and chest and felt she must cry out loud with the pain. She held her head back and stared at the gulls for as long as she was able, offering the past up to them so that they would fly away with it into the freedom of the wide sky. Her eyes were pierced with the whiteness of their wings, and her heart by the hope in their flight. She returned to the Bed and Breakfast, paid her bill, and carried her case slowly along to the coach station. She did not have long to wait after buying her ticket, and climbed wearily on board the bus which would take her away from Brighton, to a future about which she neither knew nor cared. All she knew was that her surroundings would no longer forcibly remind her of what she had lost, and that she was leaving Oliver further behind.

She put her face against the window and stared down at the ground outside. She was so tired she could barely take in her surroundings, and thankful that she had to make no more decisions for a while. It was a weekday morning and the coach was half empty, so Bethany put her bag on the seat beside her and leaned her head back gratefully. Absentmindedly she watched a pair of teenagers outside the window. They were kicking a can around on the ground, elbowing and jostling one another and raising their voices in laughter and shouts. In the pushing and shoving, one girl tripped in front of a woman who was carrying bags in each hand and almost fell on top of her. She apologised awkwardly to the impatient woman, and then collapsed with laughter as her friends jeered at her good-naturedly. One boy kicked the can harder than the rest, and it rolled under the coach. He shrugged his shoulders indifferently and then joined the larger group, who were sharing a large parcel of chips wrapped in paper. Their voices grew loud as they fought over the packet, and in the turmoil the outer wrappings came loose and dropped on the ground. Bethany turned her head away as an official shooed the teenagers away. They retreated with a burst of catcalls and whistles, and their laughter died away, leaving the coach station quiet again. The coach driver was approaching the bus, and Bethany closed her eyes once more. The hiss of the doors told her they were about to be off, and she held herself still as the coach began to move, taking her away from what she had loved.

The bus drew away. The coach station was empty. The paper wrapping discarded by the teenagers blew across the tarmac and came to rest against a bin, where it was caught. It fluttered forlornly in the wind, crumpled and greasy, but still recognisable as the front page of a local newspaper. There was a photograph of a car, so twisted by impact that the make was unidentifiable, and the headline read 'Puzzle of Mystery Car Crash Baffles Police'. Bethany would have recognised the bags flung onto the grass verge. But Bethany was not there to recognise it. She was on a coach that was taking her away from her past, towards London and a new life.

The coach ate up the miles quickly and it seemed to Bethany no time at all before she was propelled into the noisy hubbub of

Victoria Coach station. She hesitated, looking around her at the swarms of people rushing backwards and forwards, weaving around each other impatiently in their efforts to get somewhere quickly. They knew where they were going, and what they planned to do next, and were paying no attention to all the other people doing the same thing. Bethany stood still for only a few minutes, but already felt herself to be blocking some invisible path necessary for the relentless progress of the people around her. The coach had drawn away almost immediately its load was disgorged, and the space it had occupied was instantly filled with a steady stream of people intent on manoeuvring past her. Bethany removed herself from the mêlée by taking her case over to a wall covered with peeling posters advertising events long gone, and old timetables which were out of date. Someone had stuck a blob of grey chewing gum over 'Departures'. There was a polystyrene cup oozing brown liquid onto the dirty marbled flooring, and she gingerly pushed it aside with her foot, placed her case on the ground, and sat down on it. A cold draught was blowing from somewhere, and she could feel the dirt from the air settling on her skin. Already her hands felt grimy, and the air she inhaled was stale after the salty breezes of the previous weeks.

Bethany had never been in a city before, and the sheer numbers of the people around her, and the cacophony of noise generated by the coaches echoing in this high-roofed, arching space confused her. She sat on her case and realised that she was totally anony-mous. If she were to stay here for hours, no one would notice. She had no plan and no place to sleep tonight. The tenuous feeling of security that Brighton had afforded her was gone, and she was suddenly sharply aware of the seriousness of her situation. For the first time in days her mind was forced out of its numbness, and she began to think clearly. She must make a plan. Bethany rummaged in her bag and found a pen, but she had no paper. She looked out of the concourse and could see a large stationer's across the busy road opposite. A few yards along the road she could see a burger bar. The first thing to do would be to make a list of her immediate priorities, and then take practical steps to achieve each item on the list. When she knew what she was doing tonight, she would concentrate on tomorrow morning. When she had solved the problem of the morning, she would turn her attention to the afternoon. The future would tick by, minute by minute, and she would be able to cope.

Shouldering her bag, she picked up her case and set off out of the station. Immediately she had to watch where she was going, adjusting her pace to those in front and behind her, and dodging those coming out of the crowd towards her. Bethany had never been among so many people. She reached the edge of the road, and crossed with a throng of people pushing her from behind and jostling her case. Suddenly there was a blaring of horn, and a black cab screeched to a halt beside her. The driver was yelling angrily and his face was distorted and red. She could not hear what he was shouting because he kept his hand pressed on the deafening horn all the while, but his gestures told her a great deal. She hurried on to the middle section of the road, and then nervously tried to negotiate a way across the second half. Buses, cars and taxis streamed past at an alarmingly fast rate, and some were so close that she was afraid they would hit her. There was a brief gap in the steady flow, and she followed a young man with a newspaper in the pocket of his brown mac as he ran across. With difficulty she lugged her case as fast as she could, and paused panting on the pavement. She was not sure if she would get used to this.

After buying herself a small pad of paper, she got herself into the burger bar with difficulty. She realised that finding a locker for her case would have made things easier. The Formica tables and padded benches were all bolted to the floor, and the only place for her case was in the gangway, but Bethany reasoned that the place was fairly empty and that she was unlikely to be here long. She took a sip from the coffee which the pink-aproned waitress had brought her, and winced. It was very strong, and not hot. However, it gave her the excuse to sit down and devise a plan of action. Momentarily, her hand shook as she wrote 'List of things to do' at the top of her paper. She stared at the sheet. She told herself mechanically that there was no need to be daunted if she took one thing at a time.

Bethany wrote:

1) <u>Find a job.</u>
Go to an agency? Tell them I can type and have had
office experience.   Proof?
Can I take a test, or do I need to bring paper qualifications?
2) <u>Find somewhere to live.</u>
Look in shop windows for cards? Go to agency?
Look in newspaper?

A man lurched into the bar and leaned against the nearest table. He carried a paper bag with a bottle in it, and he was talking loudly. Bethany noticed that the backs of his shoes had been cut off so that they would fit his feet. He was telling anyone who would listen that he was hungry, was dying for lack of food. His voice rose in a plaintive slur. The blonde-haired waitress, who had been standing at the rear of the room behind a counter with a hot water canteen on it, now marched forward and told him in no uncertain terms that if he wanted to pay and sit down she would get him something to eat, but otherwise he should get out. The man cast his eyes around wildly and saw Bethany. Hastily she looked down at her paper, ashamed of herself but unable to cope with talking to him. A strong smell began to drift towards her.

Bethany got up abruptly. She had made a start on her list and she didn't want to stay here any longer. She knew that she had barely enough emotional strength to do what she must do, and could not try to help anyone else. All the same, the sense of shame rose hotly in her and she trembled with misery. She had never before ignored someone in need the way she was doing. Fumbling in her purse, she left some coins on the table and picked up her heavy case again. Avoiding the eyes of the waitress and the drunk, she shouldered her way out of the door. Her heavy bag swung against him as she passed, and he staggered back. She could smell the fumes on his breath but stared ahead of her, pretending he didn't exist. The was a lull in the traffic, and emboldened by her misery she half walked, half ran across the road. At the entrance to the bus station she looked back. The man was now sitting on the pavement outside the stationer's, and people were stepping over him to get past. He was on the ground, and they could look straight ahead of them without seeing him. Standing up, he was an annoyance, an embarrassment; down on the pavement he was invisible.

Her heart ached. She turned on her heel and went in search of a locker. Her case safely bestowed, she went back outside and crossed the road again. She got out her purse and bent down next to the man, who looked up at her with rheumy eyes. She pressed the money she had in her hand into his, wordlessly. His eyes widened and a look of recognition passed between them. 'God bless you, my love,' he mumbled, and she shook her head, close to tears.

'I'm so sorry.' She tailed off. She wanted to tell him that she was sorry not to be able to do more, to explain that she had nothing to give him, but she could not find the words. He was slurring with gratitude and grasped her arm as he stood up with difficulty.

' 'S all right, you're a little angel, 's all right, you've got a lucky face, you'll be lucky, I know.' She disengaged herself from his grip and moved away, breathing the air away from him gratefully. He raised his voice again in order to shout down the road after her. 'She's an angel, you know. She's got a lucky face, a lucky face.'

Bethany felt drained and hopeless. She had known she would make no important difference to the drunk, and he had been so grateful that she had given him money. The coins, and maybe the human contact, had at least made a small portion of his day better. She was beginning to get used to the idea that one could measure a life in small parts of days. He was probably doing just what she was to get through. They were not so different in spite of outward appearances. As she walked along, with little idea of where she was going, she reflected on the urgent necessity of finding a job. Her money would not last forever. On a street corner she stopped and looked around her. She was not in the touristy part of London that she recognised from brochures and advertisements. Nor was she in a residential area. Huge dark buildings with blackened windows blocked the light from the sky and overshadowed the pavements and narrow roads. Clearly this was not an area where she would find a place to live, and it was impossible to know from looking at the buildings what kind of offices they were. Bethany breathed shallowly. She hated the air here, could feel and smell the pollution and grime entering her lungs.

This was no good. She was not coming any closer to her goal of accomplishing the items on her list. She did not even know what she was looking for. It was all too big, too unfamiliar. The only way she could survive was to cut things down into manageable pieces. She dared not look too hard at her whole situation, but instead decided she must deal with smaller things. She could cope with minutes and hours, not days and months. She could manage small roads, small towns, small communities but not this sprawling metropolis with its densely packed populace. The teeming city would engulf her with its size, and she would drown in its anonymity. Bethany sank down on her heels. She felt exhausted and weak, dwarfed by the buildings around her which denied her light and air with their towering size. She was negated by the city, the crowds and the traffic, and knew that she could not stay here. She was not strong enough, might slide in her pain into the city's dark places, and then she would become invisible like the man she had met. She knew it really could happen to her that easily, and could barely summon up enough energy to care. She had to find somewhere smaller, but she needed to think properly this time. She could not afford to go blundering from place to place without a plan. Who could she ask, and what did she want?

Wearily, she retraced her steps yet again and returned to the coach station. She noted with relief that the tramp had gone, and she went into the stationer's. At the end of the ranks of newspapers and magazines there was a rack of books, luridly coloured, thick paperbacks whose jackets were designed to entice the traveller to pass his journey flipping through their thin pages. Beyond these was a small map section. Bethany browsed through them, finally picking up a thin, spiral-bound map titled 'London and the South East.' She was looking for a small town or even a suburb, where the lodgings would not be too expensive, and there would be local offices where she could find work. It was hard to tell from looking at the map what kind of places they were. Finally, Bethany took out her paper and pen and began to write down the names of suburbs and towns. It was as good a way as any, she thought. She didn't have that many options.

Armed with her list, she crossed the road yet again to the coach station, and went over to the information office. There she found a young man in a turban who looked at her through his glass partition in some puzzlement. 'Excuse me, you are asking me if I know any of these places, if I have been to these places?' He shook his head from side to side. 'Why is it that you are asking?'

Bethany smiled at him helplessly. 'I know that it does seem a peculiar thing to ask you, but I've never been to London before. I have to find work, and somewhere to stay, and I don't want to be in the city. I want to catch a bus, a short ride from here, less than two hours, say, and find a place where I can live and work, not too big a place . . . ' She broke off, aware that her words sounded strange even to her. She glanced around, hoping desperately that there was no queue of people behind her requiring this kind man's assistance. There was no one.

She turned back to see that he was studying her paper closely. 'No, no, I am indeed sorry, but I have never been to any of these places you are writing about. But I can tell you that you could not get a direct bus to here, or here. You would have to make a connection.' He made a neat line next to two of the destinations she had queried. 'And it would take . . . ' He quickly flipped through two pages of a thick manual he had in front of him, ' . . . two hours and fifteen minutes to go here . . . ' He made another neat line and then looked up at the clock on the wall behind him. 'But if you wish to be travelling to this place, there is a coach waiting at bay number eight which will be departing in exactly five minutes . . . ' He looked at her doubtfully and said, 'But I cannot tell you if it is a good place to live, because I have never been there myself.' Gratefully Bethany thanked him. The young man had been genuinely kind, and she once again felt close to tears. She told him that she would buy a single ticket. Before he returned her list, he made a neat tick next to the destination she had chosen.

Bethany retrieved her case from its locker, quickly found the bus and gave the driver her luggage. Realising that she knew nothing of her destination, she waited until he had finished loading the cases and then asked him timidly if he would tell her when they reached Sutton High Street. She then found a seat, and waited the few short minutes until they departed. She looked at her watch. She had spent only an hour at Victoria, and it was still only mid-morning. She had time to look around the town for work, or at least, a place to stay, well before it got dark. She had made a start. Fishing out her crumpled piece of paper with her list on it, she wrote underneath her first two objectives: '3. *Find a small town or suburb.* Get on a bus and go to SUTTON'.

She then put a tick against what she had just written, and put the paper back in her bag. She had accomplished the first small segment which would be her future. Suddenly, she felt great waves of tiredness wash over her. She fought her need for sleep. For weeks now it had been this way. She could not sleep at night, listening to the insects in her head, which crawled through the hours of darkness carrying their burdens of vain hope, frantic grief and bitter regret. The grey dawn light brought her relief from the darkness, but none for the cold despair in her heart. Then during the day she was overcome with hopeless lassitude, and fell in and out of sleep in spite of her attempts to stay awake. If only she could become so exhausted that she would slip into oblivion during the hours of darkness. Everything she had ever read about grief told her that time would heal her, but until it did she had to endure the grinding exhaustion that filled every week and month. She forced herself to bear the misery of endless days by cutting them into small sections of minutes and hours, but she could do nothing to banish the gnawing insects who stole her nights. They held her in a vice-like grip, endlessly marching through the darkness, feeding from her despair until she knew for certain that she was losing her mind. Each morning the grey light brought sanity again, and the cold realisation that she must drag herself through another interminable day of aching misery. She could cry no more tears for Oliver, but she ached for him every hour of every day.

Bethany woke with a start from her doze, and reached automatically for her bag. The driver had called out that they were reaching her destination, and she struggled hurriedly into her coat, which she had been too tired to take off properly. She had slipped out of the sleeves but stayed sitting on it, so it was creased and bunched up underneath her. Her mind felt fogged and confused, her head throbbing with a dull ache. Her mouth was dry and tasted unpleasant. She shivered involuntarily, her skin covered with goose pimples. Sleep had enveloped her in its own warmth, and now the air felt cold on her skin. Shouldering her bag, Bethany made her way down the gangway of the coach and stepped off the bus into yet another bus station. She knew that she could not continue this aimless wandering, and hoped that this destination would provide her with what she needed to piece her future together.

Her watch said two o'clock. She picked up her case and looked around her. Her experiences at Victoria told her that she should find a place to leave it while she investigated the town, but there did not appear to be any lockers. She reluctantly decided that she would have to carry it, and hesitated, undecided as to her first move. She looked up and down the road, which was lined with small shops and offices, looking for a newsagent or employment agency. It all appeared to be fairly anonymous – a small town street that could be duplicated anywhere in England – which gave Bethany courage. How difficult could it be to find somewhere to stay? Sure enough, in the first newsagent's window she came to, there were cards with 'Rooms to Rent' written on them. She put her suitcase down and studied them, without much idea of what she was looking for. Some of the notices were handwritten, some poorly typed on lined postcards, and nearly all stated who the owners would not rent a room to. At first sight it appeared that the good residents of Sutton were most particular about their lodgers. Some stipulated 'No pets', others 'No children or babies', still others 'no smokers', 'no couples' and often 'no DHSS'. One had 'No non-white' written in red biro across the bottom. Bethany eyed them doubtfully, and then got out her pad and paper. Some had telephone numbers at the bottom, others a single line of address. She jotted down the telephone numbers from three cards, thinking that they would come in useful when she had found some work.

She shouldered her bag again, and walked on with her case. Up ahead she could see a bright blue sign which looked as though it might be some kind of agency. If so, she would not have far to walk, and she could at least find out what the prospects of getting employment might be. The sign turned out to be for a travel agent, but Bethany went in anyway and asked if there were perhaps a secretarial agency in the town. The young girl at the desk, who was dressed like an air hostess in bright scarlet jacket and blouse, with a blue and red spotted tie at the neck, had some difficulty with her accent. She raised her eyebrows and said, 'Pardon?' Bethany repeated her question, and could see the girl mentally translating her words. This surprised Bethany, because she had never been aware that she had an accent. She had always presumed that her speech was accentless, because it lacked the twang of the Welsh valleys that Mr and Mrs Willow, and Sylvia and her family, possessed. For the first time she felt foreign, and the unfamiliar sensation unexpectedly strengthened her resolve. She had an identity, even though she was in a strange land and all alone. She waited patiently as the girl spelled out the directions with raised voice. Then she thanked her and turned on her heel, holding her head high.

Bethany followed the street names she had been given and after five minutes or so began to wonder if perhaps she had misunderstood. Just as she was about to give up and retrace her steps, she noticed a plain dark green door set into the wall with an entry-phone button at the side. Against the top button was a rather grubby label which read 'Minsles Secretarial'. Gathering her courage, Bethany pressed the button and, after a short pause and a buzzing noise, she pushed the door open. Immediately in front of her stairs led straight up to another door. With difficulty she got her case inside and shut the door to the street behind her. Suddenly she was plunged into darkness. She felt panic rise up in her. Surely she wasn't meant to go up in the dark? What if the top door was locked and she was stuck ludicrously on these narrow steps with no exit and no way forward? Firmly taking a grip on herself she fumbled around on the wall next to her and found a large round button. She pressed it and the lights came on. Bethany let out her breath in an uneven sigh, and then struggled up the stairs to the door at the top. Putting out her hand to open it caused her almost to lose her balance, as it was not latched and swung easily open and banged against the wall. It appeared to be made of hardboard. Bethany looked around her. She realised that she was sweating and shaky, and put down her case quickly.

She was in a small room without windows. Three of the walls were covered in a brown patterned wallpaper, and on the fourth there was a large noticeboard densely covered with pegs, coloured cards, maps, newspaper clippings and flyers. Some were old and curled, others appeared fairly recent, but all were pinned one on top of the other like a patchwork collage or quilt. Some of the pegs were unequal to the task required of them, and appeared ready to drop onto the floor together with the bundle of papers they held. The floor was covered with grey linoleum and there was a row of chairs against the wall opposite the board. Directly in front of her there was a small cubicle, made up of a counter, and a glass screen which slid open and shut. At the moment it was open, and there was a small lady peering interestedly at her from over the counter.

Bethany moved her case carefully to the edge of the room where it could not be in anybody's way, and approached the cubicle. She smiled and said, 'Hello.'

The little woman put her head on one side and smiled back. She took a sharp breath in through her nose and then replied, 'Minsles Secretarial, how may I help you?' through pursed lips. The phrase was delivered with a full stop at the end of it, rather than a question mark, and Bethany paused, rather disconcerted. The little woman pronounced her words in a sing-song voice that momentarily took Bethany back to the school playground. It was very like the melodic chanting of the skipping games she had watched Sylvia and the other girls singing at school. Like those schoolyard rhymes, the phrase had been spoken many times before, so often that the words ceased to have meaning of their own, but were merely an opening refrain necessary to prefix more relevant conversation.

Sure enough, as Bethany opened her mouth to speak, the telephone rang. Holding up her index finger and signalling 'excuse me' with her eyes, the little woman put her head on one side, picked up the receiver, and drew in breath through her nose. 'Minsles Secretarial, how may I help you?' she intoned, with precisely the same inflexion as before. After a pause she said, 'Please hold and I will put you through.' Bethany began to feel as though she were Alice in Wonderland, as the woman had produced the phrase with identical intonation to 'how may I help you'. She wondered if the whole conversation would be undertaken with precisely the same sing-song rhythms, and if so, if she would be expected to manage a similar construction. She thought not, though she might adopt the head-on-one-side glance if she had to. The little woman mouthed, 'sorry to keep you,' with exaggerated care, covering the mouthpiece with her other hand. Then, after a few seconds she replaced the telephone and said, 'Now. Minsles Secretarial, how may I help you?'

Bethany replied, 'Um, I wonder if you can. Help me, I mean. I've just arrived in the town, and am looking for work. I do have secretarial qualifications, though not with me. I wonder if you have offices on your books looking for typists on a temporary or part-time basis? If so, how would I go about contacting them?'

Much to her relief the little woman became instantly efficient and perfectly normal in her intonation. 'Oh, yes, well, of course, we have plenty of requirements for qualified typists. If you would just wait there, I will see if Mrs Ellis is free, and she can give you some idea of what is required and what is available right now at this present time. What is your name, please?' Bethany told her and the little lady wrote it down on a yellow pad. Bethany sat down. For some reason the lady then closed the glass panel by sliding it gently across the cubicle. She adjusted a black triangular notice which had her name on it, which Bethany noted was Miss Snite, and then spoke into the intercom. Her words carried quite clearly through it, and Bethany wondered if she knew that she could be heard. 'Mrs Ellis? I have a Miss Jones waiting in reception. She doesn't have an appointment, but she does have qualifications. She would be willing to supply references and I wondered if you could see her with a view to immediate placement in either temporary or permanent employment. You could? Very well, I will send her through.' Miss Snite had reverted to her sing-song telephone manner, and Bethany listened, mesmerised. She jumped as Miss Snite cleared her throat, and said in her more normal voice, 'Yes, it appears that Mrs Ellis can see you now, if you would like to come through.' She opened the door of her cubicle and motioned for Bethany to follow her. Seeing her hesitation, Miss Snite said, 'Your case will be quite safe there. No one will come in unless I buzz them.'

Thus it was that Bethany duly undertook a routine series of shorthand and typing tests at the Minsles Secretarial Agency and, after a short while in Miss Snite's waiting room, was informed of a number of vacancies by the efficient Mrs Ellis. Things then seemed to happen very quickly. Bethany was told that the accountancy firm of Maple and Steadbaum required a typist as soon as possible, and was given a slip of paper with their address on it. Miss Snite rang the firm and informed them that they were sending a young lady around this afternoon for an interview, and gave Bethany brief directions. It appeared that the offices of Maple and Steadbaum were very close and she could walk there. If she was found to be suitable, and if she decided to accept the position, she must inform the Minsles Agency, who would then deal with the accountancy firm directly and, in return for a small placement fee, she would be employed.

In a daze, Bethany made for the door, reaching for her heavy case as she passed it leaning against the wall. Miss Snite put her head on one side and said, 'You may leave it there if you wish, and collect it when you return.' She looked at her wristwatch and continued, 'It's 2.40 p.m. now, and so you will have plenty of time. We close at 5.30 p.m.' Bethany thanked her gratefully and was rewarded with a smile. 'Don't worry, I shall be here all afternoon. We are very quiet today, so your case will be quite safe.'

Bethany found the offices of Maple and Steadbaum quite easily, and told the receptionist that she was from Minsles Secretarial. The interview turned out to be little more than a catalogue of her duties, hours and payment, delivered by a harassed personnel officer with her eye on the clock on the wall behind the seat where Bethany sat. It was over in under ten minutes. The young woman stood up with relief written clearly on her face. 'Well, that all seems fine. Say if you can't manage this, but we are in an absolute bind at the moment and I'd be terribly grateful if you could start as soon as possible. Would tomorrow be absolutely out of the question?' Bethany hesitated, and her interviewer, who had one hand resting on the doorknob and was evidently anxious to leave the room, continued, 'Oh, I do understand. How about the day after that?' Bethany, who would have agreed to the next day if she had had more time to think, said that Wednesday would be fine.

'Marvellous, just report to reception at 8.45 a.m. and someone will show you around your desk and suchlike. Do forgive the rush, but I'm due in a meeting about now.' Without a backwards glance, the young woman clacked busily along the corridor on hurried heels, leaving Bethany mentally ticking another item off her list. She returned to Minsles Secretarial and retrieved her case.

She was not hungry, had not been for days, but she bought herself a sandwich and a cup of coffee in a small café off the high street. She pulled out her notepad and studied the three telephone numbers. It really didn't matter where she lived, she thought. A job and a roof over her head were necessary for survival, but they were purely a means of managing time. She would spend her days in one place and her nights in another, and so her life would continue, and that was something that she could cope with. If she kept moving through the days and nights, she might one day find herself on the other side of the fog of pain and loss that surrounded her. Until then she would continue to cut her life into small, manageable segments.

She rang the first number on her list. The room had been let, so she put a neat line through the figures in her book. The second number appeared to be a wrong one, as she could get no ringing

197

tone, merely a continuous buzz. Finally she dialled the third number. A woman answered and replied that the room was still available if she wanted to see it. Bethany mechanically scribbled down the directions and followed them carefully, taking a fifteen minute bus ride through unfamiliar streets and getting off at the stop opposite the recreation ground.

It was starting to drizzle as she turned into Acacia Avenue. The houses were blank and cheerless in the rain, their bowed windows like eyes staring blindly into the grey afternoon. She found the house easily and rang the bell. The woman who answered clearly didn't believe in wasting words. She led the way up the stairs and silently showed her the room. It was large and had a small gas stove in one corner and a basin in the other. There was a wardrobe near the bed, and two small cupboards secured to the wall above the stove. The single bed was covered with a purple bedcover, and sagged in the middle, but the room was clean and Bethany said that she would take it.

Her new landlady, who had specified little apart from the fact that she would prefer non-smokers, appeared grudgingly satisfied. 'I've not had the room vacant long. My rules are, I'll not have callers after eight o'clock, and no gentlemen in the room no matter what the time. If you're the sort who keeps herself to herself as I think you are, I'll not bother you and you'll not bother me. It's one month rent in advance, payable when you take the room. I prefer cash.' The woman, who was called Mrs Dawes, stood silently by the door and gave her a searching look.

'Yes, of course, that's no problem.' Bethany took out her purse and counted out several notes, noticing as she did so how nearly her supply of money was exhausted. Her new landlady counted the money quite openly, gave a brief nod, and held out a keyring on which were two keys.

'The bathroom is the first door on the left, and the water will be hot from eight until half-past nine in the evening on Tuesdays, Thursdays and Sundays. I'll not bother you further.' The door closed behind her and Bethany sank down on her bed. She stared at the ceiling, listening to the rain outside the window. The room grew darker.

That night she dreamed that Oliver was still with her. She awoke and held herself still, the tears wet on her face, her hands lying on her abdomen, knowing once again that she was alive. For the first time she allowed herself to bring out the thought that she had held closely in a protected part of her mind. Now, anchored in the unreal world between sleep and waking, she let down the walls that

198

surrounded the secret she guarded. She finally acknowledged what she had not been able to face before. She was not merely alive, she also carried life inside her. Part of Oliver was still with her. She lay numbly, wondering what this would mean for her. She did not get up from her bed the whole day, and then slept for part of the night, feeling the new life pulsing within her, and knowing that it was true. Oliver was not yet lost to her completely, not while she carried his child.

She started work at Maple and Steadbaum, travelling to and from Acacia Avenue on the bus, spending her days in mechanical tasks that held little meaning for her, and enduring the nights as best she could. Nothing seemed important to her, and she could not manage to think about her own life, only the fact of the baby growing within her, the part of Oliver that she had not lost. She thought only about guarding her last link with Oliver, and moved through her days as if sleepwalking, miserable and alone. And then, about two months after she had first arrived in Sutton, she sat at the window of her silent room watching the rain on the black streets below. Music was playing somewhere in the house and she was dimly aware of the popular tune drifting up through its rooms. Its words snaked through her nightmare. Broken-hearted people with love long departed. She would never forget the song.

She leaned her forehead against the cold window and listened to the sound of the wind outside whipping the rain into shuddering blasts against the glass. The red-black darkness began to seep into her mind and she knew that all her last hope was gone. She was finally losing Oliver, as surely as the black blood was leaving her body. She began to let herself go into the darkness, gratefully succumbing to the agony which she had resisted for so long. She paid no attention to the pain that cramped her body but instead stared unfocused into her grief. The darkness was red-black.

* * *

The late golden sunshine streamed into the living room and Bethany felt it warm on her shoulders. She reached for a tissue from the box by the fireplace and blew her nose. And that was that. Gingerly, she examined her state of mind. She was still all right. She had remembered the worst thing that had ever happened to her, the catastrophe that had shaped the rest of her life, and she was still here, unchanged. She supposed that that meant that she had been wrong for twenty years to bury it so deeply. She put her hands onto the arms of the chair and lifted herself up carefully. She made herself a blackcurrant tea and looked out of the kitchen window. She wondered what would happen next. She had finally faced all that she had dreaded, and done what the angel asked of her. She sighed deeply and sipped her tea, listening to the silent house. Norman would be home from work soon. She had better get his tea.

The next few days passed uneventfully. Bethany found that her thoughts often returned to the time when she had lost Oliver's baby, and she felt compassion and sadness for the young girl that she had been. She had been so frightened and alone, and so near the abyss of despair, but she had come back from it and gone on. She felt quiet and peaceful, and moved slowly about her household tasks. Musing gently on what had happened, she remembered small details that she hadn't thought about for years. She floated calmly through her memories and marvelled at how serene she felt. She supposed that this detatched calmness followed on from her period of intense emotion, and she enjoyed the tranquillity. She knew that she was experiencing the fruits of her lessons, and was in no hurry to rush towards whatever was coming next.

One afternoon in late September she was polishing the dining room table. Gradually she was aware of a glowing heat in her body. Her navel and chest felt warm, exactly as though she were standing in the direct path of the sun. The day was cloudy and overcast, and she wondered what it could mean. After a little while she laid down her duster, and concentrated on the heat. It really was extraordinarily like the sun's warmth, except that it was coming from the inside.

THIS IS ACCEPTANCE.

'Oh.' Bethany welcomed her angel back. 'Do you mean this warmth, or the way I've been feeling over the last few days?'

AFTER YOU HAVE COME TO TERMS WITH ALL THAT IS YOUR
LIFE, PAST AND PRESENT, AND YOU NO LONGER JUDGE
WHAT HAPPENS, THEN YOU HAVE LEARNED ACCEPTANCE.
THE SIXTH LESSON BRINGS WITH IT THE JOY OF
NON-JUDGEMENT.
NOTHING IN THIS WORLD IS GOOD, OR BAD, BUT
MERELY IS.
IT IS ALL ILLUSION, AND CANNOT BE MEASURED BY
YOUR MIND.
LET GO OF JUDGEMENT AND ACCEPT.

'Oh,' Bethany said again. 'Thank you.' She went and fetched her notebook, and pushed the Mr. Sheen and her duster to the edge of the table. She flipped through its pages, briefly glancing at her notes on Mindfulness, Action, Healing, Gratitude and Discipline, and found a blank page. She carefully wrote out the sixth lesson, and then wrote **Acceptance** at the top, and underlined it. Then she read through what she had written. At first glance it did all seem rather complicated. Bethany reflected that she was only a house-wife, had never even been to college. Sometimes she wondered why the angel bothered with her. She read back through her other lessons, beginning with the first and ending with the fifth. It was true that, at each stage, each had appeared difficult to understand. Now that she had practised them, her life itself bore out their truth. In fact, it was hard to understand how they had been so difficult. You couldn't just read about the lessons. It was only when you lived them that their meaning glowed richly in your life. Of course it would be the same with Acceptance. She just had to figure out this stuff about non-judgement and enjoy the results.

*   *   *

Norman was pleased with the way things were going. Talking with Rita made him realise how unsatisfactory his wife was. Spending time with such a sensitive, ladylike person had shown him how much he had had to put up with at home from Bethany's eccen-tricity. It really wasn't fair that one person should make all the reasonable compromises and the other do exactly as they pleased. His wife's behaviour made it inevitable. He was going round to the neat little flat behind the mauve door tonight. It was an experience that he had had last week and was looking forward to repeating. Rita had poured sherries into little pink glasses. A drop had spilled onto her hand and she had squealed and popped her finger into her mouth. Norman had offered to pour the sherries next time. There would be a next time. B seemed to be so absorbed in her own world these days that she did not really care what he did any more. She didn't even ask how his day went. It was inevitable that he would find someone more congenial to spend his time with, and he probably had no need to explain that to his wife. B probably knew it already. He had been offhand about the time that he would be home, and she had not questioned him. So that was all right.

OCTOBER

Bethany had been thinking about Acceptance for two weeks, and had made a certain amount of progress, though she wasn't sure quite how far she had got. She could understand that life was certainly easier once you could accept things as they are and not judge them as good or bad, but she had a number of problems with the practicalities. It seemed like you would have to be some kind of saint to do that, and she certainly wasn't that. Only this morning a woman had barged past her in the queue at Tesco's and Bethany had stood back politely and attempted to feel detatched and calm. But then the woman had caught her ankle with the edge of her trolley and it had hurt. Bethany tried to smile at her, but her fellow shopper looked through her coldly. Bethany felt rebuffed and foolish, and a bit cross. She tried to say, 'This is not good or bad, it just is' to herself, but was not convinced. Also, it seemed to her that one could become rather a jellyfish just accepting things. What about all the times when something was patently wrong, like tuna-fish nets killing dolphins or pesticides damaging the food chain? Her thoughts ran along these lines as she unloaded her shopping. What distinguished Acceptance from just plain Apathy?

There was no reply from the angel and she knew she had to go on thinking. After she had put everything away, she had some fruit tea, which she had come to like. She went back to the feeling of calm and peace that she had experienced after making the supreme effort to remember her past. She was pretty sure that Acceptance (alongside Forgiveness and Gratitude) must be linked to this sensation of detached well-being. There was definitely a link between Acceptance and detachment, and being detatched didn't seem to mean she couldn't care. So she could probably care about the dolphins and buy different tuna, but at the same time accept that dolphins do die sometime. She wondered if she was on the right lines. It did seem a lot easier to understand if she was dealing in abstracts. The sixth lesson was so much more challenging when you were thinking about tuna-fish. Perhaps she would

202

find it easier to be vegetarian. But she didn't really want to be. Bethany pulled herself up sharply and told herself to stick to the point.

So what she should be aiming for was to try to do the right things, live according to the other five lessons, but not get too worked up about it all. Then she could be a bit more detatched and serene. Well, it was clear she had a long way to go, but she could see that it was something to aim at. Perhaps she would leave it there for a while. There was one thing she had worked out, though. Being less involved with the way things turned out made it a bit easier to be . . . Bethany struggled for the word she wanted. It was something to do with being kind, but not patronising. She searched her mind for a while and then gave up. These things had a way of popping into her mind when she stopped trying to force them. She washed up her cup and went to get the vacuum cleaner from the cupboard under the stairs.

Later, as she cleaned Norman's hair out of the plughole, the word popped into her mind. Compassionate, that was it. If she cared but tried to be detatched, the result was compassion. She looked at the glop of hair matted together with soap and laughed out loud. It really was funny thinking about these lessons at the same time as doing the things she did in her life. A thought struck her and she became suddenly serious. It was Thursday, and the second Sunday in the month was only three days away. Bethany sighed. If there was anybody in the world who would be a good subject for Acceptance, it was her mother-in-law. She peeled off her rubber gloves and sat down on the edge of the bath. Right from the start, Marjorie had disliked everything about her. She disapproved of her accent, her name, her lack of family, the fact that she worked for a living. Most of all, Marjorie disapproved of the fact that Norman had made up his mind to marry her with or without his mother's approval.

Bethany's nose itched and she rubbed it. She caught sight of herself – rubber gloves in hand, hair in disarray, standing in her old leggings and shirt – and resolved to make a new start with Norman's mother. She would wear her new clothes on Sunday, try not to spill pilchards, and really put the sixth lesson into good practice when she saw Marjorie. Bethany gazed at herself in the mirror, remembering the day that the two most important women in Norman's life had met.

* * *

203

The long winter months had dragged on, the days marked only by the waiting at the bus stops and the journeys to and from work. Bethany seemed always to be staring out into dark streets through black windows which streamed with condensation. In the office, the harsh neon strip-lights kept the dark of the gloomy afternoons pinned against the windows, but it enveloped her when she stepped outside. Her head and eyes hurt under the lights, but she preferred them to the dark. She spoke very little, earned her money, paid her rent and ate her food. On Tuesdays, Thursdays and Sundays she had a shallow bath in the bathroom down the corridor from her room, shivering as she dried herself and dressed. Each day she made herself a sandwich that she ate at her desk, and warmed herself a tin of soup on the gas rings in her bedroom. Sometimes, when she was too weary to cook, she bought fish and chips and ate them sitting on the edge of her bed. At other times, when the tiredness and misery were too great, she got into bed without eating anything and lay with her face to the wall until it was time to get up and go to work again.

Gradually, as the days grew longer, and the darkness ebbed from the mornings, Bethany found that her numbness receded and the periods when she felt no pain grew with the lengthening days. Occasionally the grief pinned her like a moth in a glass case, but generally she knew that things were getting better. She began to look around her and take in more of her surroundings. She started to notice people in the office coming and going, and once or twice went outside with her sandwich into the fresh air at lunchtime. She took more interest in her food, and walked up and down the aisles of the little supermarket off the main street looking for things that she could cook in her small room. She bought herself a little saucepan so that she could have a hot drink at night, and a blue and white china mug from which to drink. Then she screwed a little hook into the wall beside the sink in her room and hung the mug up. Gradually her room began to look a little more lived-in, the days acquired more of a structure, and she began to dread the nights a little less.

One morning Bethany woke to hear a blackbird singing outside her window. It sounded like spring. The dark winter days were really coming to an end, and she had managed to hold on through the pain and claw her way back to life. For the first time she calculated how much time had passed since she had left her home. Sylvia and the Willows would be so worried about her. She sat up abruptly. How could she have been so selfish? Six months and she had never once contacted them. Sylvia might even be married by now. Bethany sank slowly back onto her pillow. The hot shame she felt mingled with panic at the thought of explanations. She could not go back. Her reasons for not going back were as strong as ever, and she knew that the past had to be blocked out because its pain would engulf her again. But to leave her friends without a backward glance would be ungrateful and cruel. What should she do? If she told Sylvia the truth, she would be under pressure to go home. Sylvia might even come to see her. Bethany realised with a sharp rush of anxiety that she could not bear this, could not face Sylvia after everything she had been through. Seeing her again would bring back memories of Oliver, and the pain would be too great. It was not possible to go back and salvage a future at the same time. She could not have both the past and a future where she was happy. Of that much she was certain. It would be better to sacrifice her friends and try to manage on her own, in the hope that they would all be able to begin afresh. She was so nearly there, she could bear one more parting, she would be strong enough to hold one more grief.

Bethany sat on the side of her bed in her nightgown. It was Saturday and she had two days before she got the bus back to work. She visualised them stretching out before her, empty hours which she could use. She wondered what had happened to all the weekend hours through the winter. She simply couldn't remember what she had done. But this weekend would be different. The watery sunlight was already trying to break through the grey clouds, and she was going to write to the Willows. She would send them some of the money they had given her, and write them a long, long letter about how happy she was. Once that was finished, she would write to Sylvia. It would be hard, but it was the right thing to do. She would tell her about her life with Oliver, about their house, and his parents, and the countryside where they lived. She would send her dear friend all her love and would wish for her happiness with all her heart. She would send dear Roy all her best wishes. But one thing she would not send; would forget to enclose in spite of her good wishes. She would not write an address at the top of her letter.

And so Bethany spent the first weekend of spring making her peace with her friends. Her heart ached with sadness as she wrote about her full and happy life, and expressed her fond hope that they would all meet up one day soon. Into the Willows' letter she poured her vision of how her life might have been, and she tiredly wiped the sluggish tears away as she finished. The letter to Sylvia was even harder. She had never lied to her friend before, and the contrast between the truth and the letter hurt so much that she could hardly breathe. But she didn't want them to know the truth. It was too painful for her to bear, and the only way it could be managed would be to bury it. Her dearest friends must not ache for her, must not pity her, and it was better that she create this for them. Bethany finished her second letter on Saturday afternoon. She sealed the envelope and breathed in deeply. Letting out her breath in a long sigh, she knew that what she had done was right. She must close the door on her past, and then go on. Somebody at school had told her, 'When one door closes, another one opens.' At the time it had seemed a trivial maxim, hardly worth thinking about, but now she put her faith in it. She was ready to enter into her present more fully. She must make new friends. And she would begin on Monday, at work.

That Saturday afternoon Bethany picked up her letters and walked to the recreation ground which was a place she had only become aware of recently. Through the winter months, her journeys to and from work had been undertaken in the dark. Bethany would not have been able to see her surroundings even if she had wanted to, and she had not. She had closed her eyes and listened to the bus hissing and groaning its way through the wind and rain every morning and evening, lost in the private world of grief that enveloped her. She knew when to get off at work because of the lights in the high street, and on the way home she waited until the road divided sharply, counted two stops and then got off, opposite Acacia Avenue. She did not pause to look around her in the gloom, but mechanically walked to her doorway, and so was only dimly aware that there was a recreation ground near her at all. As the days had lengthened, however, the large gates down the road from her bus stop had become clearer, and the possibility of green open spaces had pricked her curiosity.

For the first time in weeks, Bethany went out at the weekend. It was virtually her first venture out in daylight hours in almost five months. She took her letters and crossed the road diagonally, past the high, green privet hedge and towards the gates that she had noticed on her way back from work. These gates were tall, wrought-iron and did not look as though they were closed very often. They flanked a wide tarmac pathway that was lined with cherry trees. Their branches were still bare, but their bark gleamed a dull red in the sunlight. Bethany noticed that there were some patches of crocuses underneath them, and that the flower beds were showing signs of green leaves which might be daffodils. She walked to a bench and watched the pigeons hopefully stalking around her in case she dropped some food. She laid her letters in her lap, but put her gloved hands over them so that there was no possibility of them blowing away. She breathed the air and could smell that spring was coming. She wondered what it was that distinguished the air of the seasons, as each was unmistakable; if she was dropped down into any part of the year with her eyes closed, she knew that she would be able to tell if it were autumn or spring. It was nothing to do with the temperature or the light, but something from the earth and the air itself.

She shivered and opened her eyes. Although the sun shone, the air still held a chill, and the bench she was sitting on was damp. She knew that she had to post these letters. Bethany held on to them tightly and stood up stiffly. She did not notice a thin young man in a brown suit watching her curiously as she walked out through the gates. His eyes followed her as she stopped in front of the pillar-box, clutching her letters to her chest as though they were too precious to let go of. He looked puzzled when she walked on, still holding the letters, and made as if to follow her. He started guiltily as she turned and went back to the box, posting the letters that she carried. He continued to watch her until she disappeared from view.

Norman lived not far from Acacia Avenue with his mother, Marjorie. He had noticed Bethany at work, and his curiosity had been aroused by her reserved, even silent manner. She was not like the other silly girls at work, he thought, the ones who snorted with laughter as he walked past, covering their lipsticked mouths and giggling. He had not gone so far as to mention Bethany to his mother, but he had found out her name from Personnel. Norman was a young accountant at Maple and Steadman. He had worked there since he had left school at sixteen, painstakingly studying for his examinations and attending evening classes until he had gained his qualifications. It was his habit to walk in the park on Saturdays now that the days were getting longer, and he had noticed the silent young secretary from work sitting on a bench. He had walked past her twice but she hadn't noticed, and had just resolved to speak to her when he saw that her eyes were closed. Overcome with embarrassment, Norman had hesitated for a few seconds in front of her. She had sighed and opened her eyes. Sudden panic about looking foolish had seized him and he had hurriedly walked on, eyes fixed firmly on the horizon in front of him. He paused by the bus stop and watched her as she walked down the road. Norman cursed himself for his shyness, and resolved that he would find some way to talk to her when he next saw her at work. Monday would be the day.

On Monday morning Bethany had gone to work filled with resolve to make a new start, and had been only too ready to smile at the shy young accountant who asked her if she knew how to work the photocopying machine. Norman was extremely pleased with himself for creating this excuse, and had even remembered to provide himself with a piece of paper to photocopy. He introduced himself, surprised at how easy it was to talk to her. Norman did not usually talk to girls, but the young secretary with the faint lilt to her speech seemed sensible and approachable. They talked a little bit about photocopying, and Norman told her in which part of the building he worked. After a little while, as they waited for the machine to warm up, he wondered what she did for lunch usually, as he knew of a nice sandwich bar not far away. Bethany replied that she would like to try it, and they arranged to meet at her desk at 12.30 p.m.

As the weeks passed Norman and Bethany had met regularly. Bethany had been glad of the company, as she had become more conscious of her loneliness since the dark days of winter had ended. Norman liked to talk about himself and she liked listening to his plans. She learned that he lived with his mother, but wanted to move out and find a place of his own. He had been saving hard, and soon would have enough for a deposit on a little house. She knew that he worked hard, and that he was ambitious. He had been at Maple and Steadman since he had left school and wanted to better himself by taking his exams. Bethany was glad that he did not question her too deeply about her past. She had offered certain information about her home town and her friends, but Norman did not appear very interested and this had suited her well. Bethany was glad of the friendship, but did not consider them very close.

She was therefore astounded when Norman took her hand in Mick's Sandwich Bar, ('Hot and Cold sandwiches a speciality') and presented her with a small red box. He asked her to marry him, turning as pink as the ham in his sandwich. Bethany was speechless, but Norman did the talking for both of them, assuring her that he understood that the question was very sudden, and that he knew that she would need time to think, and that he would not press her for an answer straight away. He thought that they were well suited, and that they could be happy together. The tips of his ears glowed red as he told her that he cared deeply for her. Bethany swallowed silently, and he closed her hand firmly around the box which contained the little diamond solitaire he had picked out. He looked at his watch and said that they must be getting back to work.

That night Bethany lay on her bed and stared at the ceiling, the tired tears oozing out from her eyes and wetting the pillow as they had so many times before. She liked Norman but did not know if she could come to love him. But she had experienced love before, and she knew that it had not brought her lasting happiness. What was she to do? It seemed to her as though she was drifting through her life, allowing the days to flow through her fingers like sand. Perhaps Norman would anchor her, tie her to some kind of purpose and direction. But she did not know. She went to work the next day and avoided his eye. They did not meet for lunch, and she was distracted and absent-minded all day, thinking over the situation. She missed Sylvia dreadfully. If only she could confide in her and talk it over. Sylvia would have had some down-to-earth advice, and the knack of coming straight to the heart of the problem. 'But do you love 'im?' she would say. Bethany went around and around, not knowing what to do. The weekend came, and for the second time she decided to go to the recreation ground.

The sun was shining and the sky was blue with large white clouds racing across it, blown by a brisk wind. Bethany drew her coat around her and shoved her hands deep in her pockets. For the thousandth time she wondered what answer she would give to Norman. She missed Oliver so much. How could she make a decision like this without anyone to talk to? Her throat ached with the pain of it all, and she suddenly felt as though it was too much for her to bear. When was it all going to end? She longed for someone to take away the burden of her grief, to shoulder the weight that pressed on her day after day.

Bethany walked around the park until her lips were blue from the cold, and her hands were numb. She badly needed to blow her nose, and she wiped it on the back of her sleeve, hoping that no one would see her. Without realising it she had walked the whole way round the little paths that lined the recreation ground. Now she stood at the entrance to the park, on the tree-lined avenue. She sniffed surreptitiously. The cherry trees were now in full bloom, fat with pink clusters bobbing on the leafy branches. She looked up and saw the blue sky framed by the bright pink and green, and caught her breath at their beauty, surprised out of her preoccupation. She heard a delighted shriek of laughter and looked down again. A small child was running towards her, stagger-ing on ahead of its mother, who followed with a pushchair. Bethany watched the joyful little figure and her heart lifted. It was such a relief to let go of her sadness and worry. It was possible not to think about it for whole minutes on end, but instead to immerse herself in this lovely morning.

The little girl had stopped and was standing looking straight up into the branches above her. Bethany followed her glance, and suddenly there was a sudden gust of wind. The breeze took hold of the blossom and blew it down in a shower of flowers, drifting like a pink blizzard all around them. The little girl crowed with delight. 'Snow, Mummy, it's snowing!' Bethany was entranced. The blossoms continued to swirl around her until she could not see beyond the pink flowers filling her vision. They filled her eyes and her hair, and she held out her hands, catching the petals and filling her arms with pink. The child next to her was whirling around, arms outstretched, surrounded by swirling blossoms, and her mother stood open-mouthed at the beauty of what was happening. Suddenly the breeze died, and it was over as quickly as it had begun. The three of them stood on the pink ground, blossom covering every part of the grass and pathway. The two women looked at the child, who was picking up petals. Bethany smiled at the young mother, who smiled back. 'It was like confetti, wasn't it? Reminds me of when I got married, only more beautiful really.' Bethany nodded, and the mother took hold of her child's hand and they walked on into the park. Bethany walked home. The beauty of the cherry blossom had lifted her sadness, and for the first time she felt the faint stirring of optimism. Perhaps she could marry Norman. Perhaps being with him would help her forget the past. She could lay down the burden of sadness she had carried for so long and begin again. It was time to leave her grief behind if she could. Norman loved her. Surely his steadiness would give her something to focus on. They would look to the future together.

Things had moved quickly after that. From the moment that she had told Norman that she would like to marry him, events seemed to push her along with them. Norman was immensely practical, booking the registry office, finding estate agents' details of the house they were to buy, and even going with her to buy something for her to wear on the day. 'I want you to have everything you want,' he kept saying. Bethany felt something akin to rising panic about the fact that she did not seem to be making any decisions for herself. There never seemed to be a right moment to talk about things together. Apart from the first time in Mick's Café, Norman had never mentioned love, and seemed content to occupy himself with practicalities. Bethany tried several times to bring up the subject of her past, but Norman brushed her aside. 'What's gone is gone, B. We're not the sort of people who want to pick over things. We know what we want and we are going to have it, eh?' He patted her hand and smiled at her, and something in his eyes told Bethany that now was not a good time. Uncertain of herself and grateful to him for caring, Bethany told herself that things would change as the months passed. Surely when they were married they would share more, and the aching craving for intimacy that she had would be satisfied.

The day finally dawned when Norman was to introduce her to his mother. It was the weekend before the wedding. For some reason the important meeting had not come about before. Norman had always seemed busy with other things when she mentioned it, and was oddly reluctant to answer her questions about his mother. He seemed to want to spare both her and his future wife any worry about the wedding, and occupied himself with every detail. Bethany had thought that she and Marjorie might discuss arrangements, but instead Norman produced lists from which she was expected to choose. He gave her a choice of invitations, a choice of table-cloths for the reception together with a choice of matching servi-ette, and a choice of menus. Bethany lacked the energy to tell him that she didn't really like any of the choices, but instead agreed with his preferences. Norman was delighted that he and his bride-to-be were so much in accord. If he noticed her increasing listless-ness and subdued silences, he gave no sign. Bethany tried not to worry and told herself that it would be better after they were married.

On Saturday morning Norman drew up outside the house in Acacia Avenue in his car. Bethany had been watching from the window and went down to meet him, to save him knocking on the door. Norman held out his cheek for her to kiss, but seemed rather quiet. He responded curtly to her questions and was reluc-tant to talk, concentrating intently on his driving. Bethany sat nervously in the passenger seat. For the first time she wondered what Norman's mother thought about the wedding. She wondered also if she minded being left out of the arrangements, and whether she thought this had been Bethany's doing. She opened her mouth to ask Norman about it, but glanced across at his tight-lipped profile and thought better of it.

They drove the few streets to the little house where Norman lived with his mother. Bethany was startled that it was so close. She had somehow expected Norman to live not quite so near to work, but of course when she thought about it, it was obviously the most

211

practical thing to do. She wondered if all the houses that he had been looking at were this close to Marjorie and his work. Of course they would be. They would, of course, be seeing a lot of Norman's mother after they were married. No wonder Norman was so tense. It was very important that she make a good impression. She pulled down the mirror at the back of the sun-visor in front of her and tried to check her face and hair. Norman waited patiently. He seemed in no hurry to go inside. Bethany was grateful to him for understanding her apprehension. She turned to him and said, 'Do I look all right? Do you think she will like me? Oh Norman, you won't leave me alone, will you?'

Norman's nerves vanished when he saw her panic, and he looked at her fondly. 'Don't worry. Mother is the most wonderful person, and of course she'll approve of you. How could she not? Come on, she'll be wondering what we're doing, sitting here in the road.'

Bethany looked rapidly up at the house, and caught a glimpse of a hand swiftly flicking the net curtain across the window. She gasped. 'Oh, Norman, she's waiting, we mustn't keep her waiting. Come on, come on.' Smiling indulgently, Norman got out of the car and locked it carefully, while Bethany waited on the path. She had to clench her teeth together to prevent them chattering. She took Norman's hand gratefully.

As they got nearer the house, the pebble-dashed path narrowed and there was not room to walk side by side. Norman awkwardly motioned for Bethany to go first and she pressed the doorbell. The chimes of 'Rule Britannia' sounded deep in the hallway, and as soon as the verse died away the door was opened. Bethany had not heard Marjorie walk up to the door and realised that she must have been standing behind it waiting for the chimes to finish. She had not time to think about this, as Marjorie was standing in front of her. 'Come in, come in, don't be standing around in the cold, go on, go on, right in, don't stand there so no one else can get past you.' This was to Bethany, accompanied by a testy little laugh to show that the remark was humorous. With a brisk movement Marjorie ushered Bethany so firmly into the house that later she wondered if she had actually been pushed. Marjorie then squeezed past her so that she could greet Norman. Bethany stared dumbly at her future mother-in-law's back. Marjorie was holding out both her hands to Norman and leaning forward so that he could kiss her cheek. 'The drive didn't take you long then, you only left after breakfast. I hope you didn't go too fast. Where have you parked? Only you know that we all have our spaces here and Colonel Parkhurst won't be pleased if you've *encroached*, Normie.' Marjorie tittered again to show that this was meant lightly, but she looked out the door at the car before she closed it. She then moved past Bethany again in the narrow hall saying, 'Well, I don't know what we are doing standing here, come into the front room and have some tea.' Still without looking at Bethany, she led the way into a room off the hallway. Norman took Bethany's coat and hung it with his jacket on a hatstand before motioning her to follow his mother. She smiled tentatively at him and he patted her shoulder encouragingly.

'It's all right, she's nervous too. It'll be fine when we get going.' Bethany felt relief flood through her. Of course, Norman's mother would be bound to be nervous too. After all, she knew nothing about the woman Norman had chosen, and must be wondering how to handle the meeting. Norman was so sensible. She was lucky to have him. She smoothed her skirt and walked into the living room.

Marjorie was standing by an electric fire which had plastic coal on the top of it. The room was stiflingly hot. Bethany hesitated, unsure as to whether to sit down, or greet Marjorie more formally, as the shoving that had taken place in the hall could hardly count as a proper introduction. Norman obviously felt the same way, as he stood awkwardly between the two women, glancing first at Bethany then his mother. For a short moment there was a heavy silence, and then Norman cleared his throat and said, 'Mother, this is Bethany. Bethany, this is my mother, um, Marjorie ... Taylor.' Too late, he appeared to be wondering if he should have introduced his mother as Mrs Taylor, and the thought hung as clearly in the air as if he had spoken out loud.

Bethany came to his rescue by holding out her hand and saying with a smile, 'How do you do, Mrs Taylor? I'm so pleased to meet you after all this time. Norman has told me so much about you.'

Marjorie laughed gaily. 'Well, Bethanee, is it? I'm pleased to meet you at last too. Norman has certainly kept you very quiet. 'I was beginning to wonder if you actually existed.' Her eyes met Bethany's for a moment and then slid away. 'What are we doing standing around, I'm sure I've said more than once that we should sit down and have some tea.' Marjorie sat down firmly in the chair nearest the fire, and Norman and Bethany also sat. There was another silence. Bethany wondered hesitantly if she should be the first to break it and looked nervously at Norman's mother.

Marjorie was not tall, but she was solid. Her whole body seemed to be compacted and tightly encased in her clothes so that she was one pillar of firmness from head to toe. From her knees up to her neck she resembled a tightly stuffed bolster. Her face and hands were the only part of her body not constrained by her thick stockings, tweed skirt, waistcoat and blouse, and they appeared uncomfortable with the unexpected freedom they had been granted. The flesh which escaped its tight corseting pushed up out of her blouse in a series of powdered folds until it bunched up under her eyes. These were bright blue, and very piercing. She wore heavy gold chains around her neck, a large brooch pinned on her bosom, and several chunky rings bit into her fleshy fingers so that they resembled sausages bursting from their skins. Her hair, which was steely grey, was lacquered and sat in tight sausage roll curls all around her head. Bethany thought she looked formidable, and was glad when Norman began the conversation.

Norman cleared his throat. 'Mother was wondering if you liked your work, Bethany.'

Marjorie reached across and slapped his hand lightly. 'Oh, you naughty boy, do you think that Bethanee and I can't have a sensible conversation by ourselves?' Turning to Bethany she said, 'His father was just the same, always trying to take over and organise everything. That's the trouble with men, they need to be in charge, don't they? All that I was wondering was whether you were planning to work after you have married Norman. I know that the modern thing is for young girls to have a career, and you certainly seem to have managed everything beautifully so far, but I always felt that my role was to support my husband and look after him as best I could. I always think it can be so hard on the man to be working and then to come home to a cold house with nothing on the table, and of course then there's the washing and the ironing, I don't know how you young things manage these days, I really don't.' Marjorie's tinkling laugh rang out gaily once more, but her eyes were fixed intently on Bethany and waiting for her reply.

Bethany hesitated, and looked at Norman. 'Well, I don't really know. We haven't really talked, have we, but . . . ' she trailed off uncertainly.

Norman said, 'No, I suppose it would make sense for you to give up work to settle everything down at the house when we move into it, but it's really up to you . . . '

He too trailed off and Bethany hastily said, 'Goodness, Marjorie, you see how impractical we are. It's just one of those things we haven't even discussed yet, but I do see that we ought to . . . '

Marjorie drew her lips back over her teeth and said, 'Yes, well, I do think that it's up to the woman to take charge of these domestic details. Order is so important in home-making, don't you agree?

And you certainly seem to have arranged the wedding conscientiously. Norman tells me there's absolutely nothing that I can do at all. You seem to have it all decided down to the very last detail. And will your family be making the journey from, Wales, is it?'

Bethany drew breath and replied, 'Actually, there's only my mother, and she is in very poor health and won't be coming. That's why we thought we'd have a very small wedding, with not much fuss.' Again she wondered what Marjorie thought of the plans, but presumably Norman and she must have talked about them. Hesitantly, she said, 'In fact, Norman has done most of the organising, haven't you, Norman? It made sense, really, as I know none of the guests who will be coming. He said that . . . I mean, we thought that we wouldn't bother you with the work of organising . . . it's rather tedious really, and it really is going to be a very small affair.' As she looked across at Norman she saw an anxious frown cross his face, which was replaced quickly by an expression of resignation.

'Now, Mother, I know what you are like. I know I gave you the impression that Bethany wanted everything just so, but that was just to save you the bother . . . ' Norman broke off because Marjorie was talking right across him, raising her voice so that her words were clearly heard above his. She had fixed her intent gaze upon Bethany and was speaking with an insistent smile.

'Now, that's a relief. I feared that we wouldn't get on at all if you were the headstrong sort of girl, but of course I should have trusted that Normie would never choose that type. I had been led to believe that you didn't want me involved at all, but I can see there's been a misunderstanding. Now tell me all about what your plans are, and I shall see what I can do to contribute.'

Bethany had looked helplessly across at Norman, who she could see was not pleased. She felt that she was letting him down in some way, but did not know what to do. Surely it was best for them to include Marjorie? It was natural, wasn't it, for a mother to want to be involved in the plans for her only son's wedding? And she didn't want Marjorie to dislike her, as she had so evidently been prepared to do when they had first met. Marjorie seemed much more friendly now and was actually pouring the tea. What would it matter if she made alterations to some of the arrangements? For the rest of the visit she sat quietly as Marjorie subjected Norman to a barrage of questions about the wedding plans. At first reluctant, Norman soon became more enthusiastic, and laid out his arrangements for Marjorie's approval. Bethany watched, feeling more and more detatched from the whole thing. She could hardly believe

215

that she would be marrying Norman in less than a week, and that this woman sitting so close to her would soon be her family. What had happened to her? This numbness and passivity couldn't be normal. This wedding was going to change the direction of her life. Surely she ought to be more involved? But try as she might, Bethany could not seem to summon up the energy or desire to enter into Norman's conversation with his mother. They seemed oblivious to her presence and she felt as though she were shrinking, unable to muster the will to exist any more. During the hour spent in Marjorie's sitting room, Bethany drifted in and out of her thoughts in a daze. The heat from the fire and the airlessness of the room caused her to feel drowsy and light-headed, but Marjorie's ringing laughter kept bringing her back from her trance with increasing uneasiness. She had longed for a respite from her pain and grief, but was this passivity better? By the end of the morning she knew that, unpleasant as it might be, she had to talk to Norman about her misgivings.

When they had been ushered down the path by Marjorie, who had offered her cheek to Bethany as well as Norman, they climbed into the car. Marjorie retreated back into the warmth and was waggling her fingers at them from the window, her face a mask of smiling farewell. Bethany shivered in the sudden cold, and Norman switched on the ignition and the car heater. 'We'll soon get this warmed up.' He leaned across her to wave to his mother and then loosened the handbrake and drove off.

During the short drive back to Bethany's room she was very quiet, and then said, 'Norman, I think we need to talk.'

Norman said nothing as he carefully parked the car. Then he looked straight ahead of him at a small speck on the windscreen. 'Oh, do you think so? I thought we'd got everything arranged rather well.'

'No, I don't mean about the wedding, I mean about us, and about your mother. Do you realise that she hardly spoke more than a few words to me, and she's completely changed all of the plans you had made and all in the space of a morning?'

Norman rounded on her aggressively. 'Well, I hardly think you can complain, I didn't notice you taking much part in the discussion.' This was true, and Bethany tried to put into words what she had been thinking.

'I know. I'm sorry, I suppose I just don't feel that we've talked about any of the important things, and I can't seem to focus my mind at the moment.'

She was aware that the words had not come out exactly as she had meant and sighed inwardly as Norman replied, 'I know, B, but there really isn't any more to talk about. We know that we want to get married, and buy a house and live together. It's natural to be nervous, and of course you can't concentrate. That's why it makes sense for me to make the arrangements. I know that Mother tends to take over, that's why I tried to keep it all from her, but you have to admit she does know how to arrange things.'

Bethany tried again. 'Well, it's not just nerves. I feel so strange, Norman, I mean, so much has happened to me that you don't even know about, and I know so little about you and your family. I . . . '

Norman had put his hand firmly over hers and was now squeezing it so tightly that it hurt. 'Look. I want to get this straight once and for all. I don't care about things that have happened in the past. As far as I'm concerned, we should just concentrate on the here and now. What's done is done. Mother often says that, and she's right. I'm going to get cross if you insist on dredging through the past, and I won't have it, d'you understand? It's just . . . unnecessary.' Seeing the tears pricking at her eyes, he cleared his throat and said in a different tone, 'Really, it will be all right. Mother likes you, and you just have to marry me, I don't know what I'll do if you don't. I've always wanted this to happen, and now it's all so close to coming true. I'll have you as my wife; a house; and my work. Please don't worry any more, it's senseless to go on talking about the past. The future is what matters.'

The irony of what he was saying was not lost on Bethany. It was as if the conversations that she and Oliver had had were filtered through sheets of smoked glass and altered in some way, distorted, but still an ironic echo of the pact that she and Oliver had made. Bethany was unable to restrain her tears any longer. Norman awkwardly offered her his handkerchief, and patted her shoulder. 'Look, B, all of this is perfectly natural. It will all be sorted out by this time next week. Mother has said that we can move in with her until we get our own house, which won't be long, and then everything will be just perfect.'

Bethany lay in her bed that night, and turned his words over in her mind. The thought of moving in with Marjorie filled her with dread, but some of what Norman said made sense. She knew that he loved her, and surely if she took one day at a time slowly and steadily, everything would be all right. It was unfair to compare the week she had with Oliver with the time she spent with Norman, and she would never be happy if she tried to recreate what was lost. Norman was a good man, and she knew that his uncompromising attitude was his way of covering up his vulnerability and uncertainty. Now that she had met Marjorie she could understand his need to be in control, and he was bound to relax more when they were making decisions together. The lack of closeness she felt was a combination of his reserve, which would melt when he felt secure in her love, and the need she had to hold on to Oliver. She saw that the efforts she had made were not yet complete. She must consciously practice a daily forgetting, forbid herself ever to remember what had been, for Norman's sake, but mainly for her own.

Bethany thought of Marjorie's question about work. She certainly would not be in a hurry to give up work while they were staying with Marjorie, but maybe once they had their house she would concentrate on making it a home, and then children . . . Norman would like that, she thought. Bethany told herself that she was doing the right thing. She was building a future.

And so Bethany married Norman, and had tried to forget the time she had spent before she met him. The choice was made partly in a genuine belief that she had to move on with living. It has to be said also that Bethany made the most important decision of her life for the simple reason that she was too tired not to. She allowed Norman to shoulder the burden of decision-making because she could no longer bear to be miserable, and hoped that it would bring her peace of mind. When she remembered Oliver her peace of mind vanished, and she could not bear to think about the hurt that she had suffered. The more time passed, the less she had been able to distinguish between the memories and the hurt, so the memories became something to fear in themselves. She thought that she had conquered her past, put it behind her, but the dread had grown in the darkness.

For a while they had hopes of having children, but it hadn't happened. Norman did not want to talk about it, and Bethany persuaded herself that in some way it must have been her fault, some kind of judgement upon her. She put it out of her mind. Why long for something that obviously wasn't meant to be, she thought. The way forward was to resign herself to the life she had, not to wish for the impossible. She refused to listen to her aching heart, but bravely walked through her isolated days with her mind focused on her present. She exchanged her life before Norman for her life with him, bartering for a release from pain and grief and anaesthetising herself against loss. She must take the rough with the smooth. Once in a while, the sadness had surfaced, but she had always managed to push it back down deep within herself.

* * *

Bethany shook her hair back from her eyes. That was how she had been. Then the angel had come, and everything had changed. How many months had it been? Almost seven, only seven and it seemed like a lifetime. She felt a new person, a different woman altogether, although she knew that she was the same really, only healed of the hurt of her past and ready to live the present fully and gratefully. The culmination of the previous five lessons had led her to Acceptance. She was truly happy for the first time in a very long time. She felt as though she were poised on a spring-board, as though she could jump up into the future happily and joyfully. She felt purposeful.

VERY GOOD.

'Oh! What do you mean, very good? I'm not sure I'll ever get used to you just speaking like that. It doesn't make me jump like it used to, but still, couldn't you give me some warning? Sorry, what do you mean "very good"?'

YOU HAVE THE KEY TO THE NEXT LESSON.

Bethany just managed to stop herself from saying 'Oh' again, and tried to remember what she had been thinking about. She was happy, she felt she had healed her past, she had nothing to fear. Surely those were more the results of the lessons she already had and was practising, rather than anything new. There was silence from the angel so she carried on thinking. There had been something about diving in, jumping off a springboard into the blue, looking to the future . . . not really that earth-shattering, her thoughts didn't tend to be that profound really . . . Purposeful. She felt purposeful, as though the lessons clearly indicated a direction to take and that she needed to make a start.

THE SEVENTH LESSON IS THAT OF PURPOSE.
SEEK TO LIVE THE BEST LIFE YOU CAN.
TAKE THE PRINCIPLES OF THE LESSONS THAT YOU HAVE
LEARNED AND PUT THEM AT THE CENTRE OF ALL YOU DO.
DO NOT ALLOW ALL OF THE EVENTS THAT CROWD YOUR
DAY TO DISTRACT YOU FROM THE REASON YOU ARE LIVING.

219

INSTEAD, HOLD MINDFULNESS, ACTION, FORGIVENESS,
GRATITUDE, DISCIPLINE AND ACCEPTANCE
AT THE HEART OF YOUR ACTIVITY.
LET THEM DIRECT YOUR LIFE AND GIVE IT PURPOSE.
WHATEVER DAILY TASK YOU PERFORM,
ASK YOURSELF HOW IT CAN BE MADE IMPORTANT.
AFTER YOU HAVE LOOKED INWARDLY, THEN
TURN OUTWARD.
MAKE YOUR LIFE PURPOSEFUL.

Bethany, who by now found that her notebook was never far away, went to fetch it and rapidly wrote down the seventh lesson. After she had written '**Purpose**' and underlined it, she felt a surge of excitement. She really was changing her life from the inside outward. If only Norman could share this new-found sense of direction. Physically and mentally she had never felt so full of energy. Now she just had to put it all to good use.

The next morning she got up early, leaving Norman asleep in the bed, and went downstairs. She sat quietly for a while, and when she had opened her eyes she planned how she was going to relate the seventh lesson to her day ahead. It was the second Sunday in the month, a day that she did not usually relish. In the years that had passed since her wedding day, she had formed an uneasy truce with Marjorie. It had been hard won, as Marjorie would always regard her as an outsider who threatened her exclusive relationship with her son.

In the early days Bethany had tried hard to gain Marjorie's approval by seeking her opinion, something the older woman was all too willing to give. Marjorie soon established for herself that her daughter-in-law was not going to oust her from her coveted position of dominance over Norman, and she became less frosty. However, like many extremely strong-minded people accustomed to getting her own way, she was incapable of adjusting her own behaviour in order to compromise. The more that Bethany tried to consider her mother-in-law's feelings, the greater were the liberties Marjorie took. It came to the point where she was accompanying them to every house viewing that Norman arranged, as well as supervising their meals and what they wore. No house ever came up to her exacting standards, and after five weeks Norman and Bethany were still staying in Marjorie's guest bedroom.

In desperation Bethany had taken Norman aside at work and persuaded him that he must assert himself. They had secretly arranged several house viewings after work, with strict instructions to the agents that they must not be telephoned at home. When they had found their new house, they had been like excited children, giggling and half fearful that Marjorie would find them out and put a stop to it. Norman had come to see that this was a ridiculous situation for two newly-wedded grown-ups and it had been he that insisted that they keep the purchase from Marjorie until it was too late to change anything. Marjorie had been furious, but they had been too delighted to be moving in to their own home to allow her to lessen their pleasure, and things had been much better between the two of them after that.

In contrast, Bethany's relationship with Marjorie had taken a distinct downturn. Marjorie, who refused to believe that Norman was responsible for the move, convinced herself that Bethany was deceitful, a snake in the grass who had 'bitten the hand that had fed her'. Shortly after Bethany had given up work, Marjorie asked her to a coffee morning. To Bethany's growing horror she had proceeded to regale her friends with her daughter-in-law's many shortcomings amid much tinkling laughter. Bethany had left the house in tears after an hour-and-a-half, and Norman had refused to take her side, saying that his mother was bound to be upset and that she should be more understanding. Norman was experiencing a reaction to his unprecedented masterful decision-making over the house, and was terrified that he had gone too far. Never before had he defied Marjorie so openly, and he could barely bring himself to imagine the consequences. Panicked at the thought that he might have unwisely opened the battle lines with his mother, he gratefully seized on Marjorie's grievance. Consequently he put great pressure on Bethany to 'apologise and have done with it.'

The event had been a turning point for Bethany. She could not see why she should apologise, and had nothing to apologise for. She had been humiliated and hurt, and this hardened into a resolve to stand up for herself. In spite of Norman's increasingly agitated remonstrations, she refused to allow Marjorie to visit the house, and did not accompany him on his weekly visits to his mother. Unlike Marjorie, she was willing to mend the rift between them without requiring an apology, but she could not simply lie down and allow Norman's mother to walk all over her. She learned to respect herself, and tried not to look too closely at Norman's fawning behaviour, lest it lessen her respect for him. Marjorie had been unable to resist looking around the house and had been extremely affable to Bethany on the telephone when Norman was at work one day. It was true that she acted as though nothing had

221

happened, and still expressed her opinions about their lives force-fully and vociferously, but there was a small, almost imperceptible, change in their relationship. While she continued to treat her dominance of Norman as her right, she allowed Bethany a little space, and grudgingly accorded her respect.

Norman had been unaware of all this, of course, and was hugely relieved that the rift between his mother and his wife was healed. Norman had periods when he simmered with resentment over Marjorie's dominance over him, others when he was defiant and independent of her, and some where he panicked at his own daring and came running back solicitously to her side. At first, Bethany never knew how Norman was going to feel about Marjorie, but she gradually came to realise that the three behaviours fol-lowed roughly in a cycle, with the third being the most common. She was resigned to the fact that his mother would always be the prime influence in his life. Over the years he grew more like Marjorie and, although he did not possess her strength of charac-ter, he hated events to be beyond his control and developed an insistence on routine that was very similar to hers.

The afternoon tea sessions every month had fallen into a familiar pattern. For the first half an hour or so, Marjorie would steadfastly ignore Bethany, and talk to Norman at length about his work. She liked to be kept abreast of every development and held strong opinions about management, accountancy and general work prac-tices. Marjorie had never worked outside her house but felt that this gave her unique insight. Bethany sometimes wished that she had a nice peaceful hobby like embroidery or knitting, so that she could occupy her hands and mind productively while they talked.

Next, Marjorie would go out to her kitchen while she and Norman sat silently in the stifling heat. She would return bearing the teapot, which would be placed on the table between them. If it were one of the winter months they would eat pilchards on toast washed down with strong, milky tea. Bethany loathed pilchards, especially in the tinned tomato sauce that Marjorie served them in, and had to force herself to eat them. The fact that on more than one occasion Bethany had told Marjorie that she was not fond of pilchards had done nothing to sway Marjorie's firm conviction that they were her favourite food. Bethany watched her mother-in-law's fat fingers squashing the glutinous mass onto the toast and swal-lowed hard. Her discomfort was made the greater because this was the time that Marjorie elected to hold forth about articles she had read, or discussions she had heard on the radio, about topics which she felt would be beneficial to Bethany.

She would begin by asking Bethany a question, such as which washing powder she bought. As Bethany answered, she would cut right across her words with the inevitable retort that this was quite the worst washing powder one could use. It caused rashes, or research had shown it to be vastly inferior in cleaning tests, or even on one terrible occasion, that it was a contributory factor of cancer in rats. Norman would echo the concern, expressing amazement that Bethany had never heard of this, and that of all the washing powders she could be using, she had chosen the very one that caused all these problems. She must change it immediately, that very week. Marjorie would then do a complete about-face and tell Norman that his wife was perfectly capable of choosing for herself, thank you very much. She would smack his hand playfully and Bethany would smile politely as Marjorie then told her how men would always try to control things if you let them. Of course, she had never made that mistake herself. If Norman was in one of his defiant moods, he would merely lean back in his chair, fold his arms and snort through his nose. Bethany didn't really care which way he reacted, as neither was of much help to her in dealing with the situation.

Finally they would all three repair to the kitchen, which smelled of cat food, and clear away the tea things. Norman would wash, Bethany would dry, and Marjorie would put the things away. Considering they had used so few items of crockery, this seemed to take an inordinately long time. The tasks would be done silently. Norman was an extremely conscientious washer, and Bethany and Marjorie usually found themselves standing waiting for him. Marjorie bustled ostentatiously, flicking stray crumbs impatiently and piling teacups that were already stacked, while Bethany stood helplessly with her damp tea-cloth wishing away the minutes. Finally they would be done, and they would go out to the hall and put on their coats. They would kiss Marjorie and Norman would say, 'Would you like to come to us next week, Mother?' as though it were not already written in tablets of stone that this would be what she would do. Marjorie would laugh ringingly and pat her steel grey hair. 'Yes, it would suit me if you would pick me up at four o'clock, Normie.' And then the whole awful business would be over for another month. It wasn't so bad when Marjorie came to their house, Bethany thought. The pattern of the visit didn't depart a great deal from its essential dreadfulness, but at least she could eat what she liked, and they could sit in the garden in the summer.

Bethany sighed, then straightened her shoulders. How could she practice the seventh lesson in relation to Marjorie? What had it said? Don't be distracted by all the things that crowd you, but instead be purposeful by putting all the other lessons at the centre? Something like that. She really should have her notebook tattooed onto her mind these days. After reading through the seventh lesson to refresh her memory, she laid down the book and thought. First of all, the reason she was living was to live the best life she could, with the help of the lessons. Her relationship with Marjorie certainly wasn't the best it could be, she was sure of that. So she needed to keep the aim of improving her relationship at the forefront of her mind, however Marjorie might behave. She could practice acceptance more by thinking a little bit about why Marjorie behaved the way she did, and be more compassionate. She could certainly be grateful that her mother-in-law wasn't a lot worse. But how could she take action? Bethany sucked the end of her pencil and then began to scribble at the back of the book.

Sunday came, and at 3.45 precisely Norman and Bethany climbed into the car and set off for Marjorie's house. At four o'clock they drew up outside the familiar house and walked up the narrowing path to the door. After the full rendition of 'Rule Britannia', Marjorie opened the door, they hung up their coats and went into the front room. Marjorie had installed central heating a few years after Bethany and Norman had married, and she kept this on all through the summer lest any chill enter her double-glazed bungalow. Since it was now October, and officially winter, the electric fire had also been brought into service and was throwing rays of throbbing heat out from the fireplace. Bethany's skin prickled with the heat and she felt the beads of sweat begin to rise on the back of her neck. She was wearing her new light skirt and blouse, but within minutes of sitting down in Marjorie's chair, she felt her clothes beginning to stick to her back. Marjorie, as usual, was encased in thick tweed.

The years had not been kind to Marjorie. The solid rolls of fat around her neck and chin had refused to soften, but become denser and more compressed so that when she turned her head it was with difficulty, and left deep red indented lines in her skin. Her tightly corseted body strained against the heavy tweed, making flexible movement difficult. She appeared even more cylindrical, and adopted a method of swivelling her whole body when she wanted to change direction, rather than give herself the trouble of bending her limbs. The act of sitting in a chair was not one that recommended itself to Marjorie, and she had adapted the manoeuvre to obviate the necessity of bending herself in the middle. She lowered her ample rear onto the front of the chair, and almost lay at a diagonal angle until her upper shoulders made contact with its back. Her legs stuck stiffly out in front of her and continued in a solid and unbending line up to her chins. A tightly rolled bolster filled the gap between her back and the chair, and she grasped the arms firmly to prevent herself from sliding in an undignified manner to the floor. Her stomach pushed at the tight band of her tweed skirt, and the pearls that she wore around her neck appeared to squeeze the rolls of fat further upwards. She breathed heavily in the heat, and regarded Norman with a gimlet eye.

'You are rather late, Normie. Did you have difficulty starting the car? You know I've mentioned more than once that you must put anti-freeze into the engine. I always made sure that your father put anti-freeze in as soon as the nights started drawing in.' She turned to Bethany and opened her mouth.

Quickly, Bethany said, 'Marjorie, I never met Norman's father and I was thinking this week how little I know about him. You often mention him, and I would really like to hear more. Do you have any pictures of him?' She was vaguely aware out of the corner of her eye that Norman had spilled some tea, but she kept her face firmly fixed on Marjorie, who was goggling at her.

'You want to hear about Oswald? Well . . .' Marjorie appeared to be struggling with herself. It had never occurred to her to show Bethany her photograph albums, and as a rule she disliked the initiative being taken by somebody else. However, the idea was a novel one, and she suddenly rather enjoyed the thought of looking through her photograph books. Thinking rapidly, she said, 'Well, Bethanee, I have been meaning for some time to show you my albums. How odd that you should mention it just as I was about to get them out this very afternoon. I was good at photography in my day and if things had been different I might have pursued it. Normie, you will find them on the shelf in the box room. You know where they are.'

Norman got reluctantly to his feet and went upstairs. Bethany was startled to reflect that she had not been into any of the upstairs rooms in Marjorie's house since they had moved out of it all those years ago. She wondered if it all looked the same.

'Marjorie, would you like your cushion adjusting? Are you comfortable?'

Once again, Marjorie stared at her and did not reply. Bethanee was certainly acting differently this afternoon. Norman reappeared carrying a pile of grey photograph albums. 'Clear the tea, Normie, we'll eat later. Now they should all be labelled with the year.' Marjorie impatiently took the books from him and placed one on her lap. Bethany moved around so that she could see over her shoulder. And Marjorie began to take her through the albums, which documented the years from when she was married, all through Norman's early childhood. As Bethany looked, she saw that the photographs were not merely snaps, but had been taken by someone with an eye for what made a good picture. Marjorie had been telling the truth when she had said that she was a good photographer. In spite of himself Norman became interested, and the tea grew cold as Marjorie talked.

They finished the last album and Norman raised his head stiffly. 'Mother, it's nearly a quarter-to-seven. We've really overshot our schedule, and we haven't washed up yet.'

Marjorie started and pushed herself to her feet. 'Well, really, I can't think where the time has gone. This won't do. Normie, put the albums away and I'll take the tea things through to the kitchen. Bethanee can help me.' Norman gathered up the books and went upstairs and Bethany followed Marjorie through to the kitchen. It took less time than usual to wash up the cups as they hadn't eaten anything, and they were finished by the time Norman came downstairs.

If Norman was annoyed that they had departed even further from their routine by excluding him from the washing up, he did not show it. Instead, he merely said, 'So would you like to come to us next week, Mother?'

Marjorie offered her cheek for him to kiss and replied. 'Yes, it would suit me if you picked me up at four o'clock, Normie.' And they left the house, got in the car and drove home. Norman was very quiet all evening.

Before they went to bed, Bethany said. 'I enjoyed visiting your mother today. Sometimes it's nice to do something different, isn't it?' Norman did not reply, but looked at her vaguely. Bethany had the feeling that he was thinking about something else all together, but when she asked him if he was all right, he snapped that of course he was all right, what could be wrong? She put out her hand to him, but he brushed her impatiently aside and went up to bed.

Bethany sighed and sat down at the kitchen table. Some things just didn't seem to get any better. But this afternoon had been different. For the first time that she could remember she *had* enjoyed the visit, and she knew that Marjorie had too. Perhaps even Norman had liked it, although it was hard to tell. With a

226

shock of surprise she realised that she did not know much about what Norman thought these days. They had been living in separate worlds for so long now. She wondered how long this had been true. She certainly didn't think that it was a good way to go on, and as soon as she had collected her thoughts about Marjorie, it really would be time to sit down and think about herself and Norman.

Bethany went through the seventh lesson in her mind. The message it contained, that of giving her life purpose through living the lessons, had struck a chord in her mind that continued to reverberate. Bethany was by nature practical, and she loved the idea of centring the lessons within her and living a productive life according to their principles. She had already put her faith in the tenets outlined in the other lessons and was eager to put them into practice in coherent form. They would be the hub around which she could build her life, and they would effect changes that she was eager to embrace. Becoming purposeful in this way had certainly made her think differently about Marjorie. In truth, she hadn't really thought much about Marjorie at all for a long time. She hated the visits so much that she never stopped to think how Marjorie was feeling, whether she disliked the situation too, or even whether she would welcome a change. Thinking about Purpose had encouraged her to try to see Marjorie as a person rather than a hateful obligation. She was going to try to build a proper relationship with her mother-in-law which included talking together. And she must think about her marriage. Bethany sighed again and looked up at the ceiling. Norman would be lying in their bed with his back to her side of the bed. She would collect her thoughts first and then she would do something. That would be the best thing.

* * *

He stretched out his arms above his head and reached for his dressing gown. It was early, only just past six o'clock, and the garden outside was still dark and quiet. It would be at least an hour before the cold winter light would begin to filter through the bedroom curtains, and by then he would be up and dressed. He had always been an early riser, but in the first year of their marriage he and Claire had attended a course in meditation, and had enjoyed the peace that it had given them. It had been their habit to get up early and sit together in the downstairs room in calm stillness each morning. The habit was by now long established and he relished the part of the day that was his alone. He would finish his meditation, and the hours ahead would become meaningful. He dedicated his day to some higher purpose, and found that his mind and his being were clearer and more tranquil because of it. He knew from experience that it was all too easy to become mired in daily grind and forget the joys of living itself. Now that he was alone for the first time in many years he appreciated the silence all the more, and gave daily thanks that he had been blessed with so much to appreciate. Sometimes he felt very close to Claire in these moments, and could almost hear her voice as he stretched and stood up after his meditation.

She would go into the kitchen and make the early morning tea, while he drew the curtains back from the windows. If it was winter he would rake out the ashes of the fire, listening to the comforting chink of china cups and saucers and Claire moving around the kitchen in the next room. In the summer months he would open the French windows and carry a tray out onto the veranda so that they could have their tea looking out over the lawn and watch the birds feeding at Claire's beloved bird table.

Now that Claire was no longer here, he did all of this alone. As he drank his morning tea his mind ran on to the summer months. He loved the smell of the grass, the sound of the birds and the warmth of the early morning air. Winter brought entirely different joys, and he leaned back gratefully against the Aga stove that kept the kitchen warm with its constant glow. He cupped his tea in his hands and quietly enjoyed the unique sense of well-being which arose from being completely warm and at the same time seeing frost on the grass and trees outside the windows. Afterwards he went upstairs and got dressed, put on his tweed overcoat and went for a walk in the lane. The frost had covered the trees with its lacy filaments, and every blade of grass and stray leaf was transformed by a silvery coat which caught the rays of the fiery rising sun glinting over the hedgerow. His breath hung in clouds in front of him and his feet crunched with each step that he took in the quiet morning. A small vole ran across the lane in front of him, and he bent down to see if he could find where it had disappeared into the hedge. He turned back after a while and headed for the warmth of his kitchen, stamping his feet gratefully on the mat as he swung the heavy oak door shut behind him.

The postman had already called while he was out and a pile of letters lay on the mat. He stooped to pick them up and saw a thick brown envelope with a London postmark on it. He put it aside and opened the few letters and cards. Claire had been working as a nurse when he met her and had previously spent time in voluntary work abroad. Her friendships had been many, and still, almost seven months after she had died, hardly a day went by without a card or a letter from some far-flung corner of the earth from one of her colleagues or friends, expressing shock at her passing and sympathy for his loss. Many told of past memories of times they had shared, and all apologised for the tardiness of the letter, explaining that the news had only just reached them.

He answered each of the letters, sitting at the Jacobean desk that had been their wedding present to each other, thanking the writer for their kind thoughts, extending an open invitation to visit whenever they were back in the country, and explaining that she had not suffered, that it had been very sudden at the end, although not unexpected.

Claire had died in the same way that she had lived, with great courage and humour. As always, she had thought of him to the last, making him promise that he would try to be happy without her and telling him that she wanted him to remember her and be glad. In the end she had held his hand, closed her eyes and said, 'I think it's time to move on. I wonder what will happen next.' Her breathing had grown quiet and he had sat with her in the little white room at the hospice until he had known that there was no point in staying any longer.

This morning there was only one card postmarked Nigeria and he read its brief message of comfort and sorrow, and then put it back in the envelope to answer later. Then he turned to the large manila envelope which he knew was from the trustees of Claire's will. He had been made executor and, although the firm of solicitors handled the legal affairs, there were papers for him to sign and one day there would be decisions to make. When they had made their wills they had both left the bulk of their estate to the other, but Claire had two nephews whom she had been very fond of. They were still in education and she had set aside a certain amount of money to be put in trust for them to use when they reached eighteen. The letter that lay in front of him stated that, now that the legal affairs had been processed, the trust had provisionally been drawn up. They were now in a position to advise him as to the best course of action and required him to sign a number of papers. Since the papers involved were quite extensive, the solicitors felt that it would best be done in person and requested him to make an appointment at their London offices at his convenience. He folded this letter and put it back in the envelope. He went into the dining room and opened his desk, and put the correspondence into one of the pigeonholes to be answered later that day. He was not in a hurry to go up to London, but he would make an appointment and go up by train. Christmas was not far away. He could combine the trip with an afternoon shopping and looking at the Christmas lights. He would go in December.

* * *

Norman was thinking about Rita. This in itself was not unusual as he found that he could hardly think about anything else these days. They now managed to spend time together every day. Norman had taken to driving Rita home each night and coming in for a cup of tea. It was easy to tell Bethany that he was working late as she never objected. She was so preoccupied that she took indecently little interest in him at all these days. It was remarkable how knowing Rita had shown him how inferior in every way Bethany was. He and Rita were in such accord. He approved of everything about her. She dressed beautifully in a demure but alluring way which he found irresistible. He admired the way she decorated her house. Rita had been able to express her feminine, lacy personality in every room, with lavender sachets in frilly heart-shaped pouches on the tables, doilies under her pink china kitten ornaments, and even a tasteful way of concealing the toilet rolls in her 'little girls' room'. They were covered by a knitted shepherdess with flowing skirts of pink and tangerine artfully arranged over the offending article. The whole house smelled of Peachy Soft Air Freshener. Rita's manners were entrancing and she agreed with everything he said. It was extraordinary how compatible two people could be. Once he and his wife had been like that, but it hadn't been enough for her and she had let herself go badly.

It had been Rita herself who had first shown him this. When Norman had confided some of his frustrations about his home life, Rita had timidly suggested that it was shameful how some women 'let themselves go'. It was so disrespectful to the men. She herself believed that women had a duty to always show themselves to their best advantage and not to take short cuts with their appearance. As an example of this she casually mentioned that she herself would never wear tights, for instance. As she crossed her stockinged legs, Norman could only stare longingly at them and reflect that Bethany hardly ever even wore tights. His wife wore trousers.

Norman's thoughts temporarily drifted to Rita's suspender belt and his eyes glazed over. A hooting lorry hurtling towards him caused his heart to race even harder and he concentrated on the road again, and on the problem in hand. It was Tuesday and he had told Bethany he had a board meeting tonight and would be even later than usual. He would eat after work before the meeting started. In fact, he was going around to Rita's house, and he knew that he was going to begin a very serious conversation. Rita would be stunned at the possibility that he was going to raise, but he flattered himself that she would also be thrilled.

Some time ago, Rita had casually mentioned that she was lonely in her little house with just Muffy for company. How nice it would be to have a man around to do all of those wonderful jobs that they were so good at and that she found so difficult. Why, every time she needed to change a lightbulb she had to get nice Mr Fletcher from across the road to come and help her hold the ladder. Norman had felt such a rush of insane jealousy that he could barely speak, and he sat on Rita's powder-puff settee glowering and breathing heavily. Rita had hastily added that Mr Fletcher was nearly seventy, and even so she sometimes was not certain that he didn't look up her skirt while she balanced on the ladder. Blushingly, she confided that she even felt a little unsafe when he was around. Norman relaxed a little but still felt as though he would like to punch Mr Fletcher. He had told Rita that she must call on him whenever she needed to change lightbulbs. Rita had sighed with relief and been suitably grateful, but the conversation had caused Norman to think deeply. For the first time he considered the electrifying possibility that he was a man who could choose between two women.

Norman knew that Rita was so innocent and sweet that she would never even have considered the idea that he might leave Bethany for her. Once she had sighed and told him that she envied him his marriage. She appreciated his company so much, especially as she herself was a little girl left on the shelf. Almost absent-mindedly she had observed that she longed to devote herself to a man's every whim. How she envied his wife that she had had the chance to say, 'To love, honour and obey.' What a privilege! Then she had casually changed the subject. Norman had looked at her, lost deep in thoughts of his own. Rita had noticed his preoccupation and asked him what he was thinking. Norman had smiled mysteriously and told her not to worry her pretty little head about it. How surprised she would be if she could read his thoughts.

All of this and more sped through Norman's head during the journey to work each day. He had finally decided that he owed it to himself and Rita not to delay their happiness any further. He realised that his marriage to Bethany was a mistake. Why should he have to put up with it any longer? It was not as if she bothered to look after him properly any more, and any guilt he may have felt at one time had certainly vanished in the light of her recent behaviour. It would not be a shock to her, as she must certainly have sensed his unhappiness for some time now. Whereas poor little Rita would probably be overcome with confusion, so unexpected would his announcement be to her. Norman found himself looking forward to tonight.

One thing that bothered him was Marjorie's behaviour on Sunday. He knew that for years she had not approved of Bethany. Now he could fully understand why, and appreciate that, as usual, his mother had known best all along. For this reason he had been supremely confident that he could rely on her support when he confided in her. All it would take was careful handling. He had planned to visit Marjorie during the week and ask her advice. He would admit handsomely that he had been wrong, that she had known better than he, and that he would always listen to her in the future. Later, he would bring Rita along for inspection, and he allowed himself the luxury of a little daydream. Marjorie and Rita would be in total accord. 'How fortunate I am that you have rescued my beloved son from the unhappiness he has endured for so long,' Marjorie might say. The two ladies might shed a little tear and lacy handkerchiefs would be dabbed daintily. Norman had anticipated rather a pleasant interlude, with his mother graciously congratulating him on his new choice, and eagerly embracing Rita as a far more suitable choice for him than Bethany had ever been. It would be a whole new start for all of them.

But then his wife had behaved so strangely towards Marjorie last week. She had seized the initiative and had appeared to be thawing his mother's resistance. It was as if she suspected that she might need an ally in the future. Norman was beginning to wonder if he knew Bethany at all. He ground his teeth. It would be absolutely typical of her if after all these years she were to spoil everything by ingratiating herself with his mother to spite him. It had so bothered him that he had hardly been able to concentrate on what they were saying on Sunday evening. But he was determined. Not even his mother would make him stay with his unsuitable wife any longer. He had a right to happiness.

NOVEMBER

Bethany was feeling dreadful. She had a heavy cold, the kind that filled her head so that breathing was difficult at the best of times but when she lay down at night it was impossible. She had moved into the spare room so that she did not disturb Norman, as she propped herself up in bed and read for hours in the night when she could not sleep. For some reason her cold had made her far more uncomfortable than was usual. She tossed and turned in bed these days. Her limbs ached and she felt tired and unrefreshed when she woke in the morning. Somehow, she felt large and unwieldy in bed, and could not arrange her body so that she was comfortable. She tried sleeping on her back, her side, and her front, to no avail. It seemed as though since she had caught her cold she did not get more than a few hours sleep a night.

She supposed it was the lack of sleep that caused her to feel so lethargic and exhausted. Whatever it was, she felt as though she was barely able to drag herself through the day. Her cold made her breathless going up and down stairs, and housework seemed an effort. She felt as though she were walking through treacle when she went to the shops, and was grateful to sit down with a cup of tea at the end of any expedition. It was a relief to her that Norman ate so often at work recently. He rebuffed all her attempts at affection, and was curiously and blankly evasive when she tried to sit down with him to talk. She felt hurt and rejected, but tried to think about new ways to build communication between them. Maybe it was best to let him set the time and the place. He knew that she wanted to discuss things, and he obviously did not want to. Perhaps it was the wrong idea to try to force him. She would continue to practice the seventh lesson of Purpose, and wait for the right time.

She had gone to the local library to ask about Adult Education classes. Most of them had started in September, but the librarian had explained that there had been a poor take up this year, and that several classes had not filled their allocated places. If she did not mind missing a few weeks there was plenty of time still to enrol.

233

Bethany had brought the paper home and pored over it excitedly at the kitchen table. There was a poetry appreciation class on a Wednesday morning that she had almost decided to go to.

The classes were listed in alphabetical order. As she looked at Poetry, the entry above it caught her eye. It was Photography. The description underneath said that this course would be suitable for those with an interest in photography, some experience but little technical knowledge. The words of the seventh lesson passed through her mind. Before she had time to think and be frightened of Marjorie's reaction, she had picked up the telephone and dialled her number. She had had to look it up, and was aware of the fact that she and her mother-in-law never communicated by telephone. The Sunday visiting had been established about fifteen years previously, and if changes had to be made for any reason, Marjorie would ring Norman at work. Marjorie had been completely silent after Bethany had explained the reason for her call, and Bethany had leaned against the wall closing her eyes in anxiety, her heart beating in her throat. She could hear Marjorie breathing, so she knew that she hadn't hung up. Then to her amazement, Marjorie said, 'What time are these classes, Bethany, and where are they held?' Bethany had explained and said that she would post the brochure. Marjorie had thanked her and they had said good-bye. After she had replaced the receiver with a shaking hand, Bethany realised that for the first time since she had known her, Marjorie had pronounced her name correctly. She sat down shakily, leaned her head back against the wall again and smiled.

Both she and Marjorie had enrolled on their courses. They were on different days so they did not meet, but Marjorie had sent her a little card telling her that she had begun the class and thanking her for the useful information. Norman had said nothing as Bethany exclaimed over the handwriting, but silently watched her open the envelope. Bethany had read him the card over breakfast, and passed it over to him so he could look at it. Once again, he had baffled her with his reaction. He let the card drop from his fingers and brushed it aside. Instead of being pleased, or even interested in the classes, Norman had looked at her coldly and said, 'It won't work. Don't think you can change things, my mind is made up.' Bethany was totally confused. What could he mean? What was his mind made up about, and what had this to do with Marjorie's photography? She made a serious effort to detain Norman and ask him all the questions that hammered in her head, but he pushed past her brusquely and said that he was already late for work. As he rushed into the hall, gathering up his briefcase

234

and banging it against the door in his hurry, he muttered that he would be late back from work tonight and not to bother cooking. The door slammed behind him. Bethany stared blankly after him. Norman had even left his umbrella behind, which he never did after the first of October. What on earth was going on?

Bethany continued with her poetry appreciation classes. She bought the anthology the course required, and read avidly. She listened to the discussion, and shyly volunteered her opinions once or twice. There were about twelve people who appeared each week to sit at the tables arranged in rows in front of an old blackboard in one of the upper rooms of the education centre. Bethany had thought she would be nervous, but it so reminded her of school that she wanted to laugh. Most of the people were either retired or housewives like herself. The teacher was a jolly middle-aged blonde lady with bright eyeshadow, whose children attended the secondary school around the corner. She was heartily enthusiastic about her subject and thrilled when any of them made an original observation about what they were reading. She asked them to call her Jean, and was much prone to exclaiming 'Oh, good-oh, well *done*, that girl' or 'super, *what* a good idea, ladies'. All in all there was a friendly, relaxed feel to the room, and Bethany felt at home there. She particularly enjoyed the coffee breaks where they all sat in the smoky room in the basement of the building and talked. Bethany did not join in with much of the conversation, as it was often about children or husbands, but she listened and smiled. It really did remind her of school. They even had blackcurrant tea, so she did not have to drink the strong coffee that she could not imagine wanting again. The smell really was off-putting.

The next thing that happened was that Marjorie rang her. At first, Bethany didn't recognise her voice. When she realised who it was, she was so startled that she had to ask Marjorie to repeat what she was saying.

'Oh, do *listen*, I'm just ringing to say that I know we haven't always seen eye to eye about things, and I daresay it hasn't all been your fault . . . did you say something?'

Bethany had dropped the receiver and was fumbling to retrieve it.

'But I want to say that I don't approve at all, at *all*, I say. You must take charge immediately to stop this before it goes any further. I have said many a time that it's a great mistake to let them think that they can do as they like, that's where you are going wrong. It's not all your fault, I daresay, but I'm appalled that it's got this far. I will not countenance it, you can rely on that. But

I expect you to act.' Marjorie's voice sounded more strangulated than usual, and Bethany realised that her mother-in-law was in the grip of strong emotion. Marjorie continued. 'I can only do so much, but I await further developments. I shan't be hearing from them again in a hurry, you can be sure of that. I threw them out, the baggage.' On this note of grim satisfaction, there was silence, save for Marjorie's stertorous breathing. She seemed to be expecting something, but Bethany found herself so baffled that she couldn't think of anything to say at all. After a short pause Marjorie said, 'Well, I'll leave you to think.'

Bethany said yes, she would think, and thank you for ringing, Marjorie, . . . and Marjorie hung up.

Bethany walked into the kitchen in a daze. She really seemed to be losing her grip on reality. Could the angel have caused her to concentrate so much on the lessons that she had entirely missed a whole section from her life? It was like when you arrive a little late at the cinema and miss the beginning of the film. You watch the next bit, and think you are following, but then it switches to something else entirely and it turns out it's all been some kind of flashback. Norman had been so entirely predictable over the last twenty years that perhaps she had lost concentration and she had missed a whole section of the plot of her marriage. But what on earth had Marjorie to do with it? And what was 'the baggage'? One thing was certain. All this could not go on, and Marjorie was right. She had to act. She would make Norman tell her what was going on, no matter how late he arrived home tonight. She would not accept his evasions or refusals any more. She could see that waiting for him to take the initiative had been the wrong tack to take. She had to get to the bottom of it all. She began to think out some questions to ask.

That night, Norman was whistling softly between his teeth as he drew up in the drive and switched off the ignition of the car. It had to be said that the whistle was not the nonchalant warble of a carefree man. Instead it was more the anxious, distracted sort that means that the whistler is thinking deep thoughts that are not entirely pleasant. It escaped through his clenched teeth in an abstracted hiss, and it indicated a man who had been confident in the expectation that his day would go well and whose hopes had been cruelly dashed.

Norman sat in the dark bitterly contemplating his steering wheel. The afternoon with Marjorie had been a disaster. At the last minute he had changed his plans about confiding in her and asking her advice, and had decided to introduce Rita to his mother straight away. The idea had come to him in a blinding flash of inspiration. Rita would be sure to ease the slightly uncomfortable nature of the meeting due to her delicacy and charm. She would know the right thing to say. Norman saw now that it had been cowardly of him not to want to face Marjorie alone. Worse than that, it had been a serious tactical error, and his mother had seized upon it with the rapacious ferocity of a victorious general. She had taken no hostages. They had arrived unannounced late that morning instead of joining the Friday crowd at lunchtime. Norman wondered if their absence would be noticed and whether they would be the topic of conversation. Secretly, he didn't mind if they were.

However, arriving without telephoning first had been his first mistake. Marjorie did not take kindly to unexpected visitors, and had been known to refuse to answer her door. Today she had taken a long time to respond to 'Rule Britannia' and Norman had begun to experience the first ominous stirrings of doubt. Rita had no such misgivings. Sublimely confident in herself now that her chosen man had selected her over his mate, she glowed with satisfaction and happiness. When Marjorie answered the door, Rita had launched immediately into a flutter of social niceties. Ignoring Marjorie's flinty expression and sonorous breathing, she breezed past her in the hall and swept into the front room.

Things had gone from bad to worse. Rita had begun to explain at great length that Norman was unhappy, had been very unhappy in his marriage for a long time. She had laid her hand on Marjorie's arm and confided that they, as women, knew how to console an unhappy man, and she was sure that Marjorie (she didn't mind Rita calling her that, did she?) would know what she meant. Norman had felt a dull ache beginning in the pit of his stomach as he watched his mother's neck deepen in colour to a dark red. It reminded him of the day he spent his dinner money at the sweetshop when he was seven. Still Marjorie had not said a word. The final straw had come when Rita had noticed that a stray hair curler was stuck in his mother's hair just behind her ear. Marjorie had obviously been engaged in her toilette when they had rung, and they had interrupted this most intimate of feminine tasks. Norman had never in all his years seen Marjorie with curlers in, and he knew that this was as utterly a forbidden subject as those feminine harems of the East, guarded only by unfortunate eunuchs. Violation, or even mention of the mysteries of womanhood, was punishable by death.

To Norman's deepening horror, Rita had not ignored this offending item of apparel, but had actually drawn attention to it with a silvery laugh that rivalled his mother's better efforts on finer days. She had offered to remove it for Marjorie, and suggested the name of a hairdresser that she herself attended and found to be very good. She patted her own blonde coiffeur with every evidence of satisfaction. Norman was by now certain that the whole visit had been a fiasco. He did not dare speak, and could hardly believe that Rita had made such an uncharacteristic blunder. Why, even Bethany had never offended his mother like this. Marjorie was by now almost purple and was shaking with suppressed emotion. Her silence had not been due to lack of conviction, but to the necessity of choosing the choicest means of expression. When it came, her wrath was terrible, and Norman still shook when he thought of it.

She had begun with Rita, pouring scorn on her explanations of Norman's unhappy marriage. It was a well known fact that all married couples described themselves as less than happy, and only a true woman knew the value of marital strife. Others such as Rita were mere vultures, craven hyenas not worthy of the name Woman, who sluttishly fed on their sisters' leavings, or worse, stole the prize of man from under the noble gaze of those who were proud to call themselves Wife. Marjorie drew herself up to her full height and appeared to bear down on Rita, who shrank back in terror, understanding too late how dreadfully the visit was going. Norman was powerless to protect her as his mother's awful tide of vitriol poured on and on. And then Marjorie had turned her flood of invective on him. Norman did not even want to think about the things she had said. Rita at least had been given the epithet of vulture and hyena. Spineless worms and jellyfish featured large in the next portion of Marjorie's tirade.

He had remained speechless until the very end, when Marjorie had finally drawn breath, and stood, unyielding and puce, in front of him. Drawing the trembling Rita towards him, Norman had mustered every scrap of masculine dignity and defiance he possessed. He had faced his mother and said in a voice which only held the merest quiver in it, 'Nevertheless, Mother, I have made my choice, and here she is.' Rita had shrunk against him, obviously fearing she was to be thrust forward as a shield against Marjorie's recurring wrath, but Norman was made of sterner stuff. Although his knees were shaking, he managed, 'And you always try to boss me, but it's not fair.' Aware that this sounded rather childish, and wishing he could exit on a more statesmanlike note, he had paused, and then hurriedly pushed Rita before him into the hall. Thinking rapidly, the words had only come to him as they were almost outside the door. Gathering his courage again, Norman lifted his head and looked his mother right in the eye. 'So there!' he shouted, and scurried to the car with Rita close on his heels.

Norman closed his eyes and laid his head down on the steering wheel. How could it have all gone so wrong? After a while he straightened up. He did not care that it had gone wrong today. He was going to go through with it. There was no going back now. He and Rita had gone straight back to her house, and he had spent two hours calming her, as she was weeping hysterically. In desperation, he had telephoned Reg at the office and explained that Rita had been taken ill. He no longer cared what anyone thought. Rita had only stopped crying when he had reassured her that he was not to be ruled by anybody, that they would be married as soon as possible, and that nothing had changed. Rita dried her reddened eyes and reapplied her make-up at the bedroom dressing table. In no time at all she had recovered, and they had spent the rest of the afternoon together, making plans. And now he was home. The hours had sped by and now he realised that he was rather late, but of course none of that mattered any more. Norman glanced at his watch. He wondered if B had gone to bed. Who knew *what* she would do these days. Norman momentarily remembered that it was he who was deviating quite substantially from the routine, but told himself that it was Bethany's fault in the first place. In any case, it was time to look to the future, not linger in a situation that was quite pointless.

Rita and he had worked it all out. He would move in with her as soon as he had sorted things out. Of course it would all be separate bedrooms and all above board. They had both agreed to this, though Norman had tried to say that he thought that times had changed, and that perhaps ... He had tailed off in the face of Rita's suddenly icy demeanour, and hurriedly said that of course separate rooms would be most suitable. And of course it wouldn't be for long, since there would be no point in long, drawn-out divorce proceedings. Bethany would most probably be happy that he had found Rita. He had always been a good husband to her, it was only right that she be happy for him now that he could no longer continue in what was clearly an unsatisfactory state of affairs.

And then Bethany would have to sell the house. It was ridiculous that she continue to live there, as there was far too much space for one person. Rita had been adamant on this point and Norman had agreed, telling himself that Bethany would be glad to move once he had gone. She had shown herself to be indifferent to housework anyway. A small flat would be much more suitable. They would divorce quickly and then he and Rita would be free to begin their new life together. Rita had by this time recovered sufficiently to do an excited little dance around him, and he had daringly clutched at her behind and pulled her close. She had squealed and laughed. Norman had begun to feel a little better. By the time he had left Rita, with promises of a quick return, he had been confident that his talk with his wife was a mere formality, a brief interlude that would be over in a flash, leaving him free to begin a blissful state of conjugal happiness with Rita. His mind had run through to this felicitous future situation, and he had been serene and unruffled.

Now that he was actually outside his house, Norman began to feel less sure of himself. There was no doubt that the disastrous encounter with his mother this morning had shaken his confidence, and although the delightful Rita had soothed him somewhat during the afternoon, he was not looking forward to the conversation he was about to have. For a while, Norman allowed himself to drift back into memories of Rita in her bedroom, after she had applied her make-up. She had said that her stockings were chafing terribly, and asked if he would mind dreadfully if she removed them. Norman had even been allowed to help when her little fingers found the clasp of her suspenders a little too difficult. His hands shaking with excitement, he had accomplished the task without too much difficulty, and indeed had managed to say in a voice that hardly shook at all that he did not find the clasp stiff in the slightest. Rita had intimated strongly that as soon as he had dealt with Bethany, there would be so many of these little jobs that she would need help with.

Norman suddenly found that his resolve had been strengthened, and he got out of the car and strode to the front door with manly determination.

The house was dark when he got in, although Bethany had left the landing light on. He hoped that she would not be asleep. It would be so much easier if they could talk downstairs. Maybe she would help him pack his suitcases. Norman hung up his mackintosh and took off his shoes. He went upstairs and opened the bedroom door. His wife turned over in bed immediately and switched on the side light by her bed. To Norman's slight alarm, she wore an expression of determination, and before he could open his mouth, she said, 'Norman we just have to talk, it's no good putting it off any longer. I need to know exactly what is going on. I think it's best that you tell me exactly what you have been thinking and feeling, because I just can't work it out by myself.' Norman's mouth now fell open of its own accord. The unfortunate thing was that he couldn't think of any words to send out of it. He shut it again, and swallowed deeply. Now that it had actually come to the point, he did not know how to proceed. He sat down weakly on the edge of the bed. Bethany was speaking again.

'Why don't you get undressed and put on your pyjamas, and we can sit up in bed and discuss it? I could make us a milky drink and we'll just work through whatever we have to together.'

Norman gasped. He had visualised the scene as he confronted his wife, and it involved her sitting down in a chair and looking up at him while he paced in front of her, preferably with a suitable drink like a sherry in his hand. He would hold the floor, state what had to be said, and she would listen to him. Now this comfortable and masculine scenario was all being swept away with milky drinks and pyjamas.

He realised that Bethany was waiting for him to answer. She was watching him with a patient but puzzled expression on her face. He cleared his throat and said, 'B, I need to talk to you.' Before she could interrupt and explain that this was exactly what she was suggesting, he hurried on. 'I think it would be best if you came downstairs and we sat down. I should like a drink, and then I will say what I want to say.' Having managed to establish the commanding position of his fantasies, Norman was then seized with indecision. Should he wait for B to get up, pass her her dressing gown and slippers and suchlike, or should he just turn on his heel and hope that she followed him? He decided on the latter, and went quickly downstairs. He went directly into the sitting room and waited.

He tried out several positions to see which felt the most comfortable. The first was standing with his back to the fireplace with his hands on his hips. This seemed a little confrontational, so he tried putting his hands in his pockets. The pockets were a little small so that he had to stuff his hands into fists, and they caused his trousers to strain around his legs. Norman felt faintly silly, so tried a more casual stance. He leaned casually with one elbow on the mantelpiece. Then he found that whichever way he leaned he would be sideways on to the door through which Bethany would enter, and would have to swivel round, still leaning on one elbow, which would not work. Norman was beginning to become desperate. It was vitally important to get the right stance, he felt, and was losing confidence again at his inability to do so. Finally, he sat down in the chair directly opposite the door with his legs casually crossed. Satisfied, he relaxed a little. He was ready.

After a few more minutes, Norman's composure had evaporated.

Where was B? Surely she was going to come down and not leave him there in the cold sitting room all by himself? What was he going to do if she stayed where she was? Would he go up and insist that she follow him? One thing he could not do, and that was deal with pyjamas and milky drinks and suchlike. On that front he was determined.

Norman had just lost his nerve and gone out into the hall, when he met Bethany on the stairs. Startled, he panicked and scuttled back into the sitting room so that he could be sitting casually when she came in. Panting, he threw himself backwards into the chair and rapidly crossed his legs just as Bethany came through the door. Norman wondered if she had noticed that the chair was rocking back perilously under the force of his impact with it, and imagined that he saw a fleeting expression of surprise cross her face. He quickly managed to recover his equilibrium by grasping its arms firmly and shifting his weight forward again. Bethany sat down on the sofa, and Norman decided that she probably hadn't noticed anything really.

Norman cleared his throat again. The moment had arrived. He stood up. He was ready.

'Are you sure you don't want some cocoa? Or a cup of tea? I'm going to have one,' Bethany said.

Norman almost screamed at her, but she had already risen and was making for the kitchen. In desperation he reached out and held her arm firmly. 'Just sit down and listen, you can have tea later, when I, when I ... well, later.' He steered her back to the sofa and began to speak. 'It has, I think, been clear to both of us for a long while that things have not been proceeding satisfactorily between us. You are certainly aware that I have not been happy with the way that you have been behaving recently. I have sometimes been driven to my wits' end by your inappropriate, and at times bizarre, conduct. I have done my best to make allowances but am no longer content to put up with it. I ... ' Norman hesitated. He was at no loss for words when it came to cataloguing Bethany's misdemeanours, as he had run through the liturgy of complaints many times in his own mind. But he held back from the declaration that he knew he must make next, the one that explained about Rita.

He looked at Bethany to see her reaction so far. She was very pale, almost white against the peach colour of her dressing gown, and she was sitting very still, her eyes fixed on his face. She appeared quiet, and not likely to interrupt him. Norman was encouraged. For a ghastly moment it had occurred to him that his wife might behave like his mother, and he could not have coped with two such scenes in one day. In fact, if one added Rita's hysterical outburst this afternoon, Norman felt that he had had quite enough feminine dramas. He ran his hand through the sparse hair on the top of his head and continued. 'Yes . . . You must see that this unsatisfactory state of affairs cannot continue. I . . . ' Again, Norman hesitated on the brink of the announcement. He could think of no words that would not incriminate him somehow. It was one thing to list his wife's misdemeanours but another to admit that he had, well, had found someone else. The thought of poor Rita struggling with her suspenders all alone spurred him on, and his words spilled out in a rush. 'I have found somebody who . . . who fulfils everything I require in a companion, and I wish to be with her. I no longer want to continue with this marriage, and I am going to move out of this house. I am sure that this will come as no surprise to you, and I think it best not to continue trying to hide the fact that we no longer get along. Delay is pointless and I intend to pack my things and move out. We can discuss financial and legal matters in more detail later on.'

Norman looked again at Bethany. He had been staring fixedly at a point just above her head all the time that he had been speaking, and addressed his remarks to the wall. Now he saw that she had not moved, and was still staring at him, chalky white and motionless. He was glad that she was not going to make a scene. If she had cried like Rita he would not have known what to do, but B had never felt emotions very deeply. It made it easier to make the arrangements. All the same, Norman suddenly felt hesitant about leaving the room. He knew that he had said all there was to say, and was now free to be practical about suitcases and clothes, so why did he feel rooted to the spot? He must make a move, Rita would be wondering what had happened to him.

Norman tiptoed out of the room. It didn't seem right to ask his wife to help him pack after all. Norman told himself that he would exercise some sensitivity and not ask her. Bethany was obviously thinking, so he wouldn't disturb her. It was all for the best really, it would give him time to pack undisturbed. He went upstairs. It had all gone very well, considering. He began to whistle softly, and then stopped himself. Best not. Norman spent a busy 45 minutes packing. He packed a suitcase for the short term and several more containing most of his possessions. It was quite extraordinary how little he owned, he thought. Rita would most probably take him shopping and buy him some more things. She had said as much last week. He was looking forward to it.

Norman then made several journeys up and downstairs carrying his suitcases. He would ask B to help him when it came to getting them in the car. She could hold the door. It sounded as though there was quite a wind blowing up. It was marvellous how light-hearted he felt now that he had got it all off his chest, as if a weight had been lifted from him. Things were really going to work out well.

A tiny part of his mind registered that there was total silence in the living room. At first he didn't want to acknowledge the fact that his wife had not moved or spoken since he had broken the news of his departure, but gradually, as he completed his tasks, he was forced to consider the possibility that she was not feeling as sanguine as he was. Norman put the moment off as long as he could, checking the bedroom for items that he had missed (he remembered his slippers under the bed, he would have been sorry to miss those) and then gingerly pushed open the living room door.

To his relief B was still sitting on the sofa, staring ahead of her. She turned her head slowly when he came in and looked at him, saying nothing. Norman felt a bit guilty. It was obvious that she had taken it harder than he had thought. He supposed it was only to be expected, now you come to think about it. They had had some good times. Norman felt suddenly sentimental, and filled with the urge to make her feel better. B wasn't a bad old stick, he thought, and now that he was moving on he could afford to be magnanimous. She had just let herself go, which had been a big mistake. She really was a bit heavy these days. Maybe when things had settled down a bit, he could introduce Rita to her and she could give her a bit of advice and suchlike. It would be the least he could do.

Norman sat down awkwardly on the very edge of the sofa beside Bethany. He patted her hand. 'Look, I'm going to be going now. I daresay some of what I said was a little harsh. I merely wanted you to understand how unsatisfactory it all has been for me.' Norman stood up and looked down at his wife. He honestly did want to help. 'Perhaps you should read some magazines, buy some make-up. I think you've, well, you've let yourself go a bit. Go on a diet, that sort of thing. Anyway, I'd better be off now. You'll be all right. I will ring and let you know where I can be contacted.'

Still Norman hesitated. Bethany hadn't said a word. He felt a little exasperated with her. First his mother had hurled abuse at him, and now his wife was making no effort at all to respond to his very sensitive handling of what could have been a difficult situation.

244

If that wasn't just typical. If she couldn't be bothered to see him off, he would just have to go. He bent and patted Bethany's hand again, this time with rather a hard vertical pat, and gritted his teeth. He wanted to shake her.

'Goodbye, then.' Still his wife sat like a stone, and Norman finally lost patience. He couldn't wait indefinitely. He loaded his suitcases with difficulty into the car in the high wind and drove off to Rita's. He could not wait to tell her all about it, how well he had handled it all.

*   *   *

It was nearly two weeks after Norman's departure, and Bethany was lying in bed at nine o'clock in the morning. She had got up and sat in silence down in the living room earlier that day, and then on an impulse had gone back to bed. She was still there, and was considering going downstairs and getting herself some tea and toast and eating it in bed. She had not yet cancelled the delivery of Norman's newspaper, so she might even get that and make a day of it. Up until a few weeks ago, it was unheard of for her to be in bed after 7.15 a.m. She once had been so ill with the flu nine years ago that she had been unable to get up in the morning, but Norman had been so suspicious about her symptoms that she had managed to go down and boil the kettle for him before staggering back upstairs. Lying in bed merely because she quite liked the thought of it would have rocked the foundations of Norman's world.

Bethany lay back on her pillow and looked around the bedroom with satisfaction. It really was extraordinarily different in the house now that Norman wasn't in it. For morning after morning, year after year, she and Norman had proceeded through the same careful routine. Like stately dancers in a complicated gavotte they had stiffly manoeuvred around each other in the kitchen, each performing their own steps so as not to intrude on the other's business. They had occasionally met in the middle and done a sort of pirouette, an exchange of necessary information, so to speak, but in general they had proceeded on their ways unchanged for many years. When Norman had made his announcement two weeks ago she had been stunned into immobility. It was not until she heard her husband starting his car in the driveway that she had managed to absorb that it was happening. It had just been so totally unexpected, so shocking, that her mind would not take it in. She had sat there in her chair for about half an hour, saying to

245

herself, 'Norman has left me. Norman has found somebody else, and he has left me.'

At the end of the thirty minutes she had thrown back her head and roared with laughter. Just as she thought she had calmed down, another thought would come into her mind and the laughing would start again. She regained her composure and then heard 'Your inappropriate, and at times bizarre, conduct' and the mirth built up in ever increasing waves. Later she made her face serious until she remembered 'fulfils everything I require in a companion', and she let out a huge snort. It was this thought that finally sobered her. Poor Norman. Everything he required in a companion. She wondered what that was, for it had certainly not been her. For some reason, the image of him struggling with suitcase after suitcase in the howling gale had set her off again. Oh poor Norman, things just never seemed to work out as he planned. After an hour or so she had locked the front door and gone upstairs to bed, her ribs aching. For several minutes at a time before she finally fell asleep she was unable to stop the smile on her lips, but told herself firmly that this would not do. She must be serious. It was a very serious situation. Bethany let out another undignified snort and fell asleep.

The next day she had lain in the bed thinking. It was odd that she felt very little sadness at all. She could honestly say that she wished Norman every happiness, and she hoped she would find an opportunity to tell him that. In a way she felt grateful to him for freeing her. He was right, they couldn't have gone on as they were. It was just that she hadn't envisaged quite the outcome that he had precipitated.

The accumulation of the seven lessons had built up a reserve of strength and joy in her, so that she felt able to cope with whatever life might bring. Indeed, her new-found sense of purpose caused her to feel a surge of excitement at the opportunities that had suddenly opened up. On impulse she had thrown off the bed-clothes, dressed rapidly, and gone out for a walk without eating breakfast. Norman would have been horrified. When she returned she had written all her thoughts down in the form of a list. She would have so much more time now that she didn't have to condense her day into Norman's routines. But she presumed she would have to get a job now. Would Norman be making her some kind of allowance? She put telephoning Norman at the top of her list of things to do. She would suggest they go out to lunch to discuss arrangements. She was now so much freer to live life well. She didn't, of course, mean what so often is meant by 'Living the good life' in terms of money and luxuries. Bethany was excited because she could begin to see a way of fulfilling the seventh lesson, of living the best life she could. She knew that she was starting to form the habit of holding her lessons at the centre of all she did, and that this was the message of the seventh lesson. This habit imbued her life with purpose. But she realised that the inevitable consequence of each lesson was that it led to the next. She could no longer stay in one place, but was led inexorably outwards or upwards in a sort of expansion. The seventh lesson appeared to her to lead to a question. Purpose was important because it guided her actions, but what form would her actions take, she wondered. And then of course the angel had filled the silence.

Contribution.

Bethany had told herself that the next time she received communications from the angel she would definitely not say 'Oh'. It was so unoriginal. She stopped herself in time and said instead, 'Contribution?' It was a little better than 'Oh', but, she had to admit, not much.

> THE EIGHTH LESSON IS THAT OF CONTRIBUTION OR GIVING.
> A LIFE OF SERVICE TO OTHERS IS ONE THAT IS FULFILLED,
> PURPOSEFUL AND DISCIPLINED.
> ACTIVELY SEEK TO FIND A WAY OF GIVING IN
> EVERY SITUATION.
> CONTRIBUTE WHAT IS UNIQUELY YOURS TO GIVE, AND JOY
> WILL FLOW.
> GIVING IS THE KEY WHICH WILL OPEN
> YOUR UNDERSTANDING.
> ALL IS BOUND TOGETHER, CONNECTED,
> AND A LIFE OF CONTRIBUTION REVEALS THE CONNECTION.

Bethany understood immediately. Not all of it – the part about connections seemed a bit confusing – but the general sense struck a chord within her. She supposed that it was a sort of reward for her struggles with some of the earlier lessons. Now that she had incorporated them practically into her life, it was as though the path had been paved to make her progress easier. The good feeling that she had experienced when putting Marjorie on to the photography classes, for instance. She had felt so happy that she was able to help, and wanted nothing more than that. It was unlike any feeling she had had recently, and she wanted to build on it. 'A life of service' then, needn't be the one of a sort of priggish do-gooder. Bethany would cut off her arm rather than become that. But this was just a way of being truly happy. She could see that her life was going to become a lot busier. She could hardly wait. She knew that if she went about her business quietly and peacefully, holding the lessons at the heart of her day, the angel would send plenty of opportunity for practice. The eighth lesson felt like a kind of completion and she would be content to work at it for the rest of her life. She wrote it down in her book.

After a few days she began to examine the feeling that she had experienced about the eighth lesson, that of it being some kind of completion. It was the first time that she hadn't had the sense of her new lesson leading somewhere. Could it be that the angel had given her all she needed now? If so, it meant that their communication was at an end. She tried asking the angel if this was the case, but there was no answer. This raised the question that was never very far from her thoughts: the angel had said they were to meet when she had completed the lessons. When and how were they going to meet? She considered the facts that she knew. The only conclusion she had drawn previously was that she was somehow going to enter another world. She had deduced that one didn't just meet angels in one's daily life, and that pointed to the fact that she might be going to die. She had never actually talked to anybody who claimed to hear the voice of an angel. This might mean that all the people who had heard angels were now dead. She had no means of verifying this, because she didn't talk to that many people and it wasn't the sort of thing that would come up during a coffee break. People just didn't talk about angels, and for all she knew, hearing the voices of angels could be more frequent than she had previously supposed. And if she was going to conclude that, then the logical outcome of her train of thought was that it was technically possible that she might meet an angel in real life.

Bethany was nothing if not logical, and she did not shrink from what was an unpleasant idea. She knew deep within herself on an unconscious level that all was not right with her body. She was easily tired, sometimes her limbs ached and the blood pounded in her head, and she had great difficulty sleeping. Occasionally she was seized by cramping pains in her stomach. However, these were not symptoms of an illness as such, and she was easily able to dismiss them as part of getting older if she wanted to. In addition, if she was about to die, what was the point of having these lessons revealed to her? Surely it was a bit of a waste of time if she wasn't going to be allowed to put them into practice for any length of time. On the other hand, it was possible that she was undertaking some kind of spiritual crash course for the dying. So she might actually have an illness or be going to have an accident that would cut short her life, and she would meet her angel in that way.

This was not a happy train of thought, and Bethany concluded that there was no way that she could know the answer to her questions at the moment. Difficult as it was not to worry about it, she still had plenty to do with the eight lessons, and there was the question of a life to be lived as best she could. So she attempted to put it all out of her mind and began to get on with the absorbing process of living with purpose through Contribution.

DECEMBER

At the end of the second week in December Bethany was sitting on the living room floor surveying her handiwork. All the chairs were covered with dust sheets, her hair was tied back and there was a large splodge of paint on the end of her nose. In spite of the chaos around her, Bethany felt content. She had worked hard all day, with only short breaks for meals and drinks. A ladder was propped at the far end of the room and the late afternoon sunlight streaming in through the bow window revealed that the walls of the room were no longer a dusty greyish green, but instead a bright and cheerful yellow. Bethany went tiredly upstairs and peeled off her painting-clothes. She put on her new white towelling robe and ran herself a bath. As she waited for the bath to fill she reflected on the last few weeks.

Norman had telephoned her from work and they had met for lunch in the rather grimy public house that he had suggested. At first he had seemed ill at ease and kept glancing around him as though he thought someone might disturb them. After they had ordered their sandwiches he relaxed a little, and as he reached for his new leather briefcase and put it beside him on the seat, he was almost his old self.

'I like your briefcase,' said Bethany. 'Did . . . did your friend buy it for you?'

Norman looked at first startled, and then rather embarrassed. 'Yes.'

He cleared his throat. 'I'd like to get down to details, B . . . um . . . Bethany.'

Bethany reached across and laid her hand on his arm. 'Norman, before we do, I should really like to say that I don't mind. Really I don't. I think you were quite right with a lot of the things you said, and I am so glad you have found someone who can make you happy. What's her name?'

Norman raised his eyes to hers and she could read both relief and curiosity in them. He did not pull his arm away as he would have done in the past, but instead let her hand rest where she had placed it. He paused and then said, 'Rita. She's called Rita. She's my secretary.'

Bethany smiled and said, 'Is she pretty?'

Norman suddenly felt that the conversation he was having was not suitable. After all, Bethany was still his wife, and he should be making it clear that the reason they were meeting was in order to remedy this situation, not to discuss his present domestic arrangements. All the same, he felt grateful to Bethany. She was being very pleasant, not at all the way that he and Rita had imagined she would be. They had talked about it over breakfast. Rita had taken a dainty nibble of her tiny low-calorie slice of bread this morning (no butter or margarine, just the merest hint of no-added-sugar preserve) and said, 'Don't let her get round you, Norman. She'll probably want all she can get, and you must be firm. After all, we have to live too.' Norman had straightened himself and vowed that he certainly wouldn't allow Bethany to get round him in any way. But it didn't look as though it was going to be like that at all. Bethany actually seemed glad that he had found Rita. Nevertheless, it wouldn't do to discuss Rita with her. He was sure that was not the usual thing at all in such situations, so he ignored Bethany's question and instead took out some papers from his case. He began to outline matters as he saw them, laying out his papers on the table as he did so. Bethany studied them carefully, and sneaking careful glances at her face as she read, Norman saw that she was indeed taking in what he was saying. He was glad that he had put his foot down with Rita over this meeting.

Rita and he had had their first lover's tiff over Norman's proposal to meet Bethany. Rita favoured engaging a solicitor straight away, and making all arrangements through a third party. She thought that Norman should have no personal contact with his wife from now on. Norman had disagreed. He would talk to Bethany first and if they could agree without the services of a solicitor over finances and arrangements, then he thought that would be satisfactory. Rita had been a little hurt at how adamant he had been, and tried to change his mind. She had even shed a few tears at how hard and cruel he was being, not taking her opinions into account. She had left the room hurriedly, dabbing at her eyes with a handkerchief, and had not come back for a while. Norman had remained firm, and had not followed her upstairs.

Unbeknown to Rita, Reg had taken him aside at work the previous day and had a sharp word about solicitors. 'Complete arses, old boy. Take the skin off your back and they shove it where the sun doesn't shine. Avoid them at all costs, if you know what I mean. Once the little woman gets a solicitor, she'll have the bit between her teeth and be galloping full tilt down to the finishing line. I know, I've been fleeced myself. Don't you go anywhere near our friends with the poncey wigs or you'll regret it.' Norman had nodded seriously and stared into his pint. As a man of the world, Reg undoubtedly knew what he was talking about, and it made sense to try to sort things out on his own. Stubbornly holding fast to his plan, Norman had refused to be swayed by Rita's persuasion, and now he was glad that he hadn't. Bethany seemed not only to understand what he was proposing, but she was showing every sign of agreeing in principle. As far as he was concerned, Norman felt that he would be getting a very good deal if matters were sorted out today.

Norman began by telling Bethany that he didn't want to remain tied to their marriage, and would rather not pay maintenance for any lengthy period of time. Instead he proposed that he make the deeds of the house over to Bethany, to do what she wanted with it. Property values had increased in the last few years, and he thought that if she chose to sell it, she would be able to buy a small flat and retain a small sum as a nest egg. If she wanted to carry on living there, she would have the satisfaction of knowing that she had a material asset. Either way, he thought that she would have to find means of supporting herself. Norman had looked up anxiously and somewhat belligerently at this, wondering what his wife's reaction would be. He wasn't sure, but he thought that she would be within her rights to insist on a monthly sum to support herself with. Rita seemed to think so anyway. To his great surprise, Bethany readily agreed. She was saying something about training to be a teacher. Norman looked at her in astonishment. She had never intimated that this was what she wanted to do. Bethany had laughed at the look on his face, and squeezed his hand.

'Don't worry, Norman, you know well enough that it's not you who's gone mad. It is me, you know.' To his further astonishment, Norman had found himself laughing too. That hadn't happened since ... well, he couldn't remember the last time that had happened.

Bethany had agreed in principle to everything he proposed, but wondered if they could perhaps come to a temporary solution to the problem of what she was to do for money until the house was sold. Norman had already thought of this, and produced another sheet of paper from his briefcase. He would be willing to pay the bills for the house, and make Bethany an allowance each month until such time as she sold the house, provided it was not for longer than six months. Bethany thought he was being fair about this. She looked at the amount Norman proposed to give her and privately thought that he had overestimated the allowance. She decided not to mention this, as it would do no harm to save a little each month. However, six months seemed a little short, and she asked if nine would be stretching him too much. Norman, who had been prepared to stretch to a year, magnanimously conceded that he thought he could possibly manage nine months.

They concluded this part of the discussion with some relief and ate their sandwiches for a while. After a short pause, Bethany suggested between bites that they engage a solicitor to draw up an agreement between them. If it was possible, this solicitor could arrange the divorce papers, although she rather thought they might have to have one each. But she assured him that she would be quite content with the house, and did not want to impinge on his new life with Rita in any way. Norman actually patted her hand and, rather to his own surprise, suggested another drink. He found himself quite unexpectedly revealing a little nest egg of his own in the form of a few shares that had done rather well in the last few years. He had planned not to mention these, but Bethany had been so amiable that he felt uncomfortable about concealment. He had no documentation with him, an unfortunate oversight, he explained, but there was one other matter. There were a number of shares in his name that he felt it only right to divide between them. Perhaps Bethany could use hers to buy a second-hand car?

It was now Bethany's turn to be astonished. She had no means of knowing about Norman's shares and would not have investigated her rights further, since she felt the house was more than fair. How nice of Norman to be so generous. She felt like hugging him, but realised that he would be mortified by such a public show of affection. She restrained herself, but thanked him warmly for being so kind and honest. Norman felt a glow inside. He felt fully in charge and rather smug. He was glad that he hadn't mentioned the shares to Rita. Reg was right, it didn't do to . . . what was the expression he had used? To 'Let the fillies have their head'. Norman was a man of the world. If he chose to be fair and generous to his ex-wife, it was nobody's business but his own.

After they had finished their drinks, Norman had walked back to work, and Bethany had caught the bus back home. Before she had left, Norman had promised to explain all about the pension contributions she had made when she had been working. He knew all about these things and it was important that she did too. He just stopped short of inviting Bethany to Rita's house so that he could go through it all. Perhaps he had better consult Rita about this. After all, there were still protocols to be observed. All in all though, it had gone very well, and both were happy with the outcome.

Bethany had decided that she would put the house up for sale in the spring. She had asked a very nice young man from the estate agent in the high street to come around and value it. She had been astounded at the price he thought it would fetch. He had been helpful and seemed very keen to get the property on his books. He quoted his commission and Bethany had said she would come back to him when she had made her decision. After he had gone, she had done a delighted dance around the living room. There were two other estate agents in the town, and she thought it would do no harm to get second opinions. To her surprise, both had asked what her first valuation had been. As she made the third young man a cup of tea, it occurred to her that she was in a rather good position. She wondered whether they would reduce their commission? Only she hadn't really decided whom to put the house on with, and it would help her to focus her thoughts. The young man had made some pretence of looking through his folder of properties, and then had quickly reduced his commission to 1.5% 'in principle'. Although Bethany had never sold a house before, she could see that this represented quite a saving. She asked the other agents what they would do, and achieved a commission pledge from the first young man of only 1%. This she agreed and felt absurdly pleased with herself. She planned to put the house on the market in March, when the first bulbs would be out in the garden.

All of this occupied Bethany's thoughts as she lay in the hot steaming bath water. It was possible that she would be moving to a new home in March. That would be less than a year since she first heard the voice of her angel, and yet, for all that had happened, it felt like she had lived a whole lifetime. It was only eight and a half months, and she had achieved so much with the help of the lessons. She closed her eyes and thought about what she planned to do. She had decided that she had no need of a car as yet, and thought that she would put the money from the shares into a savings account. She was adding to this with a portion of the allowance Norman was giving her. She found that she could live easily on a mere two-thirds of the sum she was receiving, and her nest egg was accumulating nicely.

Bethany looked with interest at the particulars of flats that dropped onto her doormat. In the meantime she had embarked on an ambitious programme of redecoration. Norman and she had not changed the colour schemes in any of the rooms when they had moved in, and once she started she was appalled at how dowdy the decor appeared. She had begun in the bedroom, painting it a soft blue, and now had completed the living room. Next, she would start on the kitchen. Bethany sighed. She suddenly felt exhausted. It was only 4.30, but she didn't think she would bother getting dressed again when she got out of her bath. She would put on her robe and make some beans on toast and get an early night. Wearily, she climbed out of the bath and dried herself. Suddenly her legs gave way underneath her. She felt dizzy, blood was pounding in her ears, and black spots danced before her eyes. She clutched the towel rail for support and, leaning against the wall, she rested for a moment. Then rather shakily she went to lie down on her bed.

After a while, Bethany got up and leaned against the radiator while she looked out of her window. The street outside was grey and silent, as though the cold weather had frozen it into immobility. The houses stared blankly from their empty windows and there was no sign of life anywhere. Bethany understood the expression 'the dead of winter' when she looked down her road. An enormous red sun hung low on the dark horizon and cast a baleful orange glow into the wintry sky. There was a tree outside her window which raised its clawed hands skywards. Bethany glanced idly at it and was startled to notice a group of rooks in its branches who appeared to be staring straight at her. She shivered involuntarily. Suddenly, something startled the birds, and they rose as one into the air with harsh cries. She watched them as they drifted into the cold winter sky like silent flakes of ash around a bonfire. They were a mournful and somehow sinister sight and she quite understood why they were traditionally thought to be harbingers of doom and tragedy.

Bethany shook herself. These depressing thoughts wouldn't do. Here she was inside, warm and snug, and rooks were rooks, just doing what came naturally to them. Maybe she had been overdoing things a bit. It would soon be Christmas. Nothing was going to happen to her at Christmas. It was a time of year she loved. The light-headedness was probably just a result of getting out of the hot bath too quickly, and she had been working very hard. Still, it was sensible to rest. She didn't want to acknowledge that she had been frightened, but perhaps she couldn't ignore the fact that she had had what Mrs Willow used to call 'a turn'. She would leave the decorating for a while and concentrate on cheerful thoughts of Christmas.

What would she do to make it special? She had already written all her cards, and they lay in a neat pile on the hall table ready to post. It had taken her much longer than usual to write them, because she felt she owed many of the recipients an explanation of why she was only signing her cards 'Bethany'. It felt so peculiar to her, that she had made several mistakes and added Norman's name automatically before crossing it out, and then putting the wasted card in the bin. The form of wording seemed dreadfully problematic as well. It didn't seem right to wish someone all the joy and happiness of the season and add that you were getting divorced. On the other hand she couldn't be too vague; people might think something awful had happened to Norman, and cheery jubilation about her new-found freedom seemed ungracious. After much thought, she had finally settled on a brief note to the effect that she and Norman had come to an amicable agreement that they were to separate, and that she hoped they would be able to keep in touch with him as well as herself. She reminded herself to make a copy of people's addresses to give to Norman sometime. It wouldn't be an onerous task as they knew so few people.

Anyway, she had done her cards. She had also bought a few little gifts for people on her course, a token box of chocolates for the doctor and her receptionist, and a book on photography for Marjorie. Marjorie had rung her, namely to express her disappointment and disapproval at the way things were going, but Bethany had detected a hint of curiosity about the Baggage, and deduced that Marjorie was rather regretting her precipitous actions. Perhaps she had been a little hasty, especially since Norman appeared fixed on this course of action and Bethany did not seem to be standing in his way. Bethany was not able to help with information about Rita, but volunteered that Norman seemed well cared for. Would Marjorie like her to intimate casually to Norman the next time she spoke to him, that perhaps it was time to heal the breach? There had been rather a long pause and she could sense Marjorie weighing up her options. Finally, Marjorie had agreed that this might be sensible. Bethany had been about to hang up, when Marjorie had added unexpectedly that Norman was lucky to be let off so lightly. In her opinion Bethany was being very generous, and Norman did not know when he was well off. This was so nearly an expression of approval that Bethany did not know how to respond. Luckily, Marjorie had saved her the trouble by terminating the conversation with a brisk request that she be informed soon whether Norman intended to call on her.

Bethany had telephoned Norman at work, and he had made little attempt to disguise his relief. In fact, he appeared in a great hurry to get off the phone, presumably so that he could ring his mother. Since then she had not heard from either of them, but presumed that Norman would be spending Christmas with both his mother and Rita. She couldn't help feeling a little sorry for Rita. Even though she was now beginning to appreciate that Marjorie had her good points, it would be heavenly not to have to eat her Christmas dinner. Marjorie viewed cooking as an act of war, and did not emerge from the kitchen until she was satisfied that she had beaten the food into submission. Sprouts were boiled for up to an hour, and Bethany did not want to imagine the process through which she achieved the cooking of the poor turkey. It looked almost . . . mangled . . . as it sat, oddly flattened in a dispirited puddle of pallid gravy. The only colour was provided by Marjorie herself, who sat glowing scarlet, satisfied that she was the victor of the day. Bethany thought that a peaceful Christmas where she pleased no one but herself would be blissful. Of course, she would not be entirely alone, as she had her angel for company.

Thinking of the angel brought another thought to the forefront of her mind. It was one that had never been far away for some days, but it had been so daring and unexpected that she had immersed herself in frenetic painting and decorating activity while she half considered it. Now, in the peace of her newly painted bedroom, it emerged, fully formed into the open. What if she were to write to Sylvia again? Now that she had come to terms with what had happened in the past, the way that she had thrown away true friendship seemed wasteful and wrong. Instinctively, she knew that Sylvia must have felt the loss just as she did. Bethany longed to know how Sylvia had spent her life, how she had been, and if she had been happy. But was it right to go waltzing back after over twenty years? After all, she had, to all intents and purposes, lied to her closest friend and then abandoned her, disappearing without trace from her life. Could Sylvia forgive her? What about Roy? Did she have the right to ask them to forgive what she had done, and accept her return into their lives? Bethany didn't know. She did know that what she had done had been wrong, and she had to decide whether she dared take the chance to put things right.

She wondered if Mr and Mrs Willow were still alive. They would be quite old now, and she ached to think how poorly she had treated their kindness. It was true that she had gradually repaid all of the money they had given her, setting a little aside from her wages when she had started work, but Bethany knew how inadequate and ungrateful this had been. They had loved her, and she had let them think that she had turned her back on them. Bethany felt the tears well up and blew her nose loudly. Making contact was something she was nervous about doing, since she was so utterly in the wrong. But it was also a way to make things right. She owed them all an explanation and an apology that came straight from her heart. Now that she had come so far in her own mind, it was perhaps time to act. It was worth the risk, for after all, what did she have to lose?

Pulling her robe more tightly around her, she pushed her feet into her slippers and went down to the kitchen. Sitting at the table, she placed a large pad of writing paper in front of her and wrote her address firmly and clearly in the top right-hand corner. Then she began to write. She began 'Dearest Sylvia' and continued writing without pause until her hand ached and her eyes were sore. After almost two hours she signed her name, and shakily laid down her pen. Tears pricked at her eyes, but she was too weary to give way to them. After a while she put the pages of closely written paper carefully into an envelope and wrote Sylvia's name. She put Mam and Da's address underneath, although she knew that Sylvia would have her own place by now. She left the letter on the table and went upstairs to bed, where she fell immediately into a deep sleep.

The next morning Bethany woke feeling refreshed. She dressed in loose fitting trousers and top, and ate breakfast. She found that she could manage only half a slice of toast before she felt full, and tipped the rest into the bin. The letter to Sylvia lay on the Formica table beside her, and she took it out of its envelope and reread it. Although she didn't feel that any words she could write could express what she felt properly, at least it was as honest and as full an account of all that had happened to her as she could manage. It also contained a long and heartfelt apology, and a request that Sylvia find it in her heart to forgive her. After reading it, Bethany added a postscript. If Sylvia felt it was right, could she go and see the Willows, and tell her all about Bethany's letter? She wanted to give them at least an explanation of her behaviour, but thought it would be best coming from someone they knew. After reading and rereading what she had written, Bethany slowly sealed the envelope. She was glad she had written the letter, but wasn't sure if she should send it. She would leave it for a while. These things usually

258

resolved themselves, and it would be better to wait than to act hastily and wish she hadn't.

In the meantime, what was she going to do today? It was still only seven o'clock, and the early morning sun had not melted the frost on the garden. Bethany went into the living room and began to clear up. She folded the dust sheets, put the lids on the empty paint pots and put away the ladder. After she had finished, she sat down on the sofa and surveyed the room. She was very pleased with what she saw. It seemed so much lighter, fresher and even larger than it had before. Norman would not recognise it. She wondered if he would approve. She looked at her watch and saw that it was still only 8.30, and she had the whole day ahead of her. She had resolved to take it easy, and not begin decorating the kitchen until after Christmas, which left her at a bit of a loose end. It seemed an awfully long time since breakfast, and for some odd reason she felt hungry again. She made herself some more toast. After she had eaten, she went out to post her Christmas cards.

Shortly after nine o'clock, Bethany walked down the high street. They had hung the lights all down the street, and all of the shops had Christmas decorations in their windows. Bethany felt a surge of excitement. Christmas was such a lovely time of year. As far back as she could remember, she had loved the phrase 'Peace and Goodwill to All Men'. She went in and out of the shops listening to the festive music that they were playing, and found herself in the small square at the end of the street. She had been led there by the sound of a brass band playing. Carols were her favourite music of all, and they always sounded just right when played by a brass band. Bethany beamed at the Salvation Army collector rat-tling her tin, and put some coins in it. She then stayed listening, barely conscious of the cold that nipped at her fingers through her gloves. It was only as 'God rest you merry Gentlemen' came around for the third time that she reluctantly tore herself away. She retraced her steps back along the high street, and this time she began to buy things. She began with some tree decorations and some tinsel in Woolworth's, and added a beautiful silver star to her basket. She then bought some mince pies, a set of white lights and a bunch of mistletoe. After that she crammed some holly on top of her already brimming bags and made her way home. She unpacked her purchases with glee, and did not bother to remove her coat.

Norman had not really entered into the spirit of Christmas, and Bethany had always felt that her extravagances were not approved of. They had a silver tinsel tree and a fairy, neither of which Bethany liked very much, and they usually didn't bother with decorations. This year was different. She put the holly everywhere that she could reach, and hung tinsel over all the picture frames. She then laid out the new Christmas decorations and the lights, took a deep breath and went back out into the town. Right at the near end of the high street, a man was selling Christmas trees. Bethany selected a small one in a pot. Then she changed her mind and chose a larger one. The man said that 'his lad would run it along for her for a couple of quid' since she lived so close. Bethany decided that she had time to go back along the high street and went back to Woolworth's. She bought three cassettes of Christmas music, one of popular songs and two of carols. On impulse, she bought a wreath for the front door and another set of lights. She hurried back just behind the tree man's lad, who was waiting for her on the doorstep when she arrived. He carried the tree in for her and set it down in the living room. After he had gone, Bethany pushed the sofa aside and positioned the tree just in front of her window. She sat back on the sofa, still in her coat, breathing heavily. Several hours had passed since she had first set out earlier that morning, and she felt rather shaky. She felt almost too weak to get herself a drink and some food, but told herself sternly that she must pull herself together. She began to eat a sandwich, but just as her early morning breakfast had done, it seemed to stick in her throat. She made herself eat a few mouthfuls, and drank a mug of peppermint tea. She took them into the living room and looked critically at her tree.

After forcing another small mouthful, Bethany decided she could wait no longer. Although it was only 2.30 in the afternoon, the sky was leaden and overcast, and the room was darkening. What better time to decorate her tree? Bethany put on the first of her Christmas tapes. The sweet notes of the choirboys filled the air, and she closed her eyes for a minute, listening to 'Hark the Herald Angels Sing'. Pure joy filled her chest, and she wished for the first time that she had someone to share these moments with. How odd this was. In moments of great sadness she needed to be alone, and it was only when she was very happy that she felt lonely. She had always thought that it would be the other way around. But she wasn't really alone. She wondered if the angel would answer her. 'Isn't this lovely? Are you enjoying it too?' There was no reply but Bethany felt the warmth of happiness spread through her. She got down on the floor and began to unwind the sets of lights from their boxes.

After she had hung the lights, she unwrapped the silver star from its tissue paper and placed it carefully on the tree. She could only just reach, and inhaled the sharp fresh smell of the branches as she leaned close. Finally she hung her decorations, little wooden figures, and blue and silver baubles. All the time, the beautiful carols were playing and she was filled with a pleasure that was both deep and peaceful. When she had finished, she switched on the lights and sat looking at the tree. The little white bulbs glowed with a serenity that was unlike any other source of light she knew, and summed up the spirit of Christmas. She sat on the floor and gazed at her tree, smelled its scent, and listened to the carols. She vowed that she would always do this every year. One day, she might not be alone either. For the second time in as many days Bethany felt her eyes fill with tears. She really was very emotional at the moment. She supposed it was understandable, considering the things that had happened to her in the last few months.

It was four o'clock, and quite dark in the room. Bethany went to the window to draw the curtains. As she did so, what she saw in the front garden made her gasp. It was snowing, the flakes a clear luminous white, shining in the fading light and beginning to cover the ground with a thin layer. Bethany watched transfixed until it was too dark to see. Snow, and it was nearly Christmas. She wondered if Sylvia was thinking the same thing. They both loved snow. Bethany knew her mind was made up. She would definitely post the letter. Taking her unfinished sandwich and cold cup of tea back to the kitchen, she picked up the letter and put it on the hall table ready to post.

The next few days were uneventful. Bethany felt tired and stayed indoors for most of the time, apart from one brief excursion to the letter box to post Sylvia's letter, and into the garden to put crumbs on her bird table. The snow had turned to slush and a sharp wind blew around the eaves at night. Bethany played her music and drifted around her house in a pleasant, unhurried, dreamlike daze. She felt as though she were a hibernating animal, glad to be inside, snug and warm, while the world outside continued without her. She mused inwardly on the lessons, and her thoughts contained her universe. She felt detached from external events and had no desire to watch television or listen to the radio. The days passed without incident, and she would have been hard put to tell which day of the week it was.

On the fourth morning after she had decorated her tree, Bethany woke feeling different. The wind had dropped and all was quiet outside. The sun was streaming through her curtains, and she felt almost as though she would burst with energy. The need to be up and doing something propelled her out of bed and to the window in one movement. She looked out at a sky so blue it hurt her eyes. It had snowed again during the night, and whiteness lay along each branch of the tree by her window. The traffic had not yet marked the road, and everything looked pristine in the sunshine. This was definitely a day to be out and about. Bethany pulled on her clothes and wondered what she might do with the day. For once, she did not feel like sitting quietly in her living room. She simply could not concentrate, so insistent was the call to action. Perhaps she would contemplate the end of the day for a change. But what was she going to do with the hours ahead of her? She had done all the jobs that could be done, and she wanted to wait until tomorrow to buy her food. Going for a walk might be nice, but she craved new sights and sounds. She was filled with the spirit of adventure.

She went downstairs and ate breakfast. By the time she had finished, she knew what she was going to do. Her blood sang in her veins and excitement surged through her. It really was extraordinary how she had not thought of it before, but then it was only now she was free from time constraints that she considered going anywhere other than the small local community where she lived. Bethany checked her handbag and sorted out her coat, gloves and hat. She was going to have an adventure today.

* * *

It was two days before Christmas, and he was completely organised. He was rather proud that he had made all of his purchases and painstakingly wrapped them by himself. They were in a neat little pile under his tree, which sat in its traditional place next to the fireplace in the living room. He had tucked all the many Christmas cards into the bookcases and the room looked festive and peaceful. He looked around and could almost see Claire's brief nod of appreciation. She had always loved Christmas, and had created little rituals around each tradition. Her preparations began early, and she gave each enough time so that she could extract pleasure from every favourite activity. She strode through the fields in gumboots each year, gathering greenery and arriving back at the door with flushed cheeks and hair in disarray. Sometimes he accompanied her, if she had found a particular branch of holly that she just couldn't reach, or a perfect pine cone tantalisingly dangling so that she had to be lifted up to pick it. They loved these walks, returning laughing to the house, laden with booty. Claire then sorted the greenery in lavish heaps on the floor while he made the coffee. Then he would watch as she made wreaths,

262

garlands and sprigs for every corner of the house. She always played Christmas music, and sometimes sang along as she worked.

At other times she would be tucked away in the kitchen, with flour on the end of her nose and in her hair. Delicious smells would drift out, and the larder would be stacked high with tins, the fridge and freezer groaning. Claire loved to ask people in and she always seemed to be able to produce just the right delicious snack or meal for all the visitors that called, from carol singers to neighbours, dustmen to insurance salesmen. She enjoyed it so much that all around her could not but help be drawn into her infectious delight. Their house became a magnet for the village, and she was a seemingly indispensable central character in the drama that unfolded each year and culminated in a magnificent feast for all their friends after midnight mass in the village church.

It was for these, and many other reasons, that he had to confess to feeling rather tired and a little despondent. This was the first Christmas without her and, although he thought he had managed fairly well so far, it was inevitable that the feeling of loss grew sharp at times. It was made worse by the fact that so many people knew it. Claire was so much in their thoughts that, for the last two weeks, he had hardly been able to spend any time alone. His kitchen had been filled with well-wishers extending invitations to come and spend Christmas Day with them. When he had politely refused, they found it hard to take no for an answer, and suggested Christmas Eve, or Boxing Day, or what about the day after that, or before that. He had repeated his desire to be on his own as gently as he could, but the conversations seemed to be repeated endlessly in different ways. No sooner was he sure that he must have spoken to all of the kindly well-wishers in the village, than there would be another knock at the door and more smiling, slightly tentative, kindly faces would be revealed on the other side. Everyone brought offerings of food, and he thought he had been able to recycle it all fairly successfully, so that he could be hospitable to one and all.

In spite of all his efforts, the conversations had been strained, since everyone was aware that Claire was not with them, and they all felt her loss so keenly. Conversations stuttered with awkward pauses around the kitchen table, or beside the glowing fire. So often someone would casually mention her name, and then be overcome with mortification at their clumsiness. In vain he tried to say that it didn't matter, that they should all try to talk about her naturally. It just didn't seem to work. Although he knew it would take time, he felt wearied by it all. In the rare moments he was alone, he didn't know what to do with himself. The Christmas music he played brought a lump to his throat, and at times he wondered how its poignancy was to be borne.

Yesterday he had gone for a long walk across the fields and missed her easy company. His breath hung in clouds on the clear air, and memories of Claire were everywhere. He passed a holly tree laden with berries, and could almost see her standing on tiptoes with her secateurs trying to reach a particularly choice spray. Walking alongside a frosty field, it seemed to him that the bare furrows of the soil seemed to echo with their past laughter. He passed a rookery and the birds that flew up from the trees at the edge of the field seemed to mock him with their cries. It appeared that this most festive and joyful of seasons was to be sharply edged with bittersweet memories for him this year. He caught himself thinking and chided himself gently. What would his wife have made of this wallowing? There were jobs to be done, and plenty to enjoy on this desolate wintry afternoon. Sharply retracing his steps, he had doubled back for some clippers from the garden shed, and cut a few holly branches to put around the house. He returned home with an armful of greenery and felt he had earned a nice hot cup of tea.

Today, looking at the bright berries glowing near the hearth, he was glad that he had made the effort. He felt that he could be justifiably proud that he had managed a difficult time creditably well. He had delivered all his Christmas cards, wrapped his presents, shared food and drink with friends. He had spent the last week or so immersed in village life, and he had done his best to extract pleasure from all the joys of the season. In short, he had done well. He felt the need for a change of scene to recharge his strength and vitality before undertaking the rest of the Christmas period. He needed fortifying against all the well-meaning friends and well-wishers who would no doubt continue to offer him cheer and comfort in ways they alone knew how to. This would be a good time to spend a couple of days in London. He would go up to the city and stay in a hotel and drink in the atmosphere of busy hustle and bustle. He would enjoy the people, the bright lights and the anonymity, and come home on Christmas Eve. If they could fit him in, he could make an appointment to see the solicitors to sign the papers they required. He spent the rest of that morning making arrangements with the solicitors and booking a small hotel in town. He knew them of old, so they managed to find him a room for the night. He then packed a bag with various necessities.

Shortly after lunch he drove his car the brief distance to the station to catch the 1.30 train up to London. The carriage was not

264

crowded, and he found a seat with a table by a window. He folded his coat carefully and put it in the rack above him, laid his book on the table and bought a cup of coffee in the buffet car. He had just settled himself down in the still empty compartment when the train drew out of the station. He had meant to read, but the sound of the train on the tracks relaxed him, and his book lay unnoticed on the table as he stared out of the window, lost in thought. Of all the ways one could travel, he had always preferred this one. He loved the views of the countryside speeding past; the chequerboard of fields, villages and towns laid out before him in all their colours and textures. He always travelled by train whenever he could, and the railway line had been one of the main reasons why he and Claire had settled in the village.

He had disliked driving ever since he had been in a very bad car accident when he was much younger. His car had spun off the road and he had been thrown from it and knocked unconscious. Although he had suffered some physical damage, the main injuries were to his head, and he had lain in a coma for several weeks. Even when he had regained consciousness, his memory of recent events before the crash had vanished. They only reappeared gradually over the weeks, and it had been the most traumatic and painful experience of his life. Although the intervening years had softened the anguish, at the time he had come close to being destroyed by it. One long-term effect had been that, for many years, he had been unable to sit in a car at all.

Retrospectively, he realised that he had had a major breakdown, and the only reason that he had not lost his sanity completely was because of Claire. She had been a young nurse on his ward, and had been on duty late one night when the first of his nightmarish memories began to come back to him. She had calmed him, and sat with him as he ranted on in desperation about needing to get out of the hospital, to meet somebody, that it was terribly important, but he could not remember who. Night after night the nightmares had returned, and he had been transferred to a small annexe room away from the main ward. She had held him and let him rave mindlessly, had soothed his panic with her gentle presence, until the drugs they administered mercifully carried him back into unconsciousness.

Later, during the months of recovery he often lapsed into dark despair as he pieced together the fragments of his poor shattered mind. Each part of the image that formed tortured him further with the dawning realisation that the nightmares he imagined were real. She sat with him as he wept that he was too late, too late.

Eventually, one evening in November he was finally discharged from the hospital. He had told Claire everything, and they had tried to trace his lost love together. For three despairing weeks he had stayed in Brighton, endlessly pacing the streets, desperately revisiting all of the places they had been, and searching the faces of strangers in the hope that he would find her. Finally, he had been forced to accept that he had failed, and his parents had taken him, close to collapse, back to their house in Norfolk, and there had made him rest. Claire had been the one who had not given up hope, had continued to search even when it was clear to him that Bethany was gone for ever. Claire continued to write him long letters about her life, and any progress that she made in the search. At first he frantically devoured her letters in the hope of finding news of Bethany. Later, as it became obvious that there was little hope, he would reread Claire's words and was comforted by their kindness.

The love that had been lost to him had left him broken and despairing for a long while, raging against the mindless futility of what had happened and the cruel stupidity of Fate. Time after time he was nearly destroyed by the realisation of what Bethany's suffering must have been, what she must have thought of him, only to be pulled back by Claire's gentle compassion and reason. Gradually his anguish subsided, to be replaced by gnawing sorrow, and eventually to aching regret for what might have been. Claire was with him all this time, a loyal and true friend who helped him when no one else could. Eventually, when his parents encouraged him to continue with his career, he immersed himself gratefully in his work. Back in London, he found that he missed the young nurse who had offered him her friendship and compassion for so many months. He had telephoned her and they had spent week-ends together. Gradually their love had grown. Although he could never forget Bethany, and looked for her on every corner, Claire had understood his feelings, and accepted them. She had been a remarkable woman, and he had been lucky to find her, and privileged to spend his life with her.

Oliver kept his eyes closed as the train drew into the station. He could see Bethany vividly. Her dark hair was blowing around her face in the sea breeze. She was smiling happily as she looked at him, a glow in her skin and her eyes shining. He smiled back, transported to a past time long ago. Suddenly a door slammed and a guard blew a whistle on the platform beside him. Oliver returned to the present with a jump and smiled at his foolishness. He was an idiot, wallowing about in the past, but who would have thought that he would remember Bethany with such vividness after all this time? It was extraordinary that the memories were so unclouded by the intervening years. One of those peculiar things, he thought, gathering up his case and coat and briefly checking that he had left nothing behind. He went through the barrier and decided to go straight to the hotel by tube. After he had checked in he might go up to Oxford Street and look at the lights. Pausing to listen to the Salvation Army band playing carols, he put some coins in the collector's tin. The clear notes of the brass band carried out into the station concourse and he was glad that he had come. A good decision, he thought.

*   *   *

Bethany was sitting on a tube train feeling excited. The feeling of boundless energy had not left her all morning and she could hardly wait to get to her destination. She had been trying to think of the last time that she had been up to the centre of London, and she couldn't remember. The suburb where she and Norman had lived all these years was well served by shops, and the tube station was mainly for those who commuted to work. Occasionally, a housewife such as herself might venture on the tube in order to visit one of the larger West End stores, but Bethany had not been one of these. When she and Norman had first moved in to their house, they had both said how easy it would be to go sightseeing in the capital, and had planned to visit Buckingham Palace and Downing Street. They would see it all. Somehow there never seemed to be the right time. At first they had both been so busy settling in, and then the Sunday visiting with Marjorie had become established, and finally they just lost the desire to leave the house. Bethany felt sad that she and Norman had not fulfilled so many of their plans. She hoped that he would be happy with Rita. Another sudden rush of excitement swept through her. She was going to London to visit the Queen. There was a poem about that from her childhood. Bethany was prevented from following her thoughts further as the tube drew into the station and she got off.

Bethany came out of Marble Arch tube station at street level and looked around her. She had not thought what she wanted to do with the day, but the sky was blue, the air was crisp and clear, and people were thronging the pavements, busy about their business. She gave a small skip of happiness. She could barely contain the smile on her face, as the pleasure she felt was welling up inside her. What a wonderful day this was going to be. The first thing to do was to walk in that big park over there. Bethany negotiated her

267

way across the road and set off into Hyde Park. For an hour or so she strode contentedly along the wide pathways, drinking in the wide open spaces and the unfamiliar sights. She found herself by a large stretch of water and stopped to read a map at the side of the path to get her bearings. Apparently this was called the Serpentine, and if she crossed it, she would be in Kensington Gardens. A long forgotten memory stirred in her, and she wondered if she was right. She peered at the map again, and was delighted to see that Peter Pan's statue was marked. Rapidly estimating the rough direction she needed to take, she set off over the bridge towards it.

After a little while she realised that she must have taken the wrong turning. She found herself at a large lake which she knew must be the Round Pond. There were people all around it, strolling and feeding the ducks, and she stopped to sit on a park bench, grateful for the rest. She felt a little tired and her back ached, but after a few minutes sitting she felt rejuvenated. The sun sparkled on the water, and people strode, rosy-cheeked and smiling in the clear air. She watched a group of children sailing a boat and thought with pleasure that this scene must hardly have changed for a hundred years. After a little while she got up and asked a woman with a pushchair if she could point her in the right direction for the Peter Pan statue. The woman put her hand to her head. 'Do you know I must have been there a hundred times, but you've picked the wrong person to ask. I've got the most hopeless sense of direction. I *think* it's that way, but to be honest, I couldn't guarantee not to send you off on a wild-goose chase!'

Bethany laughed. 'Oh, well, don't worry. It's such a lovely day, I'll enjoy meandering a bit. I'll trust you, thanks.'

She set off, and the woman suddenly called after her, 'Oh, hang on!'

Bethany paused, as the woman called, 'Grace thinks it's that way!' She was walking back towards Bethany as she spoke, and Bethany took the few steps necessary to bring them back together.

'Sorry, we should have asked her in the first place. She's got this amazing sense of knowing exactly where she's going, and if she says it's over there, it's over there!' The woman was looking down at the little girl in the pushchair with a mixture of love and pride on her face. The child was pointing determinedly with a mittened hand in precisely the opposite direction that her mother had directed Bethany. The woman smiled helplessly once again.

'Sorry, but it probably *is* that way.' Bethany thanked her again, liking her, and thinking how nice she was to bother to come back.

'Right, I'll give this way a go. Thank you, Grace,' she said, bending down to smile at the child. 'Look after Mummy, and have a Happy Christmas!' They parted, and Bethany watched the mother and daughter until they were out of sight, blurring into the reflected light from the bright water behind them. Then she set off again in search of Peter Pan.

Little Grace had been quite right, and Bethany found the statue easily. She stood looking at the lovely polished green bronze, and found the little animals hiding around its base. *Peter Pan* had been one of her favourite books when she was a child, and she was glad to find the statue she had read about and to see it for herself.

After she had looked her fill, she wondered what she would do next. Glancing at her watch, she saw that it was nearly one o'clock, and that she had been walking for two hours. She also felt hungry. Rubbing her back, she retraced her steps back through Hyde Park and emerged by the famous Arch ready to sit down and eat something. She turned down Oxford Street, and wandered along the road amid the crowds of people in search of a café.

After eating a sandwich and drinking a bottle of water, she walked along Oxford Street for a while. The lights were not yet on, but the displays in the shop windows were magnificent. She looked with wonder at the themed grottoes, the sledges carrying Father Christmas from the North Pole, and the animated reindeer moving their heads slowly to and fro, all against the backdrop of snowy branches dripping icicles in wonderful patterns. She wandered in and out of the stores themselves, travelling the escalators up through perfumed halls glistening with sumptuous decorations, looking down on floors below crammed with people rushing and pushing to buy their last minute purchases. She stood in lifts that had glass walls, and looked in amazement as she rose high up next to huge models of laughing snowmen dancing suspended in the air, chasing glittering snowflakes through fat clouds. Each department store was distinctive, with different schemes of silver and blue, red and green, or even purple and orange, and the swathes of colour filled her eyes with delight. It was opulent, festive, and bustling, and Bethany drank it all in with pleasure.

She was on the third floor of Liberty's when it happened. She was gazing at the display of Christmas trees, some of which played their own music and had lights that twinkled on and off. Suddenly she was seized by a pain so strong that her legs gave way beneath her. It scythed through her, cutting her breath and filling her mind with fear. She sank down next to a six-foot tree covered with golden figures playing their own drums, and gasped in agony. She had never known that pain could shoot through her body so that she did not know where she began and it ended. She lost awareness of where she was, and who she was. There was only the pain which was seemingly without end, throbbing red and black so that she swam down into it and was held in its grip. Slowly she surfaced, and realised that it had ebbed away, and she was herself again. She opened her bruised eyes and focused with difficulty. She felt battered and shocked, and could barely make herself think. In front of her was a plain, undecorated tree, and she was staring without real awareness at its tip. Gradually she became aware of what she was looking at. It was a single, silver angel, standing alone at the peak of the tree, a trumpet held triumphantly aloft, exultantly announcing the arrival of the seraphim in the skies.

Bethany finally knew how she was going to meet her angel. She had to die, and it would be today. 'Please help me be brave. I am coming, but please help me to be brave,' she muttered as she staggered to her feet. One thing she knew, and that was that she must get home. She would not die here, in front of strangers, with the humiliating lack of dignity that would be her fate if she were to collapse in Oxford Street two days before Christmas. Hardly knowing what she was doing, she left the store and started to walk, trusting that the angel would lead her in the right direction, knowing only that she must get home, must quickly get back to her own small space. With her walls wrapped around her, she would be able to deal with the pain that must surely come, and try to meet her angel with some dignity.

Dazedly she walked, dimly aware that she was pushing through crowds, vaguely hearing exclamations of annoyance from passers-by as she bumped into them. She must get home. Out on the street the pain came again, as strong as before, and she almost fainted, leaning against a street light, clenching her teeth with the effort of not crying aloud. She bent forward and crossed the road blindly, ignoring the hooting of cars, focused only on moving on. While she had been inside the shops, the darkness had fallen, and the street was now a blur of light and movement. She looked ahead of her and stumbled on. At last she stopped, sick with panic and fear. She had not come to a tube station. She did not know where she was, and the pain would surely come again, sapping her strength, and forcing her finally to give up and die on the street. She made her numb brain work through her fear, and looked desperately around her, up and down the road. Then she saw them. Across the busy main thoroughfare there was a smaller street, running away from her, directly opposite. There were no cars, as it was pedes-trianised, and it appeared to be a haven from the pandemonium of traffic and people that surrounded her. But what held her transfixed was not the silence of the street. It was the decoration that filled its space with light. Up high above her there were angels. They shone silver and gentle, strong and jubilant, proclaiming their presence and filling the sky with radiance. She knew she had to go to them.

Without thinking what she was doing, Bethany stepped out into the road. She heard a shout behind her, and the screech of a car, and then the pain seized her again and she cried out. Strong hands took hold of her and pulled her back to the pavement, and she collapsed, only aware of her agony, and her need to get to the shining angels. The arms continued to hold her up as the icy pain gradually receded and she was conscious of warmth glowing around her. She was held by a man wearing a thick herringbone tweed coat. Its stitching held her numbed gaze, so beautiful and complex did its pattern appear. It was like a tapestry, woven so that each beginning met its ending, each repeating stitch joined in colour and harmony making perfect sense. She spread her fingers gently on its surface, knowing that she was behaving strangely, but unable to do otherwise. But she must focus. There was a voice, a man's voice and he was asking her a question.

Oliver could not believe what was happening. Had he stepped somehow into another time, or reality, or was Bethany standing in his arms? He looked down into her face and knew that he held her, and instinctively drew her closer to him. She was in some kind of trouble, beyond the speeding car he had saved her from. She had collapsed in great pain, and he knew that he needed to move her to a calmer place, away from the people, and get her to a doctor. Automatically, he steered her to the traffic lights and crossed the road into a more peaceful street. Still he did not trust himself to speak, but held her tightly in his arms, half carrying her along as she leaned against him, hardly seeming aware of him or her surroundings. Back from the bustling crowds they stood against a building and he looked at her again, drinking in her face, stroking her hair. Clearing his throat, he said, 'Bethany. It's me. We need to get you to a doctor. Can you manage to walk?' The banality of what he was saying seemed to him absurd, as he only wanted to bury his face in her hair, and hold her, never let her go again. Instead he took her shoulders and made her look at him. 'Bethany, can you hear me? It's Oliver. I'm here, and I'll look after you. Do you understand?'

Bethany seemed to be staring up at the Christmas decorations above her. Instinctively he followed her gaze, but saw only angels, and could not understand why they held her attention. Briefly it occurred to him that her mind might have turned long ago, as his so nearly had, but he held her to him again, and knew it could not be so. There was probably a logical reason why she was gazing at the electric angels with such rapture. He shook her gently and repeated her name. Bethany stared at him with dawning realisation, and said two things, one of which confused him further, and the other which propelled him urgently to action, and continued to echo in his brain as he sprang to hail a taxi and gave the driver urgent instructions.

So engrossed was he in his thoughts that he barely registered how miraculous it was that a taxi should be driving along without fare in this place and time. Instead, her words repeated themselves in his mind. She was now in the grip of some terrible pain, crying out in agony, and he frantically told the driver to hurry, quickly, just to the nearest hospital, but get them there quickly, it didn't matter what it cost. As the car accelerated into the traffic, he heard Bethany's words again. She had said 'Oliver? Then you are the angel. I am dying, and I need to get home.'

Oliver paused, momentarily stopped in his tracks by the extraordinarily peculiar way his long lost love was talking. Perhaps she was speaking metaphorically, and she was saying that he was her saving angel. The whole thing was so extraordinary that he was close to wondering if it was real at all. Certainly this taxi driver seemed almost to have supernatural powers, the way he was driving. Best to concentrate on what needed to be done. He had to get her to a hospital, and quickly.

Oliver held Bethany in his arms, and she looked wonderingly into his face. Her hands clutched at him and she stared speechless with amazement. He stared wordlessly back, and in spite of the gravity of their situation, he couldn't help but laugh. It was so wonderful, so impossible, so ... miraculous that she was here. Bethany said, 'Oliver? Is it really you? So you were the angel all this time. But how did you do it?'

Utterly confused, he tightened his arm around her shoulders and replied, 'Don't talk now. It won't be long, we're nearly there and we can get you some help.' Glancing quickly out of the window he realised that, incredibly, his words were true. Time seemed to be telescoping in the most extraordinary way. While they had been staring at each other, the driver seemed to have miraculously negotiated Bayswater Road and Shepherds Bush roundabout. How had it happened, with the Christmas rush and all the traffic? Even with horns blaring, an ambulance would have been hard put to it to manage such a feat. But they were speeding along Goldhawk Road and he could see a large blue hospital sign up ahead.

He had no more time to look, as Bethany was arched in terrible pain again. He tried to stay calm, but fear lapped at the edges of his mind. Surely it couldn't be true that she was about to die? Time blurred again, and he was half carrying her into the foyer of the hospital, taking his wallet from his coat pocket and throwing it back to the taxi driver, calling to him to please take all that was in it, and almost falling forwards in his haste to get help. People came to him, and Bethany was rushed away, leaving him helpless, head in hands, wondering what had happened, what could possibly happen next. He suddenly knew he had to find her, could not be separated again, even if she were dying. He had to be with her. Oliver began to run frantically along the corridor, once again searching for her. He couldn't lose her again.

* * *

Bethany lay on the bed, blissfully free from pain, encased in warmth which enveloped her both inside and out. Oliver sat beside her, holding her hand. He really was here, and he was solidly real, rather than the figment of her delirium as she had feared. She could hardly believe that they were together in this warm room after all these years. They had met in the strangest circumstances imaginable, but they were reunited, and surely nothing would separate them again. She smiled into his blue eyes, and it was as if time rolled away the years and all was as before. There were so many explanations, so much to find out and know, but they had time ahead of them. Oliver squeezed her hand and she saw her own delight mirrored in his face. Happiness flooded through her, familiar happiness that she had known only when she was with him, and now knew again. She relaxed back further into her pillow and held his hand tightly. 'Tell me what happened,' she said. Oliver knew immediately what she meant, and quietly, never taking his eyes from her face, began to explain what had happened all those years ago after he had watched her from his hotel window until she had disappeared from sight.

Bethany listened and after a while closed her eyes. It was all so sad, like listening to a tragic story that happened to somebody else. A small tear rolled down her cheek, and Oliver stopped immediately. He tenderly wiped it away and kissed her cheek. 'It doesn't matter now, does it? Any of it? All that really matters is that we are together now.' Suddenly a wonderfully familiar grin spread across his face, and her heart caught with love. He had hardly changed at

273

all. He was saying, 'And of course the very best news is that you aren't going to die, my love. I can tell you I was somewhat confused there for a while, playing the role of your guardian angel.' He smiled again, and sat back in his chair. He was teasing her in the gentlest way, but she didn't mind. It was true, and she could scarcely take in the enormity of it all. She had met her angel, and she hadn't died.

And the angel wasn't Oliver. She believed with all her heart that somehow it had been arranged so that she had been reunited with him, like the tapestry that wove its complicated pattern in repeating harmonies to its rightful conclusion, but Oliver was not her angel. He did not even know about her angel, and never had. The telepathic connection that they had had all those years ago had not been present this time, and he had been unaware of her presence right up until the moment when she had literally catapulted into his life. Rationally, it was impossible to explain, and she could only fall back on the strong intuitive feeling that it had all meant to be. And what of her angel itself?

Bethany turned and looked at her miraculously beautiful daughter lying in her crib next to her bed. Now that she knew her, it was all obvious, although she still felt that she was justified in not knowing. How was she supposed to know? The angel had shockingly intruded into her life way back in April, and it was now December. Nine months. So many of the physical changes were now explained, and the kind doctor who had talked to her had said that, although it was rare, it did occasionally happen that a woman could be pregnant, and actually go into labour without realising it. Oliver had been at first incredulous, and then amused, as he took in Bethany's bewildered expression. He was hugely enjoying the situation and had gently teased her for her unworldliness. He already knew about Norman, and seemed to be taking the whole affair in his stride. He had laid an impossibly tender hand on the baby's head, and looked at her with an expression that was difficult to read. Bethany swallowed the lump in her throat that was not quite sorrow and not quite gladness, and watched them.

Gabrielle. Her angel. She had learned so much in nine short months. The lessons, one for every month of her pregnancy save the last, had needed to be learned, before she could meet her child. She had practised Mindfulness, Action, and Healing all through the first three months as her angel had formed. Then throughout the summer months she had grown through Gratitude, Discipline and Acceptance. Finally, through Purpose she had

274

arrived at Contribution, with its message of unity and connection. And perhaps there was no ninth lesson. Perhaps it was that she must continue to take the lessons and make them part of her life and, in turn, teach them to her daughter as she grew.

Bethany knew she would never tire of looking at her child. Gabrielle was tiny and beautiful. She had translucent pearly skin, perfect little hands with miniature nails like seashells, and dark hair and eyelashes. She had not cried when she was born, and rarely since, and appeared to be adjusting tranquilly to her new surroundings without fuss. Bethany knew instinctively that she would learn much from her little daughter. She looked back at Oliver and smiled at him.

'Do you want to go and get something to eat or drink? Have we been here a very long time?'

Oliver glanced at his watch and then bent down to show her the time. It was one minute to midnight. He knelt down so that she could see the second hand moving steadily to the twelve. Then he kissed her, and said, 'It's Christmas Eve. Happy Christmas, my love.' She watched, her heart full as he gently picked up her baby and whispered something to her. He laid her precious baby in Bethany's arms and said 'I'll just go and get a bit of fresh air. I'll come back, is that all right? Is there anything you want?'

Bethany shook her head, and he opened the door. He was just about to leave when she heard something, music from somewhere, a radio from down the corridor maybe, and said, 'Wait, listen. What's that?'

Oliver smiled, thinking it would be a carol, but he too listened to catch a snatch of a popular song. When it was over, he said, 'That was pretty. I wonder what it was.' Bethany shook her head again, and reassured him that she would be fine, and Oliver left her alone with her baby.

After he had gone, Bethany tenderly kissed Gabrielle's head. Christmas Eve, and they were together. She definitely wanted to buy that song. It had said that someone had fallen from the stars, straight into her arms. She knew without a doubt that this was what had happened, and that her angel lay in her arms right now. She was happier than she had ever thought she would be. The lessons had led her here, to this private world of joy, shared by the two of them. Bethany looked into her daughter's face and saw that she had quietly woken and had opened her darkly-lashed, deep blue eyes. Bethany held her breath. Her daughter was watching her, looking deep into her eyes with a gaze that was focused and knowing. She knew that it wasn't possible, but there it was. As they looked at each other, Bethany's heart swelled and her happiness deepened. She finally understood what her angel was telling her. Of course there was a ninth lesson, and it was the most important of all. They would be learning it for the rest of their lives.

The ninth lesson was Love.